A LOVE TOO PROUD

By Kathy Keller

For information:

Kathy Keller
655 Tree Side Lane
Ponte Vedra, Florida 32081
www.KathyKeller.com

Publisher's Note: This is a work of fiction. Names, characters, places, and incidents are a product of the author's imagination. Locales and public names are sometimes used for atmospheric purposes. Any resemblance to actual people, living or dead, or to businesses, companies, events, institutions, or locales is completely coincidental.

Book Layout © 2017 BookDesignTemplates.com

Cover Art by Melissa Billman

ISBN 978-1-7370503-0-8

Printed in the United States of America

"...Do not put such unlimited power into hands of the Husbands. Remember all Men would be tyrants if they could. If particular care and attention is not paid to the Ladies, we are determined to foment a Rebellion, and will not hold ourselves bound by any Laws in which we have no voice, or Representation."

—ABIGAIL ADAMS

CONTENTS

CHAPTER ONE

Song of the Whippoorwill

April 1753—Virginia Colony

The old Negress looked up from the shelling of the last of the winter corn as the afternoon sky suddenly turned gray. The sun appeared to be ceasing its assault upon the cracked, dry land, but the temperature remained unseasonably warm and suffocating. There came no relief from even the slightest breeze; the air was deathly still. A frown creased the woman's brown features. No birds sang, no insects chirped, no bees buzzed. The silence was unnatural and her heart beat a tattoo of warning against her breast.

The other times had been much like this, and her callused hands shook as she awaited the sign—the sign that she knew was certain to follow. She leaned forward straining to hear, her large frame tensed, her eyes round with fright as she searched the horizon. Perspiration beaded her forehead, staining the faded red bandanna wrapped around her head. Then it came—three high-pitched whistles—the song of the whippoorwill.

Her heart fell. She closed her eyes and began to sway in mournful keening. The whippoorwill was a night bird. Its song then meant nothing; when heard in the light of day, it signaled death. Somewhere nearby a poor soul was lost to this world.

The skittering of a field mouse across her path roused the woman from her chanting. A thrush began to warble and with it followed the stirrings of nature once again. The spell was broken, but the question remained. Who had the Grim Reaper come to claim this time?

The old Negress raised her arms in supplication. "Dear Lawd in Hebben, don' let it be my Joe or Callie," she cried aloud.

At the crackling sound of a foot on dried brush, she quickly turned. When she spotted the slight figure dressed in buckskins and a turned down cocked hat, her chest heaved with a deep sigh of relief.

"Missy Callie, is my Joe well?" she asked anxiously.

Callie Hastings regarded the Negress curiously. "Of course he is, Lucie. I jest left him in the fields. Why wouldn't he be?"

Lucie shivered in spite of the warmth of the day. "I jest heard da song of da whippoorwill an' ye knows what dat means."

Callie gave a snort of impatience. "I told you before 'tis but a superstition, and I will not be bound by such foolishness."

"'Tain't superstition, child," said Lucie with the shake of her head. "I heard dat whippoorwill sing the day yer papa died, the day yer mama died, and on the morn of yer brother Ethan's death. Did ye not see it?"

"What?"

"Da dark when da Reaper cast his shadow 'pon da earth. Did ye not feel da stillness when ev'ry livin' creature was froze in his tracks, while dat ol' Reaper walked amongst us 'til he found the soul what he come for?"

Lucie's low, even tone held such conviction that Callie felt a chill track down her spine, and she found herself looking guardedly over her shoulder. She quickly shook herself free of the superstition, annoyed that she had allowed herself to succumb to such silliness if only for a moment. "I told ye before, 'tis all stuff 'n nonsense," she said.

Lucie fixed the young girl with a knowing eye. "Maybe so, maybe not."

Callie rolled her eyes and refrained from further comment. There was no talking to the woman when she had her mind made up to something. She tossed her hat on the ground and shook out a mass of dark red hair, tangled and damp from her labor.

"Ye is borrowin' trouble, girl, dressin' like dat in yer brother's britches," declared Lucie with the wag of a corncob.

"And who is to take offense?" challenged Callie, collapsing wearily beneath the shade tree. With Ethan dead and that no-account Abel Cane run off, I have to be the man around here anyway. I might as well dress the part."

"Humph, iffen da good Lawd intended dat, He'd a made ye a man. Ye be a mite puny and hath a yard of freckles, but ye ain't half bad to look on once yer scrubbed up some. Land above, child, as it is ye ain't got much to show for bein' female thin as ye be," said Lucie, glancing pointedly at Callie's underdeveloped body. "How a man s'pose to know ye for a woman dressed like dat?"

"Mayhap that be the idea, Lucie. There been too many strangers gettin' off the ships at Yorktown and passin' this way of late. There was one last month and two this month. Bein' that we are but a league from the main road, 'tis safer for a lone woman not to be seen. Besides, these buckskins make it easier to work the fields."

Lucie shook her head. "'Tain't right when a body crosses God's rightful intentions. Ye needs a man around here to help ye."

Callie scoffed. "Jest like Mattie Danvers' man helped her when he run off with ev'rythin' they had, leavin' her with a passel of babes to feed? No thanks. I don't be needin' that kind of help. Most of the womenfolk hereabouts do all the work anyway, whilst their men spend more time gambling and drinking than puttin' food on the table. 'Pears to me skirts was made for the wrong people."

"That ain't all men, missy. Look at Ol' Joe. Any man what calls me his beauty ain't all bad." Lucie broke into a jovial chuckle that shook her ample girth. "When I ask him what for he wants me, he jest wink his eye in dat ol' devil way and he say: 'Lucie, ye gives me warmth in da winter and shade in da summer.'"

Callie snickered and her mouth turned up into something suspiciously like a smile in spite of her dour mood. The top of Old Joe's head came to Lucie's bosom, and he was as skinny as a matchstick. If Lucie were to stand in front of him, she would completely hide him from view, but there was no mistaking who was in charge. He bossed her around as though she were half his size, and the woman loved every minute of it.

"Now, child," continued Lucie, "jest because yer mama made a mistake 'bout Abel Cane ain't no reason for ye to turn yer back on all men."

Callie sat up and regarded the Negress with a level eye. "Trustin' a man was a mistake what cost my mother her life. I may not be able to prove Cane started that fire, but I know it sure as I be sittin' here."

"How ye know dat?"

"I heard him and Mama arguin' that night. The bastard didn't even stay around to see us safe."

Callie plucked at the fragrant clover. Her lower lip quivered and lines of bitterness, made more pronounced by her anger and exhaustion at the moment, puckered her small face, nearly erasing the innocence of youth.

"Papa was so good. How could Mama have taken to the likes of Cane?"

The old Negress shrugged. "Yer mama was alone with two young'uns. 'Twas a hard time for her when yer papa died. Cane come along at da right time with da right words."

"But you and Old Joe knew him for the scoundrel he was. Why did ye not stop her from marryin' him?" Callie questioned angrily. "If ye had, Mama and Ethan would still be alive."

A long, uncomfortable silence fell between them broken only by the hum of bees and a swarm of annoying blowflies. "Old Joe and me tried to warn yer mama," responded Lucie quietly. "But Cane had already blinded her to his shortcomin's, and 'tis not a black man's place to stop his mistress from doin' anythin'."

It was a simple truth that jolted Callie back to a reality she rarely considered. She never thought of Lucie and Old Joe as servants but rather as helpmates and the only family that she had left. They had proven their love and loyalty to the Hastings many times over the years. And, in spite of the fact that Callie's father had set them free shortly before his death, they had refused to leave the family.

Callie knew that she had hurt the Negress deeply, and she reached over and squeezed Lucie's work-roughened hand in silent apology.

Lucie gave a nod of acceptance. She understood that Callie did not make the gesture lightly. The girl was stubborn and headstrong; admitting a wrong had never come easy to her. Lucie sighed. The lass was so young and already indifferent to human desires and emotions, most especially her own. It saddened the Negress to think that the little girl who used to find such joy in life, who thrilled at the discovery of Nature's gifts and secrets was now a hardened young woman, her thin shoulders bowed beneath the awesome burden she insisted upon carrying alone.

"Ye've changed much, missy," Lucie noted with sad regret. "But now da bad is over, and ye is meant to share yerself and yer burdens with a strong man. Da good Lawd intended for a man and a woman to need one another and to help each other with their problems. Dat what for He put so many on this earth."

"Men or problems?" questioned Callie with a cynical laugh. "Never mind. One begets the other." She paused. "I lost most everyone I loved, Lucie," she said, her voice low and quiet. "After Ethan died, I vowed on my mother's grave that I ain't never goin' to care for anyone ever again—'ceptin' you and Old Joe. If it ain't painful in the end, 'tis dangerous," she added, thinking of Abel Cane. "If only Papa hadna died—" Callie broke off with an aggrieved sigh and lay back on the soft carpet of grass to gaze wistfully up at the sky.

"Looks like we is finally in for a storm. The spring rains is late this year," observed Lucie, following Callie's gaze to the gathering clouds. She knew the previous subject was closed for now. "Is ye finished with thinnin' the tobaccy seedlings? Ye know the dogwood leaves was as large as a squirrel's ear last week. We gots to be plantin' da corn and da vegetable garden soon."

"'Twill have to wait until after the hilling of the tobacco fields," said Callie. "Without Ethan, our pace is much slowed."

"Humph, dat ol' devil weed take more care'n a baby. Can't eat tobaccy. Corn and wheat is what we have more need of."

"'Tis true," said Callie. "But tobacco carries the weight of silver tender." Reluctantly, she got to her feet. "I best be fetchin' up some more water to Old Joe. No tellin' how much rain'll come of this storm. Might be all bluster."

Callie gathered her hair beneath her hat, collected the wooden buckets, and headed for the river.

"Have a care, missy," Lucie called after her. "Remember dat whippoorwill."

Callie impatiently waved off Lucie's superstitious warning.

But the old Negress knew. She could feel it in her bones. Something was in the air, and it portended nothing good.

CHAPTER TWO

A Gathering Storm

The stranger squinted up at the afternoon sky. The darkening clouds and the nervous prancing of the magnificent black stallion told him that he would not make the distance to Williamsburg before the downpour.

"Easy, Saber." He patted the great beast's neck. "Easy, boy."

The man removed the dusty tricorn to wipe the sweat from his brow. It had been a long journey. Already, he was more than a fortnight overdue, and he was hot, tired, and hungry. The growling of his stomach reminded him that he hadn't eaten since morning.

Looking off into the distance, he saw the coiling smoke of a settlement. That would have to do him for the night, he decided. He hoped that the colonists' reputation for hospitality was equal to the rumors that circulated abroad. One story had it that a couple arriving for a visit in one Southern home had been prevailed upon to lengthen their stay through the birth of two children.

Others had reported that planters were so starved for conversation that they posted boys at the gates of their manors to beckon travelers to their doors. Most certainly a member of the English peerage would be that much more welcome. A smile wreathed his mouth as the man entertained thoughts of a soft bed and a well-spread table.

After traveling the remote countryside thus far, he could well understand what prompted such extremes in generosity. The loneliness was disconcerting to say the least, the silence jarring when pierced by the sudden hair-raising caw of a crow. He had passed no towns or inns along the way, and, except for a few widely dispersed farms, he saw little evidence of human existence since leaving the Landing. He found it difficult to believe that this was the main road to Williamsburg—if, indeed, one could call it a road. In places it resembled little more than a cow path, and he had met but one traveler along the way. God help the man in sudden need of aid or comfort, he thought uneasily.

This was certainly far from what Jonathan Trenholme, the eighth Earl of Eastwicke and the third son of the Duke of Lansing, had expected. In England, towns and taverns lay interspersed along each roadway and the countryside teemed with the traffic of stagecoaches, carriages, and wagons. The bloody colony was still a wilderness, Trenholme concluded irritably. Once again, he cursed the circumstances that had brought him to this place. Upon his arrival in Williamsburg, he was determined to speak to the royal governor about his immediate return to London. With that, he turned his horse in the direction of the smoke and nudged the stallion into a gallop.

Though she had scoffed at Lucie's superstitions, Callie walked with more attention to her surroundings than usual. When she reached the river, she saw something bobbing in the current near the bank. It looked like a basket caught on the branch of a fallen tree limb. Curious, Callie dropped the buckets and waded into the water to make closer inspection. She was surprised to find that the basket had been designed to float and was pitched for waterproofing. Her interest increased when she realized that it contained something of weight.

She quickly freed the basket from the tree limb and carried it back to the bank to view the contents. It was too light to be gold or silver coin, she concluded, disappointed. But perhaps it was something that could be just as easily bartered. She shifted the weight to one arm and lifted the cover. A strangled cry escaped her and tears welled up in her eyes as she stared down at the still form of a newborn baby. Judging from the construction of the basket and the care with which the baby had been laid in the makeshift cradle, Callie guessed that whoever had been responsible for this had intended for the child to be found alive. The baby was so tiny and frail that, even with immediate care, she doubted the child would have survived long after birth.

"I trust that you are aware of the penalty for infanticide," said a deep voice behind her. "God's blood, lad, have you no sense of decency?"

Callie jumped and whirled about to find a tall, broad-shouldered man scowling down at her. His dark blue wool coat and hat were covered with dust. The fearsome glare on his face and the harshness of his tone aside, the man was ominous to Callie's mind by his presence alone. His appearance was so sudden and undetected that she looked around in confusion trying to divine the source of his materialization.

Mistaking Callie's shock for guilt, Jonathan Trenholme was finding it difficult to reconcile such innocence of youth with so heinous an act. But eyes did not deceive. He had seen the scrawny, buckskin-clad youth take the basket from the river when he stopped to water his horse.

He stepped forward and took the basket from Callie's arms to examine the body. "A female child…the birth looks to be fairly recent."

"Three days I would wager—" Callie suddenly broke off when he swung an accusatory eye on her. "Oh, this child ain't mine, mister," she quickly informed him.

Trenholme snorted. "I know that, lad. I have yet to know of the birthing of a babe by the male of the species. You be too young to have a wife. Does the child belong to your sister or your mother?"

Callie opened her mouth to protest the man's impertinence, when the tenuousness of her position hit her like a shot. He thought her a boy and was still ready to hold her accountable. What would he do if he knew her to be a lass? Well aware of the harsh punishment for infanticide, Callie suddenly realized the necessity of protecting her disguise.

"Honest, mister, I jest found it. 'Tis truth!" Callie cried, noting the dubious expression on his face. "I come to draw water, and I found the basket floatin' here. I ain't lyin'. I got nothin' to hide," she continued, seeing that he was still skeptical. "Besides, this ain't an act of murder."

"Pray tell what is it, then, lad?"

"'Tis an act of love and desperation. Whoever done this hoped the child would be found alive—like Moses in the Bible."

"And how might you know that?" he demanded to know.

"'Tis obvious," replied Callie. "The basket was made of reeds to keep it afloat and tarred to keep the inside dry. Alas, 'tis plain to see the child would not survive much past the birthin'."

Trenholme gave another snort of impatience. It would seem that the lad had an answer for everything. "What is your basis for this conclusion?"

"I helped my mother bury two babes that died a few days after birth. I know the signs."

"Where is your mother?"

"She died nearly a year ago," said Callie on a more somber note. "To my thinkin', this poor babe is a bastard whose mother feared the punishment or mayhap the mother be a maidservant who found a longer indenture not to her likin'."

Trenholme studied Callie for a long moment. In the youth's tone and stance, there was a certain desperation, frustration, and anger characteristic of one being falsely accused. He had witnessed it enough times to recognize it. And the lad did make a good case. There was no trauma to the body as Jonathan could see and nothing to discount the boy's story. Nor could he attest to having seen the lad commit the crime. Still, the boy was found in possession of the corpse, and, if he wasn't a party to the infant's death, what was he so nervous about? What was he hiding? Judging from his appearance, the lad was undoubtedly an indentured field hand, surmised Trenholme. He had to know the mother's identity. She was most likely an indentured servant herself.

Trenholme whistled for his horse, and the most magnificent stallion Callie had ever seen came into view and trotted over to him.

"Who is your master?" asked Jonathan, securing the basket to back of his saddle.

He had unknowingly hit a nerve and Callie bristled. "Yer talkin' to him, mister. I be my own master. There ain't none higher, 'ceptin' maybe the Almighty."

"That may be so, lad," said Trenholme, his lips curling up in a smirk. "But 'tis the owner of the estate on which you toil of whom I speak."

Heedless of her precarious position, Callie stood with her legs akimbo, her hands on her hips goaded by his derisive tone. "You don't listen so good, mister. This land be mine to do with as I please until I die. I toil for no one but meself."

Jonathan raised a brow at this. "You do not look much like the overlord of a plantation," he responded, playing along. The more lies he could catch the lad in, the weaker the boy's defense would be.

"And jest how is one s'pose to look?" asked Callie tartly.

"Well, for one thing, a gentleman doesn't work the fields like a common laborer. For another, your manners and dress, or lack thereof, run wholly contrary to—"

"This ain't England."

"So I have noticed. While we are on the subject, since when is the responsibility of a plantation farm left to a young boy?"

"'Tis ten and seven I be."

Jonathan roared with laughter. "Ten and seven, ye say." He grasped Callie's chin and felt her forearm. "Skin as smooth as a lass, little muscle…your voice hasn't even changed yet. I would wager ye've not see more than ten and two years."

Callie angrily shoved his hand away. "Then ye would lose yer bet."

Trenholme was tiring of the exchange and impatient to see the matter resolved. The boy was plainly lying.

"Which way to your plantation, lad? I would see it now," he commanded firmly.

Callie's heart sank. She had hoped to set aside his doubts and send him on his way, but it was becoming apparent that he was not going to be so easy to dismiss. She didn't know who this man was, but his officious manner and richness of dress suggested that he held a position of authority and wasn't to be taken lightly. Anxious to satisfy his curiosity and have him gone, Callie quickly led the way up the small incline to a rough timbered dwelling some twenty-five feet inland.

Jonathan lost all patience. "Enough of your games. Take me to the manor house or I shall take a whip to you."

"This be it, mister," said Callie in bewilderment. "This be the house."

Trenholme stared at the shack in disbelief. It most certainly did not square with the description he had of a plantation home. "It cannot be. I have seen better lodgings for cattle. My resources speak of a great house and servants."

Callie stiffened. "It 'pears ye made a wrong turn, mister. An' I'll thank ye to hold yer tongue. This may not be fancy, but 'tis my home jest the same."

"Ye be a bloody tenant!" exclaimed Trenholme in disgust. The mere sound of the word left a bitter taste in his mouth. Though it had happened a score of years ago, the death of his younger brother during a tenants' uprising on one of his father's estates was still a painful memory.

"I ain't no tenant!" Callie shouted back. "'Tis freeholdin' I be, an' I'm bound that ye know the difference. I ain't beholdin' to no one, an' I ne'er shall be!"

Jonathan was astonished by the vehemence of the lad's declaration. The whelp commanded the spirit of the privileged, and he caught himself in amazement as he, a member of the nobility, was about to tender an apology to one of common stock.

"The difference is duly noted," he murmured sourly.

He entered the one-room dwelling and sniffed the air. "What is that odor?"

"'Tis a witch's bag," said Callie. At the blank look on his face, she explained. "Certain herbs, weeds, and spices bound together in a cloth are supposed to keep bad spirits out and good ones in." She threw him a pointed look. "Don't 'pear to have worked none, does it?"

Trenholme's jaw tightened, but he let the remark pass. He surveyed the crude quarters with ill-concealed disdain and dismay. A stone fireplace dominated one wall and a bedstead another. Besides the iron pots, brass kettle, and wooden utensils necessary for cooking, the only other items were a trunk near the bed and a trestle table with crude benches on either side of it in the center of the room.

"This is all that you have?" he inquired, incredulous. "Even tenants in England live more comfortably than this."

"'Tis all I need," Callie shot back defensively. It angered her that this stranger should sit in judgment of her actions, her belongings, her way of life. What rankled her most was that, given the circumstances, she was forced to allow him the privilege—whoever he was.

Jonathan opened the trunk and lifted out a simple brown wool bodice, a brown and red striped wool petticoat, and a worn linen shift. "To whom do these belong?" he demanded gruffly, his suspicions raised anew. "I had better not find that you are lying to me."

Callie grabbed the articles from his hand. "I ain't lyin'. They belonged to my mother."

Trenholme examined the coverlet on the bed and the dirt floor but found no further sign of a woman's presence or of recent childbirth anywhere. Still, he wasn't entirely convinced of the lad's innocence. He had learned long ago to trust his instincts and something didn't feel right to him. He retraced his steps outside; Callie anxiously followed after him.

"'Tis luck ye not be a lass, else your innocence would be held more in question," said Jonathan. "The casting off of unwanted children by women is a much too frequent occurrence these days in spite of the death penalty that it carries. Do you live here alone?"

Callie shifted nervously, pulling the hat lower over her face and consciously lowering her voice. "Old Joe and Lucie help me."

At this, two woolly heads peered out from the side of the cabin. Jonathan glanced at them and turned to survey the little farm. The garden alongside the crude puncheon and bark cabin was cultivated in neat rows for planting. Several yards away stood a smokehouse, another small cabin, which he figured to house the two servants, and some kind of a storage hut with basic accommodations for livestock. Next to that was a snake fence that penned two pigs. A handful of chickens, guinea fowl, and turkeys ran loose about the grounds and a cow and a horse grazed in a nearby field.

In the distance, split rail fences enclosed fields, which had been prepared for what he guessed to be corn and wheat. Opposite that, a tobacco barn stood halfway between tobacco seedbeds and fields yet to be hilled for the transplanting of the seedlings. All in all, there appeared to be a well-run order to the little farm. The boy seemed to know what he was about. Still, he was too young to Jonathan's mind to be charged with such responsibility.

"Have ye a name, lad?" he asked.

"Everyone has a name," responded Callie in a condescending tone. "It depends on whether or not he wishes to answer to it. What of you?"

Trenholme had had enough of this young pup's impertinence. "Now see here, do you know who I am?" he demanded imperiously.

Callie was undaunted. "Bein' that ye ain't never said, can't say as I do. But I would guess ye to be jest off the ship from England and a stranger to work judgin' by them hands. Ain't dressed right neither for these parts," she continued with a disdainful sniff, taking in the heavy wool cloth of his travel suit. "Ye see—"

"What I see," ground out Trenholme, visibly struggling to control his temper, "is a lad who seems to have forgotten proper speech as well as manners after a few years in this god forsaken land. Now, what be your name—if ye know it?"

Callie bristled. "I am called Callie—Cal Hastings," she quickly amended.

"Well, Cal, I am Lord Jonathan Trenholme, Earl of Eastwicke and third son of the Duke of Lansing." If he was waiting for an awed reaction, Jonathan was greatly disappointed. "You would do well to show respect for your betters," he lectured her sternly.

Callie's cheeks became flushed with anger. "Out here, mister—"

"Lord Trenholme," he interjected stoutly.

"Out here, Trenholme," Callie continued in flagrant disregard of his command, "respect is earned. Nature plays no favorites. Only the heartiest survive and title makes none the difference."

Jonathan was completely taken aback for one of the few times in his life. His birth entitled him to privilege, respect, and subservience. Never, from among even the lowest of class, had he encountered such total disrespect and indifference to his breeding. The distant rumble of thunder reminded him that he was at a disadvantage at the moment and, with great difficulty, he restrained his temper.

"Have ye a decent stable?" he inquired brusquely.

"Beside the smokehouse. Why?"

"You will have to make your bed there, while I make use of yours in the cabin."

"What? No…no, ye cannot stay here," declared Callie, hard pressed to hide her alarm.

"'Tis not my desire either, I can assure you," said Trenholme. "We shall have to take an accounting of the babe's death to the court in Williamsburg, and, by the gathering of those clouds, we would be wise to delay until morning."

"I have chores that need tendin' and fields that need plantin'. I ain't goin' to Williamsburg."

"I am bound that you are," Jonathan responded firmly. "The concealment of the death of a bastard is a capital offense under the king's law. In affairs of this nature, there are strict rules to be followed."

"Then you report it and leave me to my own," said Callie, deciding the matter once and for all.

"Hold fast, lad. The law requires the report of the most primary source."

"The law," said Callie with thinning patience, "would know none the difference."

"The law," Jonathan shot back sternly, "is what preserves civilization, and, if the whole of this community can be judged by your manners and attitude, this colony is but one step from barbarity as it is."

With great difficulty, Callie bit back an acerbic response. Instead, she repeated firmly, "Ye cannot stay here."

Jonathan glanced up at the threatening sky. "'Tis unfortunate for the both of us that I have no choice in the matter." He eyed Callie closely. "I am beginning to think that you are trying to be rid of me, lad. It gives me cause to wonder why."

"I have not the space or quarters to offer ye—as befittin' your station," she added with thinly veiled sarcasm. "And the stable is but a poor lean-to. If it rains, I shall be soaked and taken with fever, which would serve neither of us."

Again, Jonathan regarded the youth. Something didn't track here, but he couldn't put his finger on it. Perhaps it was more prudent to keep the lad on a short leash. "Your concern is most valid, Mr. Hastings."

"What is that to mean?" asked Callie warily.

"It means that I accept your argument. You shall make your bed by the hearth."

The smile that had started to form on her lips quickly faded. She opened her mouth to protest, but Trenholme didn't give her the chance as he continued to bark out orders.

"Call your man to bed my horse now. Have a care for I have brought Saber all the way from England with me and lay great store by him." Jonathan untied the basket and handed it to Callie. "Keep the corpse safe from preying animals. The court shall have a need to examine it." He unfastened his saddle, then, and carried it into the dwelling.

Callie's jaw dropped. This was not what she had intended at all. And how dare he order her about like a servant in her own home. Make her bed by the hearth indeed! Suddenly, she was seized by the frightening realization that the secret of her gender was becoming less secure by the minute.

CHAPTER THREE

A Ruse Exposed

I hope you have enough food in that pot," said Jonathan, when Callie returned from carrying out his orders. The aroma of simmering food was bringing protests from his stomach once again.

Callie grudgingly filled two wooden tankards with cider. "I wasn't expectin' to take vittles for awhile, but I s'pose 'tis fittin' enough to eat—even for you."

Ignoring the youth's insolent and sullen manner, Trenholme sat down expectantly on the bench. He took the proffered tankard and drank thirstily. "Ye do a woman's job quite handily," he noted, as Callie deftly lifted the kettle off the pot hanger in the fireplace and placed it on the hearth. Once again, he was struck by a sense of incongruity but couldn't quite figure it.

"Out here a body does the work of both a man and a woman to survive," Callie responded smoothly, making a mental note to watch her steps more carefully. She ladled out stew into a large wood bowl and placed it on the table.

"What is this?" asked Jonathan, his mouth twisting into a grimace at the sight of the steaming mash.

"'Tis stewed pumpkin with boiled beans, peas and corn. What does it look like?"

"I dare not say," muttered Trenholme.

When Callie handed him a long-handled wooden spoon, he tentatively sampled the mash. "'Twill do," he announced at length.

In truth, the taste was rather bland but, given the choice between the concoction and hunger, he was happy to accept the stew. When washed down with the sweet cider, he had to allow that the mash was palatable.

Callie seated herself on the bench across from him. She dipped her spoon into the bowl, and when she brought it to her lips, she looked up to find Jonathan staring at her in disbelief.

"Somethin' amiss?" she asked.

"What are ye about?" he demanded to know.

Callie looked at him in perplexity. "'Tis eatin' I be about."

"Have ye no other bowls?"

"'Tis just me. Ain't no need. Besides, hereabouts most everyone uses the general dish."

"What about trenchers?"

"Can't eat stew off a flat trencher," she scoffed as though addressing a simpleton. "That be for eatin' meat."

Jonathan spread his arms wide and gripped the edge of the table, at great pains to restrain his temper. "You are missing the point," he responded crisply. "Surely, you do not expect us to partake from the same vessel."

"Why not? Say, ye ain't got some disease, have ye?" Callie asked in sudden alarm.

"Certainly, not!" he exploded.

"Then what's the fuss about?"

"I am a member of the nobility. Alas, you are not. You do not eat with me; you serve me."

Callie stiffened and her eyes flashed. "I told ye afore. I ain't no servant, Trenholme, an' I ain't no slave. I serve no man."

Jonathan was taken aback for a second time by the passion and conviction in her tone with such a declaration. "Even so, I am not sharing my vessel with a commoner," he flatly stated.

"Be there a law against it?"

"No. But 'tis hundreds of years of English tradition. There are rules. Someone of my class simply does not partake with commoners."

"Then wait until I finish and ye can have the bowl all to yerself," replied Callie, matter-of-factly.

Trenholme was flabbergasted. He had the same thought only he hadn't intended to be the one to wait. "Does no one understand etiquette in this god forsaken land?"

"What's that?"

"Manners! Court society commands that you—"

"Maybe ye don't hear so good. This ain't England," interrupted Callie impatiently.

Jonathan stared at her. In his world, no lowborn would ever consider interrupting a nobleman. "Be that as it may," he ground out, "you are still subjects of the king and as such are subject to the same customs and societal restrictions."

Callie fixed an unwavering eye on him. "There ain't no king an' his fancy court here, Trenholme. Rules be different in Virginia."

Trenholme glared at her as that realization was beginning to sink in, and he had the uncomfortable feeling that his stay here was going to be worse than he had anticipated.

"Keep your spoon to your side of the bowl," he ordered sourly.

Callie peaked up at him from under the brim of her hat and covertly studied her uninvited and most unwelcome guest as they ate. He was taller and broader of shoulder than most men of her acquaintance, and he wore his light brown hair pulled back in a queue in the style of his class. His features were strong and well drawn though, at the moment, arranged in a scowl. And his deep-set brown eyes, flecked with gold, were intelligent, sharp, and uncomfortably assessing.

Callie supposed women might find him attractive—probably most women. But he was a man not given to humor or forbearance, as she could see, and he was much too overbearing for her taste. While he did not possess the sinister air of her stepfather, he did carry an air of authority apart from his noble status that kept her on her guard.

Jonathan took his fill of the mash. "What other courses have ye?" he asked. "Fowl…fish?"

"This and this here corn bread is all there is," said Callie.

Trenholme looked at her with an equal measure of disbelief and disappointment. Again, the world from whence he came served no less than twenty dishes and two courses at the main meal and at least three different liquors. Though he didn't expect so lavish a spread in this wilderness, he certainly thought to encounter better than this meager fare.

"Do ye not fish or hunt game?"

"Ain't had time."

"What about the fowl running about the yard?"

"'Tis certain ye ain't never farmed or cooked," said Callie with a hint of condescension. "'Tis 'bout all the three of us can do to get the crop fields cultivated in time."

Jonathan ran a critical eye over her person. "Little wonder ye be so bloody thin."

"If I know'd ye was comin', I'd a brought out the china and made a puddin'."

"No need to be sarcastic, lad. Are all you colonists so bloody genial?"

Callie bristled. "I thank ye not to be callin' me names that I don't be knowin' the meanin' to." She suddenly eyed him with suspicion. "If yer such an important nobleman, how come ye to be travelin' alone? People like ye always have servants about."

"I left my manservant at the port to tend to my trunk while I rode on ahead to Williamsburg. He is to follow by coach."

"What business have ye in Virginia? By the way ye been complainin', 'tis certain ye ain't here by yer own hand."

Trenholme leaned forward to lend full emphasis to his words. "I am here because a woman once sought to take me for a fool and a man endeavored to capitalize on it. 'Tis fitting to say that they met their just rewards. I was sent here to wait, shall we say, for calmer winds to prevail." He knew certain satisfaction when Callie quickly drew back.

"Ye killed two people?" she asked, her eyes wide with alarm.

Trenholme's mouth curled up in a half smile. "No, not killed but something almost as satisfying. You will find, lad, that I am not a man to be trifled with."

There was a note of warning in his voice, and Callie gulped hard thinking of the deceit that she was attempting to practice on him.

"How is it you that find yourself here?" he asked. He couldn't imagine that anyone would choose to come to a place like this.

"I was born here," said Callie, careful to keep a distance between them.

"How unfortunate."

"Now jest a bloody minute—" She started to protest, then thought better of it. After his disclosure, she was even less certain of what manner of man he was.

"Go on," prodded Jonathan.

"Nothin'. Don't know what concern 'tis of yers is all."

"Perhaps none, but you inspire curiosity, Mr. Hastings. Please enlighten me about your family."

Callie twisted uncomfortably on her seat. She was loath to tell him anything about herself. But he had her at a disadvantage for now.

"If ye must know," she said with a huff of annoyance, "my father was a carpenter and a joiner of note. Lord Robert Randall brung him from England to oversee the building of Randall Hall. Lord Randall give him this land to farm as a weddin' gift. We had a nice house, then," she added in a wistful tone.

"What happened to it?"

Callie shrugged, trying to project an air of indifference she was far from feeling. "Papa died some years back, and Mama married a scoundrel by name of Abel Cane. One night, the house and barn burned. My brother Ethan was asleep in the loft when the fire broke out. Mama went up to get him and got trapped. She had to jump from the loft window and died some days later. All Lucie and me was able to save was the pots, the kettle, and that trunk over there with a few clothes. Cane had disappeared with the first spark, the bloody no-good bastard. 'Twas him to blame. He weren't no good at nothin' anyways 'cept gettin' babes."

Callie caught Trenholme's penetrating gaze on her and knew that he was still trying to connect her to the baby. "Well 'tis truth I tell ye!" she exclaimed angrily. "If ye do not believe me, go look at my mother's grave."

Jonathan put up a hand to stem her outburst of temper. "All right, I believe you. Calm yourself and finish the story."

"Ain't much more to tell. Old Joe helped me and Ethan to build this cabin."

"Where is your brother?"

"Ethan come down with a fever after last harvest and died. He was a good boy just ten and two." Callie's voice trembled, and she quickly looked away to hide wounds not yet healed.

"I am sorry for your trials, lad," said Trenholme more gently. "I lost a younger brother as well. 'Tis the will of Providence—or so I was told," he added on a bitter note. "In any case, 'tis best not to dwell on such things as cannot be changed."

He rose from the bench, took off his coat and waistcoat, and threw them on the bed. "Come along, lad. We have a chore to address."

Callie quickly dashed away a tear with the back of her hand and jumped up to follow after him. "What chore?" she asked warily. "Where is it we go?"

"To the river. We should have enough time before the storm breaks."

"For what?"

"A bath."

Callie stopped dead in her tracks. "I ain't takin' no bath."

"I am bound that you are. I have a great need to wash the dust from me, and you…what were you doing this morning, lying in manure?"

Callie stiffened. "I was spreadin' some about in the fields. It keeps the soil from gettin' poor. Farmers hereabouts don't do that and—"

"I don't need a lesson in farming, lad, and I will not suffer the malodor," said Jonathan with firm resolve.

"I took a bath near a month ago," protested Callie. "Do ye wish me ill?"

Trenholme snorted at the long held belief that dirt and odor kept sickness at bay. "I am of another mind. Come along now. I have had a bellyful of unwashed bodies on the ship."

The man was not to be dissuaded, and Callie cast about desperately for a way to delay the task. "I have to take up the meal first. Lucie is busy with other chores. I-I'll be along directly."

Jonathan hesitated. "See that you are," he warned.

He left the dwelling and sauntered off to the river, wondering what he had fallen into this time. God's teeth! He would have faired better at the hands of his enemies in England.

As Callie placed the remains of the meal back into the kettle for breakfast the next morning, the Negress entered the cabin. "What ye gonna do now?" she whispered urgently. "Ye go in da water and dat man gonna know for sure ye ain't no boy lessen he be blind, missy."

Callie nervously bit her lip. "Oh, Lucie, what am I to do? If I do not go, he will come after me. And if that is not enough, he is forcing me to go to Williamsburg to give an accountin' of that poor babe."

"I told ye dat ol' whippoorwill spelled a mess of trouble. Iffen dat man don' know ye for a female now, he sure enough gonna know it by the time ye reach town."

"Damnation but this day has turned for the worst!" exclaimed Callie in frustration.

Lucie cocked a brow as if to say I-told-you-so. "Ye best have a care, child. Dat be a man what don' take kindly to bein' fooled."

A chill passed through Callie as the Negress echoed Trenholme's sentiments. Again, she wondered what he had done to that couple in England to warrant him having to take refuge in a land he so disliked.

"Ye best tell him you is a female afore he finds out on his own," Lucie warned her.

Callie shook her head. "No, 'tis too dangerous. He already believes I may have had a hand in the death of that poor child. If he knew me to be a lass, he would think me the mother and be that much more certain of my guilt."

"'Tis for sure he ain't gonna believe ye iffen he discovers it for hisself," said Lucie. "Too often a body can't see beyond da lie to da truth then."

"I shall have to take that chance. More is the time men don't see what's before their eyes anyway."

"Honey, you gots the curves of a board, but ain't no man dat blind for dat long." Lucie shook her head and mumbled dire forecasts under her breath as she lumbered out of the cabin. "Ye best not forget to lay da broom 'cross yer door this night to keep out dem evil spirits. Ye don' need no more trouble," she yelled back over her shoulder.

Callie dallied until she could no longer ignore Jonathan's impatient shouts. As she walked slowly to the river, she mulled over various excuses in her mind. She could say that Lucie needed her help. No, he would most likely respond that Lucie could wait. A servant was at the beck and call of his or her master, not the other way around. Perhaps she could tell him that she had a deformity of some sort—a deformity that must be kept dry. Callie immediately cast aside that thought. He was possessed of a suspicious nature and would most certainly demand a show of proof. What about an illness? She smiled. Yes, that was it. She would tell him that she was too ill to risk a chill, and she began to cough for effect as she approached the river bank.

"This day is hotter than a poker iron. I cannot fathom how you suffer those buckskins," said Jonathan, crouched low in the water.

"'Tis no worse than them wool clothes of yers," she countered.

"Quite so and all the more reason to shed them. The water is most refreshing."

Callie coughed again and regarded him with calculated woebegone eyes. "I fear there is an illness comin' in me, and I would not put myself to more risk."

He looked at her somewhat amused. "You weren't coughing earlier."

"It—it just come on."

Jonathan snorted. "I swear you are as jittery as a cat around water."

He stood up and emerged from the river to stand unabashedly naked before her. Callie's jaw dropped and her eyes widened as they traveled his body from the broad shoulders and muscular chest down to the tapered waistline and sinewy thighs.

Regaining her senses, she quickly turned her back to him. "What do ye think ye are about!" she exclaimed.

"'Tis customary to remove one's clothing whilst bathing," Jonathan replied dryly, maneuvering to stand before her again. "Now, enough of your tricks."

Looking up in time to see his intentions, Callie backed away from him. Suddenly, she felt space beneath her feet as she stepped off the bank. Her arms flailed, and she grabbed for her hat just in time. The next thing she knew she was sputtering up from the depths of waist-deep water. Jonathan's rumble of laughter did nothing to help her bruised dignity. When he waded in to pull her to her feet, Callie sidestepped him and scrambled up the bank to run back to the cabin.

A short while later, she heard the approach of heavy footsteps. The wet buckskins had molded to her body, and she grabbed the coverlet off the bed to wrap it around her, lest her secret be discovered. When Trenholme entered the dwelling, she peered up from under the brim of her hat and nervously fingered the quilt. When he shut the door, she swallowed hard.

"What is amiss with you?" he demanded to know.

"I-I cannot swim," she replied, forgetting her earlier decision to plead illness as she stared at his imposing figure. His shirt was slung carelessly over one shoulder, and in the small cabin, he seemed even more hulking to her.

"I doubt that you will drown in knee-deep water," he remarked.

"'Twas waist deep."

Jonathan shook his head as though she defied explanation. He pulled on his shirt and tucked it into his breeches "Is that hat a permanent attachment?" he asked.

"What?"

"The hat…you never take it off. Do you have lice?"

"No! Now, leave me be!"

Jonathan shrugged matter-of-factly. "I guess living out here in this barbarous land can turn one strange sooner or later."

Keenly aware that his gaze remained on her, Callie shifted uncomfortably from one foot to the other. She was sweltering beneath the quilt, the soggy hat sat heavy on her head, and the wet buckskins were making her skin itch. She tried to be inconspicuous in her scratching, but it was too much for Trenholme. Uttering an oath, he snatched the coverlet from her, picked her up, and tucked her under his arm.

"What—what are ye doin'?" she sputtered, struggling to break free.

"I will not lie down with bugs and whatnot," said Jonathan. "This time I shall see to it that you have a proper dunking."

Callie wriggled free from his grasp. "I ain't got louses. 'Tis the wet buckskins what make me itch."

"Then take them off."

He reached out to yank off her shirt, but Callie bolted and he was left with a handful of fringe. She frantically flung open the door and started to run when she tripped over something lying across the doorsill and hit the ground with a thud. The fall knocked the wind out of her, and it was a few seconds before she realized that Trenholme, having lunged for her at the same time, now lay on top of her. He sat up and flipped her on her back. When she saw the astonishment on his face, she realized that she had lost her hat.

Jonathan coiled his fingers around the long, tangled hair in disbelief. "Ye be a lass!" he exclaimed. He patted his hands over her body as though in need of further confirmation. "No wonder things did not ring true—God's teeth, ye let me parade around ye as naked as a jay bird!"

"Well, 'twasn't by my invite," retorted Callie. "Take yer hands off me!"

Jonathan felt like a complete idiot. He stood up and furiously hauled her to her feet. As he shoved her back into the cabin, Callie looked to see what she had tripped over. She groaned at the sight of the broomstick that Lucie had laid across the sill to protect her mistress against the evils of the night.

"Why the devil did you not tell me that you are a lass?" railed Trenholme.

"I was afraid," said Callie. "Ye was so certain that I had a hand in that poor babe's death, I feared ye to think me the mother."

"And what should I think now that I have caught you in this lie?"

"I didn't lie. 'Twas you who decided that I was a lad."

Trenholme glared at her. "With good cause, I dare say. Do you always go about dressed in buckskins, denying your gender?"

"A man is more likely to pick a quarrel with another man or to press unwanted advances on a lone woman. A young boy is often ignored. Now that there are so many strangers travelin' about, I thought the disguise to serve me better."

"So many strangers—I saw only one the entire way from the Landing."

"And now there is you," said Callie, considering she had proven her point.

"Good Lord, ye have nothing to fear from me! I could never be so sorely tried as to bed a lass against her will—much less one smelling of manure." He raked a critical eye over her in the dim firelight. "How many years have ye seen, Cal?"

"The name is Callie, and I told ye afore 'tis ten and seven I be."

"Ten and seven—ha, ye look to be more a child than a maiden."

Callie may have balked at advertising her womanhood, but it stung her pride that Trenholme should so casually dismiss it. She bit back a stinging retort, however. She didn't know this man's full nature and her low regard for the male species was such that she had no wish to test his character.

"What is to happen now?" she asked haltingly.

"You will still stand at court."

There was a sudden clash of thunder and a downpour of rain that seemed to portend her future.

"But I ain't guilty of anythin', and, accordin' to you, 'tis likely they will think me to blame."

"When testimony is given that the babe was found on your property and that you are a female of childbearing age, suspicion will naturally fall on you," Trenholme admitted unhelpfully.

Callie paled. "How am I to prove my innocence when my own witness scarce believes the truth?"

"If you *are* innocent, 'twill be proven. At this moment, I am more concerned with getting a good night's rest," replied Jonathan dispassionately. He closed the shutter against the driving rain. "Where are you going?"

"To sleep in the tobacco barn," snapped Callie.

"You will be drenched before you get a foot outside the door, and, as you pointed out, 'twill serve neither of us if you fall ill."

"Afraid it will rob the hangman of his pleasure?" she asked snidely.

Trenholme let the remark slide. He was too tired to cross swords. "Now where are you going?" he demanded impatiently.

"To stay with Lucie and Old Joe in their cabin."

"I will not stand for a mistress to share her slaves' quarters."

"Lucie and Old Joe ain't slaves. They be freemen."

Jonathan heaved a sigh of exasperation. "You will stay the night here," he declared firmly.

"'Tis better for an unmarried woman to share her lodging with a strange man?" challenged Callie.

"It has been done upon occasion," replied Trenholme, deliberately fanning her ill ease.

Callie stood resolutely with her hands on her hips, a determined glint in her eye. "Mister, I ain't gonna share Sadie Hanks' fate no matter what."

"Who the deuce is Sadie Hanks?"

"Sadie was caught beddin' her man afore marriage and they was flogged and obliged to stand afore the whole church in robes of shame."

Trenholme snickered. "Well, do not overly concern yourself. I bed neither commoners nor children." As she continued to regard him with marked uncertainty, he picked up the quilt and threw it to her. "Make your bed by the hearth. The warmth will dry out your clothes, and you can tend the fire throughout the night. Move it, lass! I am short on temper this night and the morrow promises to be a long day."

Callie dragged the damp quilt over to the fire. She knew that further argument was useless and might only provoke him to a more undesirable act.

Trenholme pulled off his boots and flopped on the bed only to bolt upright again rubbing his back. "What the devil makes this mattress? 'Tis hard as stone and as prickly as a porcupine."

"Hemlock boughs," said Callie.

"How the deuce can a body be expected to rest comfortably on hemlock boughs!"

"A hard day's work makes for a soft bed—sir," she quipped smartly.

Trenholme's jaw tightened. That an impudent, lowborn child should derive amusement at his expense did not sit well with him. Twice now, she had made him look the fool. It soothed his bruised ego somewhat that, given her thin frame and manner of dress, anyone would have mistaken her for a lad. Just the same, no one got the better of Lord Jonathan Trenholme. Such impertinence, he decided resolutely, deserved redress.

CHAPTER FOUR

Day of Reckoning

For the next few hours, Callie tossed and turned beside the spitting embers, keeping the fire alive just enough to easily revive it in the morning. Usually, Lucie saw to it, bringing hot coals as a starter from her own cabin. But she knew that the Negress wouldn't venture near here as long as Lord Jonathan Trenholme were present. Callie also had an idea that this man did not take kindly to waiting for his meals. 'Twas a malady of both his gender and his class, she thought disparagingly.

She laid a small log on the fire and flopped back on the quilt. Perspiration beaded her forehead, and her clammy skin begged to be separated from the buckskin trappings. Damnation she was hot, and she yearned to trade her clothes for the thin linen shift that she usually wore.

Callie's irritation only increased as she looked over to see Trenholme's long form peacefully stretched out on her bed. A long, lean, muscular form—Callie gasped, mortified as her mind's eye shamelessly recalled every detail of his virile body. She immediately shook her head to dispel the disquieting image of Jonathan emerging naked from the river. She had never seen such a sight.

Her mind returned to her predicament, and she asked herself, again, why this stranger newly arrived from England should be so insistent upon involving himself in a matter that was of no concern to him, whether he thought her guilty of the infant's death or not. To be sure he spouted a lot of words about civilization and the law, but there was more to this than met the eye, she concluded.

At the thought of being dragged before the court, she was gripped by panic. What if no one believed her? She knew justice in this matter to be swift and terrible, for far too many women were still driven to this desperate measure despite the consequences. Rumor had it that one indentured woman had been burned at the stake for drowning her baby. And she imagined the justices, one by one, passing a similar sentence upon her. All too clearly, she saw herself being tied to a pole and the dry kindling around her set afire.

The picture became that much more vivid and horrifying when a spark flew from the fireplace to land on her leg. Callie uttered a cry and jumped to her feet, slapping at the smoldering legging. She glanced over her shoulder at the bed praying that she hadn't awakened her guest, for she had just made a decision that she knew would not meet with Lord Jonathan Trenholme's approval.

When he didn't move, Callie slowly let out her breath and quietly made her way to the door. Trenholme didn't strike her as a man who left much to chance, and she questioned why he hadn't anticipated this action. But, with the thought of freedom within her grasp, she didn't belabor the point.

As she reached out for the leather door handle, her options scrolled across her mind. Although she knew plenty of hiding places in the area, Jonathan Trenholme knew her identity now, and he didn't seem likely to give up the hunt so easily. The couple in London on whom he had exacted revenge would undoubtedly testify to that fact. He would probably hound her until her dying day, and she certainly had no wish to spend the rest of her life in hiding. To run now would only make him that much more certain of her guilt and that much more set in his resolve to see her before the court.

Callie's shoulders slumped in defeat and she released the handle to creep silently back to her fireside bed. It would seem that the only way she was ever going to be rid of this man was to go to Williamsburg and declare her innocence.

She had just settled herself, when Trenholme's deep voice penetrated the silence. "Well chosen, lass."

Callie gasped. What little presence of mind she yet possessed completely dissolved. She had the eerie feeling that her thoughts were no longer her own. He seemed to anticipate her actions before she knew them herself. Any thought of sleep Callie might have entertained was beyond her now, and she passed the night in anxious turmoil. God's teeth! What grievous sin had she committed to warrant such ill fortune?

* * * * *

Callie greeted the first rays of light that squeezed through the cracks of the wooden shutter with mixed emotions. Her sleep had been fitful at best as she worried about her fate.

She could hear Jonathan talking with Old Joe outside. Soon he would be demanding to eat, she thought irritably, and she got to her feet to stir the fire to greater heat. By the time Trenholme entered the cabin, she was setting breakfast on the table.

He frowned when he saw the reheated pumpkin mash before him. "This again?"

"We eat what we cook 'til all is done," said Callie, clearly out of sorts.

With a sigh of resignation, Trenholme sat down to appease his hunger. Callie, however, found it difficult to swallow as that knot of apprehension in her stomach tightened, and she laid aside her spoon after one mouthful of the mash.

"I recollect that you have a horse," said Jonathan.

Callie nodded.

"Good. Then, if you have done with your meal, you may finish with your chore of last eve."

She eyed him warily. "What might that be?"

"Judges tend to look with more favor upon a person as clean in body as in spirit."

Callie jumped up from her seat. "If yer talkin' 'bout me takin' another bath—"

"I don't call falling into a river fully clothed a bath."

"Water is water."

"Not to my thinking."

Callie saw the threat in his narrowed eyes. When he moved to stand, she quickly reconsidered. "All right, I'm goin', but I had better not catch ye within a hundred paces of the bank."

"Have you soap?"

"Some lye jelly for washin' clothes."

"Use it. And see if you can find something more suitable to wear than buckskins."

Callie's eyes flashed and her face flamed with indignation, but she held her tongue as she stormed across the room to rummage through the trunk for her shift and her mother's petticoat and bodice. She draped them over her arm, and, throwing Trenholme a thunderous glare, she stomped out of the cabin. Outside the door, she stopped to fill a tin cup with lye jelly from a barrel.

Her furious strides kept pace with her temper as she covered the short distance to the river. Reluctantly, Callie shed her buckskins behind a tree, casting suspicious glances over her shoulder for any sign of voyeurs, and plunged into the water. Muttering curses under her breath, she took the jelly and half heartedly rubbed it across her body and washed her matted hair.

While Callie finished her bath, Jonathan set about readying the horses. He smiled with pride as Old Joe led the handsome and spirited stallion from the lean to. When Old Joe brought out Callie's horse, Jonathan's face fell at the sight of the swaybacked old gelding. He had given the horse scant attention the day before when he saw it grazing in the distance; he couldn't believe it was the same animal. He had to wonder what kept it on its feet, and he chafed at the speed that was certain to be lost.

"Come along, lass," he shouted irritably. "I should like to cover these miles before the morrow. With this old bag of bones ye call a horse—"

"No need to holler, Trenholme. I am here," said Callie, her annoyance matching his.

Jonathan whirled about, surprised by her stealth.

"Well?" she demanded peevishly as he raked a critical eye over her person.

"I suppose 'tis the best we can hope for," he said, taking in the tangled wet hair and drab attire.

The striped petticoat was well mended; the bodice was faded and worn; and the ruffled sleeves of her shift were tattered. Jonathan didn't know which detracted most from what—the shabby apparel from Callie's thin figure or Callie's figure from the shabby apparel. Decidedly, neither did anything to compliment the other.

His tactless dismissal of her efforts hurt and angered Callie. Her appearance, such as it was, had not come about without considerable work and discomfort to her thinking. Never mind that he had made her vulnerable to disease. Even more degrading, he made her feel like a slave on an auction block.

"Do ye wish to check my teeth, sir?" she asked sarcastically.

Trenholme ignored her comment, wondering what ailed her now.

He finished saddling his horse and secured the basket that contained the baby's corpse to the back. "Where is your saddle?" he inquired, turning back to her.

"I have no need of a saddle," she haughtily informed him.

To demonstrate her point, Callie led her bridled horse to a tree stump and lithely swung herself atop the beast. Jonathan gawked at the sight she shamelessly presented with her petticoat hiked up in the front and back, leaving her thin legs to dangle bare from the knees.

"What is amiss now?" she demanded impatiently.

"Have ye no stockings?"

"Ain't got no need of 'em with buckskins."

"What about shoes?"

"These moccasins is all I got."

"I suppose 'tis pointless to ask if you have a cap or a hat."

"Jest my brother's field hat." At this, Lucie came forward with the turned down cocked hat, and Callie jammed it on her head.

Jonathan sighed heavily, considering the matter hopeless.

"I told ye everythin' was lost in the fire," said Callie, growing more perturbed with his criticism of her dress and lifestyle. She turned to Lucie and Old Joe. "I shall return forthwith."

"No need to worry, child. All will go well with ye now that no lies stand in yer path," said Lucie. "Remember, when ye comes to da crossroads, sing yer heart out so's ye can get past dem devil forces of da other world."

"Hush woman," said Old Joe. "The missy don' need no mumble jumble to make her way. She gots da *will*," he pronounced solemnly.

His eyes held a strange glow as they stared into Callie's. Suddenly, she knew the strength and confidence that seemed to have deserted her since Jonathan Trenholme had intruded into her life. Old Joe smiled and nodded as she straightened her back and squared her shoulders. She was ready to face whatever might come her way. Even Jonathan sensed a new determination in her as she rode out ahead of him, her head held high.

"Hey, Trenholme," said Callie when he had drawn up alongside of her, "I had a saddle once—afore my stepfather lost it in a cock fight. I had lots of things once," she added in a brittle tone.

She didn't know why it mattered that he knew. It just did. She may be only a farmer and the daughter of a carpenter, but her pride demanded respect.

"Trenholme?" she ventured again.

Jonathan gave a sigh of annoyance. "What is it now? And 'tis *Lord* Trenholme to you."

Callie made a face at him. "How long will I be at the court?" she asked. "I must return to the farm afore dark. The road is too dangerous for travel at night."

Trenholme shook his head in wonder. For all of her distrust, the girl was amazingly naive. "You had best plan to stay in Williamsburg three days at least," he replied.

Callie brought the old gelding to an abrupt halt. "Three days! 'Tis not possible," she flatly declared. "The tobacco fields need to be hilled and the corn and wheat fields need to be planted."

"Old Joe and Lucie appear capable enough. If you are worried about them running off—"

"No, 'tis not a concern. But I cannot be away so long. Without Ethan, 'tis all the three of us can do to keep up. The loss of one hand for three days is the loss of one week's work."

"I am afraid that you have no choice, Callie. You must wait until your name comes up on the roster."

"Then I will come back to town when it does."

She moved to turn the horse around to return to the farm, but Jonathan grabbed hold of her reins and stopped her.

"'Tis not that simple."

It seemed simple enough to Callie. "Why not?"

"The court cannot sit idle waiting for you to be notified and brought back to Williamsburg."

"Are there not others being brought before the court?"

"Most likely there are."

"Then the court shall not be idle waitin' for me."

Jonathan took a deep breath to contain his impatience. "Still, there is a process to be observed."

"And this process says that I must be taken away from my farm in the midst of plantin' time until the court decides to call my name. It don't 'pear to be sensible or fair to me, Trenholme."

"It is not a question of sense or fairness. One simply does not inconvenience the court. The court exists to bring order to an otherwise lawless society, not to accommodate criminals."

Callie bristled. "I ain't a criminal."

"The court shall decide that." Jonathan dropped her reins and moved forward.

When Callie fell silent, he glanced back to find that she had dropped farther behind and her small face was pale and worried. "Now what is troubling you?"

"Trenholme, what if the court decides wrong?"

"How mean you?"

"You just said that it is more concerned with convenience than with sense or fairness. What if the court makes the wrong finding in haste?"

Jonathan let out a groan of exasperation. She had an annoying way of nuancing his words. "You mistake my meaning," he said. "In any case, the truth will out."

He could see that his reply was of little consolation to her, but he coldly reminded himself, as a twinge of conscience sought to creep in, that if she were innocent it would be proven. If she were guilty, then justice would be served. In any case, it would be a humbling experience, and God knew that her spirit could do with a good deal of humbling.

He nudged his horse to a faster pace. "The sooner we get to Williamsburg, the sooner this business will be ended," he called out impatiently.

Callie spurred her animal to greater speed. To Jonathan's amazement, she kept an even pace with him after that. Her horse had a half lumbering, half rolling gait. After an hour on the road, he had to wonder how Callie's bones hadn't been jarred to pieces or why the poor beast hadn't collapsed in a dead heap.

The storm had drenched the countryside the night before, but the air was becoming more oppressive as the morning wore on. The bloody place was as bad as the Indies, Trenholme concluded irritably. Once again, he made a mental note to speak with the royal governor with immediate dispatch about his release to return to England.

"Trenholme, what of lodgings?" Callie suddenly asked. "I have no coin."

Again, Jonathan was amazed by the degree of her naïveté. "The court will see to it," he said.

When they finally reached the city limits, Callie held back.

"What is the matter now?" he demanded to know.

"I don't take much to towns. Too many people knowin' ev'rybody's business and too much noise. 'Tain't healthy."

Trenholme snorted. "As a child living in the backwoods with only two old people for comfort, I should think you would welcome the company of others."

"I do not want or need anybody—and I am not a child!" Callie responded with an intensity that surprised him.

Jonathan shook his head again. He had never seen such temper and cynicism in one so young, except maybe in the dirty-faced urchins who lived by their wits on the streets of London. He fervently hoped that he would find people with more sophistication in Williamsburg.

CHAPTER FIVE

Darkness Descends

As they entered the town and rode down the Duke of Gloucester Street, Callie wrinkled her nose. The humid air was pungent with the odor of animal waste. Sounds of rooting pigs, chickens, and grazing sheep and cows mixed with the shouts of irate pedestrians dodging the heavy traffic of coaches, carriages, wagons, and two-wheeled riding chairs. It was late morning, but already the heat was suffocating, and Callie plucked at her petticoat and bodice.

Jonathan caught the disapproving lift of the ladies' brows as they rode past them. Callie wore her brother's hat instead of a cap and broad brim straw hat; the sleeves of her shift came just to her elbows instead of covering her arms; her legs were bare and exposed to the knees; and she wasn't wearing proper shoes. He wondered if Callie was unaware or simply uncaring of the ladies' stares. In her case, probably a bit of both, he decided.

The General Court sat twice a year—April and October—and people from miles around swarmed the town for weeks to share in the social events of Publik Time. There was a conjurer on one corner, a juggler on another. A puppet show and an auction were drawing crowds to the common. In the evening, Callie knew there would be parties and dances for the common folk, formal dinners and balls for the elite.

She and her brother had accompanied their parents to town during Publik Time on more than one occasion, and her eyes had been wide with excitement, her heart filled with joy and laughter. But those had been happier times then. The festive air on this occasion did nothing to lighten her heavy mood or to allay the fear she felt.

In direct contrast to Callie, Trenholme surveyed the colorful sights along the neat, tree-lined street with happy amazement, noting with approval the richness of dress and the clean uniformity of the brick and frame establishments. The atmosphere was one of gaiety and congeniality; underlying it all was an air of prosperity. Trenholme smiled to himself. The place was more civilized than he had dared to hope. Here, he would find the respect due him. This certainly wasn't London by any stretch of the imagination, but, for the first time, he had hope that his banishment to this barely civilized country might not be quite the punishment he was anticipating after all.

When they came to the Capitol building, Jonathan turned to Callie. "Wait here," he said. The tone of his voice and the stern expression on his face warned her that he had better still find her here upon his return.

As Callie watched him swing himself down from his mount and disappear into the brick building, her uneasiness increased. The public grounds surrounding the building teemed with men of every rank and profession, and Callie busied herself for the moment wondering what business each had come to transact before the court. Given the conviviality of the men, however, she doubted that any shared her fearful circumstances. The palms of her hands became sweaty and she was beginning to fidget nervously, when Jonathan finally emerged to take up his mount again.

"Follow me," he said.

"Where do we go?" she asked suspiciously as he led her to a narrow dirt road that ran behind the Capitol to Nicholson Street.

Jonathan hesitated. "We go to the gaol. There are some papers to see to," he quickly added when he saw her balk.

Callie continued to hold back, her manner wary. "Where might we be stayin' the night, Trenholme?"

Once a victim of it himself, Jonathan hated trickery and deceit, and he could carry on the ruse no longer. He reined in his horse until she drew up alongside of him.

"Callie, your lodging will have to be in the gaol until this matter is decided to the General Court's satisfaction."

A small cry escaped her, and her eyes mirrored her sense of betrayal. All of her fears of the previous night were now firmly rooted in reality. She turned the horse to flee, but Trenholme, anticipating her actions, reached out to catch hold of her reins. The horses stamped and snorted as she fought to break his hold.

"Ye planned all along to see me in that foul place!" she cried. "Ye took my bed and ate my food, and this be your payment? I have done nothin' I tell ye!"

She pounded and slapped at his arm to break free from him. In a last desperate effort, she threw her leg over the side to slide off the old gelding. Trenholme caught her around the waist and pulled her over to his horse, firmly anchoring her in front of him. She was so thin it was like lifting a feather, he thought fleetingly.

"Settle yourself, Callie," he ordered. "You are quite right. I should have prepared you, but I did not want you to worry."

"You mean ye feared me to run off from ye," she spat contemptuously.

Jonathan couldn't deny the charge credibly and didn't try. "'Tis only for a few days," he said as they rode up to the gaol. "I am not without influence, and I shall see to it that your case is called before the end of the week."

Callie shoved his hand away and slid off the horse, nearly falling to the ground. "Do me no more favors, Trenholme. The next one may put the rope around my neck or the torch to my stake."

"Come now, 'tis not as bleak as all that. Justices can be a fair-minded lot, and, if you are innocent of the charge, 'twill be proven."

"I ain't got much of worth but my name, and 'tis proud I am to bear it," said Callie. "Now, thanks to ye, I'll not have that. Since ye come along, I ain't seen nothin' but trouble, so stay away from me. I would see this through on my own."

She drew herself up, raised her chin, and squared her shoulders. Without so much as a backward glance, she walked up the dirt path to the gaoler's door and pounded on it. It was a few minutes before the door opened. The gaoler adjusted his spectacles on the end of his nose and peered down at her in astonishment.

"Why my stars and moon—Callie Hastings, that you, lass? Ain't seen ye since Digger was a pup. 'Twas right sorry I was to hear of your mother and brother. What can Tom Wilson do for ye?"

Callie jerked her thumb over her shoulder. "Ask him."

The gaoler looked behind her to see a young man of obvious means and status imperiously sitting astride a magnificent stallion, and he quickly negotiated the path to Trenholme.

She waited for Trenholme and the keeper to finish conferring, her irritation and anxiety mounting as they discussed her future as though she were immaterial to the subject. The gaoler nodded a few times, and when he turned to regard her with a mixture of surprise and pity, she shifted nervously wondering what Trenholme was telling him.

When the two men had finally concluded their business, the gaoler called for his son. Within minutes, a gangling, pimple-faced youth no older than Callie came from around the side. He gawked with unabashed curiosity at her until, annoyed, she stuck out her tongue at him. Startled, the boy nearly fell over his feet. Observing the exchange, Trenholme snickered.

"Willie, mind your business!" Tom Wilson berated his son. "Take this basket to Dr. Blackmore for him to examine." He removed the basket from behind Trenholme's saddle and handed it to his son. As Willie looked at him in confusion, his father sighed impatiently. "The contents, lad… 'tis the contents what need be examined."

Willie mouthed a silent "Oh," and his father shook his head as one having to endure much.

"Now get ye goin'. I haven't all day for ye to stand here gawking."

His arms loaded with the basket, the boy quickly left to do as he was told.

"I swear that lad has mush for brains," mumbled Wilson resignedly. He turned back to Jonathan. "Ye've no need to worry, Lord Trenholme. I shall watch after Callie."

The gaoler's assurance was small comfort to Callie. As she followed Tom Wilson inside, she threw Jonathan a scathing look.

The room into which she stepped was not the dungeon of horrors Callie had expected. The walls were freshly whitewashed and fragrant rushes had been strewn across the floor. A pig was roasting on the spit in the fireplace, carefully tended by a small, round woman who gazed up at her compassionately. A long, rough-hewn table had been set with pewter and wood trenchers, and, in a cupboard in the corner, various pieces of chipped china were proudly displayed. Callie guessed that this was the Wilsons' living quarters, and she reluctantly left its comforting warmth to trail the gaoler down a dark, narrow corridor.

He unlocked a door and swung it wide. "'Ere ye go, Callie," he said, his tone sympathetic.

Callie cautiously entered the dark cubicle. When she heard the heavy wooden door close and lock behind her, her determined spirit was at odds with the growing panic inside her, and she silently cursed Trenholme every which way she knew.

CHAPTER SIX

Retribution

Her cell was one of eight and measured ten feet by ten feet. It was located on the north side of the gaol and overlooked the gallows, giving no comfort to anyone awaiting sentencing. There was a small window with a grill, but it emitted little light and Callie blinked trying to adjust her eyes to the dimness.

"What they get ye for, honey? Stealin'…doxyin'?"

Callie jumped at the sound of the gravelly voice that issued from the far corner of the cell. Peering closely, she could make out the figure of woman.

"'Tis all a misunderstandin'," said Callie in a hesitant voice.

The woman laughed huskily and came forward. "A misunderstandin' she says, Mae."

Callie's attention was drawn then to a form lying quietly on the straw.

"Listen, honey, everyone that comes in here says that," continued the woman. "Sometimes it's true, most times it ain't. The court hath heard it too often to believe it. If I was you, dearie, I'd find me a better story than that."

"Leave her be, Sally," said the reclining woman in a soft voice. "She be a child, and a body that scared can't have done nothin' that bad." The woman's voice grew fainter with each word before a paroxysm of coughing seized her.

"Easy, Mae, or ye might not live long enough to birth that babe in yer belly."

Mae sighed. "Death by childbirth would be the kinder justice if 'tis the rope I'm to draw for me sentence."

Callie's eyes had adjusted to the light, and she could more clearly make out the lines of despair etched in the young woman's face. "You are with child?" she asked in surprise.

"Aye…five months into my increasin' time."

"Surely, the court will show you some mercy. Can ye not plead yer belly?"

"Aye, that she can," interjected Sally. "'Tain't no reason for her to fear the worst."

"'Tis no small thing I done," Mae reminded her cellmate.

Sally snorted. "Humph, from what ye told me, 'tis a deed I'd a done in good conscience I can tell ye."

Callie looked at Mae curiously. "What deed did ye do?"

"She killed her husband, the no-good bastard. That's what she done," said Sally. "Beat her night an' day, he did, for the fun of it. Then he beat her some more when she couldna work the fields for her bruises whilst he spent the day tiltin' the bottle. Was about to split open her head, he was, when Mae reached for the pitchfork an' the drunken brute fell on it. 'Twas him what shoulda been hanged."

"Sally, 'tis enough words ye speak. I told ye afore there be things ye not be privy to," said Mae hoarsely.

"Go on with ye. What be ye sayin', gal?"

"I be sayin' that Jack…well, maybe this time he had cause to raise his hand." Mae's voice was barely above a whisper now and her eyes held a faraway look. "He was alive when I went to fetch help. When I come back—" Mae shook her head. "Poor Jack, it ain't right to die alone like that."

Callie couldn't take her eyes off Mae. She couldn't believe that this frail, young woman could possibly be guilty of murder whatever the situation.

* * * * *

For two days, Callie languished in the cell, her emotions running the gamut from confusion and frustration to anger at the injustice of it all. Why her? What twisted fate had conspired to curse her with Jonathan Trenholme and bring her to this end?

The keening, moaning, complaining, and crying of the other inmates—men and women awaiting trial or waiting to be whipped, branded, or hanged—grated on Callie's nerves until she thought she would go mad herself. And always there was the waiting, the wondering when the gaoler entered the passageway, and the dashed hope each time he continued on past her cell. The dankness of the gaol bred such despondency and fear that Callie despaired of ever waking from this nightmare.

Then there was Mae. Gentle Mae, who valiantly struggled to hide her pain as the cough continued to decimate her body and the guilt her mind. Callie and the coarse, gruffly attentive Sally did what they could to ease the ill woman's discomfort, but the dampness of the cell only exacerbated her condition. Though the keeper's wife provided them with a palatable fare, Mae ate less and less. Neither spoke her thoughts, but Callie and Sally knew that Mae, whether sentenced to death or not, wouldn't last a month in these surroundings, let alone four until the birth of her baby.

The next day, a summons came and the three women looked at each other with hope, fear, and anxiety. When only Sally's name was called, Callie and Mae didn't know whether to be disappointed or relieved that it wasn't one of them. With a gritty display of bravado that fooled no one, Sally followed the guard out with a saucy sway of her hips and bawdy banter on her lips.

In the gaol, there was little concept of time. Each minute seemed like an hour, each day an eternity. As one hour melted into two, Callie became increasingly restless.

"Mayhap Sally's been let go," she said hopefully.

"Mayhap," replied Mae.

But Sally was a prostitute and a con artist with a long list of chicaneries to her name. Both knew that the courts traditionally wasted little patience or mercy on such felons.

When the door finally swung open, it was a different Sally who returned to the cell. The ribald banter was subdued; the tough veneer had disappeared.

"Sally, what happened?" asked Callie.

Slowly, Sally lifted her eyes. "I've been indentured for seven years. I'm to be put on the block day after tomorrow."

"I am sorry for ye, Sally," said Mae.

The sympathy in Mae's words and the pity in her voice seemed to snap Sally out of her despondency.

"Ain't no one gonna be sorry for me. Mayhap 'tis for the better," she declared, recovering some of her swagger. "All me life I been left to find me own way. Now 'twill be another's job to see me fed and clothed, ay ladies." She laughed huskily, and Callie and Mae joined in to play her game.

When Mae had fallen asleep, Sally took Callie aside. "Listen, missy, there be a judge what be a bastard of a man. He wanted to give me the rope, but the others voted bondage. I seen his kind afore. Somethin's eatin' at his gut and it takes little to draw his displeasure. And there be another one what takes the law as gospel. Ain't no in-between for him. Ye best watch yerself good."

Callie nodded. She had come to trust Sally's instincts for all of the woman's flaws. "What of Mae?" she asked worriedly. "How can she defend herself against such judges?"

"'Twas as she said. Death by childbirth would be the kinder justice for her," replied Sally with painful honesty.

The next day, there came the clank of the key in the lock. A wary glance passed among the three women, and Callie rose cautiously to her feet as the door opened.

"The court has called for you, Callie," said Tom Wilson. "The guard will escort ye to the Capitol."

At one point, Callie would have done anything to escape that cell—even appear before the court. But now she was reluctant to leave. The three women had formed a union, bonded by the harsh realities and inequities that life had thus far dealt them.

Mae threw her a tremulous smile. "Go along, Callie. 'Twill be fine. 'Tis time ye cleared up yer misunderstandin'. Iffen ye ain't done what they said, look 'em square in the eye and say so. Only the truth can stand the test."

"Good luck, dearie," said Sally. "Remember what I told ye."

Callie reluctantly followed the guard out. She threw a last backward glance over her shoulder at the two women who had become her friends, despite her every intention to hold herself apart from the world.

As she was led across the street to the H-shaped brick building, her thoughts were ponderous. Sally was to be put on the indentured block on the morrow, but Callie knew she would survive. As Old Joe would say, "She gots da will." But what of Mae and her child? And what of herself? What was to be her fate? She had only her word. How was she to prove her innocence of such a charge?

The west building of the Capitol housed the General Court. Callie was taken to a small room where she was obliged to wait until her name was called. The chamber was small and stuffy with wooden benches and a small window set high in the wall. Three men and two women waiting for their moment in court looked at Callie with mild interest when she entered, then turned away.

She had just settled herself on the bench, when a burly guard appeared through another door and shouted, "Callie Hastings, step to!"

Callie jumped up, but it was a second until she could make her legs move.

"Step to, I say!" the guard shouted impatiently.

She hurried over to him. He took her by the arm and shoved her roughly through the door. The bailiff took charge of her then and marched her to the front of the courtroom. He directed her to take a seat on a bench in an area called the bar that was separated from spectators by a railing.

Callie looked around her. The room was handsomely paneled in a warm dark wood. Three large, round windows set in the semicircular wall behind the judges' bench and two arched windows located on either side of the bar emitted much sunlight. But Callie found the room chilling, the day even more dismal when she looked up at the curved, elevated platform to see twelve justices staring down at her with little mercy in their eyes. At the center, sitting in a throne-like chair was the royal governor.

"Callie Hastings, rise and approach the court," commanded the colonial secretary.

Callie rose uncertainly and moved to the railing that enclosed the well where the secretary sat.

"You stand accused of drowning your newborn child. How plead you?" he asked.

Callie looked anxiously over her shoulder and searched the spectators. Trenholme had said that he would be here to help her. Where was he? She had told him that she would see this through on her own; she hoped that he hadn't taken her at her word.

"How plead you?" asked the secretary again.

Callie turned her attention back to the man. "I ain't guilty," she said. "'Tis a misunderstandin'."

As Sally had predicted, a titter of amusement went around the room until a justice banged his gavel on the desk.

"Mr. Procter, present your case," said the secretary.

The attorney general rose from a table draped with a green cloth and addressed the court. "Your Honor and Milord Justices, Miss Hastings was found to be in the possession of the corpse of the female infant."

"Under what circumstances?" asked one of the judges.

"A witness was watering his horse, when he saw the accused remove a basket from the river. Finding Miss Hastings' behavior strange, he approached her and saw that the basket contained the body of the infant."

"Did your witness see Miss Hastings drown the child?" the judge continued to question.

"No. But he reported that the accused sought to conceal her gender," replied the prosecutor.

"How so?"

"Miss Hastings was dressed in the clothes of a lad."

"Then how did the witness discover she was a lass?" inquired another judge.

"Her hat fell off in the course of an altercation, Milord Justice."

"What kind of altercation, Mr. Procter?"

The prosecutor hesitated. "The witness was, uh, attempting to force Miss Hastings to a bath."

As the crowd burst into laughter, Callie wanted to melt into the floor.

The judge who sat nearest the governor banged his gavel again for silence. "Callie Hastings, plead your case," he commanded sternly.

Callie looked up at the judge. His face was large and fleshy and his brow and mouth were drawn down in a perpetual scowl, but it was the glittering malevolence in those small, dark eyes that filled her with apprehension. As he openly assessed her, Callie became conscious of the contempt he held for her. Already he had convicted her, she realized with growing alarm, and she knew that he must be one of the judges that Sally had warned her about.

Remembering Mae's advice, Callie squared her shoulders and willed her voice to be clear and steady. "'Tis as Mr. Proctor said. I was at the river drawin' water and saw the basket in the water. It was caught on a tree branch, so I waded into the river and brought the basket back to the bank to see if it held anything of value."

"Why were you dressed as a boy?"

"'Tis easier to work the fields."

"Why did you not divulge your gender to the witness?"

"I was afraid he would think me the mother and hold me to blame for the poor babe's death," replied Callie.

"And yet here you are," the judge observed coldly. "One cannot escape the truth."

"I ain't lookin' to escape the truth, sir."

"Have you anyone to speak for you, Miss Hastings?" inquired another judge.

"Yes, sir. The man who brung me here said he would speak for me."

"Mr. Procter's witness said he would speak for you?" questioned the governor in surprise.

"Yes, sir."

The governor looked at the attorney general. "Mr. Procter, who is your witness?"

"Lord Jonathan Trenholme, Your Honor," replied the prosecutor, himself surprised by Callie's revelation.

The judges immediately focused their attention on a justice sitting at the end of the bench to the left of the governor.

"Surely, there must be some mistake—" began one of the judges.

"There is no mistake," interrupted the justice in question.

At the sound of his voice, Callie turned to look at the man in disbelief. Her view of him had been blocked by the prosecutor during the proceedings, but barring that, she hadn't thought to look for Jonathan Trenholme on the justice bench, and she swallowed hard already feeling the noose tightening around her neck. She instantly knew that this was the other jurist Sally had warned her about.

"Justice Trenholme, it is most unusual for a jurist to bear witness at all, but to bear witness for both the prisoner and the prosecutor is highly irregular," admonished the judge with the gavel.

"I am aware of that, Justice Smythe, but the circumstances permit nothing less," said Jonathan.

"Do you or do you not believe the accused to be guilty?" Smythe demanded to know.

"I do not believe that Miss Hastings is responsible for the child's death," replied Trenholme.

"Then why are you wasting the court's time? The docket is full enough."

Jonathan looked at the governor. "If you will permit me, Your Honor, I should like to have the secretary read my report."

Governor Dinwiddie nodded. "The secretary shall read Lord Trenholme's report."

Jonathan handed his two-page brief to the secretary. The room was deathly still as the man proceeded to read it. But Callie didn't hear a word. She was still reeling from the shock of seeing Trenholme on the judges' bench. No wonder he had been so determined to drag her to court, the bloody sop!

When the secretary had finished, the judges were silent for a moment.

"Justice Trenholme, your report does not deny the guilt of this girl," Smythe pointed out.

"Nor does it confirm it," countered Jonathan. "It is merely a presentation of the facts, which I believe speak for themselves. The infant had been covered with a linen cloth. I made a thorough search of the Hastings farm and found no similar linens and no laying of childbed linen. In short, there was nothing to indicate that a recent birth had taken place or that Miss Hasting was in any way connected to this child. Nor do I believe that a crime of infanticide has been committed. Dr. Blackmore's findings were that the infant's death did not result from drowning or any ill will. Given the best of circumstances, the child was too frail to survive."

"Even so, the fact remains that the prisoner was in possession of the corpse when you came upon her, and she sought to hide the nature of her gender. Your search proves nothing. Knowing the penalty for infanticide, this young woman could have destroyed all evidence of childbirth beforehand. I submit that the defendant is still guilty of delivering a bastard and trying to conceal the fact."

"I believe the findings of a jury of matrons will decide the matter," said Jonathan.

Justice Smythe snorted derisively. "I do not think it necessary to waste the court's time any further with a jury of matrons."

Trenholme locked eyes with Smythe for a long moment before continuing his appeal to the other jurists. "Gentlemen, as it was unclear that a crime was committed on the Hastings property, I believed it to be in the defendant's best interests to present her to the court, not to cast blame upon her person but to absolve her of any future misunderstandings on the matter. Are we, then, to convict her without allowing her a rightful defense? If that is to be the case, this colony is in danger of becoming a land of laws without justice, for to dispense with one person's rights is to eventually dispense with the rights of all, save those in authority."

"'Twould appear that Justice Trenholme would do better to stand for the defendant, as well he argues her case," quipped Smythe sarcastically.

"Truth be told, I find merit in Justice Trenholme's argument," said another jurist after a moment's deliberation.

"In view of the circumstances, I must agree," spoke up another.

The governor nodded. "Justice Smythe, convene a jury of matrons," he ordered. "Considering the penalty this young woman faces, the court should be certain of her guilt."

Smythe glared at Trenholme. "Very well. The prisoner will be returned to her cell to await examination by a jury of matrons. The decision of the court shall rest upon the findings of the matrons. Next case."

Callie didn't know what a jury of matrons was or how it pertained to her, but she knew that she didn't like the sound of it. As she was being led away, she shot Trenholme a look full of fear and recrimination that made his conscience squirm.

In truth, he had adjudged her to be innocent before they had reached Williamsburg and not just for the very reasons he had put forth to the court. In the two days he had spent with her, he had found her to be too honest a creature to commit such an act.

Even so, Trenholme had decided that it was necessary for her to appear before the court to establish her innocence and prevent any further accusation of so serious a charge. He could have remanded her to another's custody than that of the gaoler, and he could have used his influence to have her case called after the appeals of the first day were heard. But, he had been determined to teach Callie a lesson and break that insolent disrespect for position that she refused to curb. He might have succeeded in humbling her this day, but the satisfaction he felt was fleeting.

The next morning, the four-member jury of matrons solemnly trooped into Callie's cell. She had a passing acquaintance with two of the women, but neither greeted her. One tersely ordered her to undress. Callie balked at first. But Mae reminded her that her future and quite possibly her life hung in the balance, and she reluctantly did as she was told. She didn't know what to expect and was totally unprepared for the humiliation she was forced to suffer as the women silently poked, prodded, and examined her to most intimate lengths. When they were done, they nodded to each other and left.

An hour later, Callie again stood before the stern justices.

"Matrons, have you concluded your examination?" asked Justice Symthe.

The head matron rose. "Aye, that we have, sir."

"How find you?"

The room was wrapped in silence. In a loud clear voice that Callie was certain carried to all corners of the colony, the woman announced: "The lass be yet a virgin."

Snickers broke out in the courtroom and men jabbed each other in the ribs. Callie wanted to die from shame. No amount of pride could have lifted her gaze from the floor at that moment. Tears pushed through her eyes in spite of her determination not to crumble.

Smythe banged his gavel to command order and, again, addressed the head matron. "The jury is quite certain of its findings?"

"Aye, sir."

"The secretary shall record that the accused Callie Hastings has been found innocent of all charges and is hereby released," he declared brusquely. "Case dismissed. Next."

Case dismissed…just like that. No word of apology for disrupting her life and humiliating her beyond measure. Callie's anger sparked and ignited. She shook off the guard's hand on her elbow as he sought to hasten her departure.

"Has the defendant something to say?" asked Smythe impatiently.

"Aye," said Callie. "I would ask a question."

"What is your question and be quick about it?"

"My name has been shamed and my morals questioned before the whole town. I was forced to spend days in the gaol. Had not my innocence been thusly proved, my penalty would have been death. 'Twas in the name of justice I am told. Would it be so for a man who kills his child?"

"A father is recognized by English law as being owner and master of his children," replied a jurist. "His penalty would be the loss of service and income the child might provide."

"And what of a man's wife?"

"She is chattel and servant as well."

"I see." Callie drew herself up and lifted her chin to look the judges in the eye one by one. "Then I say to ye, sirs, yer justice better serves the devil for it serves not woman or child."

The judges recoiled in shock and the spectators gasped. As murmurs of disbelief escalated into nervous laughs, Smythe furiously pounded his gavel.

"Silence! Silence!" he shouted.

Callie stood her ground. Her outrage was such that she cared little about the consequences at this point. Her only satisfaction lay in the stunned look on Jonathan Trenholme's face as he rose from his seat in incredulity

CHAPTER SEVEN

Turnabout

Y ou fool! You bloody little fool!" railed Trenholme. "Such a show of disrespect for the court, English law, and the royal governor will not go unforgotten. Had I not interceded on your behalf and talked the other justices and the governor into placing you in my custody, you might have been pilloried or flogged through the town for contempt of court."

"At least then I would be guilty as charged," retorted Callie.

Trenholme's nostrils flared, his anger further fanned. The pressure of his hand under her arm was such that Callie's feet barely touched the ground as he pulled her down the street with him, and she winced at the firmness of his hold on her.

"I should have washed my hands of you," he continued to rant. "At the very least, you might show some gratitude for my efforts."

"Gratitude! 'Tis well I rue the day I first set eyes on ye, for 'tis naught but trouble ye brung me," retorted Callie, her anger matching his. "Ye speak of honesty, fairness, and justice, but they seem not to apply to you. Why did ye not tell me ye was a judge?"

"'Twas not of importance."

"Not of importance! I was thrown into the gaol and threatened with punishment of death for a crime I had no hand in, and ye thought it not important to tell me that ye was one of them who would convict me?"

Jonathan glared down at his charge as he continued to pull her along, little given to consideration for her smaller size. It had not been said in so many words, but he knew the justices ultimately blamed him for Callie's behavior. It was by his hand that she had been dragged before them in the first place, and it was by his hand that she had been exonerated. To their way of thinking that made him responsible for her.

Once again, the little chit had made a fool of him. She seemed to have a talent for it. What infuriated him most was that he so handily played the part for her. He wasn't stupid, quite the opposite. How was it, then, that this ignorant, little hoyden was continually able to blindside him?

Callie struggled to jerk her arm free from his grasp. "Let go of me!" she demanded. "I know yer madder than a whipped beehive at me, and I can't say as I like ye much better, so unhand me and I'll be on my way home. We ne'er have to lay eyes on the other again."

Jonathan came to an abrupt halt and fixed her with a look of astonishment. "You think you can impugn the integrity of the court and go on your merry way?"

Callie wrinkled her brow in perplexity. "What say you?"

"Does no one understand proper English here?" exploded Trenholme. He took a deep breath to bring his temper under control. "Listen, Callie, you cannot be disrespectful to the court and expect to be let on your way."

"Why not? The court disrespected me. The Good Book says an eye for an eye. We're even now."

"No, you are not! The law assumes guilt and 'tis up to the accused to do whatever necessary to prove his innocence."

"So for a body to prove his innocence, he must stand to be humiliated and disgraced before all?"

"Yes—no—well, perhaps sometimes it might seem that way," sputtered Trenholme. He took another deep breath to collect himself.

"Look, Callie, the law is the law. It may not always be convenient, but if civilization is to endure, it must be countenanced."

"And this law is what separates us from the savages?"

"Aye," said Jonathan, relieved that she was finally getting the point. But his relief was short-lived.

"Truth to tell, Trenholme, I think I find the Indian's law more just," she said, after a moment of consideration. "Unhand me. I am goin' home."

Jonathan rolled his eyes heavenward and prayed for strength not to strangle her. "You cannot go home to your farm, Callie," he sternly informed her.

Callie looked at him in bewilderment. "Why not? The court released me."

"Did you not hear anything I said? The court has placed you in my charge. You are not free to leave the town."

"For how long?"

"Until you have learned respect for the law and can tender a proper apology to the court."

"When the devil wears a halo I will!" exclaimed Callie. "'Tis them what owes me an apology."

Jonathan sighed heavily. "I was afraid you might see it that way. And as ignorance continues to breed contempt, I am placing you in the charge of Mrs. Whithers."

"That woman who runs a school for planters' daughters?"

"She closed the school some time ago to enjoy the leisure of her remaining years. I'll warrant ye'll learn a few social graces from her, whether you are of a mind to or not." Jonathan's temper abated somewhat at the thought of the iron-willed Martha Whithers shaking Callie into line.

"Trenholme, jest who the bloody hell do ye think ye are!" exploded Callie.

"Now, now, Callie, a child of your age using such language…'tis exactly what I mean. You need some guidance and a lesson on manners."

Before she could protest further, he propelled her on until they came to a two-story, white clapboard house with green shutters and two dormers cut into the attic. The brick foundation was three steps high and brick chimneys flanked both sides of the dwelling. It was a modest but respectable home that pointed to an owner of a certain level of social acceptance.

A young servant girl neatly dressed in a blue petticoat and bodice and a white cap and apron answered Jonathan's knock on the door.

"Is Mrs. Whithers at home?" he asked.

"Yes, sir. Who shall I say is calling?

"Lord Trenholme."

The servant girl glanced curiously at Callie and showed them into a small parlor to the left of the foyer. "I shall tell Madam you are here."

Callie looked around the room. It was simply but comfortably furnished with a secretaire, a camel-backed settee, two comb-back Windsor chairs, a candle stand and a tea table. The walls were a cream color with green trim, which complimented the red, blue, and yellow tones woven into the floral pattern of the fabric that covered the settee.

"Lord Jon, 'tis true then. My sources did not deceive me that you had arrived in Williamsburg," trilled a feminine voice.

Callie turned to see an elderly woman enter the room. She was fashionably dressed in a green and yellow print gown and white mobcap, and her bearing was erect, her carriage graceful in spite of her years.

Jonathan gave the woman a wry smile. "Indeed, Madam. Imagine my surprise to find that you make your home here as well. How well you look, Whithers. Nary a year has touched you since last we met."

Mrs. Whithers raised a brow. "Still trying to get around me with your charm I see. Well, what is it this time? What brings you to the colonies—and to my doorstep?"

"Come now, Whithers. One can't fool an old fooler," responded Jonathan pointedly. "Might I assume that a letter from my father accompanied my arrival asking you to keep watch of me?"

Martha Whithers laughed heartily. "I never could hide anything from you."

"I know my father and his penchant for keeping a hand in my affairs," said Jonathan with some annoyance.

"Perhaps with good reason, Lord Jon. I know not the details, but the event in England must have been quite fractious for you to be sent to Virginia."

"Never mind that," Jonathan responded brusquely. "I am not here about me."

"Well, whatever the circumstances, 'tis pleased I am to see you. And do not think that you are too big to keep in line. I am still capable of taking a stick to your backside."

"No doubt and for that reason I have brought you a new pupil to keep you preoccupied and out of my business." Jonathan pulled Callie to the fore. "This be Callie Hastings. I wish for you to instruct her on the proprieties."

Mrs. Whithers looked at Jonathan quizzically for a moment, then set her pince-nez atop her high-bridged nose to critically assess the urchin before her. As the old woman surveyed Callie's dirty, rumpled clothes and the mass of tangled hair with shafts of straw sticking out here and there, she gasped and melodramatically clasped a hand to her heart.

"Dear me…dear, dear me. Lord Jon, I was governess to the duke's family until you boys were old enough to be sent off, at which time I came here and opened a school. I have taught girls from the finest of families and have yet to know failure. But this child…" Mrs. Whithers shook her head. "Lord Jon, I still have a name to consider, though retired I be. One cannot make a silk purse from a sow's ear."

Callie bristled at the insult. "Lady, I ain't no more keen on me bein' here than ye are."

Mrs. Whithers' jaw dropped. "'Tis worse than I thought," she murmured. She looked helplessly at Trenholme. "I fear this task too formidable, sir."

Jonathan glared at Callie and took Mrs. Whithers aside. "Come now, Whithers, I have never known you to avoid a challenge. I am not asking you to make the lass presentable to society, merely to instruct her on a few manners. 'Tis at the request of the governor and the court," he added slyly, appealing to the older woman's pride.

Mrs. Whithers glanced dubiously at the petulant Callie. "The governor you say—oh, very well. But I shall expect a fee and a very handsome one at that," she warned with the wag of her finger.

"Done," said Jonathan. "If you have further need of me, I shall be residing at the Samuels' house while they are away in England."

Whithers clapped loudly. "Jane!"

The young girl who had answered the front door appeared. "Yes, Madam?"

"Jane, this is Miss Hastings. She is to be a student—of sorts. She can share the attic room with you."

"Yes, Madam."

"We shall need to see to a proper bath for her immediately."

"I just had a bath," protested Callie.

"Indeed. When?"

Callie shrugged. "Three maybe four days ago. A body tends to lose track of time in the gaol."

"The gaol!" The old matron rounded on Trenholme. "Lord Jon, I demand to know what manner of person I am taking into my house."

"I ain't no criminal if that's what ye be thinkin," broke in Callie angrily. "Tell her Trenholme."

Mrs. Whithers eyes widened in further shock at the failure of this young commoner and apparent convict to properly address a member of the peerage. Even more surprising to her was that Lord Jon, a stickler for protocol, hadn't bothered to correct or upbraid the girl.

"I would know, sir, what this is all about," Mrs. Whithers demanded firmly.

Throwing Callie a look that warned her to keep silent, Jonathan explained, in the best light possible, the circumstances of Callie's appearance before the court and of the custodial arrangement.

Mrs. Whithers reacted with varying degrees of disbelief, shock, and amazement with each new revelation, and her eyes swiveled to Callie, not quite certain what to make of her new charge.

"So, you see why I thought to bring her to you," finished Trenholme, again fixing Callie with a warning glare as she opened her mouth to speak.

"What I see is that I have my work cut out for me," returned Mrs. Whithers. She looked Callie over again. "Gracious, child, are these all the clothes you have? No doubt they are riddled with lice."

"I ain't got lice—" Callie started to protest.

But Mrs. Whithers officiously cut her off. "Lord Jon, I shall require an extra sixty pounds I should think. I will not have a student of mine appearing as a rag-a-muffin."

Jonathan nodded, agreeable to the demand.

"No! I ain't takin' a farthin' from that man. I take nothin' from no one!" Callie burst out.

"So, the urchin has some pride," said Mrs. Whithers. "Good, then, perhaps this won't be the exercise in futility it first appears."

"I mean what I say. I ain't takin nothin' from him," reiterated Callie. "He's what started my troubles to begin with."

"You are not taking money from him. I am," replied Mrs. Whithers definitively. "And from here on, miss, you will not render an opinion unless asked for it. You may leave now, Lord Jon. Jane will see you out."

As Jane led Trenholme to the front door, Mrs. Whithers' no-nonsense tone carried into the foyer.

"You will find my disposition to be a pleasant one, my dear, when you mind my instruction. If not, well then, I am afraid you shall find your stay here rather tedious. Just remember one thing: Madam Whithers never fails."

Jonathan grinned broadly. Whithers was a shrewd, tough old bird, and he and his brothers had the stories to prove it. She would whip Callie into line. And he left the house whistling a jaunty tune, secure in the knowledge that all was well in hand.

CHAPTER EIGHT

The Punishment

Mrs. Whithers lost no time in taking control of her charge. She marched Callie into the back yard to a small brick building that was the laundry, handed Callie and Jane buckets, and instructed the girls to fill a large wooden washtub with water from the well. Callie grumbled and protested, but Mrs. Whithers turned a deaf ear to her. When the task was done, Mrs. Whithers dispatched Jane on a scavenger hunt to borrow the necessary clothing for Callie until a new wardrobe could be made for her.

The old matron next turned her attention to her charge. "Now, miss, you will strip to the skin and get into that tub of water."

True to form, Callie resisted, but, once again, Mrs. Whithers' resolve won out. Muttering under her breath that she hadn't had so many baths in a year as she had seen in the last four days, Callie grudgingly undressed. As she discarded the petticoat, bodice and shift, the old matron picked up the garments by the tips of her fingers and threw them into the corner. She made a mental note to instruct Jane to burn them.

Clearly unenthused, Callie stepped into the tub and sat down. The bath water was cold and after a brief acquaintance with it, she started to rise.

"Oh, no, you don't, miss," said Mrs. Whithers, quickly advancing on her charge with a long handled scrub brush. "You will not quit this bath until you have had a proper scrubbing from head to toe."

The next thing Callie knew the older woman was lathering her hair with soap. It was lye soap, but it was made from pearlash and a better quality tallow than the harsher wood ash and lard of Callie's jelly lye. A scent of lavender had been added to it, as well as salt to render it into a solid cake. Callie had never seen the likes of it.

As Mrs. Whithers poured pitchers of water over her head to rinse her hair, Callie coughed, sputtered, and complained so loudly that Jane came running into the laundry with the armful of clothes she had gathered.

"Madam, I heard the cries. What be amiss?" she asked worriedly.

"The only thing amiss here is this dirty water," said Mrs. Whithers, next attacking Callie with the scrub brush in one hand and soap in the other. "Jane, I shall need you to prepare a second rinse."

In the three hours that she had been under Mrs. Whithers' care, Callie figured that she had borne more than a body should have to bear. She had endured a scrubbing from head to toe and suffered a comb being painfully pulled through the heavy entanglements of her hair in search of nits. After that she was clothed in a clean shift and hustled across the yard to the house and up the stairs to Mrs. Whithers' bedchamber, where she was now being forced into articles of dress that she was unaccustomed to wearing.

Callie loudly objected as Jane gave another yank on the laces of the stays. "Stop! I cannot breathe. I ain't wearin' this thing."

"Nonsense," said Mrs. Whithers. "Every female young or old, rich or humble wears stays."

"To what purpose, except to torture a body?"

Mrs. Whithers was undaunted. "It provides support for the back, forces good posture, and enhances the bosom—in most cases," she added, eyeing Callie's flat chest. "In any event, a woman of good moral conduct does not go unloose from her stays."

Callie's renewed protests were muffled as Jane and Mrs. Whithers pulled a small-hooped petticoat over her head, followed by a gown of blue dimity. Lastly, they tied muslin ruffles around her sleeves below the elbow.

When the old matron stood back to observe her handiwork, she frowned. The dress hung loosely on Callie's thin frame. "Jane, I believe we shall have need of one of your short aprons."

Jane nodded and hurried from the room. A few minutes later, she returned with a white linen apron. As she tied it around Callie's waist, pulling in the gown for a shapelier fit, Mrs. Whithers nodded her approval.

When the older woman picked up a white cap, Callie balked. "I ain't wearin' that."

"But you must," said Mrs. Whithers. "'Tis part of a lady's wardrobe."

"'Tis an annoyance."

By now, Mrs. Whithers resolution was wearing thin. "Oh, very well. We shall take up this matter later," she said with a weary sigh. She picked up a looking large glass from her vanity and held it up in front of Callie. "Have a look, my dear."

The fashionably dressed figure that looked back at her was a stranger to Callie, and she stared in amazement at her reflection. It was as though she had stepped into another person's body. She couldn't breathe, she couldn't move, and the high-heeled shoes hurt her feet. She wanted her buckskins and moccasins. The strain of the last four days and emotions she had repressed for far too long suddenly welled up and bubbled over, and, much to the astonishment of Jane and Mrs. Whithers, Callie burst into tears.

* * * * *

The passing days hadn't improved Callie's disposition. She couldn't yet reconcile the perception she had of herself to the properly dressed young woman in the looking glass. Neither would she ever become accustomed to such uncomfortable and impractical dress, she decided.

On top of it all was the continuous rigor of what Callie had come to regard as mindless instruction from serving tea to curtsying. It had been a particularly exasperating morning and afternoon this third day, and, when Mrs. Whithers brought out the needlepoint, Callie rebelled. Standing at loggerheads with the imperious matron, toe to toe, nose to nose, vivid blue eyes flashing in stubborn defiance of sharp gray eyes demanding complete obedience, neither was willing to back down from her resolve.

"I am takin' my leave," repeated Callie resolutely.

"And let me remind you, my dear, that you have no leave to take," her mentor countered firmly. "Due to the leniency of the court, you are doing your atonement here rather than in the gaol."

"'Twould be far easier in the gaol."

"For both of us, no doubt," responded Mrs. Whithers curtly. She kneaded the ache in her temples and dropped into a chair exhausted. "Look, child—"

"I told ye afore, I ain't no child."

"Well, neither are you a lady."

"I ain't aimin' to be."

"What then, pray tell, *are* you aiming to be?"

"Jest me—Callie Hastings. I jest want to be left alone to farm my tobacco as best I see fit. I want to be beholdin' to no one, an' I want no one to be beholdin' to me."

Mrs. Whithers sighed heavily. "In all my years, I have never failed with a charge, but I fear you defy all reason."

"'Tis what Trenholme said," remarked Callie, proudly considering it a badge of honor.

Mrs. Whithers shuddered. "Callie dear, 'tis *Lord* Trenholme. One must always refer to a member of the nobility with correct title."

"Why? He ain't my lord—or my master."

"'Tis a mark of respect for one of higher class."

"From whence I come, respect is earned, not born to."

For once, Mrs. Whithers had no response. She, herself, had not been born to a state of privilege and her position in Williamsburg society had been hard won. For the first time, she began to understand her difficult charge.

"And it matters not a diddly damn neither whether I can pour tea, dress in fancy clothes, or spout fancy words," continued Callie. "Them things ain't goin' to tell me when a frost or a storm is comin' or how long a drought is goin' to last. They ain't goin' to feed me when the corn don't come in or the tobacco crop fails. I may not know how to make pretty flowers with a needle, fix my hair, or drop a proper curtsy, but do you know how to live on three ears of corn and a pumpkin for a week? Miz Whithers, nature is my teacher," said Callie more calmly. "'Tis the best one I could have."

Mrs. Whithers was taken aback by the crude eloquence of Callie's passionate outburst, and she began to see the girl in a new light. "Dear me, I guess people tend to forget there are other worlds. While some may be easier than others, you are right, Callie. Who is to say which is the better? In yours, I dare say you are quite knowledgeable and I quite the dunce."

"Then I can leave?" asked Callie hopefully.

"I wish you could, dear, but Lord Trenholme has instructed that you are to remain until such time as the court summons you for an apology."

"And if I refuse to make one?"

"I wouldn't test the patience of the court," warned Mrs. Whithers. "I rather think you can forfeit a little pride than more time away from your farm right now."

Callie nodded glumly. Stubbornness had always been a difficult bone for her to bury, but she recognized the wisdom in the older woman's words.

"Come now, miss, it cannot be as bad as all that. Perhaps we can come to terms."

"What sort of terms?" asked Callie guardedly.

"Well, let us say that if you promise to face the court with proper humility, I shall overlook certain lessons in decorum—but not all, mind you."

"De-decorum…what's that? If I don't know the meanin', I don't figure I need it."

"On the contrary, miss, sometimes we do not always know what we will need. Now, have we a bargain?"

"No more tea parties or sewin'?"

"Agreed. But I must insist upon napkins and handkerchiefs in place of your sleeve."

"Buckskins?"

"Proper dress," said Mrs. Whithers, her tone firm.

"I ain't goin' to be trussed up like a chicken ready for the pot," declared Callie.

"Well, I suppose that we can dispense with the stays within the confines of the house. But the stockings and shoes remain," warned Mrs. Whithers, anticipating the next line of negotiation. "And you shall not go out without a cap and hat upon your head. Agreed?"

Callie let out a sigh of resignation. "Ye have my word on it, ma'am." She spit on her hand and soberly extended it to the old matron.

Mrs. Whithers inwardly shuddered. "Your word shall suffice, my dear. But now you must not say anything to Justice Trenholme about this. Lord Jon can be a real stickler for rules, you know."

Callie had come to know that all too well and readily nodded in agreement. The less he knew about her business the better.

"Miz Whithers, there be one other thing I need to do."

"What might that be?" asked the older woman, preoccupied with gathering up dishes from the afternoon tea.

"There be a woman—a friend—I wish to visit."

"I cannot see the harm in that. Where does she live? Perhaps I know of her."

"Ain't likely, ma'am. Mae be in the gaol."

Mrs. Whithers dropped the tray noisily on the table and clutched her chest in a familiar gesture. "Dear me, I should say not!" she exclaimed. "The gaol is the last place you should be seen in your circumstances. Communing with felons, thieves and murderers—'tis not to be considered."

"But ma'am—"

"No 'buts', miss. You shall not get around me on this one."

Mumbling under her breath, Mrs. Whithers rearranged the dishes on the tray and carried it from the room. She missed the stubborn set of Callie's chin and the determination in her blue eyes.

* * * * *

Callie watched impatiently from her bedroom window, mentally giving Mrs. Whithers an extra boost as the lady climbed into the carriage. Jane had told her that every week at this time Mrs. Whithers visited her friend across town, and Callie thought she would go mad before the carriage finally pulled away from the house.

"Jane," she called urgently.

A few minutes later, Jane appeared uncertainly in the doorway with a curious dress of clothes draped over her arm.

"Hurry! Help me shed this gown," ordered Callie.

"Oh, miss, I do not think ye should be doin' this. If Madam finds that ye was at the gaol, she will have me position," said Jane, casting worried glances toward the doorway as she struggled with the laces on Callie's gown.

Callie impatiently wiggled out of the garment and threw it aside. "She will not find out. Did ye see to a hat and shoes as well?"

"Aye, they be under the britches. The clothes belong to Dickie Campbell, the apprentice to the cooper. 'Twas curious he was, but him bein' sweet on me he give 'em over easy enough. He's grown so he can't wear 'em anyway. He says to keep 'em. The shoes be over large. Ye shall have to wrap yer feet in rags."

As Callie threw off her petticoat and shift, Jane quickly moved about the room gathering up the discarded clothing. The clock struck the noon hour when Callie stood ready to go.

"How do I look?" she asked, stuffing her hair beneath the cocked hat.

"Like a young lad," said Jane. "Now, do not forget. Madam always returns by late afternoon afore the setting of the sun."

Callie nodded. "Leave this window open."

With Jane looking anxiously on, Callie straddled the window until her arm and foot connected with the tree just outside. She pushed herself off, caught the limb, and shimmied down the trunk to the ground below. With a wave to Jane, she cut across the back yard to Waller Street. As she passed the tavern, she pulled the brim of the hat lower over her face. It would be just her luck to run into Trenholme, she thought nervously.

When Callie arrived at the gaol on Nicholson Street without incident, she breathed easier. But as she walked up the front steps, she suddenly felt less certain of herself. Perhaps this was a fool's errand as Jane had said. Tom Wilson had a keen mind and eye. Would the disguise be good enough to get by him? She took a deep breath and knocked loudly on the door. When it finally opened, she was relieved that it was Mrs. Wilson who answered it.

Callie put a hand to her hat and slightly tipped it. "Good afternoon, ma'am. I be Mae Bailey's brother, and I've come to visit with her," she said, lowering her voice and keeping her eyes down.

"The mister ain't at home now," replied the gaoler's wife kindly. "I regret ye shall have to return at another time."

"Please, ma'am, I come a long way."

The good-hearted Mrs. Wilson wavered. "Well, seein' that the poor soul is so ill, I don't s'pose it can hurt none, ye bein' her brother an' all. Might cheer her up some. She is such a sweet, gentle creature. Never a bother to no one…not like that hussy Sally that was here—"

"Uh, ma'am, might I see Mae now?" interrupted Callie, struggling to hide her impatience.

"Oh, yes." Mrs. Wilson beckoned Callie inside. "My boy shall see ye back. Willie! Come here an' take this lad to the Bailey woman's cell."

The boy who appeared was the same gangling youth who had gawked at her when Trenholme had brought her to the gaol for the first time, and Callie carefully avoided his eye.

"Mama, ye know Papa don't like us lettin' visitors in to see prisoners when he ain't here," he said in a whiney voice.

"Hush, boy! This be a special case. The lad be her brother. Now, do as I say."

Willie hesitated, then took the key from the hook on the wall and led the way through the dark, narrow corridor that Callie knew all too well.

"Miz Bailey, yer brother come to see ye," the boy announced, stopping before the familiar cell and unlocking the door.

Callie entered the cell, and, even in the dim light, she could see that Mae was alarmingly weak as the young woman struggled to sit up.

"There must be some mistake," said Mae, her voice barely above a whisper. "I have no—" She stopped as Callie put a finger to her lips and gave a slight shake of her head.

"I'll be back in a quarter hour," said the gaoler's son, finding nothing untoward in the reunion.

When she heard the boy retracing his footsteps down the corridor, Callie whispered: "Mae, 'tis me."

"Oh, Callie," cried Mae, her voice catching in her throat. "Now what would ye be doin' here? I heard tell ye was found innocent, though I recollect something of a ruckus about it."

"Never mind about me. I am fine." Callie knelt down and took Mae's hand. It was so cold and limp. "What of you? Has your case been called yet?"

Mae nodded. "After the babe is born, I'm to be hanged for murder."

"But why? 'Twas an accident."

"The law cannot see it that way."

"Ye mean that Justice Smythe can't," said Callie. "'Twas him what give ye the rope, wasn't it?"

"'Tis of no concern now," replied Mae wearily. "'Tis the babe what matters more. I need to find a place for it…a safe place where it can know more than the wretchedness of my poor life."

"Surely, they cannot mean to keep ye here for four more months."

"'Tis not so bad. Mr. Wilson allows me out in the yard when I have strength enough to walk. And the missus sees to it that the cell is cleaned regular. She is very kind."

"Mae, yer too ill to stay here, and I'm bound to see ye released—leastwise until the birth of yer babe."

"Callie, let it be," pleaded Mae. "There be things ye not be knowin'."

"What things?" demanded Callie. "What could possibly keep you from fightin' for yer life?"

Mae turned her face away in shame. "I have made a pact with the devil. There be no hope for the likes of me and only danger for anyone who tries to help."

Callie scoffed. "Bah! There is always hope somewhere." And it suddenly came to her just where to look for it in this case. She squeezed Mae's hand in reassurance. "Take heart. I shall be back for ye. I have a plan."

CHAPTER NINE

Justice Denied

Jonathan Trenholme entered Raleigh Tavern in a heavy mood. The lively political debates, the toasts of fellowship, the pungent odor of tobacco smoke in the air, and the animated sound of dice boxes did nothing to pierce his dark humor as he made his way to a quiet table in the far corner of the tap room.

Having taken care of one problem by delivering Callie into his old governess' hands, he now turned his attention to Governor Dinwiddie. The man seemed never to be available to him each time Jonathan requested an audience to discuss his return to England. He was beginning to suspect the unseen hand of his father in all of this.

"Milord Justice Trenholme?"

Jonathan looked up to see an attractive, middle-aged man of impressive stature. The brown and gold brocaded silk coat and matching waistcoat, the powdered wig, and the silver-handled walking stick told him that this was a gentleman of no small distinction.

He stood and gave a slight bow. "I fear, sir, that you have the advantage."

"Perhaps now but not for long. Please sit down, Lord Trenholme. May I join you?"

"But of course," said Trenholme, his curiosity piqued as the distinguished man took a seat across from him.

"I was told that you are a man of handsome features, though somewhat willful in demeanor," remarked the gentleman. "A black sheep of sorts, ay?"

"I beg your pardon, sir."

"I am Lord Randall, Earl of Sedgefielde, and a friend to your father."

"Oh," replied Jonathan in a dull tone. "I see now why Father was so intent upon King George banishing me to Williamsburg. Not only is my old governess present to report my every movement, but it would seem a friend as well. Might I assume you had a hand in having me appointed to the General Court, sir?"

"You may."

"I wondered how my father had accomplished his ends so quickly. I would guess you to know something of my situation then."

Lord Randall nodded. "Your father wrote me of the furor you created with the Westmont Affair. He was quite worried for you. Nasty business that."

"Lady Westmont got exactly what she deserved."

"Banishment from the peerage? Perhaps."

"Perhaps!" exclaimed Jonathan. "God's teeth! Lord Westmont was caught embezzling funds from his brother's estate to cover his gambling debts. And his wife had me disqualified from the bench on the charge that I had seduced her when I refused to destroy any proof against her husband. No doubt she was trying to redirect the attention of the case. She might have succeeded had I not learned that she had been supporting her husband for years with her seductions and blackmail of key members of the peerage. Who knows what Crown secrets she holds into the bargain."

"Yes, 'tis a most unfortunate state of affairs," replied Lord Randall. "Lady Westmont is a comely woman with uncommon cleverness and undeniable charms, but that doesn't excuse the fact that you were indiscreet enough to take her into your bed as well."

Lord Randall smiled as Jonathan shifted uncomfortably in his seat.

"At ease, lad. As you are well aware by now, you are not the first to make that mistake, and I'll warrant that you will not be the last. Twenty and five can be a rather unsettling age for measuring discretion against desire and prudence against pride. But was it necessary to expose her other victims to prove your case? It nearly ruined some of the most powerful men in the peerage. You have your father's connections and sway with the king to thank for the leniency shown you."

"I would hardly call banishment to this place a show of leniency," grumbled Jonathan.

"It could have been worse," countered the earl. "King George, as I hear it, is still quite angry. The scandal will live long, and he regards you the culprit. Suffice it say, Lord Trenholme, you have made enemies."

Jonathan scoffed. "Had Father left it to me, I would have handled the matter, and I yet intend to. As soon as I can secure an audience with the royal governor to release me from my duty on the court, I shall return to England to clear the case against me."

Lord Randall chuckled at the brashness of youth. "I take it the governor will not see you."

Jonathan looked at the older man in surprise. "How did you know?"

"The governor is not so foolish as to get caught in the middle between you and your father—and certainly not between you and the king. You forget that Lady Westmont is the king's goddaughter."

"Even so, I will play the fool for no man and least of all for any woman," responded Jonathan resolutely. But even as he spoke, Callie's face rose to the fore to taunt him.

"Well, enough of this," said Lord Randall. "I did not come here to chastise you about past deeds but to welcome you to the colony. I trust the Samuels house that I secured for you is adequate."

"Aye—for the short time that I intend to stay."

"Good, then I shall take this opportunity to extend the hospitality of Randall Hall to you as well."

When the earl showed no inclination to leave, Trenholme eyed him speculatively. "Apologies, sir, if my experience has burdened me with an overly suspicious nature, but I wonder if you have not sought me out for another reason."

Lord Randall smiled again. "You are as astute as you are brash, Justice Trenholme."

"I prefer the word honest, sir," said Jonathan.

"Perhaps at times you are lacking in judgment, but, yes, I do believe that you have more than a fair measure of integrity," acknowledged the earl. "You are quite right. I have sought you out more specifically to discuss the matter of Callie Hastings."

Jonathan straightened to full attention. Now he remembered where he had heard the name Randall before. Callie had mentioned that he was the proprietor of her land.

"Go on, sir," said Trenholme, his manner guarded.

"I understand that Callie has been remanded to your custody."

"It took a bit of doing, but the justices were good enough to be lenient."

Lord Randall sighed. "Indeed. I heard of Callie's unfortunate outburst. The lass can be rather headstrong at times."

Trenholme snorted. "That, sir, is an understatement. With the court's discretion, I have placed Callie in the care of Mrs. Whithers until she learns proper respect for authority."

"I know of Mrs. Whithers and I do not question her credentials. But Lord Trenholme, where Callie comes from, Nature is the only authority to which she bows. It doesn't distinguish between class, wealth or gender, and she and her kind have a very healthy respect for it. Indeed, they seem to have a special kinship with the land that many of us can only hope to understand."

"How is it that you have continued to allow her the land after her father's death?" asked Jonathan, curious.

"The General Assembly has decided that acreage of large estates no longer needs to be entailed," replied the earl.

"And what does King George think of this?" asked Jonathan, recalling something of a heated debate on the matter in Parliament.

Lord Randall shrugged. "The king is in England and understands little of our problems here. Rulings can take a year or more to reach us. Sometimes it is necessary for us in the General Assembly to take matters into our hands and make rulings of our own," he explained diplomatically. "Docking entails and allowing freehold in exchange for a crop lease has been one of them as the colony has a great need for labor to work the land. The practice has strengthened our population and is aiding in the settlement of our western frontier."

"'Tis still tenant farming, even though Callie may think different," remarked Jonathan dryly.

"Under Virginia's new system, more autonomy is granted and I, perhaps, allow Callie more latitude."

"Regardless, the lass splits hairs."

The earl chuckled. "Callie does tend to see things in a different light."

Jonathan snorted. "That is my discovery. In any case, 'tis fair rich land to entrust to a young girl."

"While I shall always be the proprietary owner, John Hastings, as was his right under Virginia law, bequeathed the property to his wife Anne to hold in custody for his son until Ethan reached his majority."

"And now they are both deceased."

"Yes...such a tragedy. Ethan was a bright, young lad, and Anne was a lovely woman. She was pretty, smart, and spirited—Callie is very much like her." The earl looked at Jonathan. "Callie does right by the land. While she may still be below her majority, I see no reason for circumstances to change."

"She has no custodial guardian?"

Lord Randall's mouth twisted into a grimace. "There is a worthless stepfather, but he is gone from sight. I do not expect him to reappear."

He paused. "Lord Trenholme, John Hastings grew the best tobacco in the colony, and the lass is continuing in that tradition. With the quality of Callie's crop, the profits on the small acreage that she has in cultivation are nearly equal to that of my own larger fields."

"Perhaps you might try some manure," murmured Jonathan wryly.

"I beg your pardon?"

"Nothing. Please go on, sir."

"The fact of the matter is that the merchants in England hold most large planters here hostage, and I am no exception," continued the earl. "They allow us less than the market worth on our tobacco because of our debts to them, thereby increasing our obligations all the more. In short, for all of my holdings, material assets, and position, I am in bondage to those leeches."

"Increase your yield, then," said Jonathan.

Lord Randall smiled indulgently. "You do not know much about growing tobacco, do you? Because of the crop's susceptibility to even the most minor of changes in climate and soil, less than thirty acres out of a thousand are suited to that cultivation. Then, too, one must take into account that one worker can tend only three acres."

"The crop hardly seems worth the effort," commented Trenholme. "Why take all the risk? At best, the practice of investing so heavily in one crop is foolhardy."

"Undeniably so," agreed Lord Randall. "Unfortunately, tobacco is accepted as legal tender here. It is as precious as silver or gold, and the merchants in London have successfully thwarted any efforts to change that custom." Lord Randall sighed heavily. "As did those who settled Virginia over a century ago, I, too, came to the colony to escape the power of the merchants and the stranglehold they have over my estates in England. Too late did I realize that the founding fathers of Virginia, in all of their wisdom, had unwittingly repeated history by establishing a simple economy based upon one crop."

"Which must be brokered through merchants," finished Jonathan, beginning to understand the earl's problem."

Lord Randall nodded. "Rather ironic, isn't it, when one considers the care these forefathers had taken to prevent the power of the merchants from reaching across the ocean by setting up a feudal system and breeding a great disdain of the trades."

"I sympathize with your situation, Lord Randall, but why tell me?" queried Jonathan.

"The point is, Lord Trenholme, I have a special fondness for Callie. She has pluck for a lass. And I need the profits from her tobacco crop that her tenure brings in to restore a balance to my accounts in London." He eyed Jonathan meaningfully. "I should hate for anything to upset that alliance."

"I hardly think that a lesson in humility will do Callie any harm," replied Jonathan.

"Perhaps not, sir, but 'tis like taking a bear cub out of the wilderness. Upon its return, it forgets how to survive. In our world, the lass might be little better than a savage, but in her world, I dare say she could teach us a thing or two. And I would wager that hers would prove to be the more valuable lesson. To be blunt, sir, I am charging you personally responsible for Callie's well being while she is forced to remain in our midst."

Lord Randall rose from his chair. "By the bye, as a member of the Council, I do have some influence with Governor Dinwiddie. Perhaps, when you have dispensed with this duty to my satisfaction, I might secure an audience for you. I trust you will have a good day, Lord Trenholme."

Trenholme stared after Lord Randall as the older man left the tavern. The message was clear. Jonathan inwardly fumed. Even in her absence, the chit had managed to trump him. She was supposed to be at his mercy. Instead, he now found that his well being hinged upon Callie's. The son of the Duke of Lansing was expected to play nursemaid to a young wilderness heathen!

Jonathan was just recovering from one blow, when he was hit with another.

"Lord Trenholme, sir, the boy by the door wishes to see you on an urgent matter," announced a servant.

"What manner of urgency?"

"Somethin' 'bout yer horse, sir."

Jonathan looked up in alarm. "Saber? What has happened?"

The servant shrugged. "The lad did not say."

Trenholme jumped to his feet and hurried over to the slight figure waiting by the door. "What of my horse, lad?" he demanded anxiously. "If that drunken stableman has mishandled my stallion, I shall have his—" Trenholme choked on the rest of his words as familiar blue eyes peeked up from under the brim of the hat. "Callie, what the deuce are you doing here!"

"Well, I—" Callie gasped as a gentleman very publicly relieved himself into a chamber pot supplied by a servant.

Following her eye to the scene, Jonathan grabbed her arm and propelled her roughly out the door. "There is a reason why women are not allowed in taverns," he said sternly. "Now, what is this all about— what have you done to Whithers?" he demanded in new alarm when he suddenly took note of her apparel.

"I ain't done nothin' to Miz Whithers," retorted Callie indignantly. "She be out visitin' with a friend."

"You mean to say that she left you alone?"

"Well, I ain't a prisoner, Trenholme."

"Never mind. I shall have to have a talk with Whithers. How did you find me?"

"I heard ye tellin' Miz Whithers ye was usin' the Samuels' house whilst they was in England. The housekeeper wouldn't tell me where ye was 'til I thought to say 'twas a matter of yer horse." Callie giggled at the recollection of the stern old busybody turning pale at the news. "She told me fast enough where ye was then."

Trenholme was not amused. "I must remember to warn Mrs. Bendel of your tricks. I thought you did not lie."

"'Twas not a lie, but a fib."

"What is the difference?"

"A fib is in furtherance of a just cause."

Trenholme snorted. This was so typically Callie. "And what 'just cause' do you seek to further?" he asked warily.

"Mae Bailey."

"Bailey…the woman who murdered her husband?"

"The man was lower than a snake. He was beatin' her and would have killed her had she not—had not fate taken a hand," Callie quickly rephrased.

"You do not know that," responded Trenholme.

Callie looked at him, incredulous. "Are ye sayin' she should have allowed her husband to keep beatin' her with the hope that he didn't kill her?"

"No. You are twisting my words."

"What are ye sayin' then?"

"The man was drunk," said Trenholme. "I'm sure Mrs. Bailey could have escaped his hand without killing him."

"You do not know that," returned Callie, throwing his words back at him.

Jonathan glared at her.

"'Twas an accident, Trenholme. Mae was jest tryin' to protect herself."

"'Tis a defense that can be claimed only by men. While I may agree that this is an unfortunate situation, a wife is her husband's property to do with as he pleases. The court told you that. There is nothing for it. 'Tis the law," said Jonathan, brushing her off as one might a pest.

But Callie was not to be brushed off. "What kind of law allows a woman with child to be hanged for protectin' herself, but does not punish a man for killin' his wife or child?"

"Granted, it may have a few imperfections," agreed Jonathan, "but, on the whole, common law has served England quite well since the Norman Conquest and the Magna Carta."

Callie looked at him blankly. "The Magna what?"

"The Magna Carta…the great charter that King John granted in the year 1215 guaranteeing certain liberties. 'Tis the basis of our judicial system today," he explained, losing patience.

"Then that be the problem," declared Callie, matter-of-factly. "It needs be changed after all these years."

"Says you. We are all surviving quite nicely, thank you."

"Mae ain't and neither are women like her."

Jonathan sighed heavily. "Callie, what do you want?"

"I want Mae Bailey released from the gaol until she births her babe. Like ye done with me…released in your cus-custom—"

"Custody," supplied Jonathan. He gave a short laugh. "You are joking, of course." The look on her face told him she most definitely was not, and he took a deep breath to collect himself. "See here, Callie, custody in itself is difficult to achieve. And 'twas upon Justice Smythe's arguments and by the governor's hand that this woman received the death penalty. 'Tis unlikely that they will sanction her release."

"I am not askin' ye to have her sentence set aside, Trenholme, jest to have her prison changed for awhile. Mae is ill. She will die before the rope reaches her neck. 'Tis doubtful she will last another fortnight without proper care."

"Perhaps 'twould be the kinder fate."

"'Tis a thought I've heard too often of late," retorted Callie. "I doubt the church would agree if 'tis at the needless expense of an innocent babe."

"And you shall see to it that the church is fully informed," said Jonathan, following her thoughts.

"There be something amiss with a law that condemns to death an unborn babe for its mother's crime."

Jonathan ran a hand wearily across his face. God help him, he was beginning to see the logic in her argument.

"If I were to agree to help in this matter, who would care for this woman should she be temporarily released?"

"Miz Whithers be a good woman, and she has plenty of room in her house. Mae won't be a bother to no one."

Jonathan shook his head emphatically. "'Tis out of the question."

"Trenholme, if ye do not do this for me, I will stay in Williamsburg and make yer life a bloody hell. And if Mae and her babe die in the gaol, I shall bring charges against the court for infan-infanti—what they charged me with."

"For God's sake, Callie, have you lost your mind? No one has ever charged the court. What of your tobacco?" he asked, trying to redirect her thoughts.

"It ain't important no more."

Trenholme's alarm increased as he recalled Lord Randall's veiled threat to him. If Callie weren't returned to her farm to harvest her tobacco crop, he would be trapped in this god forsaken land indefinitely. Add to that now, her headstrong promise to charge the court. Smythe would have her head for sure. It didn't take Jonathan long to conclude that he had no choice but to accede to her wishes. Callie had gotten the upper hand again.

"All right," he said, greatly aggravated. "If Whithers is agreeable, I shall see what can be done. But you must promise to tender your apology to the court, return to your farm, and let me to my peace!"

Though Callie nodded soberly, Trenholme had the feeling that somehow she would find other ways to test him for the duration of his stay.

* * * * *

Just as Jonathan had predicted, it had taken considerable finesse on his part and great influence from Lord Randall to achieve Callie's request. Justice Smythe had strenuously opposed the condemned woman's temporary release. It was only by Jonathan securing consent from a quorum of the justices and Lord Randall intervening with the governor that Mae Bailey was transferred into Mrs. Whithers' care.

As Mrs. Whithers stood at the window watching Callie help a thin, pale young woman alight from the carriage and slowly negotiate the steps to the door, she briefly wondered how she had allowed herself to be maneuvered into taking responsibility for a woman found guilty of murder and her unborn child. But in her heart, she knew the reason.

When told the facts, Mae's case had struck a chord with her. It was all too vivid a reminder of the cruelty that she had suffered at the hands of her own husband. It was many years ago, but Mrs. Whithers could well understand Mae's desperation. Had not James Whithers died when a horse trampled him, the old matron was forced to admit that she might have been driven to lend Providence a hand herself.

Aside from that, Martha Whithers felt that she had a purpose in life again since closing her school—a purpose that she found more satisfying than that of instructing spoiled, young rich girls. Until Callie was foisted upon her, she hadn't realized how superficial her priorities had become or how lonely she had been. If Callie behaved herself in court, the lass would be returning to her farm at the end of the week, and, with that in mind, the older woman no longer had any doubts about the arrangement. She needed someone to care for.

As Jane opened the door for Callie and Mae, Mrs. Whithers was galvanized into action.

"Jane, fetch the cooper to carry Mrs. Bailey upstairs," she ordered. "The poor woman is near to collapse. In the meantime, lay her down on the settee, Callie."

Callie gave Mrs. Whithers a grateful smile. It was all she could do to support Mae's weight as far as the parlor.

Tears welled up in Mae's eyes as she tried to acknowledge her own gratitude, but a feeble smile was all she could manage in her weakened state.

Over the next hour, in a flurry of orders, Mae was transported upstairs, bathed, dressed in a clean linen shift, given a bracing toddy for her cough, and tucked into a freshly made bed where she immediately slipped into deep slumber.

"Shall I bring up some food?" asked Callie worriedly. Mae was so still, her breathing so quiet.

Mrs. Whithers shook her head. "'Tis best to allow Mrs. Bailey to regain strength with some sleep for now. I shall send for Dr. Blackmore to examine her when she awakens."

"She looks awful sickly, Madam."

"Tch, tch, with a little fresh air, proper food, and rest in an environment where she isn't reminded each day of her unfortunate circumstances, the poor soul will be fine."

"But she has no will to live beyond the birth of her babe. I cannot say as I blame her in her position," fretted Callie.

"Indeed. But perhaps the fates shall intervene," replied Mrs. Whithers.

There was a strange, conspiratorial twinkle in the older woman's eye that heartened Callie and she broke into a smile, the first in a very long while, as she suddenly felt the lifting of one of the many burdens that she had assumed over the months.

"Ye be plannin' somethin', Miz Whithers?" she asked hopefully.

"Let's just say that I have an idea in mind," replied the old matron. She led Callie out of Mae's room and into her bedchamber. "I am afraid these old bones cannot stand up to much rigor in a day," she said, wearily easing herself into a chair. "Fetch me my shawl, dear, if you please."

Callie snatched the blue covering from the foot of the bed and placed it gently around Mrs. Whithers' shoulders. Mrs. Whithers had proven to be a tough taskmaster over their time together, but Callie had developed respect and affection for the old woman.

"If ye needs me to stay and help with Mae—"

"No, no, dear. Between Jane and myself, we can handle what must be done. 'Tis time for you to return to your farm."

"I shall visit as often as I can."

Mrs. Whithers took Callie's hand and patted it affectionately. "I am counting on it."

"Madam, what did ye mean about the fates helpin' Mae?"

"Well, as laws appear to be set with no mind to circumstances, leastwise for women, then 'tis up to us to do something about it."

"But what, Madam? We cannot change the law."

"No, but we can use it to our advantage," said Mrs. Whithers.

Confusion rippled across Callie's features. "How? What are we to do, Madam?"

"For now, we are going to get you back to your farm and Mrs. Bailey on her feet. Everything must appear commonplace. I shall commence with some correspondence. Perhaps in a month or so, I shall have an answer for you."

Callie's curiosity wasn't satisfied by Mrs. Whithers' evasive answer, but she knew it would have to do for now. And, for the time being, she was content to let hope rule her emotions.

CHAPTER TEN

Sentence Served

Callie heaved a sigh of relief as she stepped from the Capitol building into the sunshine. She had managed to swallow enough of her pride to render a credible—if less than heartfelt—apology to the court and was now free to go. Today, she was going home. She breathed in the fragrant air that smelled of roses, Sweet William, and jasmine. For the first time in many months, she felt lighter in spirit, released from the somber malaise that had held her in its grip for so long.

She had missed Old Joe and Lucie, and she wondered how the tobacco crop had fared in her absence, but, strangely enough, it no longer dominated her thoughts. No longer did her problems seem to be at the core of her being. It had been gradual and ever so subtle that Callie had yet to realize she had violated her rule not to care for anyone again, that she had, in fact, opened her heart to include Mrs. Whithers and Mae.

Mae's health had greatly improved over the past few days, allowing Callie to return to her farm in good conscience. Thanks to Mrs. Whithers' plasters and possets, the young woman's cough was nearly gone, and she was resting peacefully and taking more nourishment. Now they must all turn their minds to staying her execution, thought Callie.

"Callie, hold up."

Callie turned to see Jonathan walking toward her. "Trenholme, what think ye now?" she asked, when he had reached her side.

Jonathan's lips curled up in a resigned smile. "I think Mrs. Whithers has succeeded admirably in her task in *most* respects," he said, taking a mental deduction for Callie's continued lack of awe for his position and refusal to acknowledge his title.

"And what of my dress?" she pressed, twirling around. "Do I look to deny my gender now?"

There was an impish side to her personality this day and a sparkle about her that he had never glimpsed before. She had always been so resentful and insolent in his company that he had never considered humor to be a part of her character as well. A grin flicked at the corners of Trenholme's mouth as he lazily examined her with an eye that would have sent any other young girl into nervous titters.

She wore a simple but fashionable white dress imprinted with small red and blue flowers, and the skirt was split open in the front to reveal a blue and white-stripped petticoat. Her hair was gathered beneath a cap and a wide-brimmed straw hat. She was still too thin, but she had filled out a bit and the freckles were fading due to her lack of exposure to the sun. Gone, too, were the cynical twist to her mouth and the bitter despondency that had marked her features, allowing the brilliance of her blue eyes to shine through. She might actually be pretty one day, thought Jonathan in surprise.

"Well?" demanded Callie, becoming perturbed by the long, silent perusal.

"Your dress is a credit to your womanhood," pronounced Jonathan.

Callie eyed him narrowly for a moment as she measured his sincerity, but she detected no hint of mockery on his face or in his tone and decided to accept the compliment on its merit.

"I do believe, however, that these have yet to gain favor amongst the couturieres," he said, pulling out a pair of breeches that she had tucked under her arm.

"Well, I can't be farmin' in dresses, Trenholme. 'Twouldn't do to get them fine things dirty."

Jonathan suppressed a grin. "Indeed. Might I assume that you are returning to your farm now?" he asked.

Callie nodded.

Jonathan signaled to a groom who came forward leading a sturdy bay hooked up to a chaise with Trenholme's stallion tied behind it.

"What is this?" she asked, her brow puckered in bewilderment.

"That old gelding won't get you a mile out of town," said Jonathan. "You can keep Ginny and the chaise until I have further need of them."

Callie considered the offer for a minute. "Ye know I ain't one to take handouts, but seein' as how it is a loan and given all the trouble ye caused me—"

All the trouble he had caused her! That wasn't the way Jonathan saw it. But he bit back a retort for his part would be done soon and they would be out of each other's lives forever.

"Why is Saber tied behind?" asked Callie suspiciously.

"There have been reports of attacks on women in the countryside. 'Tis most likely an itinerant. And while I have little doubt which of you would come out the victor in an encounter, I mean to see that you are safely returned to your farm."

"What of court?"

"Yours was the last case to be heard today."

"Well, my thanks to ye, Trenholme, but I can look after myself."

"If you think wearing those britches will fool anyone—"

"It fooled you on two occasions," Callie reminded him.

Trenholme was not amused. "Be that as it may, the matter is not up for argument," he replied firmly. "A young lad can be almost as much amusement to scoundrels as a lass. In any event, I am taking no chances." With that, Jonathan lifted her off her feet and deposited her on the seat of the chaise. "Can you handle the reins while I ride Saber?"

"Ain't never done it afore, but I'll manage," she assured him pertly.

"I have no doubt of it. Allow me to supply you with a few instructions just the same."

He climbed up beside her to show her how to hold the reins and guide the horse. When he was confident enough of her ability to handle the chaise, he got down and untied Saber.

She started out a little unsteady.

"Hold the reins tighter," Jonathan called out to her.

"I know how to do it," she yelled back impatiently.

Jonathan shook his head and mounted his stallion. It was safe to say that he had never met anyone quite like Callie Hastings. She amused him even as she annoyed and exasperated him, but he had to admire her pluck.

"Trenholme, how come ye to be a justice if yer s'pose to be a nobleman?" asked Callie, as he pulled up alongside of her.

"Primogeniture," said Jonathan.

"What is that?"

"'Twas my misfortune to be the third born in a noble family. By English law, primary title and holdings are passed to the eldest living son," he explained. "Other sons receive lesser titles not in use from other branches of the family. My own lordship is descended from an uncle who had no children. The second son is usually groomed for the military and held in waiting in the event of the untimely death of the first; other sons are given a choice between the clergy and the law."

Callie cocked her head as she considered him. "I cannot fathom ye a preacher man."

Jonathan threw her a wry smile. "Alas, neither could I."

Callie let out a little giggle. What a curious man Jonathan Trenholme was. He could be arrogant and hot-tempered one minute, disarmingly charming and considerate the next. And while they found each other barely tolerable, here he was lending her a horse and chaise and accompanying her home as though she were a highborn lady.

"Trenholme, why be ye doin' this?" she suddenly asked. The longer she considered the matter, the more she found his actions suspect.

"What is that?" asked Jonathan.

"Seein' me home and lendin' me this fine horse and carriage."

Jonathan shrugged. "I told you. A wanderer appears to be attacking women about the countryside, and I still feel responsible for you."

"Why?"

"God's teeth! Do I have to have a reason?"

"'Tain't human nature not to. Say, ye ain't expectin' to share my cabin again, are ye?" she questioned suspiciously.

Whatever the response Callie had expected, it wasn't an outburst of laughter.

"Well, I cannot see that it is anythin' to laugh at!" she snapped. "Miz Whithers said as how she's seen a man take to looks far worse'n mine, and Lucie said that, scrubbed up some, I ain't half bad to look on."

"I am sure," replied Trenholme, still chuckling. "But I can assure you, Callie, I have no reason for seeing you home other than concern for your safety. As I told you before, I do not bed children."

"I ain't a child! 'Tis ten and eight I'll be end of September," she retorted, her cheeks flushed with anger.

"Be that as it may, I am not your enemy. You have more to fear from nature than from me."

"I can understand nature. I cannot understand you," responded Callie testily.

She lapsed into silence then. What was the matter with her? Her opinion of men was such that she went out of her way to discourage their notice. And now that she was succeeding with that most overbearing of the species, she was angered by his disinterest. She paraded as a boy, yet she sought to convince this man that she was a woman. It was all too confounding to her.

Jonathan glanced at Callie in bemusement, wondering what had triggered her temper this time. The lass was as prickly as a thornbush. Never had he met anyone so complex wrapped up in such simplicity. She was unworldly, illiterate, and possessed not an ounce of sophistication, but she was intelligent, clever, and had an understanding of human nature that, when balanced against her youth, was damnably irritating to him. With a little education, the lass could be downright dangerous, he concluded.

The remaining miles ticked off with agonizing slowness as they rode in silence, each trying to figure the other and how it was that their lives had become so entangled. When they turned onto the lane to Callie's farm, she slapped the horse to greater speed, impatient to get home and be free of Jonathan's presence. Caught off guard, Trenholme uttered an oath and spurred his mount to a gallop, fearing that she might be spilled out of the carriage and thrown beneath the wheels.

Quickly, he closed the distance between them. "Are you trying to kill yourself?" he shouted angrily, reaching out a hand to rein in her horse.

Callie ignored him and cried out for Lucie and Old Joe.

Lucie lumbered cautiously out of the cabin, a little confused and frightened by the commotion. When she saw that it was Callie, she shouted excitedly and hurried to meet her mistress. She was so anxious to enfold Callie in her arms that she nearly ran underfoot of the horse, and Jonathan had to struggle to bring the excited animal under control.

Callie jumped down from the chaise and was immediately engulfed in large brown arms. "Lucie, I cannot breathe," she said, laughingly breaking away from the Negress' exuberant greeting. "Where is Old Joe?"

"Him is yonder hilling the tobacco fields," said Lucie, blowing her nose and wiping her tears on her apron. "Ye was gone so long, I didna know whats to think. But Joe, he know'd ye was comin' back. Let me looks at ye, child. I hardly know'd 'twas ye dressed as ladylike as ye is." Callie fidgeted self-consciously as the old Negress assessed her from top to bottom. "Now ye looks like somethin' a man can lay an eye to," Lucie declared with satisfaction.

Her gaze moved to Jonathan and the horse and chaise.

"Now, Lucy, it ain't what ye be thinkin'," said Callie, following the woman's train of thought. "Dilly wouldna made two miles afore droppin'. Trenholme was jest helpin' me to get home to make amends for the trouble he caused me. Ain't that right, Trenholme?"

Jonathan bristled, once again, taking exception to Callie's interpretation of events. "That point is a matter for debate," he replied crisply, dismounting from his horse.

Callie looked quizzically at him for a moment and shrugged. "She usually didn't understand half of what he said anyway, but it didn't matter. He was going to be gone from her life soon.

"Ye both be in luck," said Lucie. "I has two rabbits turnin' on the spit. Ye must be near to starvin'."

"Trenholme is returnin' to town straight-away," said Callie.

Her curt dismissal of him made Jonathan adamant in his own resolve. "I accept your invitation to eat, Lucie," he countermanded firmly.

Lucie broke into gales of laughter and ambled back to the cabin.

"Why did ye do that?" demanded Callie, rounding on him in a fit of pique.

"Saber could do with a rest and some water, and I am in need of nourishment." Jonathan looked her squarely in the eye. "Beyond that, I will not have my mind made up for me by any female—least of all you. Is that clear?"

Wide-eyed, Callie nodded.

As he strode off toward the cabin, she stared after him. Her father had often told her that for a man to control his destiny, he had to control his environment. He had taught her nothing about how to control the man.

CHAPTER ELEVEN

In Furtherance of a Noble Cause

Lucie and Old Joe had noticed the change in Callie almost immediately upon her return from Williamsburg. Although she still preferred breeches to proper dress, nothing else was the same. The bleak, heavy moods, which had colored Callie's personality since the deaths of her brother and mother, no longer seemed to dominate; her industriousness was no longer driven by bitterness and anger.

However welcome the change, the superstitious Negress began to fear that her mistress was beset by spirits when Callie announced that she would be making periodic visits to Williamsburg over the next four months. When Lucie came upon Callie actually singing one day, she was certain of it.

"Ye ain't been layin' da broomstick outside da door at night, missy" she scolded one morning. "For sure dem spirits gots a hold of ye."

"I ain't beset by nothin'," Callie retorted impatiently.

"Den it gots to be a man. Ain't but two things what sets females on end—evil spirits an' men."

"'Tain't neither. I told ye afore I have no belief in the one and I got no use for the other."

"Well, what 'bout dis Mister Justice fellow? A man don' see a gal home all dis way for no reason."

"Well, nothin'," said Callie. "I told ye how it was. Besides, he is gentry and thinks me a child."

"Dere be more to dis than ye be sayin'," insisted Lucie with an emphatic wave of her finger. "I knows ye, miss. Ye'd as soon be hung by yer thumbs than go into town after yer papa died."

The woman was like a dog with a bone. With a sigh of exasperation, Callie finally told her about Mrs. Whithers and Mae. "So if ye must know, 'tis them I go to see in town," she ended on a note of finality. "Now I will hear no more on the matter. Is that clear?"

Lucie nodded, but she vowed to lay a broom outside Callie's doorway each night for good measure just the same.

* * * * *

Callie winced as she straightened to full position. It felt as though an unseen hand sought to twist her backbone against the natural curvature of her spine. Massaging the dull, stabbing ache at the small of her back, she surveyed the rows of tobacco plants that lay on the ground wilting and absorbing moisture, which made for a heavier leaf and a higher price.

"How much more to be cut?" she asked wearily.

Old Joe continued to swing his knife in rhythmic motion never missing a beat. "Some ain't ripe yet, but there be 'bout two acres more, missy."

Callie moaned as she dipped her kerchief into a bucket of cool water and knotted it around her neck. It was so hot in the fields.

Old Joe stopped to regard his mistress worriedly. "Ye best rest a bit, missy. Da sun takes a better likin' to dark skin. Ye been pushin' yerself too hard these past months."

"I ain't quittin'," said Callie, wiping the perspiration from her flushed face. "Ye cannot do it alone. When first we planted, 'twas with my brother's help in mind. Now I fear 'tis more than the two of us can handle. Papa freed ye and Lucie. I cannot fathom why ye stay. I got nothin' to offer but hard work."

"Ye gives more'n ye knows, missy," replied Old Joe soberly. "By my count, respect is dearer than silver. Ain't no way Lucie and me is leavin' ye 'ceptin' by Providence's hand. Now we best stop flappin' our jaws and start cuttin'. We still gots to pole da plants afore ye go off to town."

Callie looked at him in surprise. "How did ye know I was fixin' to go to town?"

"'Tain't hard to figure. Ye been off to visit round 'bout this time for the past three months. And Lucie says as how ye always starts singin' and actin' a mite queer jest afore ye goes off. Moon-eyed she calls it." Old Joe grinned. "Her thinks ye gots a man."

"Oh, that Lucie!" exclaimed Callie. "I swear she has corn cobs for ears. I told ye 'bout Mrs. Whithers and Mae. 'Tis them I go to see and none other."

"Ain't no need to tell me, missy."

As he moved down the row of tobacco plants to resume his cutting, Callie could hear his laughter ring out. She gave a snort of annoyance. She thought she had nipped Lucie's curiosity in the bud, but apparently a little more nipping was in order.

After two more days of cutting and poling plants, Callie decided that she could leave the farm. The last acre they had planted wasn't ripe enough to cut, but Old Joe figured it would be ready when she returned from Williamsburg.

In preparation for her trip, Callie immersed herself in the cool water of the river and half-heartedly rubbed the jelly soap on her body. Mrs. Whithers seemed to be in that small camp of people who laid great store by the practice of frequent bathing, despite the risk. And Callie was not about to be subjected to another one of her scrubbings.

It would appear that Trenholme shared his old governess' viewpoint on the subject as well, thought Callie wryly, as the image of him emerging naked from the river suddenly came to mind with disturbing clarity. She shook her head to dispel it, much annoyed with herself. She seemed to be having difficulty ridding herself of that particular memory.

She quickly rinsed the soap off her body and waded from the water, impatient now to be on her way to town. When she stepped onto the bank, Callie let out a shriek. "Lucie! Lucie, come quickly!" she cried, cowering behind a stand of bushes.

The old Negress answered the summons with amazing alacrity.

"Lucie, where did ye come from so quickly? Never mind. I cannot find my breeches. I laid them on that bush."

"Oh, missy, a body run through da yard and took yer buckskins right off da line," said a seemingly distraught Lucie. "Him was headin' dis way. 'Twas him what musta taken the breeches."

"My buckskins! He took my buckskins, too? What body?"

Lucie shrugged with wide-eyed innocence. "Musta been one of dem trash what roams da woods ev'ry now and again."

"What am I to do now?" cried Callie. "I must leave soon if I am to be in Williamsburg afore noon."

"Ye gots dat nice dress ye was wearin' when Mister Justice brung ye home," suggested Lucie.

Callie didn't have time to argue. "Oh, all right! Fetch it straightaway—afore another body has a mind to run through this copse."

"I be quick, missy."

Crouched behind the cover of bushes, Callie scanned the perimeter as she awaited Lucie's return, sourly belaboring the fates that appeared to work overly hard at making her life difficult. It seemed an eternity before Lucie's large figure was seen negotiating the hill and even longer before the Negress finally appeared huffing and puffing at the bank's edge. It certainly wasn't with the speed that she had answered Callie's first summons.

"Here ye be, missy," said Lucie.

Callie grimaced and grabbed the clothes and pannier hoops. She pulled on the shift and stockings, tied the smaller-sized side hoops around her waist and donned the petticoat. Lucie helped her with the odious stays. Buckskins had never been this much trouble, she grumbled to herself.

As Callie slipped on the gown and laced the bodice, she eyed Lucie suspiciously. "May a bolt of lightning strike ye silly if ye've played me false 'bout my clothes."

Lucie nervously licked her lips and gazed uncertainly up at the sky, finding little relief in the clear blue color. For good measure, she crossed her fingers behind her back.

"Here, let me do somethin' with dat hair," she said, anxious to change the subject. "Ye shove dat mop under a cap and ye is gonna get a tangled mess ye ain't never gonna undo."

"Never ye mind. I venture to say ye've done quite enough already," responded Callie, gathering the unruly curls at the nape of her neck and securing them with a length of vine.

Finally dressed, she started off in an unsteady gait. The high, curved-heel shoes, which favored neither the left nor right shape of the foot, felt awkward, and twice she stumbled before impatiently casting the footwear aside in favor of her moccasins. At least the thief had left her these.

Neither did she have the temperament nor time to walk in the mincing steps that Mrs. Whithers had tried to teach her. Lucie rolled her eyes heavenward as Callie impatiently hiked the skirts to her knees and resumed a stride up the incline to the cabin that would have curled Mrs. Whithers' hair without benefit of a curling iron.

Issuing last minute instructions, Callie climbed into the chaise that Jonathan had left behind for her use. "I shall be back in a few days," she said, setting the wide-brim straw hat atop her head. She glared down at Lucie. "When I return, we *will* take up the matter of my britches."

Old Joe looked on in puzzlement as Lucie shifted uneasily beneath Callie's stern eye, but no one sought to enlighten him.

"Ye take yer time, missy," he said. "Lucie and me'll see to everythin' here. Ain't no cause to worry none."

"I ain't worried, Old Joe."

With a wave of farewell, Callie snapped the reins and the horse lurched forward into a brisk trot. After about a mile, she allowed the bay to lapse into a more leisurely pace. The cutting of the tobacco plants had exhausted her more than she had realized and it felt good to rest.

Ruefully, she regarded her rough, stained hands that were neither improved by the numerous little cuts that covered them nor the broken nails. Callie grinned. She could just hear Mrs. Whithers' scandalous intake of breath at the sight of them, followed by a lecture on the importance of presenting a clean and polished appearance. At least, Mrs. Whithers couldn't take issue with her dress.

Callie entered the trace where the trail narrowed and felt more ill at ease than usual. She disliked the narrows. Surrounded with thick vegetation and tall trees, the span was dark and forbidding. With Trenholme's warning about women being molested in the area, the narrows seemed even more ominous. Still, she had made the other trips to Williamsburg without incident, she reminded herself. She was about to relax her guard, when birds suddenly fled their perches and there was a skittering of small animals. Callie stiffened. Something or someone had disturbed them.

Her heart thudded hard against her chest as she scanned the dense woods. She saw nothing, but she sensed that she wasn't alone, and she whipped the horse into a run, giving the bay its full head. At one point, the wheel hit a stone and she was nearly spilled onto the road, and she struggled to bring the horse under tighter rein. She couldn't risk breaking an axle or being thrown out of the conveyance at this point.

As the sun broke through the clearing, Callie breathed easier. No one appeared to be following after her, and she forced Ginny to a slower gait. Nothing untoward occurred for the remainder of the trip. By the time she pulled up in front of the Widow Whithers' house, she had decided that her imagination had gotten the better of her and set the incident from her mind.

Jane greeted her warmly at the door and showed her into the parlor. Mrs. Whithers was bent over her needlepoint. When she glanced up to see Callie, the corners of her mouth turned up into something suspiciously like a smile.

"Well, I see you have dressed yourself appropriately for once," she said with a hint of triumph in her voice. "No cap, but at least you are wearing the stays and hoops." When moccasins peeked out from underneath Callie's dress, the matron arched a brow and sighed resignedly. Some things would be slower to change. "Come here, lass, and greet this old woman properly," she commanded. "'Tis small reward, indeed, for turning my life upside down."

The twinkle in her eyes belied the gruffness in her tone, and Callie gave her mentor a kiss on the cheek, still cautious about opening her heart too wide.

"How is Mae?" she asked.

"See for yerself," said Mae, standing in the doorway.

With each visit, Callie could see that Mae was thriving, but she couldn't believe that this was the same sickly woman she had half carried out of the gaol four months ago. Gone was the haunted look of years of hopelessness and fear and in its place was revealed a quiet, dark beauty enhanced by a newfound serenity and robust health.

"Mae, you look wonderful!" exclaimed Callie.

"'Tis a pity we cannot say the same for you," remarked Mrs. Whithers. "That farm of yours is going to kill you, miss. Each time you visit you are thinner than before, and you have more rings around your eyes than an old tree."

"Never mind me," said Callie. "Mae, I can scarce believe 'tis you."

Mae smiled shyly. "I know. 'Tis all Miz Whithers doin'."

"Pshaw!" blustered the old woman. "Mrs. Bailey was a most cooperative patient—and I dare say a more willing student than another I can call to mind," she added, glancing pointedly at Callie.

"Madam taught me to do needlework and to write my name," said Mae. She proudly pulled out a piece of parchment from her pocket with some crude scrawling on it. "I be learnin' to read some, too." She smiled wistfully. "So many things to know and so little time."

A heavy pall settled over the room.

Looking from Mae to Mrs. Whithers, Callie sensed that something was wrong. "What's amiss?" she asked apprehensively.

Mrs. Whithers looked at Mae, and Mae gave a slight shake of her head. Neither wanted to burden Callie further, but Callie caught the silent exchange.

"Something has happened. Tell me," she insisted.

The old matron sighed heavily. "Lord Jon was here this morning. 'Tis less than a month until Mrs. Bailey births her baby, and the court is ordering her return to the gaol in two days for the remainder of her increasing time."

Callie reeled from the news. She knew this day would come. They all did, but it had seemed so far off that it had been easy to ignore. Now, the day of reckoning was here staring them in the face, demanding payment in full.

She turned to gaze moodily out the window. "I had hoped that Mae would slip between the cracks."

Mrs. Whithers gave a sniff borne of experience. "When you have lived as long as I have, you learn that trouble never goes away, my dear. Mayhap it disappears for a spell, but it always comes back around bigger than before if one does not address it at the start."

"What can we do?" asked Callie. "If I hide away Mae on my farm, 'twill be the first place Trenholme looks."

"Please, Callie, ye've known enough trouble with the court already," said Mae. "I will not have ye know more on my account. We all knew this day would come. You and Miz Whithers done so much for me already. I ain't lettin' ye risk more. In these few months, ye've given me a lifetime of happiness, and I will always be beholdin' to the both of ye. In the time left to me, I must find a good home for the child."

"You will do no such thing, Mrs. Bailey. You shall raise that baby yourself," declared Mrs. Whithers. "Some time ago, I wrote to my sister in Carolina telling her of your situation. Priscilla lost her husband this past winter; I thought you to make an admirable companion and the child a wonderful distraction for her. She loves children. 'Twas one of her greatest sorrows that she was never able to bear a child."

"And ye think she might take in Mae and the babe?" asked Callie excitedly.

"She has already consented to do so. But we must move quickly now, and the authorities must never suspect a thing. Not even Jane can know. I fear that she can be easily duped by Lord Jon should he prove skeptical. To that end, we must have a well-worked plan."

"Please, I cannot allow you to endanger yourselves," said Mae.

"'Tis not your decision to make," responded Mrs. Whithers brusquely. "Callie, how say you? If your part is discovered, you could be indentured."

Callie nodded in agreement without a moment's hesitation. "But how are we to spirit Mae away?"

Mrs. Whithers smiled. "You just said the word, my dear."

At the perplexed look on both girls' faces, the widow explained her plan.

"As far as the court is concerned, Mae is going to die giving birth prematurely," she began. "We can say that the birth was brought on by the distressing news that she was being returned to the gaol. Death in childbirth is common enough and an occurrence that men can readily understand but do not care to probe. Then we shall lay Mae out in a coffin in such a way as she can breathe properly." Mrs. Whithers looked pointedly at Callie. "Her 'brother' who was seen visiting Mae in the gaol shall claim her body and presumably return home to Maryland with it."

"You know about my trip to the gaol?" asked Callie in surprise.

"I told you that Jane couldn't keep secrets. The guilt lies too heavily on her. Now, to get back to our plan—Callie, you shall drive Mae to an old abandoned farmstead on the road to Richmond. My sister's overseer will meet you there and claim the wagon. His name is Jake Tyler. Mae will finish the trip posing as Jake's wife. Well, what say you?"

"Who shall bear witness to the death?" asked Callie. "Trenholme will never accept our word for it."

"I have already considered that possibility and have spoken to Midwife Gilbrett. She is sympathetic to our cause and most trustworthy. She shall be our witness," said Mrs. Whithers, quite pleased with herself.

Callie and Mae looked at her in astonishment. Who would have thought this respectable old lady and a stickler for rules capable of such delicious deception?

Mrs. Whithers laughed merrily at their reactions. "As a governess, one learns to be clever to survive the antics of her charges."

"There is one problem," said Callie. "I ain't got the britches with me, and we can't have Jane ask her friend for more. Both will suspect something for sure."

"Hmmm, I had not considered that Callie Hastings would appear on my doorstep without a pair of britches in hand," said Mrs. Whithers. "Well, never mind. In the attic is a trunk full of clothes my students used for costumes in their plays. I am certain we will find something suitable there."

"No, please, ye must not do this," pleaded Mae. "Ye do not know Justice Smythe. Ye do not know—"

"Mae, the Widow and me ain't goin' to let you die," said Callie with firm resolve. "Nothin' else matters. Like Mrs. Whithers said, the risk is all ours. The decision ain't yers to make."

As Callie and Mrs. Whithers became caught up in the excitement of their daring plan, Mae realized that it was out of her hands and that she could better ensure the safety of her friends by cooperating. The secret that she had been harboring for so long and had now tried to impart could add nothing to the success or failure of the plan and might only prove distracting in the end, she decided. No, the secret was better left buried along with the anguish deep in her heart.

As the waning sun cast long shadows across the room, all came to know their parts. For Mae, there was a burgeoning hope where none had existed before; for Callie and Mrs. Whithers, there was a new purpose in their linear lives that far outweighed any risk. Each carefully went about her duties knowing there could be no rehearsal before the first and only performance—a performance that could impact the rest of their lives.

CHAPTER TWELVE

In the Spirit of Justice

Jonathan arrived within a half hour of the urgent summons to find his old governess and Callie anxiously pacing the floor of the parlor room. Callie's exhausted state held her in good stead. Not having seen her since escorting her home after her apology to the court, Jonathan was shocked by her worn appearance, which lent further credence to her performance.

"What has happened?" he asked in alarm.

Anguished screams and moans, capable of piercing the reserve of even the most stalwart, suddenly filtered down from the upstairs bedroom.

"What the deuce is that!" exclaimed Trenholme.

"'Tis Mrs. Bailey," replied Mrs. Whithers soberly.

"The news that she must return to the gaol day after the morrow sent her into early labor. Midwife Gilbrett says that Mae ain't likely to live," said Callie, sniffing back tears.

Jonathan looked at them nonplussed. "But I just saw the woman yesterday. She looked to be in the best of health."

Mrs. Whithers shook her head sadly. "Depression and shock can be dangerous to a woman nearing the end of her increasing time."

Trenholme's features were inscrutable as he shot each of them a considering look, making it impossible now for either lady to judge the quality of her acting. "I shall return this evening to look in on Mrs. Bailey," he said.

At the front door, they could hear him talking with Jane, just as they had expected. Callie and Mrs. Whithers held their breath. When he finally left, apparently satisfied, they exchanged smiles of relief.

"His lordship is no fool, miss, and this is but the first step," cautioned Mrs. Whithers. "We can afford nary a stumble."

When Trenholme returned a few hours past nightfall, Jane showed him upstairs to a room where Callie, Mrs. Whithers, and Midwife Gilbrett solemnly surrounded their moaning and writhing patient. The room was dimly lit, and, due to the talents of Mrs. Whithers and a bit of powder, Mae looked the very image of impending death. If somehow the ladies' performances had fallen short of the mark in this scene, Jane's sudden and honest eruption of heartfelt sobs sealed the moment.

Jonathan drew Callie out into the hallway. "Send me word when the poor woman expires—ah, never mind," he amended, seeing the aggrieved look on Callie's face. "I shall drop by in the morning."

The compassion that Callie saw reflected in his usually stern features surprised her, and, for a moment, she actually felt guilty deceiving him. But then she reminded herself it was for a noble cause. In Jonathan's eyes, the law was the law whatever the circumstances. If Mae had failed to win the court's sympathy during her pregnancy, the court would surely turn a deaf ear to her once she had birthed. It was clear to everyone concerned that the only way to save Mae's life was to smuggle her out of Williamsburg.

Early the next morning, Mrs. Whithers waited anxiously for the telltale sounds of a wagon drawing up to the front of the house. The ticking of the mantel clock was an uneasy reminder that more and more precious time was passing.

What could be taking Callie so long? she wondered. Midwife Gilbrett would be notifying authorities of Mae's death soon and there was no telling when Lord Trenholme would show up to examine the body, which wouldn't do at all. Then, too, Jane would be returning from her errand to compound matters.

Mrs. Whithers walked over to the wooden casket and tapped lightly on the lid. "Mrs. Bailey, are you well?" she asked in a whispered tone.

"Aye," came Mae's muffled voice.

Just then, the old widow heard a wagon pull up. Quickly, she summoned the carpenter and his apprentice who were standing by outside and directed them to carry the casket to the conveyance.

Callie and Mrs. Whithers held their breath, knowing a full moment of heart-stopping anxiety when the apprentice tripped on the step and nearly dropped his end of the pine box. Inside, Mae had covered her mouth to keep from crying out at the jarring.

"Careful there! Have some respect for the dead," Mrs. Whithers admonished the men.

When the box was finally placed in the bed of the wagon, Callie climbed atop the seat and touched her hat in farewell. "Thank ye kindly for yer trouble, ma'am," she said, deepening her voice.

Mrs. Whithers nodded solemnly, and Callie started off slowly so as not to arouse suspicion. When she reached the edge of town, she coaxed the horse to a faster pace, taking care to keep her hat low over her face and ever mindful of her precious cargo. A coded tap on the lid of the box assured Callie that Mae had survived the clumsy handling by the two tradesmen.

The day had already turned sultry and it was barely midmorning. No one followed them. Five miles outside of Williamsburg, Callie pulled off the road into a stand of trees. She took out a jug and cornbread and jumped to the bed of the wagon. Hurriedly, she pried off the lid of the coffin with an iron bar.

"Mae, I have some water for ye," said Callie, helping the woman to a sitting position.

Shakily, Mae accepted the jug and a square of the cornbread. "'Tis a mite warm in here," she said with a weak smile. The coffin was well lined with quilts, but it was still a hard bed on rutted roads. Suddenly, Mae winced and grabbed her stomach.

"Are ye well?" asked Callie in alarm.

Mae smiled. "Aye, 'tis jest the babe kickin'. Ye mustn't worry over me, Callie. I am strong now, and, for the first time in years, I have hope thanks to ye and Mrs. Whithers. I will make it through. Come, we must be on our way. Ye must return to town before ye're missed."

Callie nodded. She helped Mae return to her reclining position and replaced the lid. Slowly and cautiously, she pulled onto the main road again. So far, they had met only a frontier family on their way into town, and Callie prayed that their luck would hold. They had several miles to go.

The sun was high in the sky when she finally came to the shell of a burned-out barn and remnants of an old farmstead. This had to be it. But there was no one around, and Callie knew her first real feeling of panic. She brought the wagon to a halt, stood up, and scanned the surroundings. It was so quiet.

"Jake...Jake Tyler," she called out tentatively, cupping her hands around her mouth. "Be ye here?"

Callie jumped as a large, burly figure suddenly appeared by the side of the wagon.

"Ye be Jake Tyler from Carolina?" she asked nervously.

If he wasn't, she was no match for this giant of a man if he sought to steal her horse. His size alone was frightening, but the rough-cut features and hard dark eyes bespoke a man rarely challenged. The black shaggy hair that brushed the top of his shoulders and the scar above his eye made him appear even more fearsome.

The man nodded. "Aye, I be Jake Tyler."

Callie struggled to hide her ill ease and continued to regard him with suspicion. "Who be yer employer then?" she asked, her heart in her throat. She was ever conscious of the fact that, with one swift movement, he could break her in half if he had a mind to.

When the bearlike man made a move toward her, Callie snapped the reins, but he was too quick for her and had a hand firmly on the horse. Giving him her most menacing glare, she threw up her fists to fight.

The man burst into laughter. "Ye gots gumption, boy, takin' on a body thrice yer size. Ye has smarts, too. Miz Priscilla Bates sent me to meet a Miz Bailey. Ye must be Hastings."

As he continued to chuckle at the bold defense of one of such meager stature, the man's harsh, frightening features relaxed. And they took on a warmth and good naturedness that surprised Callie.

He looked Callie up and down. "So, the Widow Whithers hath sent a boy to do a man's job, ay."

Callie nimbly jumped down from the wagon and, with an impish grin, removed her hat to shake out a wealth of auburn curls.

Miz Whithers hath sent a *woman* to do a man's job and quite ably so. When ye've found yer tongue, ye may call me Callie," she said, enjoying the astonishment on the huge man's face. It quite reminded her of Trenholme's reaction to the discovery.

Jake Tyler nodded appreciatively, giving Callie her due. "Where be my passenger?" he asked.

When Callie pointed to the coffin, Jake climbed into the wagon and pulled off the lid of the box. Despite the cleverly disguised holes in the wood designed to give ventilation, the box was as hot as an oven now and Mae was barely conscious from the heat. Loose strands of hair clung damply to her face and neck and her lips were dry, in spite of the water Callie had given her along the way.

Jake quickly scooped up the young woman in his arms. Seeing the condition of her friend, Callie gave a cry of alarm and rushed forward to support Mae's limp body when he handed her down. Jake jumped to the ground then and carried Mae to the side of the road where he laid her on the sweet-smelling grass beneath the shade of an oak tree.

"Have ye more water?" he asked.

Callie nodded and quickly fetched the jug. He took the kerchief from around his neck, wet it, and lightly bathed Mae's face.

"Is she all right?" asked Callie anxiously, as he forced water between Mae's lips.

"She'll come 'round. Miz Bates said nothin' 'bout a babe bein' on the way. "'Twill slow us down considerable."

Mae choked on the water. Her eyes fluttered open and color returned to her face. Upon seeing this coarse mountain of a man looming over her, she cried out and shrank back in terror.

"Easy, Mae. Ye be safe," Callie hurriedly assured her. "This be Miz Bates' overseer come to take ye to Carolina."

"Jake Tyler, ma'am," he said, introducing himself. He looked at Callie. "I will let ye womenfolk to yer farewells whilst I switch the horses."

As Mae's eyes followed him apprehensively, Callie patted her hand in reassurance. "Ye can trust him, Mae. He ain't as fearsome as he first appears."

"Oh, Callie, ye mustn't think that I am ungrateful, but—"

"I know. By both our counts, men ain't got much to recommend 'em. But, as my Negress Lucie is always tellin' me, ev'ry now and then a good one comes along. Do not ye worry. Jake will see ye safe."

The two girls embraced then, and Callie prayed that Jake was, in fact, a "good one."

As she watched him seat Mae in the wagon making her as comfortable as he could, any misgivings Callie had of him began to fade. There was respect in his manner toward Mae and warmth in his eyes when he looked at her.

"I shall take good care of yer friend," he said, coming to give Callie a leg up on her horse.

Callie smiled. She believed him.

When Jake took his seat beside Mae on top of the wagon, Callie no longer feared for the young woman's future. She and Mae exchanged tremulous smiles and raised their hands in silent farewell. As the overseer clicked the reins and set the horse on a brisk pace, Callie wiped a tear from her eye. She wondered if she would ever see her good friend again.

With a heavy sigh, she turned her horse in the direction of town and suddenly froze. Coming toward her on his magnificent black stallion was Jonathan Trenholme. Her mind raced with questions. How much had he seen? Would he recognize her despite the disguise? Of course he would recognize her—if not her person, most certainly her mount. It was the horse he had lent to her.

She considered trying to outrun him, but as quickly as the thought came to her, she realized the futility of it. The powerful stallion could easily overtake her bay. She was trapped and he knew it. The ruse was up. The couple he had avenged himself on in London immediately came to mind as she wondered what action he would take with her. All she could do now was to keep him from going after Mae.

There was no greeting, no animosity, no bravado, no attempt to deceive him further, just a despondent resignation in Callie's manner as he drew up to her. Jonathan dismounted and pulled her from her horse. He didn't say a word, but she had never seen such a black look on his face, and what courage she had left completely dissipated.

"How did you come to know?" she asked, struggling to keep her voice from quivering.

"It was not difficult to figure, though your performances were quite above par," he responded coldly. "I could find no evidence that Mrs. Bailey had a brother in Maryland or any place else for that matter, so it did not take me long to realize who the young boy was who had claimed her body. After that, everything fell into place. Mae Bailey was alive in that coffin, wasn't she? That is why you were all in such a bloody hurry to get the body out of Williamsburg before I could make an official examination."

Callie nodded dully. "How did you track me here?"

"A few questions put to Jane yielded the fact that Whithers has a sister in Carolina, and I took the chance that you would be somewhere along this road. Was that Mrs. Bailey on that wagon?"

When Callie didn't answer, Jonathan shook her roughly by the shoulders. "Do you know what the punishment is for helping a prisoner to escape? You could be indentured or exiled for the rest of your life! Whithers and the midwife could be jailed and forced to forfeit all of their property real and personal! Is that what you want?"

"No, but who has to know? The court is satisfied," said Callie.

"If I found you out, it will not take long for Justice Smythe to draw the same conclusions, were he of a mind to investigate the matter. 'Tis easy enough to test your story, and I can assure you that he is possessed of a far more suspicious mind than I."

Callie bit her lip nervously. She had thought that the court would consider the matter closed with the report of Mae's death. Clearly, she hadn't taken into account Justice Smythe's vengeful nature.

"Can ye make a note in the record that Mae had a brother?" she asked hopefully. "A headstone can mark her grave somewhere in Maryland, should Justice Smythe decide to check."

Jonathan glared at her. "Always the schemer, ay, Callie—and why the blood hell are you not on your farm where you belong?"

"Trenholme, what's to be served by anyone knowin' that Mae be yet alive?" pressed Callie, ignoring his temper.

"The law," he answered succinctly.

"But not justice," she countered. "Did ye not tell me once that justice is what matters? Mae is no killer. She was a woman protecting herself and her unborn baby from the brutality of her husband, and, even so, his death was an accident. Where would be the justice in taking her life, too?"

"The law says a person must pay for his or her deeds. Justice is implied."

"Mae Bailey already paid for her deed ten times over—every time that brute took a hand to her and for all those months she suffered the gaol. Do you know what it is like to be even a day in that place? I do," she said, giving him a pointed look. "It tears at the soul."

Jonathan inwardly winced at the guilt he still felt for his part in her incarceration.

"Trenholme, the law might be black and white," continued Callie, "but justice ain't."

Privileged and male, Jonathan had never been forced to consider before that law and justice could mean two different things. He let out a heavy sigh of frustration. He was a man ruled by logic; Callie wasn't—at least not by any that he understood. Raised and bound by the convoluted conventions that he was, she confounded him time and again by her simplistic views.

What the bloody hell was he to do with this girl? He had thought to see her impetuous spirit quelled beneath the iron will of Martha Whithers, but now he had to wonder just who had tamed—or corrupted—whom? In any case, to expose Callie's complicity was to expose his old governess' involvement as well as that of the midwife.

"Get on your horse," he ordered gruffly.

Jonathan gave her a hand up on her horse and swung himself into his saddle.

Callie looked at him. "Are ye goin' after Mae?" she asked anxiously.

He was silent for a long, tense moment. "It is as you said. Mrs. Bailey has paid her debt," he said, turning his horse in the direction of Williamsburg.

Callie let out a sigh of relief. "Ye ain't half bad for a gentry, Lord Trenholme."

Jonathan glanced at Callie in surprise. *Lord Trenholme.* For the first time in his life, he felt that the acknowledgement of his title was for an honor earned.

CHAPTER THIRTEEN

Trouble Returns

Callie looked up at the gathering black clouds in dismay as she raced the storm home from Williamsburg. When the chaise rounded the lane to the farm, she could see Lucie and Old Joe carrying long poles of tobacco plants to the curing barn. She shouldn't have stayed the extra two weeks in town, but Mrs. Whithers had fallen ill and Callie couldn't bring herself to leave until the old matron had been nursed back to health.

The first drops of rain began to fall, and Callie hurried to unhitch the horse from the chaise. She led the bay inside the corral to the lean-to and rolled the chaise to a more protected area under the overhang. She had just entered Lucie and Old Joe's hut when the downpour came. It was such a driving force that the fire danced and hissed from the raindrops that found their way down the chimney. She figured that Lucie and Old Joe would wait out the storm in the curing barn, and she settled down to wait.

It was an hour later when the rain finally abated and Callie heard their footsteps. She flung open the door. Her heart fell when she saw the grim expression on their faces.

"How much was left?" she asked.

"Nearly a quarter acre on the ground and three quarters of an acre in the field I figure," said Old Joe.

Callie slumped dejectedly on the bench. "We was too long with the plantin'. All that work for naught."

Lucie patted Callie's shoulder in consolation. "Ain't nothin' done without reason, child, 'ceptin' when da evil spirits is to blame."

Old Joe gave a derisive snort. "Spirits got nothin' to do with it, woman. Missy Callie, da plants will mold if left on da ground. My bones is tellin' me dis rain gonna be around a few days more. 'Tis lettin' up some now. We can gets more plants poled afore dark iffen we hurry."

"No. Workin' in the rain is how Ethan come down with the fever."

"Da clime was colder then. Asides, I ain't heard no whippoorwills singin'," said Lucie, trying to be helpful.

Callie shook her head adamantly. "If those plants ain't wilted, the tobacco will be of a lesser grade anyway. Ain't worth the trouble or the risk. We'll make up the loss with the last cuttin'."

Old Joe ran a hand across his face and looked away for a minute. He hated to burden her with more bad news. "Missy, da frost is comin' early this year."

Callie looked at him in alarm. "Be ye certain?"

He nodded.

Old Joe's instincts were rarely wrong, and Callie went still. An early frost was the bane of tobacco farmers. "Will there be enough time for the plants to dry on the ground after cuttin' the last field?" she asked.

Old Joe shrugged. "Depends on how many days of sun and rain we gets."

Callie sighed dismally. She could not cut back on the acreage already in cultivation. She would not be able to meet the terms of the lease next year and still have barter. Indeed, only if her tobacco were of an excellent grade would she be able to meet them this year. The answer was obvious.

"There be too much land for us to handle ourselves," she said resignedly. "As soon as the tobacco is in hogsheads, I will go to town and post some acreage. Hiram Finch always wanted that stretch of woods what lays next to his. Mayhap then I can hire on more help for the fields we got left."

Old Joe nodded in agreement, but Lucie protested. "I can helps ye. I gots hands big enough for two."

Callie clasped the Negress' hand and gave it an affectionate squeeze. "My thanks to ye, Lucie, but I need ye to oversee the kitchen garden. Ye and Old Joe best get out of them wet clothes and get some rest." She rose from the bench to leave. "Lucie, don't be botherin' with my meal. I ain't hungry."

Lucie opened her mouth to protest again, but Old Joe motioned for her to remain silent.

* * * * *

Mother Nature both blessed and cursed Callie. She obliged with the moisture needed for the humidity to cure the tobacco already cut, seasoned, and hanging on poles in the barn, but the rain cost Callie the critical loss of most of her last acre of crop.

For the next five weeks, Callie and Old Joe carefully tended the fires in the humid, tightly closed curing barn around the clock. Mold was always a danger during the process and they kept a vigilant eye to that end. The heat from the smoldering fires on the floor sapped their energy. The smoke, as it circulated around the suspended stalks of tobacco before escaping through the eaves, stung their eyes and burned their throats day and night. Callie was conscious of nothing outside of this narrow world, and her eighteenth birthday came and went without notice. Miraculously, the vagrant who had stolen Callie's breeches and field hat had mysteriously returned them.

With agonizing slowness, the leaves began to change from a greenish yellow to a light tan color. Finally, Old Joe judged the tobacco to be ready for striking. Callie and Old Joe carefully stripped the leaves, sorting them by quality as determined by their position on the stalk, their color, and the number of defects. Then, they piled the leaves into small bunches and stacked them five feet high to ferment.

Nearly two weeks later, the day had come. Callie nervously held her breath as Old Joe stretched out the glossy leaves. If they were too moist, they would decay in shipment; if too dry, they would crumble, and the inspectors would burn the shipment. All would be lost. If the leaves were *in case*, then the tobacco had absorbed the correct amount of moisture.

One by one, Old Joe smoothed out the leaves grading them, sniffing the aroma, and fingering the texture of each. A quarter hour stretched into a half and a half into three-quarters until Callie could no longer endure the suspense.

"Well?" she asked hesitantly, when she felt that he had graded enough of the crop to make a judgment.

Anxiety clawed at her insides as Old Joe laid aside a leaf. Why wasn't he smiling? Callie groaned, bracing herself for the worst.

"'Tis of the finest quality yet," pronounced Old Joe, breaking into a wide grin. "Lord Randall should be well pleased."

Callie closed her eyes against tears of relief that threatened to spill down her cheeks. They had been long, hard months. Not even the happiness she felt could dispel the marks of that hardship. Suddenly overcome by exhaustion and an onslaught of emotions left unresolved, Callie broke down and cried.

Unperturbed, Old Joe gently placed a hand on her shoulder. He knew this moment had been a long time in coming. "Let it go, missy. 'Tis time ye rid yer body of the poison."

After several minutes, Callie self-consciously wiped away tears with the sleeve of her shirt. "I-I'm sorry."

"Ain't no need to be sorry," replied Old Joe. "Now, whilst I finish with the gradin' and put these tobaccy leaves in hogsheads, ye best rest a spell, or we ain't never gonna roll dem barrels down to da ship when she comes."

Completely spent, Callie raised no argument. Old Joe was right. In her present state, she would be of no help to him at all. She stumbled to her cabin and fell fully clothed upon the bed.

When Callie awoke, she looked around her in confusion. She wore her shift beneath the covering, and she could see through the open window that the position of the sun was wrong. It was early morning when it should have been late afternoon. She must have slept through the night! She was trying to bolt out of bed on legs that refused to hold her weight, when the door opened and Lucie entered the cabin.

"Oh no ye don't, missy!" the Negress staunchly declared at finding her mistress half sprawled on the floor. "You gets back into dat bed 'til I tells ye different. Go on now. Get back in there."

Reluctantly, Callie complied. "But Lucie, I will miss the ship," she protested.

"Honey, dat ship come and gone. Ye been asleep for nigh on two days."

"No, 'tis not possible!" cried Callie. "What of the tobacco? Why did ye not wake me? What am I to do now?"

"No need to carry on so, child. 'Tain't good for ye. After ye went to bed dat afternoon, ye come down with a fever. Dat nice Mister Justice come 'round and—"

"Trenholme? Trenholme was here? Why?"

"Now I is gettin' to dat, missy," responded Lucie indignantly.

Callie groaned. When Lucie had a story to tell, there was no hurrying the moment.

"As I was sayin'," continued the Negress with maddening deliberation, "yer young man—"

"He ain't my young man," corrected Callie.

Lucie put her hands on her hips. "Do ye wants to know what he had to say or don't ye?"

"Yes, yes, go on."

The Negress took a deep breath. "As I was sayin'," she repeated, sending Callie a look that warned her not to interrupt again, "he say da Bailey records is set straight. He say ye'd know what dat means."

Callie gave a quiet sigh of relief. Trenholme had been able to enter into the record that Mae had a brother living in Maryland without arousing suspicion.

"Anyways," Lucie went on, "when I comes to fetch ye, ye was sick with fever. Mister Justice was fit to be tied I can tells ye."

Callie looked at her in surprise. "He was?"

Lucie nodded. "Wanted to bring a doctor and all, but I showed him my possets was jest as good. When he see'd Ol' Joe needed help with da hogsheads, he rolled dem barrels hisself down to da river. Now dat one be a man," she declared, her black eyes shining. "Yes sir, 'tis all done and yer tobaccy is at the inspector's warehouse waitin' to be shipped to England. Ain't nothin' to worry on now 'cept gettin' yer strength back, missy. Now, ye stays in dat bed 'til I tells ye to get out."

With Lucie standing guard, Callie did as ordered and within a few days, she was back on her feet again.

With her tobacco on the way to England, she turned her attention to the posting of her land. She was just returning from staking out the parcel she intended to sell, when she saw Lucie and Old Joe frantically waving her down. The look on their faces and the presence of a worn-out nag grazing nearby were all the warning she needed, and she approached warily.

"What's amiss?" she asked, dismounting.

Lucie's mouth twisted into a grimace of disgust. "Yer stepdaddy is in yer cabin eatin' all yer vittles. Says he come back to be with his family. He come back all right to make trouble I say."

When Callie didn't respond, Old Joe and Lucie exchanged worried glances.

"Missy?"

"I heard you, Lucie," she replied tonelessly.

She went to her horse and removed her father's hunting rifle from the saddle scabbard that Old Joe had fashioned for her. Her features set in a tight line, she leveled the gun to a spot just above the doorframe and fired. A resounding blast splintered the wood.

Instantly, Abel Cane came bellowing out of the cabin. "What the bloody hell do ye think yer about! Ye near to took my head off!"

"Then 'twould seem I missed my mark," said Callie with icy reserve.

The look on Cane's face changed from anger to confusion as he stared back at the buckskin-clad figure before him.

"Ethan? I heard ye was dead."

"Ethan is dead. 'Tis me…Callie."

Cane's eyes narrowed. "I shoulda know'd 'twas you. Always did have a nerve twice yer size. Why ye dressed in them buckskins?"

Callie ignored his question. "What be ye doin' here, Cane?"

Cane shrugged. "I come back to be with me family."

"Ye've a nerve of yer own comin' back here after startin' the fire what killed my mother."

"Here now, ye ain't fixin' that on me. 'Twas an accident. Yer mama and me was arguin', and she knocked o'er the candle."

"Ye was stealin' coin begot by our labor from the box, and she found ye out. The candle was knocked over when ye hit her and knocked her senseless."

Cane was unapologetic. "Can't steal what's mine. I be the master of this house. I can take what I want. Yer mama ne'er could learn that."

"She learned ye was a leech. Now get out of here afore I shoot ye for a trespasser. Ye ain't got no family here."

"Ye changed some, Callie," said Cane, looking her up and down. "Ye be a hard, little bitch now."

"You ain't changed," she shot back. "Ye still be the same connivin', lazy bastard ye always was."

"Now that ain't no way to talk to yer stepdaddy what come to help ye."

Callie laughed contemptuously. "Ye figured the fields to be harvested by now. Ye come to help yerself to the profits ye mean."

"I am a mite short on barter," admitted Cane, flashing her a disarming smile that usually worked well with women.

But Callie was immovable. "I got news for ye. There ain't no profits to speak of this year."

Cane's show of amiability disappeared. "Wha'd'ye mean there ain't no profits?"

"The tobacco crop was too much for me and Old Joe to handle by ourselves. We wasn't able to harvest it all in time. I have to post some of the land to get coin for more field hands. Looks like ye'll have to find yerself some other widow with the means to keep ye, Cane."

Instead of the outburst of temper she had expected, Cane smiled again with such complacency that Callie was immediately put on guard.

"Go on. Sell the land," he said. "But make certain that the coin lands in my hands."

"In a pig's eye, I will!" spat Callie.

"Iffen ye don't, gal, I will have ye afore the court for stealin'."

"And how might ye be thinkin' to do that?"

"'Tis my land."

Callie laughed mirthlessly. "Mama is gone. Ye ain't the master of nothin' no more."

"That ain't so. Accordin' to the law, when I married yer mama all of her property become mine—the land, the horse, that fancy chaise there I see'd ye drivin' through the trace."

The blood drained from Callie's face. "Ye been watchin' me all along ye low-bellied snake...just waitin' for the tobacco to be harvested."

"Let's jest say I been keepin' my eye on my profits," said Cane.

"Ye ain't never been inclined to the truth, and I don't believe yer claim now."

"'See for yerself. 'Tis truth I speak."

"Ye ain't that smart. Who told ye this?"

Cane stiffened at the insult, but apparent victory within his grasp brought the easy smile back to his lips. "That Miz Sanders told me," he said with an air of self-importance. "She see'd me walkin' the streets of Alexandria some weeks back. She told me I got rights and I should come back to claim what's mine."

Olivia Sanders. The mention of the name was enough to raise Callie's hackles. The woman was a viper and Lord Randall's sister. Left widowed and penniless by a husband addicted to gambling, Lady Sanders had arrived a year ago from England with her daughter Lilibeth to live on her brother's charity. For reasons Callie had yet to fathom, the woman had taken an intense dislike to her and had been a thorn in her side ever since. But Callie had never thought the woman would go to such lengths as to see her dispossessed of her land.

"If this be the case, then ye best be prepared to get them hands dirty cause yer tied to the terms of the lease," said Callie, struggling to conceal her alarm.

"Why should I do that when I got ye and them darkies there?" he questioned carelessly.

"Because Lucie and Old Joe ain't yers."

"Of course, they is. They go with the l," he said, proud of his new-found knowledge.

Callie smiled. "Not if Papa freed 'em afore he died. They only stay for me. The horse and chaise ain't mine neither. They was lent to me. And I'd sooner starve than lift a finger to do yer work. So ye see, Cane, ye ain't gettin' nothin' but hard labor." Callie grabbed the rifle that Old Joe had quietly reloaded. "Now get out of here afore I put buckshot betwixt yer legs." For emphasis she fired, barely missing his foot, and had the rifle half loaded again before Cane had recovered.

"Ye batty, female!" he cried, angrily shaking a fist at her. "Ye'll rue the day ye set Abel Cane off his land."

Callie sent another volley past his ear, and Cane quickly jumped astride his mount and headed down the lane as fast as the nag could carry him, anxiously looking over his shoulder at Callie's raised rifle until he was safely out of range.

"Dat man is worse den a wart on a hog," said Lucie. "Can he do what he says?"

"I can't rightly say, but I am goin' to find out," declared Callie resolutely.

CHAPTER FOURTEEN

Grist for the Mill

Jonathan gave himself a vigorous scrubbing in the bronze tub. Callie's tobacco was harvested, and, by his calculations, his account was paid in full. He had done more than his share in keeping her out of trouble and on her farm, though he knew an anxious moment when he had arrived that day to find her ill with a fever. Now, it was time for Lord Randall to make good on his promise. And Jonathan intended to see to it that the man lived up to his part of the bargain by securing an audience with the governor for him. *If all goes well,* thought Jonathan happily as he rinsed off the soap, *he will be on his way home to England soon.*

This new, raw land, where the development of towns was discouraged and the practice of law placed in the hands of laymen appointed at the favor of the governor, was wholly enigmatic to him. Although they were all Englishmen under the king's rule, he could feel a disturbing undercurrent, a growing schism developing between the colony and England. Virginia, Jonathan decided, was definitely not to his liking.

The valet entered the first-floor bathing room then to set out Jonathan's clothes for the afternoon. Suddenly, a commotion broke out in the outer room. Thinking he was under attack, Jonathan quickly stood up and was reaching for his pistol, when the door flew open and an all too familiar buckskin clad figure burst into the room.

He hurriedly sat back down in the tub. "What the bloody hell is this all about!" he exploded angrily.

The distraught housekeeper came rushing in. "I told him ye was fixin' to leave and was too busy to see anyone, but when my back was turned—oh! your pardon, sir," the woman stammered red-faced when she saw they were interrupting his lordship's bath. She quickly averted her eyes and grabbed Callie firmly by the arm. "Come along, lad, and let Lord Trenholme to his privacy."

Callie resisted, losing her hat in the scuffle, and the housekeeper dropped her hold to gape at the dark red hair that tumbled down Callie's back. The poor woman didn't know if she was more shocked by the fact that it was a young woman who had brazened her way into a gentleman's bath or that a lowborn had dared to trespass in such a fashion upon a nobleman and justice of the court. For his part, the valet sounded as though he had received a blow to his midsection, so sharp was his intake of breath.

"Ye can all stop yer gapin'," snapped Callie. "I seen him afore when he didna have no tub to hide in."

At this candid disclosure, the monocle popped from the valet's eye to roll noisily across the floor, and the housekeeper clasped a hand to her bosom to still her heart.

Trenholme moaned, sinking lower into the tub. By evening he knew that he and Callie would be the main topic of conversation at every supper table and in every servant's quarter.

He looked at Callie and ordered tightly: "Get out!"

He was careful not to use her name. The servants were fairly new to the employ of the Samuels and were not natives of the town, and the valet had come with him from England. If they could not identify his unexpected visitor, then perhaps the gossip mill would be deprived of some of its grist, he reasoned hopefully.

But Callie in her single-mindedness was oblivious to the ramifications of her brashness. She had come to Jonathan seeking a refutation of her stepfather's claim and the world could very well hang until she got it.

"Trenholme, ye have to hear me out."

"And how do you figure that?" he demanded crisply.

"Ye ate my vittles and slept in my bed. That be how."

The valet and the housekeeper gasped in unison, and Callie threw them a look of annoyance as she wondered what the fuss was all about.

At this, Jonathan firmly took control of the situation before Callie ruined both their names. One more scandal and his father might bury him in this god forsaken land for good.

"Mrs. Bendel, escort the young lady to the drawing room," he ordered curtly. "I will speak with her there."

Callie started to protest, but the steely look in his eyes silenced her. Reluctantly, she followed Mrs. Bendel from the room.

In the drawing room, Callie paced the floor anxiously awaiting Jonathan, too worried to notice the housekeeper's audible sniffs of disapproval each time the woman passed by the room. It seemed an eternity to her before Trenholme finally appeared and closed the door behind him.

His large frame seemed to fill the room and Callie swallowed hard. Even in her distress, it was difficult to ignore his attraction. He was casually dressed in a white linen shirt and close fitting gray breeches. Wavy brown hair hung loose above his shoulders lending him a more boyish appearance. But there was no mistaking a lighter mood as he glowered down at her.

"Now, suppose you tell me what has compelled you to place at risk both our reputations," Jonathan demanded. At the blank look on her face, his constraint dissolved into temper. "God's teeth! For someone who was so worried about her good name, even you must realize the tat you have so handily provided gossips by bursting into my bath and announcing in the company of two servants that I have slept in your bed!"

Callie blushed when she saw his point, but it didn't supersede the fact that she was in danger of losing her land. "Never mind that, Trenholme, I got me a bigger problem."

Jonathan looked at her in dismay and groaned. "What have you done that could set aside such a predicament as this?"

Callie bristled. "I ain't done nothin'." Quickly, she told him about her stepfather's visit to her farm that morning. "Can he do what he says, Trenholme? Can he take my land?" she asked tensely, searching his face for an answer in her favor.

Jonathan's anger deflated somewhat in the face of this new situation. "I am sorry, Callie, but when he married your mother, everything became his property."

"Papa meant that land to pass to Ethan and now 'tis mine," she argued.

"It matters not your father's intentions, and unless your mother made some prior arrangement in the event of her death, your stepfather is the custodial head of house."

Callie felt as though the bottom had fallen out of her world, and she staggered beneath the force of this new blow. She had pinned every hope on Trenholme and now that was gone.

Her eyes misted over. "Mama wouldna married Cane if she know'd it would mean our birthright," she said in a choked voice.

"Unfortunately, ignorance of the law is no defense," said Trenholme. "If your stepfather is as irresponsible as you say, he will no doubt welcome you to continue farming the property. Nothing needs to change. He will probably drift around and show up now and again for some coin or a meal."

"No!" exclaimed Callie. "The likes of him will not profit from my labor. I promise ye that."

"I fear you have little choice in the matter. Now, I must be about my business."

As Jonathan opened the door to leave, Callie called out to him. "Trenholme, there is always a choice. 'Tis jest a matter of finding it. Ain't nothin' this unfair that can't be undone—law or no law."

Jonathan turned and studied her for a moment, once again struck by the contrast between the force of her resolution and the size of her stature. She looked so small, so lost and vulnerable standing there—like that day in the courtroom. But the flash in her turbulent blue eyes, the set of her chin, and the manner of her stance all bespoke a stubborn determination to prevail, the likes of which he was quite unaccustomed to in the young women of his acquaintance.

"The law is clear on such matters, Callie," he said, becoming irritated with her refusal to accept the unchangeable. "See for yourself." He walked over to the desk, picked up a book, and plopped it into her arms. "It is one of Coke's *Institutes* on the common laws of England."

Callie's initial surprise as she caught the heavy book swiftly turned to anger. "Ye know I cannot read. Do ye mock me at a time when most I need yer counsel?"

"I have given you my counsel, but you seem intent upon discounting it," retorted Jonathan. "Now I invite you to seek your own."

As he strode from the room, he took all of her hopes with him.

Callie tentatively fingered the book, finally turning over a page, then another and another. Her father had started to teach her to read shortly before his death, and she found that she could make out a few of the simpler words. But taken out of context, they made little sense to her, merely adding to her frustration. She closed the book and tucked it under her arm. Sweeping past the curious housekeeper who hovered outside the door, Callie departed the house and set out on a determined pace across town.

Martha Whithers had always prided herself on being prepared for the unexpected. But she was caught totally off guard this day when Callie marched into her parlor and dropped a tome on common law into her lap with the most astonishing request that she, Callie, be taught how to read it.

"It seems to me that a certain young woman once told me that what she does not miss, she does not need," said the Widow Whithers when she found her voice.

Callie winced as her brash statement came back to bite her, and she could see by the smug look on the old lady's wrinkled features that Mrs. Whithers would not be satisfied with anything less than that Callie eat her impetuous words.

"All right, so it was true then; it ain't now," said Callie.

"And it appears that this young lady is not content to begin with the basics but must commence with a book of laws no less," continued Mrs. Whithers with a melodramatic flair. "My dear, Callie, I know that you are a most extraordinary person, but even a baby must learn to crawl before walking."

"I ain't fixin' to learn to walk, Madam, and I ain't no baby. Ye just learn me the words, and I will figure the rest. I ain't got nothin' to offer in return but my hands and a strong back. Mayhap Jane could do with some help with her chores."

"Mayhap," replied Mrs. Whithers. "But why this sudden need to learn to read? What about your farm?"

Callie told the old matron of her stepfather's visit and of his claim to her land.

"I see," said Mrs. Whithers, "but I fail to understand how learning to read can wrest your land from his grasp."

"I thought 'twas only the weak that was easily bested, but I know now that 'tis the ignorant as well. I ain't gonna be one of them what goes down without a fight. 'Twas the law what took my land away, and 'tis the law that's gonna give it back." Callie's eyes glittered with determination, and there was no mistaking the passionate resolve in her voice.

Mrs. Whithers was pensive as she considered Callie's request. "While I sympathize with your position, my dear," she said at length, "alas, I fear that I cannot aid you in your quest."

Callie blinked in surprise. Clearly, she had not expected to be refused. "But why, Madam?"

"'Tis no small task that you ask, and 'tis no small fee that I would charge."

Callie's shoulders slumped. "I hoped ye might accept my labor for coin."

"'Tis not coin I would require of you but a debt of a different sort."

"I have nowhere else to turn, Madam. Whatever debt ye ask, I shall pay," said Callie, unable to conceal the desperation in her voice.

A slight smile lifted the corners of Mrs. Whithers' mouth. "Very well then, just remember who first requested the bargain. I shall stand for no scandals, indiscretions, or questions to my authority. Once balked, twice excused, miss. You will get no second chance with me," the old woman warned with the wag of her finger.

Again, in her single-mindedness, Callie saw only a means to her end, and she nodded solemnly as she submitted to the lady's terms without question.

"'Tis in good time I dare say," said Mrs. Whithers. "It shall take all of my talents to repair your brashness this day."

"You know of my visit to Trenholme?" asked Callie in surprise. "But I just left—"

"My dear, by this time everyone in Williamsburg is well acquainted with your lapse in good judgment. 'Tis the stuffing of gossip. And there is nothing that travels faster than the servant's tongue for news of this nature. 'Twould seem that Lord Trenholme's housekeeper lost no time in imparting the story to the cook, whom Jane happened to be visiting at the time. Thank heavens Lord Trenholme and Jane had the good sense not to mention your name."

"That ain't the way it was."

"It does not matter. There are many who delight more in falsehoods than in truth. They are the more interesting. Now to begin, those odious breeches shall be burned and—"

"I have a business to see ended first," interrupted Callie. "I shall return on the morrow."

"Here now, what are you up to? I know that look and it usually bodes trouble."

"I have a visit to make, and then I mean to see that Cane gets no more than he is due," said Callie, her features set in a tight line.

She left the house with Mrs. Whithers sputtering out warnings of consequences, but they fell on deaf ears.

Callie galloped recklessly through the countryside and down the avenue of majestic oaks to Randall Hall with no mind to her safety. The narrow, dirt lane twisted and turned through the private forest for nearly a mile before a large, brick house finally broke into view. Bypassing neat, whitewashed buildings that housed the plantation's office, laundry, and kitchen, Callie brought the horse to a stop directly in front of the mansion. She threw the reins to a young black boy standing by and ran up the front steps to bang on the door. Within minutes, the door opened and the servant's round brown face dissolved into a wide grin when Callie took off her hat.

"Missy Callie, ain't seen ye in an age. Ye grow'd some I'd say."

"Hello, Juba, is Miz Sanders at home?" asked Callie, her mouth twisting with distaste.

Juba's eyes widened with surprise. "Lady Sanders be at home, but is ye sure 'tis her ye be wantin' to see?"

Before Callie could answer, a voice trilled haughtily from inside the house. "Callie Hastings, is that you I hear at the front entrance? Tenants go to the back door."

Callie stiffened. She didn't have to see her to know that the source of the unpleasant voice was Lilibeth Sanders, Lord Randall's niece. There was a defiant gleam in Callie's eye as she sidestepped Juba and entered the house. An attractive, young woman meticulously groomed and coiffed in the latest fashion of the day was descending the stairway.

"I ain't no tenant, Lilibeth, and ye ain't mistress of this house," retorted Callie.

"How dare you!" sputtered the girl, stopping midway on the stairs. "And how dare you sully this house with your presence. Juba, if you cannot keep out the riff raff, I shall have you removed to the fields."

"I be here to see yer mother," said Callie, "and I'll not waste time with a spoiled brat living off her uncle's kindness."

Lilibeth looked as though she had been slapped across the face. Her wide-set eyes were huge with disbelief. Her chin quivered as she struggled to stammer out a response. All she could manage in the end was a shriek of indignation, and she turned and ran up the stairs screaming for her mother.

A dumbfounded Juba stared after Lilibeth. "Oh, missy, ye shouldna done that," the black housekeeper warned nervously. "No one crosses the likes of her and Lady Sanders without knowin' a heap of trouble."

Callie was too angry to be worried.

"Here now, what is all the ruckus about?" demanded Lord Randall, emerging from the drawing room. "Callie? What brings you by?" he asked in surprise, adjusting his glasses on the bridge of his nose. "Juba, did I just hear Lilibeth carrying on like a banshee?"

"Yes, suh."

"What did she do…tear a nail again?"

"No, sir," spoke up Callie. "Lilibeth and me had words."

Lord Randall looked at Callie quizzically. "I see," he said, ushering her into the drawing room. "You do not like my niece, do you?"

Callie was taken aback by the question. She had been prepared to defend her behavior. "Do ye wish me to be honest, sir?"

"Of course. God knows 'tis a quality in short supply in this house nowadays," he remarked dryly.

"In that case, sir, I ain't got time for the useless who are otherwise able."

Lord Randall chuckled at Callie's candor. "Neither do I, my dear, but I fear that Olivia and Lilibeth are my crosses to bear. I presume that you are here to see me. My factor tells me that the quality of your tobacco will meet the terms of your lease. 'Tis a pity the entire crop could not be harvested."

"Truth to tell, sir, I have come to see Miz Sanders."

Lord Randall looked at Callie in surprise. "You wish to see Olivia? Why? What has she done?" he asked, suddenly chary.

"Ye might ask her," replied Callie as a tall, thin woman with narrow, pointed features and dark, glittering eyes swept angrily into the room.

"Robert, I must insist that you put this lowborn tenant out of the house immediately," the woman said in a strident voice. "That girl nearly attacked Lilibeth. The poor child is most upset."

"Be quiet, Olivia, I want to hear what Callie has to say. Go on, lass."

"Robert, really—"

"I said be quiet, Olivia."

Lord Randall's sister snapped her mouth shut and fixed Callie with a hostile glare.

Callie didn't flinch. "My stepfather has returned to claim my land under the law of guardianship, and ye have her to thank for it."

"What!" Lord Randall rounded on his sister. "Olivia, what have you to do with this?"

"Nothing. She is just trying to cause trouble."

"I would know the truth, Sister, and I would know it now!"

"Calm down, Robert. I saw the poor man wandering around Alexandria a few weeks back without a farthing to his name, and well, I might have mentioned that he had some rights to the land."

Lord Randall became livid. "Do you know what you have done? You have put my best crop of tobacco in the hands of a wastrel who has never done a lick of work in the whole of his worthless life!"

"Now, Robert, you said this girl was able to harvest only part of the crop this year. I just thought—"

"You do not think, Olivia. That is your problem. What do you suppose will happen when that man fails to meet the terms of tenure?"

"For one thing, this little heathen shall no longer be a bother to us. For another, the land will revert to you, and you can settle it on Lilibeth for a partial dowry," replied Olivia, having considered the matter carefully.

Lord Randall stared at her as though she had lost her mind. "No, Olivia, I cannot," he said, visibly struggling to control his temper. "Aside from the fact that the parcel would count for but a fraction of the dowry, that land makes it possible for me to meet my debts. And now, not only shall I lose a year's revenue waiting to foreclose on Cane, but it will also be necessary for me to use the coin I have been saving for Lilibeth's dowry to buy more slaves to work that land myself."

"But, Robert—" The rest of Olivia's words died in her throat as her brother fixed her with a withering glare.

Lord Randall turned back to Callie. "If you have nothing further to discuss with me, I must see my solicitor on this matter."

"This is all I come to say," said Callie.

Throwing a last angry glare at his sister, the earl strode swiftly from the room.

Olivia turned pale as the ramifications of her actions set in. This had not been the plan. She had expected to secure a piece of Lilibeth's dowry and be rid of Callie Hastings into the bargain, once and for all.

As Callie turned to leave, Olivia grabbed her arm. "If you think you have won this set to, miss, think again."

"Nay, we have both lost," said Callie, jerking her arm free.

"I would not be so high and mighty if I were you. Were it not for the bargain struck between Lord Trenholme and my brother, you would be rotting in the gaol."

"What bargain?"

A nasty smile spread across Olivia's narrow features. "My brother promised Lord Trenholme an audience with the governor so that he might plead a case for his return to England."

"In trade for what?"

"Lord Trenholme was charged with seeing that you stayed out of trouble long enough to harvest your tobacco crop. Wait, I have not yet finished," said Olivia as Callie charged out of the room.

But Callie had heard enough. She rushed out of the house, past an astonished Juba, and grabbed the reins of her horse from the stable boy. She had always respected Lord Randall, and she had begun to place more trust in Trenholme. Despite her intentions, she was even growing to like the man. And, once again, she had been deceived. The horse, the chaise, changing Mae's files, helping Old Joe roll the hogsheads of tobacco to the river—his actions had all been part of a bargain. She climbed astride her mount and galloped out of the yard, berating herself for having let her guard down.

CHAPTER FIFTEEN

Ashes to Ashes

Callie returned to the farm just before dark. The hope that Old Joe and Lucie had harbored since Callie rode off to town this morn vanished with one look at the thunderous expression on her face.

"What's to be done 'bout yer stepdaddy?" Lucie asked anxiously.

"Nothin'," said Callie.

"What ye gonna do, missy?" questioned Old Joe.

"I am goin' to learn to read."

Lucie and Old Joe looked at each other nonplussed.

"Take yer rest for the night," continued Callie. "I have some thinkin' to do."

As Callie walked to her cabin, Lucie was about to start after her, but Old Joe put a hand on her arm to stop her. "Let the missy to her figurin'."

Just before dawn, Callie roused Lucie and Old Joe and instructed them to set their belongings outside in the yard near the road, to harvest what vegetables were left, and to gather the food and animals. She had already dragged out her few possessions. When all was made ready, she mounted the horse.

"Old Joe, fetch me a torch," she ordered.

Old Joe quickly did her bidding. "What are ye about, missy?" he asked, handing the lighted torch up to her.

"Cane shall find his claim in the manner that he left it," replied Callie.

When she rode to the tobacco fields and began to torch what they had been too late in cutting, Lucie cried out. "No, child, no! Joe, stop her."

"It ain't our say so," he replied solemnly. "The crop ain't no good anyways."

For the next half hour, Old Joe and Lucie watched as a grim-faced Callie methodically set fire to the cabins, the out buildings, and the harvested wheat and corn fields. The air was soon thick with the acrid smell of smoke.

The sunrise was blood red, eerily complimenting the orange glow of the blazing fire. Lucie took this to be an ill omen and fervently mumbled incantations. When Callie finished with her destruction, she came to stand beside the couple. No one moved or spoke.

Callie finally broke the spell when she lifted the heavy brass kettle, the most prized possession of colonists fortunate enough to own one, and set it with the couple's belongings. Lucie understood what the gesture meant and began to cry.

"We ain't leavin' ye, child," the old Negress sobbed. "Tell her, Joe."

"'Tis time now for ye and Old Joe to go yer own way," said Callie. "There ain't nothin' left here for ye. I hear tell the land out in the western frontier is free to anyone who farms it for a year. Fresh land'll mean better crops anyways, and no one'll bother ye out there. The hard work and know-how was mostly yers, Old Joe; so should the rewards be, too."

"We ain't leavin' ye," Lucie insisted stubbornly. "Why, what's to become of ye?"

"This was my family's home. I will not let Cane take it away without a fight."

"What are ye up to, missy?" asked Old Joe, concerned. "Ye ain't 'bout nothin' foolish, is ye?"

Callie shook her head. "Don't ye worry 'bout me. The Widow Whithers is takin' me in for a spell. She is learnin' me to read and write so I can find a way to get back my land."

"Then we's stayin' with ye," declared Lucie stoutly. "I's sure this Miz Whithers ain't gonna say no to some extra hands and—"

"No, we ain't," cut in Old Joe decisively. "Missy Callie is steppin' into a world where we ain't no more help to her. She needs this Miz Whithers now."

Callie looked at the couple who had become her family, her heart heavy with what would be another loss in her life. Lucie clasped Callie to her breast in a hail of tearful sobs. After several seconds, Callie gently extricated herself from the woman's arms and wiped away her own tears.

"Come, we have much to do before we can leave," she said, her voice hoarse with emotion. "Old Joe, gather up the nails. Ye'll be needin' 'em to build yer shelter when ye settle. I am off to the Tobias farm. The mister agreed to sell me a horse and wagon for ye."

"Ain't no need, missy," replied Old Joe. "Lucie and me has served a master all our lives. We is too old now to serve ourselves. If 'tis all the same to ye, Lucie an' me'll ask Lord Randall if he gots room for us."

Callie looked at Old Joe in surprise. "But what of your freedom?"

Old Joe shrugged. "Lord Randall be a good man, and 'tis enough for Lucie and me to know we is free in our hearts and minds."

Callie turned to the Negress. "Lucie, what say you?"

"Whatever Old Joe say," Lucie answered quietly.

Callie nodded. "I will take you there. But we are still in need of the extra horse and wagon."

It was a strange little caravan that pulled up to Randall Hall hours later. Callie led the procession with the chaise full of smoked ham and vegetables. Old Joe and Lucie followed behind with a wagon filled with their possessions, more foodstuffs, chickens, and the cow tied up to the back. Callie was grateful to find that Lilibeth and Olivia Sanders were not at home to bait her temper. Her emotions were too raw and too close to the surface for her to credibly do battle with them.

As a surprised Lord Randall listened to Callie plead the black couple's case, his anger over his sister's high-handedness was mitigated somewhat by the sudden good fortune of adding Old Joe's know-how to his tobacco fields and Lucie's hand to the kitchen. Since the death of his old cook, he hadn't had a decent meal in a month of Sundays, he complained. Thus, the earl was only too happy to accept Lucie and Old Joe into his "family." It was with the stipulation, however, that their free status be kept secret, lest it should breed envy and discontent among the other servants and field hands.

With the futures of Old Joe and Lucie settled to everyone's satisfaction, Callie guided the chaise leisurely through the trace to Williamsburg with less anger and a more determined spirit. She was too preoccupied with her thoughts to notice the sudden scurrying of animals and the flight of birds. It was only when she heard the pounding of hooves and a crashing through the bracken that she turned to see Abel Cane bearing down on her.

He looked ridiculous clinging precariously to the nag he rode. But there was nothing laughable about the dark expression on his face or the distance he was closing between them in his pursuit of her. After a paralyzing moment of disbelief and fear, Callie desperately rallied her horse to greater speed. But the animal, having come to enjoy the easy pace, was slow to respond to her commands.

Cane was nearly beside her now. Callie grabbed the whip to beat him back when he reached out for her, but he tore the lash from her grasp. When she brought forth her father's hunting rifle, Cane knocked it from her hand and pulled her from the seat. She hit the ground with a hard thud, and it was a minute before she could catch her breath and scramble to her feet.

Cane dismounted and collared her before she could run more than a few yards. She winced when he grabbed a handful of her hair and jerked her face up to his. "Ye little bitch! Iffen ye think ye can burn my place to the ground an' ride away, ye'd best think again." He cuffed her so soundly that Callie would have sunk to the ground had he not had so firm a hold on her shirt.

"I left it for ye jest the way ye left it for us," spat Callie with as much force as she could muster. The effort earned her another vicious slap that drew blood from the corner of her mouth.

"Since ye enjoy playin' the part of a lad so much, I shall punish ye like one. And then, miss, ye'll set up house for me like a woman."

He took out a length of rope and threw her spread eagle against a tree.

"What devil thing do ye do?" cried Callie, as he looped the rope around the tree trunk and tied her hands with lightning speed.

The color drained from her face when she looked over her shoulder to see him pick up the whip. Her shoulders sagged with the first stinging blow. She hadn't recovered yet before she felt the whip a second, third, and fourth time in rapid succession. Despite the clench of her teeth, cries escaped her. With the punishment of the next lash, her legs buckled and a haze enveloped her.

When Cane raised his arm to strike again, the whip was wrenched from his hand, and he turned in surprise to find a tall, robust young man scowling down at him.

"If you ever touch that lass again, I shall see you whipped throughout the town," said Jonathan Trenholme. His voice was like a low rumble of thunder, and there was no mistaking the fury just below the surface.

Cane cowered. "I-I be exercisin' a father's right," he stammered.

"You are Callie's stepfather?"

"Aye. The lass be under my governance, sir. Who might ye be?"

"I am Lord Trenholme and a justice of the court. In your absence, the General Court placed Callie in my custody. Any authority over her shall be mine." Trenholme didn't mention the fact that the custody had been temporary and had, in fact, ended with Callie's last appearance before the court.

Jonathan's pronouncement, however, only emboldened Cane. "Your pardon, sir. I thank ye for yer interest in me girl. Whate'er she's done, she won't be no more bother to ye. I be here now to release ye of yer duty."

"I am afraid that I do not choose to relinquish it," said Jonathan, eyeing Cane coldly. "Now, I suggest you be gone before I take this switch to *your* hide."

As Trenholme took a menacing step toward him, Cane's brief moment of courage deserted him, and he scurried to mount his nag.

"Ye've not done with me yet, Callie Hastings!" he shouted over his shoulder, hurrying off as fast as the played-out horse would carry him.

Trenholme swiftly untied Callie's hands. She sank half conscious into his arms, and he lay her down on the ground. When he smoothed her hair away from her face and saw the bruise on her cheek and the swollen, bleeding lip, he angrily clenched his jaw. If he had Cane before him now, he would beat the scoundrel within an inch of his worthless life. Gently, Jonathan rubbed the circulation back into her wrists.

"Callie, I must examine your back," he said. She didn't respond, but he could see her stiffen at the suggestion. "I have some balm in my saddlebag. If the skin is broken, the salve should be applied before infection sets in. Callie, do you hear me?"

She nodded faintly. He carefully turned her over and raised the tattered shirt, exposing to view several nasty welts. Three were laid open. Again, his features tightened with anger. She was so slight that the markings covered her entire back.

Jonathan quickly returned with the balm. Callie flinched as his fingers began to gingerly work the soothing ointment into her wounds. "Easy now," he said. "'Twill soon ease the pain as well."

Callie rallied somewhat and recalled Olivia's disclosure of the bargain he had struck with Lord Randall. "Why did Lord Randall send ye this time?" she asked.

Her voice was weak, but Jonathan detected the cynicism in her tone, and he furrowed his brow in bewilderment. "Lord Randall did not send me. Whithers became worried when you were late to arrive. She asked me to find you."

"Was the terms as good?"

"Terms? Callie, I know not of what you speak. We will discuss it another time," said Jonathan.

Suddenly, Callie began to shiver and her teeth chattered. "Trenholme, why am I so c-cold?"

Jonathan lowered her shirt. He took off his coat and placed it over her. "'Tis the shock," he said. "It will pass."

He turned her over and picked her up, mindful of her injuries. As he carried her to the chaise, Callie whispered: "Trenholme, Cane didna best me." Her voice trailed off as she drifted into unconscious sleep wrapped in the comfort and security of his arms.

Jonathan had to smile at the familiar sentiment that was Callie to the end. She may have been soundly whipped, but she wasn't defeated. He was relieved to know that, however bruised her body might be, her pride was still intact for he was beginning to realize that her spirit was what made her so unique.

CHAPTER SIXTEEN

Carrot-and-Stick

When Callie came fully awake, she found herself in a bed in Mrs. Whithers' home. And it was much against her will that Mrs. Whithers insisted that she stay abed for a few more days. To keep a close eye on her young charge, the old matron had Callie installed in the bedroom next to hers. With the careful ministrations of Mrs. Whithers and Jane, Callie rapidly regained her strength. Thanks to the balm that Jonathan had applied and left behind with strict instructions for continued use, the scars were healing.

While Callie was grateful for Trenholme's timely intervention with her stepfather, she was still angered over what she considered to be his deception. She thought that he had lent her the horse and chaise, escorted her home that day, altered Mae's files, and helped Old Joe with the tobacco out of the goodness of his heart or perhaps out of a sense of debt for the ordeal he had put her through.

It confounded her somewhat that it should make any difference to her what his motives were, but, try as she might, she couldn't banish the hurt she felt that his interest in helping her hadn't been all that altruistic. She furiously upbraided herself for having let her guard down and vowed not to let it happen again.

When Callie was released from her convalescence, she had no official function in the house except that of a student. Gradually, Mrs.

Whithers came to depend upon her more and more as a companion. Callie lapsed willingly into the roll. She was fond of the old woman, and, considering what Mrs. Whithers had risked to help Mae Bailey, she figured that she owed the lady a great debt.

This time around, Callie proved a much more willing student, though she chafed at the other things she was made to learn which, to her mind, were senseless and had little bearing upon her goal. This particular afternoon, she was at the peak of her frustration as she awkwardly poured tea into a cup.

"No, no, Callie," chided the older woman. "The tea must not splash. Hold the teapot closer and pour slowly."

Her patience tried to the limit, Callie set the pot down and jumped up from her seat to pace the floor. She was unused to the wider more formal pannier hoops, and the undisciplined swoosh of her skirts came dangerously close to upending a delicate porcelain figurine more than once.

"Callie, do sit down before you make a shambles of the room," pleaded Mrs. Whithers.

As Callie dropped onto the settee in a very unladylike heap, the old matron winced. The process was going to take longer than she thought.

"Madam, I fail to see how pouring tea, pricking my fingers with needles, or wearing skirts twice my width can learn me to read or write," complained Callie.

Mrs. Whithers was almost at her wit's end as well. "You shall have to trust me that everything has its purpose," she replied.

"Like what?" challenged Callie.

"Well, take the needlework for instance. When first you came here, you had little knowledge of numbers. By having to count stitches, you have learned to add and subtract correctly and to count to fifty…which will help you to better determine your crop yields."

Callie mulled this over for a minute. "I suppose, but what about Mr. Plinn? He constantly corrects my speech and makes me sing silly verses. That doesn't help me to figure my crop yields. What purpose does he serve?"

Mrs. Whithers was determined to transform Callie into a refined young woman with or without her cooperation. And she did not see the wisdom in explaining to her student just yet that the real duty of the music teacher was to replace the coarse, lowborn tone of her voice with that of a more genteel quality. The old matron quickly searched her mind for an explanation that would satisfy Callie.

"Music aids in your command of numbers and your ability to read," she said.

"How so, Madam?"

"Do not you count beats and learn to read more words with the songs that you sing?"

Callie eyed her mentor skeptically but accepted it. "Then what of this tea business?" she challenged.

Mrs. Whithers sighed, momentarily stymied. The other lessons she had managed to cloak in the guise of Callie's own interests, but what could be said for the importance of learning how to serve tea?

"Well," she began haltingly, "serving tea requires a sure hand…just as does writing," she ended on a more confident note. "It steadies and coordinates the hand to better form letters correctly."

Callie again threw her mentor a dubious look, but she did have to admit that the words she was able to write were beginning to resemble less the uncertain scrawl of a child and more so that of a mature individual. Still, she restlessly twisted a stray curl around her finger showing little inclination to return to her tea exercises.

Mrs. Whithers sighed again in anticipation of a wasted afternoon, when a clever thought suddenly came to her. "Callie, it occurs to me that you are making so little progress with your law book because, although you may recognize the words, you do not understand the context of them. It would seem to me that you would benefit more from the guidance of one who has studied law."

"And who might that be?" asked Callie moodily. "Certainly not Trenholme. The man ill-stands my company as it is for he has yet to pay a single visit."

"I was not thinking of Lord Jon. Mr. Plinn read law at the Inner Temple in London for a time before resigning to pursue his musical interests. I might be able to convince him to take on an extra duty were you to promise to make his others—and mine—less arduous," Mrs. Whithers proposed craftily.

Callie saw the trap. But, again motivated by her own self-interest, she quickly agreed to the bargain.

When Mrs. Whithers approached Mr. Plinn about instructing the ignorant and temperamental Callie on the law, he was flabbergasted— if not horrified—at the thought. His patience was tried to the limit with just one simple music lesson. The intricacies of law were out of the question, he stoutly informed the matron. Only when Mrs. Whithers promised to make this exercise in futility financially worth the anguish it was certain to cause him, did Mr. Plinn agree.

With new incentive to propel her over the tedium, Callie stopped fighting the lessons. Over the next several weeks, her diction improved rapidly thanks to Mrs. Whithers' unrelenting correction of her grammar. Her vocabulary, too, had noticeably expanded from pouring over the primers. And her tone was slowly losing the rough, harsh edges indicative of her common background as Mr. Plinn took advantage of her more even temperament to expand the voice exercises.

Callie continued to scoff at the dance lessons that were secretly designed to improve her carriage, and her continued sessions with the tea service and needlepoint nearly drove her to distraction. But she accepted it all in good stride, knowing that she would be rewarded with a lesson on the law two evenings a week.

Had her drive been any less, she would have found it impossible to advance beyond the first paragraph of the law book. But as it was now, when the evening sessions with Mr. Plinn were over, she continued to study the passages long into the night, making careful note of points she desired to have clarified at the next session.

Mr. Plinn thought the change in his, heretofore, recalcitrant student no less than a miracle and found it incredible that she was the same ill-mannered ruffian of a few months ago. Her aptitude for learning and her grasp of the rudiments of law, though she continually railed at the injustice of it, was astonishing to him. Knowing nothing of the bargain between Callie and Mrs. Whithers, he pompously credited Callie's new interest in her studies to his erudite manner and expert instruction.

As he came to appreciate her intelligence, his scholarly eye began to acknowledge her physical attributes as well. Now that she did not have to be concerned with eking out an existence and was comfortable in her obsession, Callie found an appetite for food that she had never had before with her simpler fare. She added weight and was quite unaware that she now possessed, at last, the rounded curves of a woman to please the most particular of men—of whom Mr. Plinn was no exception. And he suggested additional evening sessions at no extra charge.

Had Callie not been so absorbed in her task, she might have noticed that Mr. Plinn was now using cologne and choosing his clothes and dressing his wig with greater care; or that he found countless excuses to touch her face, ostensibly to correct the shape of her mouth during the singing exercises. Thus, she was shocked to the core one day when he suddenly broke from character to grab her around the waist and plant a wet, slobbery kiss on her mouth while his other hand fumbled with the laces of her bodice.

"Mr. Plinn!" exclaimed Callie, shoving him away and wiping her mouth with the back of her hand in disgust. "Just what do you think you are about!"

Pale, thin, possessed of a hooknose and protruding eyes in a long, narrow face, Mr. Plinn hardly brought to mind the image of a lothario. His priggish manner and patronizing contempt for the less than scholarly made him seem older than his twenty-eight years. And it was with great disbelief that Callie watched the tutor's eyes narrow and his thin lips curve into a salacious grin as he once again lunged for her.

Totally consumed by his now frequent fantasies of Callie, Mr. Plinn reached out to acquaint himself with the treasures of her womanhood. Instead, he encountered a force of resistance that left him momentarily dazed when Callie promptly thumped him on the head with a book. The blow seemed to bring him to his senses, and he recoiled in contrite horror at his loss of control.

He was stammering out an apology and tenderly massaging the bruise on his head when Mrs. Whithers quickly entered the music room at the sound of the commotion. With one glance at the thunderous expression on Callie's face and her disheveled appearance, she correctly assessed the situation.

Though it might be said that the situation had not been handled in the most discreet way possible—Callie had proceeded to chase the poor man into the street hurling curses at him—it was clear that she had handled it. Nevertheless, it was time to find a suitor for her charge, Mrs. Whithers decided.

CHAPTER SEVENTEEN

An Awakening

With the quick exit of Mr. Plinn, Callie stole more and more hours from the day for the study of her law book. Between her duties as a companion, her tutelage under Mrs. Whithers, and the time she spent examining her precious book, Callie barely slept, though her appetite remained steady enough.

Even when she accompanied her mentor on social outings or was busy with a duty, her mind was bent on one thought—the law book. Mr. Plinn's indiscretion had been most ill timed for her purpose, but at least she had managed to pick up enough of an understanding of the legalese before his hasty departure to carry on by herself. Of course, there was always Trenholme, but that was an option she refused to exercise.

The sun was well past the rising hour this morning when Mrs. Whithers burst into Callie's room. Callie groggily lifted her head from her arms and looked around in surprise to find that she had fallen asleep at the desk.

"Really, miss!" Mrs. Whithers huffed indignantly, still in her nightgown and cap. "Were your reason for being here to act as my companion, I should have dismissed you long ago. The hour is so late I might as well remain dressed for bed. Look at you—pale, hollow-eyed, neglectful of your person, studies, and duties. I must insist that you put aside that book and assume a more regular schedule."

"My apologies, Madam," said Callie, stifling a yawn. "I promise to be more attentive in the future."

Mrs. Whithers sighed in exasperation. "'Tis been nigh on three months. Surely you have learned something of the law by now."

Callie shut the book. "Yes, I have learned that a single woman has few rights and a married woman even less. Oh, Madam, I can find little hope of regaining my land from Cane until I have reached my majority," she said in dismay.

Mrs. Whithers' cross features softened. "I am sorry, dear. But something will turn over. I am certain of it. In the meantime, perhaps this letter will cheer your mood."

Doubtful that anything could cheer her, Callie took the parchment from Mrs. Whithers. When she recognized Mae's childish scrawl, she gave a cry of joy. The spelling was sometimes difficult for Callie to follow, but Mae's happiness and contentment shone through every word.

"Oh, she birthed a daughter before reaching Carolina…and Jake helped her to deliver the babe." Callie had to laugh at the thought of that bearlike man tending to such a delicate task.

"Yes and the man married her," finished Mrs. Whithers, eager to be about the day's tasks.

"Imagine that." Callie sighed wistfully. "Oh, how I wish that we might see Mae again."

"Perhaps one day we shall. But in the meantime, miss, time waits for no one."

"Do ye wish me to help you to dress now, Madam?"

"No, Jane can do that. I wish you to make yourself presentable and be off to the mantua maker. You are in need of a ball gown."

Callie looked at Mrs. Whithers warily. "Why is that, Madam?"

"The Raleigh Tavern is hosting a holiday ball, and we shall be attending."

"I have no wish to attend."

"Well I do and we shall, miss. A bit of revelry will set us both in good stead. Planters and merchants alike will be present. 'Tis time for you to make their acquaintances."

"Why?"

"Perhaps you might meet someone helpful to your cause," replied Mrs. Whithers.

Meeting eligible young men was more what the old widow had in mind for Callie, but she knew better than to say so. The incident with Mr. Plinn had opened her eyes to the fact that Callie had turned into a most fetching young woman and was quite in need of marriage. Were the girl to keep a rein on her impetuous spirit, she could make a comfortable match with a respectable merchant, thought the old widow. She had done her part in softening the edges. It was time now for the unveiling.

She held out a piece of parchment. "Here are instructions for Mrs. Stanhope on the construction of your gown. Mind you, do not dally. We have lessons to review upon your return. And do not forget to change to street shoes and pattens," she added, knowing how Callie hated the hard leather footwear.

Callie groaned as Mrs. Whithers exited the room, effectively putting an end to any further discussion on the subject. Muttering under her breath, she poured water from the pitcher into the bowl and splashed it on her face. Since she had no choice in the matter, she was anxious to get the deed done and return to her book. She fussed uselessly with her hair and gown until Jane arrived to help her. It seemed an eternity before she finally stepped out into the December morning.

The air was cold enough to take one's breath away, but it was a clear sunny morn and Callie felt her melancholy mood lifting. Christmas was four days plus a fortnight away, and she found that even she was not immune to the holiday spirit that hung in the air. People called out cheerful greetings; the front doors of homes and shops were decorated with wreaths of nuts, berries, and pinecones; and vendors on the street corners offered cups of hot mulled cider.

As Callie walked down the Duke of Gloucester Street, she suddenly heard her name called in a tentative fashion, as though the person wasn't quite sure of her identity. When she looked up, she saw Trenholme astride his prized stallion.

"It *is* you!" he exclaimed, quickly dismounting and walking up to her. He shoved back the hood of her red cloak to better view her face. "I can scarce believe my eyes," he murmured in amazement.

The gray, gaunt-like appearance was replaced by a palette of color. Her cheeks and lips were rosy red from the cold air; her eyes, unclouded by stress, were bright blue; and her auburn hair shimmered with shades of gold and red in the morning sun. Jonathan also noticed that she possessed a more confident, less defensive bearing and seemed to project a newfound maturity. She was no longer the wanton child of his acquaintance, he realized with a shock. Somehow she had grown into a fetching young woman when his back was turned.

Callie began to fidget beneath his scrutiny. "Trenholme," she snapped impatiently, "I ain't—I am not a horse on auction. If there be something amiss about me, say so."

Jonathan laughed heartily. While her appearance may have changed, her spirit certainly hadn't. His ear had also caught a new softness in her tone and her quick correction of grammar. He began to wonder what was going on in his old governess' home.

"On the contrary, Callie, I dare say there is much that is right about you," he said in open admiration.

Callie flushed and lowered her eyes, suddenly feeling unsure of herself. She was desperately searching for a response before she started to babble mindlessly, when she remembered that she was still angry with him.

"I figured you to be in England by now, since you earned your fare," she remarked curtly.

Jonathan gave her a quizzical look. "The governor is away on a trip, and I must await his return to present my petition," he replied. "How have you been getting on?"

"Who is asking—you or Lord Randall? Why should you care anyway?"

Jonathan was surprised by her manner toward him. He thought they had achieved a new level of understanding in their rather ambivalent relationship when he had allowed Mae Bailey to escape. Callie's peevishness told him otherwise.

"All right, Callie, what is troubling you? If memory serves, something was bothering you the day I stayed your stepfather's hand against you, and apparently, it still stands between us. What is it?"

"I do not play the fool twice, Trenholme. Good day to ye, sir."

Jonathan took hold of Callie's arm as she started past him. "Ho there, miss, you do not get away that easily. I would know the meaning of that remark."

"Do you deny that Lord Randall promised you an audience with the governor in exchange for my safe conduct until the tobacco was harvested?"

Jonathan chuckled and released her arm. "So that is it."

Callie's eyes flashed angrily. "I can take care of myself, Trenholme. I do not need a keeper, and I'll have no truck with a body who ain't—isn't—truthful about his actions."

"I dare say we are both guilty of that charge," countered Jonathan with the lift of his brow.

He had a point. She hadn't been completely truthful with him either in her actions concerning Mae. "I-I guess this makes us even," she conceded. "Still, I will not be bargained over like a hogshead of tobacco."

"I have come to understand that, Callie, but at the time the plan seemed expedient for all concerned. I can assure you I will not make that mistake again."

Callie nodded stiffly. She wasn't sure what the word "expedient" meant and his wasn't an unqualified apology, but she decided to accept it. Her eyes were drawn to his, then, and she became flustered and dropped the note of instruction that Mrs. Whithers had given her for the dressmaker. As the paper fluttered behind her, she quickly turned and bent over to pick it up, unwittingly exposing more than was deemed appropriate.

Jonathan smiled, much amused. "May I suggest that, given these ridiculous hoops you women insist upon wearing, you not bend over in such a manner?"

Callie quickly straightened, her cheeks a bright pink that had nothing to do with the cold. "How is a body to pick up anything?" she asked.

"Well, if a gentleman is not available to do the deed, then it behooves the lady to bend at the knee and stoop."

"Oh. I don't know why females have to wear half the things said to be necessary," she grumbled. "They ain't comfortable or practical."

Jonathan chuckled again. Despite the changes, the old Callie still maintained a presence. He cast about for further conversation. He wasn't ready to let her go. To his surprise, he realized that he had actually missed not seeing her. "I trust your stepfather has kept his distance."

"I have not seen him about," said Callie.

"Good. I doubt that he will bother you again."

Just then a closed carriage drew alongside. If Callie hadn't recognized the Randall crest, there was no mistaking the haughty voice of the occupant.

"Lord Trenholme," trilled Olivia Sanders, poking her head out the window, "how opportune to find you here."

Jonathan moaned inwardly. He found the woman to be singularly overbearing and her daughter, although pretty enough, dangerously close to following in her mother's footsteps. "How so, madam?" he asked, struggling to be polite.

"I understand that you are to partake of my brother's hospitality this afternoon. As Lilibeth and I have done with our shopping, we are returning forthwith to Randall Hall. Perhaps you will do us the honor of an escort."

"It will be my pleasure," replied Jonathan haltingly. He turned to Callie and smiled. "I look forward to seeing you again. Perhaps we might have a longer conversation then."

Callie stood spellbound as he took her hand and pressed his lips to it in a light caress. Her color rose again, and she was certain that Jonathan could hear the rapid beating of her heart. In the back of her mind, she wondered if a kiss on her lips from him would be more pleasant than Mr. Plinn's had been.

Olivia heard the note of affection in Jonathan's voice when he addressed the young woman, and she did not miss the fleeting intimacy that had passed between them when he had taken her hand. When Trenholme went to tie his horse to the back of the carriage, Olivia's sharp black eyes turned to the redheaded woman. The girl possessed a beauty not as refined as that of the blonde Lilibeth, but there was a clarity and definition that was just as likely to catch a man's eye. Unlike the giddy, flirtatious nature of her daughter, this girl radiated a reserved, earthy sensuality that Olivia immediately found threatening to Lilibeth's interests.

Olivia's eyes narrowed. There was something familiar about this young woman, she thought, and she pulled back into the carriage to confer with her daughter.

"No! It cannot be!" Callie heard her exclaim.

Olivia's head reappeared in the window. "Callie Hastings, you were supposed to—I mean I thought you left town when you lost your land. What are you still doing here bothering decent gentlemen the likes of Lord Trenholme?"

Callie bit back a caustic retort and, in her very best tone and grammar, answered: "I am a student of Mrs. Whithers."

Olivia gave an unpleasant laugh. "A student—what, pray tell, could *you* learn?"

"I may never be able to stitch a tapestry to your satisfaction," said Callie, exercising what Jonathan viewed as remarkable restraint for her, "but I will know enough not to marry a man who would gamble away my daughter's dowry and throw me on the charity of my family."

Inside the carriage, Lilibeth let out a shriek. Olivia's features turned ashen, and the shocked woman pulled her head back into the conveyance so quickly she knocked her hat askew.

Callie had just insulted the sister of an earl, a member of Jonathan's precious nobility, but she was unrepentant. Her features set in a defiant line, she looked over at Trenholme daring him to upbraid her for her impertinence. Instead, he grinned and tipped his hat to her before hoisting himself inside the carriage.

Even from the street, Olivia's shrill voice could be heard. "Lord Trenholme, I must insist that any gentleman with an interest in my daughter refrain from associating with such dregs of vulgarity."

Callie smiled when she heard Jonathan's prompt reply. "Madam, I am not aware that I am paying court to your daughter, and I have no notion to what vulgar association you refer. I was conversing with a charming young lady."

Silence followed and the carriage took off. Callie could imagine a most awkward ride to Randall Hall, and with uplifted spirits, she practically skipped the remaining distance to the mantua maker's shop.

Mrs. Stanhope, proprietor of the shop, appeared to Callie to be a much beset woman. Her dark hair was turning prematurely gray, her brow was furrowed with worry, and her manner was anxious. From the moment that Callie had entered the shop and handed the dressmaker Mrs. Whithers' note of instruction, the woman hadn't stopped flitting.

She led Callie to a dressing room and instructed her to strip to her shift. After measuring her from head to foot, the dressmaker set about yanking bolts of cloth from the shelves and threads and bric-a-brac from baskets. She chattered on hardly giving Callie time to answer, and it took a little while for Callie to realize that Mrs. Stanhope was not really soliciting a response.

All of a sudden, the woman sat down on a stool and burst into tears. Dumbfounded and not knowing quite what to do, Callie hesitantly put a hand on the dressmaker's shoulder. Thanks to the friendship of Mrs. Whithers and Mae, Callie's emotional scars were healing, and she was beginning to recover a more compassionate nature. But she still found it difficult to extend herself to strangers. To her relief, Mrs. Stanhope soon calmed herself.

"Your pardon, miss," she said, choking back sobs. "My circumstances will not permit me to serve your needs. I had to release all my seamstresses and cannot produce the gown in time. I fear I shall be forced to close my shop soon."

"But why?" asked Callie in surprise. She knew the dressmaker to have a fine reputation, and, while the wealthier ladies of the colony sent to England for much of their wardrobes, Mrs. Stanhope was not without an impressive clientele.

Mrs. Stanhope pulled out a handkerchief and dabbed at her tears. "Alas, my husband spends in gambling debts the coin with which I must pay my seamstresses and buy new cloth and threads. The only material I have left to ply my trade is what you see before you. 'Tis not even a full wardrobe, and I lack the selection of wools, silks, and satins required by my customers."

Callie looked around the shop, taking note of the bare shelves that had earlier escaped her notice. "I am sorry, Mrs. Stanhope, but perhaps—" she stopped midsentence as a thought suddenly came to her. "Mrs. Stanhope, if you wish to save your trade, I know of a way—unless you fear your husband's temper."

Mrs. Stanhope looked up at Callie with renewed hope. "I shall do anything. My man is given more to poor judgment than to temper. It is mostly by my labor that we live, and now he will soon see us thrown out on the street. What must I do?"

"You must take an advertisement in the *Gazette* declaring yourself a sole trader in business," said Callie, eager to practice her newfound knowledge. "In that event, you cannot be held liable for your husband's debts and no one shall take his wagers."

"Oh, miss, I've never heard of such a thing. Be ye certain?"

Callie nodded, confident in her advice. "'Tis no doubt a secret well guarded by men," she added disdainfully.

"Then I shall do it." The woman wiped her tears and squeezed Callie's hand in gratitude. "As payment for your counsel, I shall fashion ye a handsome dress from the very finest material."

Mrs. Stanhope disappeared into the back room for a few minutes and returned with a half finished gown made of silk of a most extraordinary color. It was neither blue nor green but a cross between the two, and the flowers and leaves embroidered on it with silver threads shimmered in the light. Callie had never seen such beautiful cloth, and Mrs. Stanhope smiled at the expression of awe on her face as Callie gently fingered the material.

"The fabric came from France," said the dressmaker. "With a bit of tweaking, the gown will be perfect for ye."

"France?" Callie looked at the woman in surprise. "I thought the colonies were permitted to trade only with England."

"That is true. Smugglers brought it in, but that shall be our secret," said Mrs. Stanhope with a twinkle in her eye.

Callie smiled and looked at the fabric again. "'Tis quite beautiful. But is this gown not being fashioned for another?"

"It is."

"Then how can I take that which is spoken for?" she asked, disappointed.

"Lady Sanders holds a rather large debt with me. I am not in a position to add to it now," replied the dressmaker. "I think the color to be better suited to you than to Miss Lilibeth anyway and, alas, a more useful advertisement for my trade."

Callie smiled to herself. It would be sweet revenge, indeed, to show up to the ball wearing Lilibeth's gown. "I shall accept your kind offer," she said with a glint of mischief in her eyes. "But my counsel was freely offered. I will insist upon making full payment for the gown—after you declare yourself sole trader. The coin will be yours to use then to restock your shelves."

Mrs. Stanhope nodded. "I shall take out the advertisement today."

CHAPTER EIGHTEEN

Metamorphosis

Callie, I must insist that you stop dispensing legal advice from my parlor to strange women. Ever since you aided Lydia Stanhope, my house is never empty. The menfolk take a dim view of such things," warned Mrs. Whithers, her voice becoming muffled as Callie and Jane pulled the petticoat down over her head.

"But why?" asked Jane, drawing in the skirt at the waist.

"Because," interjected Callie as she helped Mrs. Whithers into the robe of the ball gown, "if women were to know their rights—such as they are—they would be less under a man's thumb and fewer would be inclined to marry. I recollect you once saying, Madam, that as laws appear to be set with no mind to the circumstances of women, it is up to us to do something about it."

"Well, yes, I did say that," admitted Mrs. Whithers uncomfortably. "But though I may agree with your sentiments, miss, I will not have the town fathers appearing on my doorstep with tar and feathers. 'Tis better for a young woman to marry an older man of comfortable means and limited years. Ow! Jane, have a care with those pins. I am not a pincushion."

Mrs. Whithers patted her skirts into place and twisted around to take a last critical look at her debutante. A pleased smile crinkled her face and her eyes shone bright with pride. "Ah, you look lovely,

Callie. Mrs. Stanhope certainly outdid herself on your gown. 'Tis such an uncommon color. Wherever did she come by the material?"

"I cannot say. 'Twas intended for Lilibeth, but Lady Sanders hadn't paid her account," said Callie, strolling out of the room.

Mrs. Whithers' eyes widened. "What? Have you lost your mind, miss!" she exclaimed, hurrying after her headstrong charge. "Of all the people to cross—consider the consequences, lass."

"I have," said Callie, gliding down the stairs.

The old matron cast her eyes heavenward. "Dear Lord, have mercy upon us," she murmured.

The Raleigh Tavern, at any other time the strict purview of men, was tonight awash with candlelight and the resplendent finery of men and women alike as they moved about the Apollo Room in time to a complicated minuet.

At a table spread with delicacies and sweets, Olivia Sanders had the ear of a circle of gossipy matrons. "Can you imagine the incompetence of that woman losing the material for Lilibeth's ball gown? Lydia Stanhope should be run out of town," she ranted. "My poor Lilibeth has been forced to a gown this night that she has worn once before, though 'twas in England. Isn't that right, dear?"

"Yes, Mother," Lilibeth answered dutifully.

"This never would have happened in London I can tell you."

As Olivia droned on, Lilibeth rolled her eyes in boredom and looked about the room for one person in particular. Instead of Lord Trenholme, however, her gaze fell upon someone else and her mouth dropped open in astonishment.

"Mother," she said, tugging on Olivia's arm. "Mother, look there."

Olivia yanked her arm away. She could not abide being interrupted, but Lilibeth was not to be put off.

"Mother, look!" insisted the girl.

Olivia gave a huff of annoyance, and her eye followed the point of her daughter's finger. She gasped when she spied Callie entering the room with Mrs. Whithers.

Indeed, Callie escaped the attention of few. Her gown, gathered in the back in the style of the popular saque dress, was beautifully fashioned to her petite figure. The unusual turquoise color brought out the blue in her eyes in heightened contrast to her dark red hair and cream-colored complexion. An eschelle of silver bows decorated the low-cut stomacher, enticing the more interested eye to the soft swell of cleavage above a strategic line of lace. Aware of the stares she was drawing, Callie nervously twisted the ivory and silk fan in her hands.

Jonathan stood inconspicuously in the far corner of the room attempting to escape Lilibeth's notice. He lounged against the wall, his arms folded across his chest, bored and indifferent to the gaiety of the evening. Suddenly conscious of a stirring, Jonathan turned. When he saw Callie, he slowly unfolded his arms and straightened to full attention. He had had a glimpse of her incredible transformation when he met her on the street that day, but he never imagined a metamorphosis such as this. And he watched her with undisguised interest.

Mrs. Whithers was proudly introducing Callie around the room, when she caught sight of Olivia Sanders furiously marching across the crowded floor toward them with her daughter in tow. And she squeezed Callie's arm in warning.

"Callie Hastings!" shouted Olivia, her strident voice catching the ears of everyone around them. "How dare you steal my daughter's gown, a common planter no less! You do not belong here in the first place."

A hush fell over the crowd as the music came to a stop. Jonathan was about to come to Callie's aid, when he saw the familiar set of her chin and the flash in her eyes and knew that she was equal to the task.

"Madam, I fear there has been some mistake," said Callie in a firm, well-modulated voice. "I have not stolen the gown. Mrs. Stanhope bade me to accept it to lighten the strain of the debt that you owe her."

The blood drained from Olivia's face, and Lilibeth looked as though she might swoon from embarrassment. The last thing they wanted was for their financial straits to be bared to the town at a time when Olivia was trying to secure a husband for Lilibeth.

"Furthermore," continued Callie, "were it against the rules of the ball to admit planters, I dare say that nearly every man here would needs be expelled."

As murmurs and nervous titters reverberated through the room, Olivia realized her enormous blunder. Though the colonial elite emulated the English aristocracy and sought their acceptance, even the largest plantation owners proudly considered themselves planters as well as landowners. Callie had neatly set the Sanders' women in front of Williamsburg's most distinguished citizens, and Olivia's cheeks flamed with humiliation.

"You will pay for this, miss," she hissed in a voice low enough for only Callie and Mrs. Whithers to hear.

"Apologies, Miss Hastings, for my sister's poor manners," said Lord Randall, coming to the rescue. "Come, Olivia…Lilibeth. I think you have made spectacles enough of yourselves for one evening." Before they could utter another word, he sternly ushered the two women out of the room.

With their departure, the music started up, and the ball resumed. Mrs. Whithers slowly let out her breath in a sigh of relief. "Nicely done, my dear, nicely done. And now, I find myself much in need of refreshment. Will you join me?"

Callie shook her head. "I find myself more in need of a chair than of refreshment at the moment."

Mrs. Whithers patted Callie's hand in a motherly fashion. "It was not a pleasant scene, to be sure, but that woman needed to be put in her place. You did what had to be done and rather deftly at that. You mustn't let this spoil your evening."

As the elderly lady went her way, Callie found a secluded corner and snapped open her fan. The encounter with Olivia Sanders had drained the last of her courage for the evening, and she wished she could leave as well. She had expected an unpleasant exchange with the Sanders women, but she had not anticipated that it would be so public. She raised the fan to her face, her blue eyes peering over the top, as she sought to shield herself from the world.

Jonathan grinned and continued to watch Callie from across the room. It was all he could do to keep from laughing aloud when he saw three young men head toward her at a fast trot. This time she would have need of his help, he decided, and followed in their path.

Callie blinked in bewilderment as the young men presented themselves to her at the same time, then immediately began to argue with one another.

"Perhaps the lady will settle the matter once and for all," said one of them. He turned to Callie. "Miss, will you be so kind as to inform the others that 'twas me whom you summoned."

"Summoned? No—I—you must be mistaken," Callie stammered helplessly.

"The young lady is spoken for this evening, gentlemen," said Jonathan, stepping in to decide the matter.

The men turned intending to voice their protests, when they realized who had usurped their position. "Oh, Lord Trenholme, your pardon, sir." They turned back to Callie and gave her a slight bow. "Apologies, miss."

As they made a hasty departure, Callie stared after them speechless. She had no idea what had just transpired.

Jonathan chuckled. "I fear Whithers has neglected to school you in the art of the fan." When it was obvious that she still didn't understand, he explained: "The fan has a language of its own, depending upon how a lady holds it. The positioning of your fan a few minutes ago was signaling your desire for an assignation—a private meeting—with the man whose eye you caught."

"But I was looking at no one," said Callie.

"Apparently, those three men beg to differ with you."

Callie let out a groan as she remembered now how Mrs. Whithers had tried to instruct her on the use of the fan, but failing to see how it related to her goal, she had paid no attention. Her debut was turning into a disaster. "Olivia Sanders was right, Trenholme. I do not belong here," she said, disheartened.

Jonathan smiled. "I dare say that, in the future, 'tis you who will be the more welcome here. You look most elegant tonight, by the way."

His expression and tone held no hint of mockery, and Callie quickly lowered her eyes to hide the damnable flush that she seemed so prone to of late in his presence.

"How about a dance to display your new talents?" he suggested. "Whithers tells me you do quite admirably by a reel."

Callie paled at the thought of performing before so many eyes. "No, I cannot. I—my head throbs. Please, I wish only to leave."

Trenholme studied her for a moment. He was acquainted with her well enough to know that it wasn't an act. She was trying hard, but the transition was not yet complete.

"I shall arrange your leave-taking with Whithers and collect the cloaks," he said. "In truth, I am rather desirous of escaping the evening myself."

As Callie waited near the door for Jonathan, a voice behind her commented: "Miss Hastings, I had not expected to encounter you here tonight. It would seem that you are full of surprises and quite clever out of court as well as in."

Callie's heart sank as she turned to face Justice Smythe. She didn't have the strength to wage another battle this evening.

"There is nothing clever about the truth, sir," she responded evenly.

"Not even in the case of Mae Bailey?"

Callie struggled to maintain a calm, cool demeanor. "I am at a loss to understand your meaning, sir."

"Oh, come now, Miss Hastings. You must admit that Mrs. Bailey's death was a trifle convenient and, shall we say, strangely coincidental."

"Convenient perhaps for her, though I much prefer to think 'twas fate laying a kind hand on her for once," replied Callie. "But I see no coincidence here. The poor woman was never strong, and she was subject to much physical and emotional strain for many months. I am sure that Dr. Blackmore and Midwife Gilbrett will tell you that as well."

"Perhaps. Still, there is the curious matter of a brother who suddenly appeared from Maryland on two occasions."

"What is strange about that?" asked Callie.

Smythe smiled. "It seems another one of those convenient coincidences, don't you think? By the bye, Lady Sanders tells me that you are quite fond of wearing breeches."

He slipped in the comment so casually that Callie almost took the bait. To confirm the fact would prove some kind of guilt in his twisted mind, and a denial could be easily disproved, implying that she had something to hide. Either way, Callie realized that she couldn't win.

Instead, she answered noncommittally: "Lady Sanders says many things. After tonight, I should think you would not find her a worthy source."

The smile on Smythe's face faded, and his eyes narrowed to dark slits. "If you want to play cat and mouse with me, Miss Hastings, you shall find yourself out of your element. I will know the truth of this Bailey business, and my judgment shall not be lenient."

"Smythe, you are charged with trying cases, not creating them," Trenholme broke in sharply. "The Bailey case is done. I trust you will not be bothering Miss Hastings about it again."

There was a clear warning in his tone, and Smythe gave a slight bow and a smile that was more of a sneer and moved off into the crowd.

Jonathan draped her cape around her and drew his cloak across his broad shoulders. As he steered her toward the door, neither of them observed the man across the room whose dark eyes followed Callie's every movement.

"You leave her be," said Justice Smythe coming up behind the young man. "That woman is dangerous. She has the protection of a powerful adversary."

The young man slowly turned, lazily shifting his gaze to the justice. "'Tis a pity, Father, that you never learned 'tis the danger what makes the game. Is it any wonder that my mother left you?"

Smythe was livid and raised a hand to strike his son, but the young man caught his father's wrist in a bruising grip. "I am no longer the boy to take the beatings for a wife you could not hold," he sneered. He cast off his father with contempt and strode across the room.

Callie stepped out into the night and raised her hood over her head. She breathed in the cold air, feeling a welcome release from the tension of the evening. Jonathan set his hat and signaled for the carriage.

"Wait. If it makes no matter to you, I should like to walk," she said.

Trenholme nodded and waved off the driver. "As you wish."

They walked for a few minutes before Callie broke the silence. "I fear Smythe knows about Mae."

"He is suspicious by nature. He can prove nothing in this case. I have seen to that. But, Callie, you must watch yourself. Smythe will continue to test you. The man harbors a special resentment toward women in general and, it would appear, toward you in particular."

"But why?"

"As the story goes, Smythe's wife ran off with another man years ago, leaving him with a young boy. Smythe came to Virginia with his son to start a new life, but he has never been able to forgive or forget his wife's betrayal. Not only are you a female born to betray in his eyes, but you also dared to challenge him in his court," said Jonathan. "Have a care."

Callie suddenly recalled her old cellmate's warning. Sally had said that it would take little to draw this justice's displeasure, and, once earned, it was for life. It would seem that she was right. A shiver ran through Callie but not from the damp chill in the air.

Mistaking the nature of her discomfort, Jonathan put an arm around her shoulders and enveloped her in his great cloak to shield her from the wind gathering at their backs. Her first impulse was to pull away, but mounting insecurities from the trying evening refused to allow her to leave the comfort and warmth of his embrace. For the first time in a very long while, she felt a measure of safety. For his part, Jonathan was a little surprised that she hadn't balked at his gesture. But, then, that was Callie, unpredictable to the end.

It was late and the night was quiet with only the stars and a few cresset torches left burning to light their way. Neither spoke. Both were content to enjoy this moment of peace in an otherwise fractious relationship.

When they reached Mrs. Whithers' house, Callie turned to him. "Trenholme, would you kiss me?"

Jonathan was taken aback. He had never sought any woman's permission to kiss her. Most certainly none had ever requested his. It was just something that quite naturally and instinctively happened between a man and woman when the mood served. Not knowing how else to spare her the awkward moment, he replied gallantly: "It would be my pleasure to oblige you, Miss Hastings."

She stood stock-still, her lips parted, her eyes closed as though to mitigate any displeasure there might come from it. Jonathan smiled. This was obviously her first kiss. The top of her head came to his shoulders. He put a hand beneath her chin to raise her face and bent to lightly brush his lips across hers.

In a second, it was over and Callie opened her eyes in surprise. "Is that it?" she asked, clearly disappointed. "I dare say that Mr. Plinn's kiss was the more ardent if perhaps the least desirable," she proclaimed matter-of-factly. "Bound if I know what all the fuss is about. A good night to you, Trenholme."

Jonathan was speechless as he watched her walk up the steps to the house and let herself in the door. When he recovered himself, he was both galled and flabbergasted. That Callie had compared his passion to that of another man and found it wanting was wholly intolerable to him. More to the point, who the bloody hell was Mr. Plinn, and why was she kissing him? Most definitely, he was going to be raising the matter with Whithers.

CHAPTER NINETEEN

Requisition

Callie tucked the box containing her new gown securely under her arm and walked out of the shop to find a white, swirling mist blanketing the street. Snow was not one of the town's more common sights, and there was an air of excitement and conviviality heightened by the fact that it was Christmas Eve.

Callie smiled as she watched children gaily slide down the icy street. Unable to resist the temptation, she set down the dress box, lifted her skirts, and tried her own hand at it. For a moment, she was the child she had never had the time to be. Tendrils of hair came loose from under her cap and blew in the wind, and her nose and cheeks were rosy from the cold air. To those who chanced to notice, she made a fetching sight.

She looked away for a second and suddenly collided with an object that nearly knocked her off her feet.

"'Ere now, what do ye think yer about!" a voice growled in ill humor.

The speech was slurred, but it was distinctive and all too familiar to Callie as she struggled to regain her balance. She hoped against hope that Abel Cane wouldn't recognize his stepdaughter. She could smell the liquor on his breath and guessed that he had just come from a nearby tavern. But Callie hoped in vain. Despite his inebriated state,

Cane's bloodshot eyes were sharp as he surveyed the young woman that had ploughed into him.

"God's blood! 'Tis ye, Callie." He reached out a dirty hand to stroke her face as though to satisfy his befuddled mind that she was real.

When Callie recoiled in disgust and turned to leave, Cane quickly sobered. "Hold fast, lass," he said, laying hold of her arm. "I been lookin' for ye."

Callie shook off his hand. "What do you want?"

"I mean to take ye home with me to keep me house. Built myself a hut don't ye know."

Callie pulled the woolen cloak tighter around her as his gaze slid over her from head to toe. The salacious gleam in his eye told her that he had more in mind for her than the keeping of his house.

"I would sooner be dead than be under the same roof with you," she spat contemptuously.

"Ye forget, lass, I be yer guardian. The law says ye'll serve me," Cane reminded her smugly.

"In a pig's eye I will," spat Callie.

She started to walk away from him, when he grabbed hold of her arm again. "I give ye seven days hence to come back to the farm, lass, or I shall sell the land and ye will make yer bed where I decide it."

"Let go of me," she said, trying to break free of him.

At a sudden sharp blow to his hand, Cane pulled it back with a yelp of pain, and both he and Callie looked in surprise to see a well-dressed young man of medium height and slender build holding a walking stick.

"Who do ye think ye are?" demanded Cane, rubbing his hand.

"Certainly not a drunk molesting a young woman on the street," replied the man. "'Tis a curious thing about this walking stick," he continued, examining the ivory handle. "It seems to have a mind of its own when its patience is tested. I suggest you take your leave before it finds its way to your worthless hide." He looked meaningfully from the stick to Cane.

"Ain't no need to take on. I be on me way," said Cane, backing away. "I was jest havin' a chat with me daughter is all. That be my right."

When the man made a sudden move toward him, Cane turned around and ran to the tavern across the street, nearly colliding with exiting patrons in his haste to gain entrance.

Despite the gravity of her situation, Callie had to laugh at the undignified retreat.

"That is better," said the man, surveying her with an appreciative eye. "You are much prettier when you smile."

Callie's cheeks turned a brighter pink. "My thanks for your help," she replied, feeling self-conscious and awkward. "'Twas well timed."

As she turned to leave, he stuck out his cane to bar her exit. "Hold on there. Am I to know no payment for my service then?"

Callie stiffened. "What have you in mind?" she inquired warily.

"Your name, fair lady, is all that I seek."

A warm grin split his boyish features. While not what one would call handsome, the man held a certain attraction. He was something of the dandy with his powdered hair and cane, but his swaggering charm, light humor, and infectious smile outweighed that disadvantage to her mind.

Callie relaxed. "'Tis small payment, indeed, that you ask, sir," she said. "I am called Callie Hastings."

"Is it true that man is your father?"

"Stepfather," she corrected him tightly. "And now, sir, I believe one good turn is deserving of another. Might I know your name?"

"Charles Smythe at your service."

Callie stiffened and Charles let out a sigh of resignation. "I see that my father's notoriety precedes me. I warrant he nurtures enmity like others foster friendship, and I seem destined to forever suffer the stigma of his ill will. I pray that you will not hold me accountable for it as well."

Callie didn't understand some of the words Charles Smythe said, but she got the general idea. The man looked genuinely upset and Callie felt contrite. "Apologies, Mr. Smythe," she replied, finding it difficult to say his name without grimacing. "'Tis my nature to judge a body on his own merits than on those of another. But I must confess that I do not think kindly of your father."

"Few do, Miss Hastings, I assure you." He picked up her dress box. "May I help you home with your package?"

"No—I mean there is no need. I live only a short distance away," said Callie, the moment turning awkward again for her.

"Your stepfather is just across the street," he reminded her.

"I am grateful for your concern, Mr. Smythe, but I will be fine."

Smythe smiled. "I understand. I shall endeavor to prove to you, Miss Hastings, that the sins of the father are not visited upon the son. Perhaps, in time, you will allow me to call."

"Perhaps," said Callie with some reticence. "Good day, sir."

She took the dress box from him and quickly crossed the street. She soon forgot young Smythe as her thoughts turned to her stepfather and his ultimatum. It made little difference whether Cane gave her a week to make up her mind or a year. Either way she lost.

If she didn't willingly submit to his authority, she ran the risk of losing her land forever, and the court would remand her to his custody anyway. Could she survive living under his roof until she reached her majority and could legally lay claim to her land? She knew the answer to that the minute Cane had touched her face and that gleam had come into his eye.

She may be inexperienced, but she wasn't ignorant in the ways of men, especially not after Mr. Plinn's ardent attack upon her person. Barring that, Callie knew that she couldn't trust Cane not to sell the land at some point while both she and it were under his control. There had to be another way. With a new sense of urgency, she picked up her step.

When Callie arrived at the house, she burst threw the front door, ran past an astonished Jane, and tore up the stairs to her room as though Lucie's demons dogged her heels. Nothing else mattered now but that she discover a way to stop Cane. She threw the dress box carelessly on the bed and began to thumb desperately through the pages of the law book.

"Callie, did you not hear me knocking?" chastised Mrs. Whithers, letting herself into the room. "What devil torments you now to race up the stairs like a lunatic without so much as a word, frightening Jane by half?" Consternation overrode her annoyance when she saw Callie's face. "What is it, dear? What has happened? You look most upset."

Callie quickly described her encounter with Abel Cane, omitting any mention of Charles Smythe. She didn't want to confuse the issue, and she didn't expect to see him again anyway. Her eyes shimmered with tears. "What am I to do, Madam?"

"I will tell you what you are to do," said the old widow stoutly. "You will go and stay with my sister in Carolina where you will be beyond his reach."

Callie shook her head. "No, I cannot leave or Cane will sell my land for sure. Besides, Justice Smythe watches my every move. I cannot chance leading him to Mae."

At this, Callie's thoughts jumped to young Smythe as she suddenly wondered if their encounter really had been coincidental. Had the justice sent his son to gain her confidence and spy on her activities? Still, she couldn't discount the bitterness in his tone and the hard glint in his eyes when he spoke of his father. She knew that to be genuine, for she was no stranger to that emotion herself when it came to Abel Cane. Also, Charles hadn't tried to press her when she declined his offer to see her home. Nor had he made any attempt to disguise his identity.

"Well, you certainly cannot give sway to that no-good stepfather of yours," Mrs. Whithers was saying. "I shall speak to Lord Jon straightaway."

"What good will that do?" asked Callie, returning her attention to the matter at hand. "Cane is within his rights. It says so right here on this page. And the law is the law," she added, parodying Trenholme.

Mrs. Whithers patted Callie's hand, her features set in a determined line. "I am bound we shall find a way around this."

CHAPTER TWENTY

Horns of a Dilemma

Callie was of one mind. Nothing else was permitted to intrude—not even thoughts of Trenholme. Christmas had come and gone, and she had not joined in any of the festivities. Her only concession to the holidays had been her attendance at services at the Bruton Parish Church upon Mrs. Whithers' insistence.

Charles Smythe had been in attendance as well and had made his presence known to her within the bounds of propriety. Though she remained wary of him, she hadn't gone out of her way to discourage his attention. Half a head shorter than Trenholme and lacking the nobleman's rugged good looks and muscular frame, the younger Smythe still cut a dashing figure, and she found that his light humor and easy-going manner lifted her spirits.

But that time was past now.

The day of reckoning was upon her. Tomorrow, she would have to give Cane her decision. If she didn't go willingly to him, Cane would force her to his rule and sell her land. And her precious law book had yet to yield a solution to her dilemma.

There came a light knock on the door and Jane called out tentatively: "Miss Callie, Madam wishes a word with ye in the parlor."

Callie groaned. She could imagine what Mrs. Whithers wanted with her. No doubt the well-intentioned widow had another young man for her to meet. The would-be suitors always seemed so uncomfortable that Callie sometimes wondered if Mrs. Whithers had kidnapped them off the street.

When she entered the parlor, she was surprised to see Lord Randall. He greeted her warmly and escorted her to a seat on the settee, but his manner was preoccupied and Callie immediately sensed that something was wrong. She looked at Mrs. Whithers, who sat at the tea table. When the older woman avoided her eye, Callie knew something was in the wind.

"What's amiss?" she asked anxiously as Lord Randall seated himself in a chair.

He sighed deeply. "It pains me to have to tell you this, Callie, but word has reached me that your land is posted."

Callie stared at him in disbelief. "It cannot be. Cane promised me. I have until tomorrow to submit to his authority."

"I am sorry, Callie. There is nothing that I can do to stop him. I understand that he has a buyer."

"A buyer—who?"

"I am not at liberty to say."

Callie clutched the arm of the settee as she absorbed this latest blow. "I knew Cane couldn't be trusted, but I hoped this time he might hold to his word. Are ye quite certain there is nothing to be done?"

Lord Randall paused. "Well, there is one other way for you to sidestep the man on all accounts," he said. "But I fear that you shall find the cure worse than the illness."

Her eyes locked on him as she seized this new ray of hope. "What is it? Surely nothing could be worse than losing my land and being forced to live under my stepfather's roof."

Lord Randall looked at Mrs. Whithers, and the widow quickly busied herself with the preparation of tea.

"Well, sir, if you have a plan, I would hear it," prompted Callie impatiently.

Lord Randall took a deep breath, wishing he could be anywhere but here. "Were you to…were you to marry," he finally got out, "the land would be returned to your control as a dowry for your husband, and you would no longer be under your stepfather's rule. I understand from Mrs. Whithers that you have a few suitors."

Mrs. Whithers braced herself for Callie's explosive reaction. When there came only silence, she looked up from her task to find Callie staring at the nobleman as though he had lost his mind and Lord Randall shifting uncomfortably beneath her gaze.

"I am well aware of that option and have already discounted it," said Callie in a clipped tone. "Marriage is no solution at all. 'Twould be trading one gaoler for another, and still the land would not belong to me but to my husband."

"Perhaps that could be remedied," replied the earl after a moment's thought.

"How?"

"If I, as proprietor, were to grant you the land as a gift and your husband were to sign a document renouncing all rights to the property, the land would remain under your control." he said.

Lord Randall and Mrs. Whithers exchanged hopeful glances when Callie appeared to be considering the matter. In actuality, the old earl knew that it would be easier by half to change the flow of the river than to find a man willing to give up all rights to his wife's dowry. But he would cross that bridge when he came to it. Right now, it was more important to get Callie to agree to a marriage at all.

"Lord Randall, if you are willing to gift me the land, why must I be married?" Callie suddenly asked.

"Because your stepfather will have prior claim as your guardian. Marriage is the only way to suspend his guardianship as long as you remain below your majority. But you must act quickly before the day of the sale, or I can do nothing to save your farm."

"Forgive me, sir, but that is not entirely true," said Callie. "As I recall, the proprietary owner can petition the court for an injunction to block such a sale. When my stepfather fails to meet the terms of the lease, as he most certainly will do, the land will revert to you and you can gift it to me when I reach my majority."

A look of wonder came over her face, and she gave a little laugh. "How did I not think of this before?"

Lord Randall was thrown completely off balance by her sudden moment of inspiration, and he took out a handkerchief to wipe the perspiration from his brow. He couldn't possibly tell her that the General Assembly had charged him with the responsibility of seeing her married one way or another. And the only plan that seemed to have presented itself was for him to secretly approach Cane as an anonymous buyer of the land in order to force Callie's hand.

If she agreed to a marriage, Cane would lose control of the land and the sale could not go forward. No one would be the wiser. If she refused, there was the probability that the scheme would be exposed and Callie would never forgive him.

"Yes, I suppose I could petition for an injunction against the sale," Lord Randall replied slowly, trying to think. "But that will not solve your other problem in regards to Cane's guardianship of you," he said, realizing his trump card.

Callie gave a huff of frustration and fell silent as she pondered her options—surrender her personal rights to a husband for life or her freedom to her stepfather for three years until she reached the age of twenty-one. Neither one was acceptable to her. The tension in the room was palpable as she struggled to find a solution. At one point, Lord Randall coughed and cleared his throat to prod her to a decision, but Callie paid him no mind.

"Lord Randall, the court released me into Trenholme's custody once. Can it not do so again?" she asked after long consideration.

"That was only temporary, Callie, and not a legal custody per se. Lord Trenholme's authority cannot supersede that of your stepfather. Besides, Lord Trenholme will be returning to England soon."

"How soon?"

"I expect the governor will release him from his duties here in five or six months."

She fell silent again as she reconsidered her options. "I shall marry," she finally announced. "But my betrothed must be Trenholme."

Lord Randall broke into a coughing fit, and there was a loud clatter as Mrs. Whithers dropped the cup she was about to fill with tea.

"My dear Callie, I do not think that you understand," said the matron. "Lord Trenholme is a member of the nobility, while you, alas, are of common stock."

Callie was undaunted. "Trenholme told me, himself, that sons after the second born are generally left to their own desires as no woman of account would settle for the lesser lands and title."

"That may be true—of others. But his father the Duke of Lansing is a man who jealously guards his lineage. Whether Lord Jon is the third or the sixth born, I can assure you that His Grace will not allow a son of his to marry outside of his class."

Callie was not to be dissuaded. "It must be Trenholme," she insisted. "I will have no other."

"But why Lord Trenholme, dear?" asked Mrs. Whithers, still somewhat flustered. "There are a dozen nice young men more fitting to your station, two of whom have already shown a desire to take you to wife."

"I find Trenholme to be the least offensive of them," said Callie, thinking of his light, innocuous kiss on the night of the ball. "He appears to lack a passionate nature outside of his precious law, and 'tis more probable that I shall not have to suffer his attentions as I might those of another more enthused about such matters."

Mrs. Whithers' eyes widened at Callie's candid assessment of Lord Trenholme, wondering how the young woman had ever come to such a conclusion, while Lord Randall dabbed at his mouth with a now limp handkerchief in an attempt to hide his snicker of amusement. Jonathan Trenholme was a lot of things but certainly not a man lacking in passion were his reputation to be believed. The old earl couldn't help wondering, as well, how Callie had come to such a determination.

"I am afraid that a match with Lord Jon is clearly outside the realm of possibility," Mrs. Whithers declared firmly. She turned to her co-conspirator for support. "Lord Randall, what say you, sir?"

Lord Randall shrugged. "I have learned that the seemingly impossible is sometimes easier to accomplish than the simplest of tasks."

"Perhaps I should speak with Trenholme myself to be certain that he understands the terms," said Callie thoughtfully.

"Terms?" inquired the earl.

"This is a marriage of convenience, sir."

"Oh. Yes, well, I think it best if you leave the matter to me," replied Lord Randall.

"What of Lucie and Old Joe?" asked Callie. "Are they also part of the bargain?"

The earl winced at the thought of losing two such valuable servants. "They are freemen," he reluctantly allowed. "They can do as they choose."

"Then I shall leave the details to you, sir," said Callie. She stood and left the room, considering the matter settled.

Mrs. Whithers swung an incredulous gaze on Lord Randall. "Your pardon, sir, but I fail to see how this end is to be accomplished. The duke is not one to overlook such a breach of convention, I can assure you. And Lord Jon can be rather a stickler for protocol, himself."

Lord Randall remained unperturbed. "I dare say that Lord Trenholme would have us think so, Madam. But if I have learned anything at all about the man over the months, it is that Lord Trenholme makes his own rules when it suits him to do so. As for his father, suffice it to say that I do have a certain amount of influence with the duke. I think I can persuade him to accept this marriage."

Mrs. Withers regarded the earl with surprise and skepticism. "Indeed, sir. Should that be the case, what of Callie? She does not belong in that world."

"This is the colonies, Madam. England is a long way off."

"Be that as it may, Lord Jon intends to return to his home…and, contrary to what Callie may think," said Mrs. Whithers, suddenly realizing Callie's line of thought, "I find it highly unlikely that he would leave behind a wife."

Lord Randall smiled. "Much can happen between now and then."

Mrs. Whithers was still doubtful. "There is yet the matter of Lord Jon's consent," she reminded the earl.

"Has not Callie drawn the eye of several admirers?" questioned the earl.

"Yes, much so."

Lord Randall's smile widened. "Lord Trenholme is a man, Mrs. Whithers. I dare say he has taken notice as well."

Taken aback by the idea, the widow was slow to respond. "Even were that the case, sir, I cannot see Lord Jon agreeing to terms much less to a marriage of convenience. He views marriage in much the same light as Callie, and you have no means of persuasion to bring to bear against him." Mrs. Whithers shook her head. "I fear, sir, it would take Providence, itself, to secure Lord Jon's cooperation in this matter."

"In that case, Madam, I shall leave that task to an elite group of gentlemen, many of whom consider themselves to be the equal of Providence," replied Lord Randall.

He leaned back in his chair, comfortable in the knowledge that he had done well in his task. He had gotten Callie to agree to marriage and into the bargain had honored one deathbed wish of Callie's mother without betraying the other. In truth, once he had recovered from the initial shock of Callie's pronouncement that she would accept a marriage with only Jonathan Trenholme, Lord Randall found that he rather liked the idea. His kind could do with some new blood.

CHAPTER TWENTY-ONE

Pride Goeth Before the Fall

Jonathan eagerly strode through the double doors of the Capitol and raced up the staircase to the second floor. At last, the long-awaited summons from the governor had arrived. Lord Randall had certainly taken his time in arranging the meeting, he thought with some annoyance. It struck him as odd that the audience was to take place in the Conference Room where burgesses and councillors held joint conferences rather than at the Governor's Palace, but he immediately shrugged it off. He didn't care if the meeting was held in the gaol as long as he secured his release from this retched colony.

He knocked on the door. When he was admitted to the room, his step faltered and his smile faded as he came face-to-face with the grim countenances of the illustrious membership of the General Assembly. In addition to Lord Randall, Jonathan was acquainted with some of the councillors as fellow justices on the General Court, and he was familiar with other burgesses and councillors through various social functions. But as he looked around the long mahogany table at the somber faces this day, Jonathan had the uneasy feeling that this was not going to be the meeting he had anticipated.

"Lord Trenholme, please be seated at the end of the table," instructed Governor Dinwiddie. "I understand that you are requesting a release from your duties so that you may return to England."

"Aye, that is correct, sir," replied Jonathan guardedly, taking the appointed chair. "Am I to assume that the matter requires an order of the General Assembly as well?"

The stout royal governor allowed himself a smile. "No, Lord Trenholme, but then yours is a special case."

"I beg your pardon, sir?"

"I believe that you are acquainted with Miss Callie Hastings."

A muscle flicked in Trenholme's jaw and his body tensed as he looked from one man to another trying to divine the real purpose of this meeting. "What has Miss Hastings to do with my return to England?" he asked warily.

"'Tis no small favor that you ask of me, Lord Trenholme," said the governor. "In reducing the length of your term in Virginia, I run great risk of incurring the king's displeasure. It has occurred to me that one good favor should be deserving of another."

Jonathan remained guarded. "Of what favor might you be thinking, sir?"

"Perhaps you are aware, Lord Trenholme, that…well, the fact of the matter is that Miss Hastings is creating havoc with our manner of justice."

"Making a bloody damn mess of it would be more to the point!" expounded a crusty old man, whom Jonathan knew to be a very powerful proprietor. "If left to her own, this young woman will set the colony on its ear. I have a line of husbands and fathers already pounding on my door to lodge complaints."

"What has Miss Hastings done?" asked Jonathan with a sinking feeling. Though he hadn't conversed with her since the holiday ball at the Raleigh Tavern, he hadn't been aware that she was creating any problems. But then with Callie, one never knew until the damage was done.

"What has she not done!" exclaimed a burgess indignantly. "She advised Lydia Stanhope the dressmaker to change her business to sole trader so that Sam is not able to touch a farthing of the profits now."

"And, now that the word is about, other women who have trades are following suit as well," said another. "By Miss Hastings' hand, too many men are suffering grievous injury to their pride and finances."

Jonathan gave a slight snicker. It was on the tip of his tongue to advise that these men would better protect their pride and finances by staying out of taverns and away from dice and drink but thought better of it.

"If that is the extent of Miss Hastings' offense, gentlemen—"

"Nay, that is not the extent, Lord Trenholme," interrupted another irate councillor. "The girl has ruined a match that has taken me months to arrange between my daughter and Channing Galt. She advised Mary that a man must assume the debts of his betrothed at time of marriage. To discourage the suit, my daughter has taken it upon herself to accumulate several debts of large note. Naturally, Galt has refused the match until the debts are disposed of—to great expense from my pocket!" the councillor exclaimed, his face turning a mottled purple. "Do you know that this Hastings woman is actually petitioning the county court on behalf of women under coverture?' he continued to rant. "God's blood! 'Tis not to be believed!"

"Miss Hastings is committing no crime in advising these women of rights allowed them under common law," said Jonathan, hard pressed to hide his amusement.

"Bah, the only say that a woman should have is that which her husband permits her," blustered the crusty old proprietor. "Just as riches should be confined to the wealthy, rights should be limited to men, as only they know how to put them to best use."

"Aye," agreed a colleague worriedly. "'Tis dangerous practice to inform women of rights of which they are ignorant. Soon they will be of a mind that they are the equals of men. We have trouble enough with the French and Indians on our western frontier and the Crown overturning our petitions. We do not need this woman stirring up discord into the bargain."

"The point is, Lord Trenholme," the governor cut in, "this situation could be laid to rest and peace restored were Miss Hastings to marry—"

"Because only single women have the right to petition the court," finished Jonathan, following the members' train of thought now.

The governor smiled, pleased that Jonathan understood the predicament. "Exactly."

"Well, gentlemen, I do not envy you your task. I cannot imagine Miss Hastings accepting a marriage proposal from any man."

"She cannot refuse, Lord Trenholme, if she cares about her land or being returned to her stepfather's custody. Lord Randall tells us that her stepfather has posted the estate and has already received an offer. Next, he intends to petition the court if needs be to force her under his roof. Unless she marries immediately to negate his rights—"

"Yes, I see that," interrupted Jonathan impatiently. "What has this to do with me and my return to England?"

"Miss Hastings has agreed to marry you, sir. She will accept no other suitor," Governor Dinwiddie informed him.

Shock registered on Jonathan's face, and he was speechless. He didn't know whether to burst out laughing or explode in anger. He became conscious that all eyes of the General Assembly were upon him as members leaned forward in their seats to gauge his reaction, and he struggled to regain his composure.

In his circle, marriage was many things. It was a convenience, an alliance, a business intended to strengthen as well as to preserve one's lineage and to increase one's legacy. It was rarely a love match. His own parents' union was a prime example, and he had come to learn from experience that commitment and love were by no means required in the face of such practicality and sense of duty—as long as discretion was practiced.

Thus, it was with a jaundiced eye that he viewed marriage and had decided long ago that he could do very well without the legal entanglement. As for his legacy, he was happy enough to pass on his title to his nephew.

"Gentlemen," said Jonathan after a long moment of reflection, "while I sympathize with your problem—having come to know Miss Hastings well—I am afraid that the match is not possible."

"If you are worried about your father's approval, Lord Randall has agreed to take Miss Hastings into the family to provide her with acceptable pedigree if needs be," a councillor quickly assured him.

Jonathan glared at Lord Randall. "The earl is overly generous, but were I desirous of wedding Miss Hastings, I would do so with or without my father's permission and Lord Randall's assistance."

"Good. Then the matter is settled."

"The matter is not settled!" exploded Jonathan.

"Come now, sir, what is the nature of your objection?" a burgess impatiently demanded to know. "Though her spirit is in sore need of tamping, the lass is quite comely. And Lord Randall is prepared to settle on her the dowry of her land as well as some other property in the frontier. Miss Hastings does not come empty-handed."

No one was about to explain to Jonathan at this point that he would have to waive his rights to the dowry. That information, they had just silently and unanimously agreed, could wait.

"You are missing the point," responded Jonathan tightly. "I am not prepared to wed *any* woman."

"No, Lord Trenholme, 'tis you who is missing the point," interjected the governor. "If you do not marry Miss Hastings and put a stop to her meddling, you may consider your stay here more permanent than you might wish."

Jonathan bristled at the overt threat. "Marrying Miss Hastings only prevents her from petitioning the court. How do you propose that I keep her from practicing her right to advise?"

"That will be up to you," replied the governor. "As you well know, a husband's authority is unconditional."

"A babe at her skirts and one in her belly would do the trick I'll warrant," quipped a burgess, his remark drawing titters of amusement from around the room.

Jonathan raked the Assembly with cold brown eyes. "Do what you will, gentlemen. I will not bow to blackmail."

"Perhaps you will bow to witchcraft then," said Justice Smythe. He had kept quiet throughout the proceedings, and his manner now bore a smugness that gave Jonathan to know that the man had been biding his time for just this moment.

Jonathan's eyes narrowed. "What trick have you up your sleeve this time, Smythe?"

"I am not the one with tricks," replied the justice pointedly.

The others looked on in bewilderment and with gathering interest at the strained exchange between the two men.

"As I was saying, Justice Trenholme, there have been allegations of witchcraft made against Miss Hastings that the others have prevailed upon me to set aside if you agree to the marriage," said Smythe.

"What allegations?" Jonathan demanded to know.

"A certain Mr. Plinn will testify that Miss Hastings wove a spell upon his person which caused him to act in a less than gentlemanly manner. Her own stepfather openly accuses her of putting a conjure on his land that disallows his crops, thus forcing him to a sale."

Jonathan started to laugh at the absurdity of the charges, when he realized that Smythe was serious and that no other member was coming forward to countermand him. Trenholme quickly sobered. Witchcraft was a dangerous charge. Though to his mind Smythe's case was ridiculous and his witnesses ludicrous, superstition was almost a religion to many. It wouldn't be too difficult for Smythe to whip up a frenzy of fear and direct it toward Callie. Most certainly, he would enjoy the support of the men in the community upon whose toes she had already stepped.

Jonathan leveled a cold, steady eye on the vengeful justice. "Smythe, if you dare to bring that charge to bear, I shall personally plead the case on Miss Hastings' behalf and make a fool out of you before the entire town. As was so readily brought to my attention, Miss Hastings is a very comely woman," he said, directing his remarks to the Assembly as a whole. "I would suspect that Mr. Plinn's actions resulted from his own lack of self-control rather than from a spell. As for Abel Cane, I doubt that the man would know a hoe from a shovel or a plow from a rake. I can assure you that the only sowing he has ever done has been in taverns for ale."

For the moment, it appeared that his arguments had been effective; no one said anything.

Jonathan stood up. "Now, if you will excuse me, gentlemen, I have better things to do." He didn't wait for an answer, making it clear that he didn't care if they excused him or not.

As he started for the door, he missed the signal that passed between Lord Randall and the governor. They had prepared themselves in the event that the young man proved resistant and all argument failed.

"Lord Trenholme," called out Governor Dinwiddie, "perhaps the spirited maiden is more than you can handle. I am told that Miss Hastings has chosen you above the others, sir, because she does not deign to overly suffer a man's hand and thinks your touch to be the least ardent of her other suitors."

Jonathan was stopped dead in his tracks.

A short while later, Trenholme burst forth from the Capitol in a furious temper. The snickers of the burgesses and councillors still buzzed in his ears. To have his manhood called into question before the entire body of the General Assembly was more than he could tolerate. And he knew that he had been deftly maneuvered into a corner the moment a flurry of papers suddenly appeared before him to sign. That he had actually signed them still astounded him.

How the bloody hell had it come to this! he raged. The Callie he knew would never have taken part in such trickery. She would have found another way to solve her problem. Barring that, she would have approached him first with the request that he marry her, not employ the governor and the General Assembly to coerce him into it. He didn't know what enraged him more—that the General Assembly had manipulated him into a corner or that, once again, this child-woman was directing his life. It never occurred to him that perhaps his pride and vanity might have played a sizable part in his predicament.

Jonathan angrily walked up one street and down another, his direction aimless, his eyes unseeing until he was forced to a stop by a carriage in his pathway.

"Lord Trenholme, will you do me the honor?" asked Lord Randall, opening the door of the conveyance.

"Have I honor enough left?" inquired Jonathan with heavy sarcasm.

The look that he flashed the earl as he climbed into the carriage was so full of recrimination that Lord Randall swallowed hard. He had hoped to wait a few days to allow Jonathan's temper to subside before charging him with this new task. But the governor had insisted that Jonathan be apprised of the bargain struck between his father and the king for there was need of the young man now.

"Lord Trenholme," began the earl hesitantly, "'twas not by accident that you were sent to Williamsburg to do your penitence."

Jonathan snorted. "I have become well aware that my father has connections here through whom he seeks to further direct my life—of which you are one," he added with a glare.

The earl smiled. "That may appear to be the case, but I assure you that there is a more primary and pressing concern."

Jonathan regarded the older man closely, still wary. He would be damned before he let himself be maneuvered into another corner. "Go on," he said, his tone contentious.

"The truth of the matter, sir, is that France is encroaching upon lands in the Ohio Valley that the governor has granted to Virginia land companies," explained the earl.

"Were not the French there first?" questioned Jonathan wryly.

"That is beside the point," replied Lord Randall. "The Iroquois signed a treaty with the British government in 1744—the Treaty of Lancaster—that extended Virginia's charter west to the Pacific Ocean. When word came last year that the French were building strategic forts in the area, the governor sent a young man by name of George Washington to the valley to warn the French to abandon their folly. Washington returned with a note of refusal."

"'Tis not surprising," remarked Trenholme.

"Perhaps not, but neither does it bode well," countered the earl. "It was Washington's observation then that the French were working to steal the allegiance of the Indians away from the British and that the French government was planning to reinforce the camps with a large military force. The governor later sent out three scouts to assess the strength of French arms in the area. None of these men have returned, and time is of the essence now. If we can stop the French before they build up an army, we might possibly avert a war."

"What has this to do with me?" Jonathan demanded to know.

"The governor has reason to believe that there is a traitor in our midst," confided Lord Randall. "Any strategy discussed in the General Assembly appears to find its way to the enemy's ears as well. The French seem to anticipate our every move. When the governor had first suspected as much, he requested that the king send an emissary who could be trusted to ferret out the spy. In light of your need to quit England, it was brought to the king's attention that you might have value in this matter."

"No doubt by my father," muttered Jonathan. He fell silent for a few moments. "Should I agree to expose your spy, Lord Randall, my price is an end to this farcical marriage with Callie and my leave to return to England."

"I can guarantee you the latter. As for the marriage, you signed papers," the earl reminded him. "The matter is out of both our hands."

"But not out of Callie's. I shall reason with her," said Jonathan.

Lord Randall sighed at the young man's stubbornness. "Were you to ennoble yourself in this matter before us, Lord Trenholme, your indiscretions would be overlooked. You would be welcome again at the royal court…hailed as a hero and, perhaps, with some reward. Is that not recompense enough?"

"Some things cannot be valued, sir," responded Jonathan curtly. "But I will expose this traitor for the Crown. The matter with Callie I shall handle afterwards and be off to England in a fortnight."

"I-uh-fear this concern will take longer to dispatch," hedged Lord Randall.

Jonathan eyed him with suspicion. "Why?"

"'Tis a complicated matter."

"How complicated?"

"The governor requires that you travel into the Ohio Valley to make contact with the missing scouts and return with a report of the situation," Lord Randall hurriedly explained. "With your command of the French language, you can pose as a French fur trader if challenged. Washington once surveyed that land as a youth and knows the territory well. He also knows the location of the French camps. I would advise you to seek his counsel."

"This is more than the simple task of exposing a spy. 'Tis a bloody mission!" thundered Jonathan. "Why was I not told of this before?"

"It was not readily known how you might be used to best advantage. And given your temperament when you first arrived, the governor thought it advisable to wait until you had become more, shall we say, resigned to your surroundings," replied the earl diplomatically.

"God's blood! I have been languishing in this bloody colony for these many months only to find 'tis by design?"

Jonathan's anger flared anew when he realized that the governor had had no intentions of allowing him to return to England before this task was done, no matter how many interviews he might have secured. He felt twice the fool when he saw how empty Lord Randall's earlier bargain had been—the governor's ear in exchange for Callie's welfare. As for the marriage—Jonathan nearly exploded at the realization that this mission had been deliberately withheld from him until after he had been maneuvered into marrying Callie, rendering useless his only bargaining chip.

He glared at Lord Randall. "When am I to leave?"

"In a fortnight—*after* the wedding."

Jonathan laughed humorlessly at the timing. "The General Assembly fears that I will choose not to return?"

"'Tis a dangerous mission, Lord Trenholme. The choice may not be yours to make. And the General Assembly would know its remedy one way or the other," replied Lord Randall with a wry smile.

Jonathan regarded the earl resolutely. "It matters not, for I shall be seeking my own remedy."

CHAPTER TWENTY-TWO

Honor and Obey

Handsomely attired in a suit of silk brocade patterned with white on gray, Jonathan stood before Reverend Peters in the parlor at Randall Hall waiting for the ceremony to begin. He had been in a temper for the past two weeks and this day was no exception. The "remedy" he had sought did not bear fruit.

He had tried to see Callie several times to convince her to choose another suitor, but Mrs. Whithers, acting upon instructions from Lord Randall, he had come to suspect, always managed to thwart any meeting. In a last act of desperation, he had posted a boy to keep watch for when Callie left the house, hoping to intercept her on an errand. Mrs. Stanhope and other vendors trooped in and out of the house, but Callie never appeared. He was cynical enough to imagine a conspiracy. To add insult to injury, he had been forced to sign an agreement that disallowed him any rights to Callie's property. In truth, he didn't care a fig about the dowry; it was the principle of the matter.

Jonathan's anger flared. He had the sense that events were leading him instead of he controlling them. After his talk with Lord Randall, he readily saw how the wheels had begun to turn even before he left England. He found it convenient to ignore his own part in the events that had led up to that point. Now, he was about to be bound to a willful child he knew all too well and a budding woman he knew not a whit. He was no longer just the protector but a partner now as well in a legal institution in which he placed no merit and very little respect.

His mouth curved up in a tight smile. He wondered what his father was going to say about this—a son of the Duke of Lansing marrying a lowborn farmer from the Virginia colony. Jonathan doubted very much that this had been part of his father's plan. His Grace was very particular about his lineage. He suddenly frowned as the question came to him. How was it that Lord Randal was so confident of the duke's blessing?

Jonathan glanced about him. The cold, gray January day accurately reflected the mood of the room, given the sobriety of the guests. Their somber faces called to mind more a funeral than a wedding. Lilibeth and Olivia Sanders sat glowering in a corner. Several members of the General Assembly in attendance watched his every move as though fearing that he might bolt. The obvious fact that these illustrious citizens were present only to make certain that the deed was done incensed Jonathan all the more, as did the obvious inference in their last minute warning that they would stand for no annulment.

"And what proof of consummation would you have, sir?" he had demanded to know of one councillor.

There was a nervous titter of laughter among the assemblage before the men had hastily assured Jonathan that the matter would be left to his discretion. At least something still remained in his hands, he thought sourly.

Only Lord Randall seemed to be enjoying himself, making no apology for his part in the scheme, and Jonathan was given to wonder at the man's motives once again. Clearly, there was something more to all of this than met the eye.

Servants moved quietly about the room lighting candles. When they had finished, the first strains of music issued forth from the fiddles and flutes of the slave quartet, and Jonathan turned with the others to watch Callie enter the room on Lord Randall's arm. He had gotten a hint of the transformation taking place on a few occasions, and most certainly, the holiday ball at the Raleigh Tavern had opened his eyes. But he was still unprepared for the striking beauty that moved gracefully toward him now.

The fact that Lord Randall had spared no expense on the bride's indigo gown of figured silk, or that Mrs. Stanhope's seamstresses had done their finest stitching to date on the white silk petticoat and low-cut stomacher was of little note to Jonathan. He was staring at Callie the woman.

Her eyes were a vivid blue beneath long, dark lashes. Her dark red hair was drawn up in the back and caught in loose buns, leaving ringlets free to frame her heart-shaped face. Pearl drop earrings adorned her ears, and a matching pearl necklace encircled her long, slender neck. Jonathan drew in his breath. Try as he might, he could find nothing of the recalcitrant waif in her. Callie gave him a shy, uncertain smile as she came to stand beside him, and the Reverend had to address him a second time before Jonathan turned his attention to the ceremony.

There was an impatient edge to his tone, but Jonathan's voice was clear and steady as he repeated the marriage vows by rote with only a half conscious mind to the words. By contrast, Callie's voice was low and halting as she repeated her vows. Jonathan glanced sideways at her, inwardly amused when he realized that she was having difficulty pledging to honor, obey, and to submit to her husband in total unity. He could hear her uncertainty increasing with each word, and he promised himself that he would hold her to every vow.

When the Reverend prompted Jonathan to kiss the bride, Callie dutifully presented her cheek to him. Goaded by the fact that she had mistaken his last kiss for a less than ardent nature, Jonathan pulled her into his arms and pressed his lips firmly against hers. This time, he would give her no cause to question his skill. As his kiss became more intimate, a sigh escaped a despondent Lilibeth, and the ladies present began to fan themselves with their handkerchiefs.

The Reverend cleared his throat, and Jonathan released Callie satisfied that she was flustered. There was a crimson glow on her cheeks that had nothing to do with the touch of rouge, and she refused to meet his eye. Now, he would know whom she judged the least ardent of her suitors, he thought smugly.

At the end of the ceremony, he drew her arm through his and led her into the dining room to a simple buffet of fish, stewed oysters, roasted pig, potatoes and pumpkin casserole. A smaller table held trays of nutmeats and blocks of maple sugar candy and a wedding cake made of spices, dried fruits and nuts. Tankards of spiced hard cider were passed around to toast the couple. Those men who had so recently sought her head now charitably wished her well, having considered the moment of crisis passed.

The solemnity that had marked the ceremony soon gave way to a more convivial atmosphere as attendees liberally partook of food and drink. The only guests of Callie's acquaintance were Mrs. Whithers, Lydia Stanhope, who had come to help with the gown, and Lilibeth and Olivia Sanders. There were but a handful of other women present and this would not be the usual two-day celebration of feasting and dancing, but Callie did not feel slighted or disappointed. This was a business arrangement as she saw it and nothing more.

Even so, she felt that Jonathan could be a little less rigid. He was stiff and remote as he accepted congratulatory greetings without so much as a smile. He seemed to be enduring the occasion with the stoicism of one being greatly put upon. She knew him well enough to know that he was angry, but she couldn't fathom the reason.

When the group of burgesses and councillors beckoned Jonathan across the room to them, Callie felt conspicuously alone and awkward. Mrs. Whithers and Mrs. Stanhope had departed, and she was a stranger among strangers. She felt weary and longed to be away from this place and these people. Suddenly, she felt a vicious pinch to the back of her arm and winced.

"That, you hussy, is my congratulations to the bride," Lilibeth hissed in her ear. "I should have been standing up with Lord Trenholme, not you." She and her mother flounced from the room then, throwing murderous glances over their shoulders.

Callie was massaging the painful bruise, when the wife of a burgess approached her. "My dear, how very fortunate you are," said the woman, glancing from Jonathan to her short, portly husband. "Lord Trenholme is a most uncommon man." She let out a sigh as her gaze returned to Jonathan. "How I should like to have your seat at the table this night."

Callie looked at her in puzzlement, but the lady moved on without further comment.

When Jonathan returned to her side, Callie was aware that he was more perturbed than before. "Is anything amiss, sir?" she asked.

"That is a matter of viewpoint," he replied crisply.

She sighed, out of sorts herself. "'Tis been a long day. Dusk is already fallen, and 'twill be long dark by the time we reach Williamsburg. Can we not let these people to their amusements and take our leave now? I know not why they are in attendance in the first place."

"Indeed," murmured Jonathan tightly.

When he made no move, Callie repeated more firmly, "Trenholme, I wish to leave."

"Why, Madam, you would cut short this celebration?" he asked, his deep voice laced with sarcasm. "Is not all of this by your command?"

Callie glanced up at him in confusion. "I do not understand your meaning, sir."

"Never mind. You are quite right, my dear. We have more important things to tend to this evening."

Callie continued to stare quizzically at him. He was acting most strange this day, and she couldn't reason his mood. Before she had time to consider it further, he pulled her across the room to Lord Randall.

"My wife and I shall take our leave now and wish to tender our appreciation for this wedding," said Jonathan, his manner stilted. "I trust everything is to your satisfaction." He was barely polite, and, again, Callie shot him a curious look.

Lord Randall was unperturbed. "Quite so, Lord Trenholme, and I believe you shall find it to your satisfaction one day as well. There is a carriage in readiness for your departure outside. Juba will meet you with your cloaks." He took Callie's hand and kissed it respectfully. "Permit me to say, Madam, that you make an exquisite bride. This day has been my greatest pleasure."

Unused to receiving such compliments, Callie smiled and self-consciously lowered her eyes as a telltale blush spread across her cheeks. "My thanks for your kindness, sir," she replied shyly.

Jonathan ushered her to the front door. He snatched the garments from the servant's arms, flung Callie's cloak around her shoulders, and donned his. He barely gave her time to pull the hood over her head before hustling her outside to the carriage.

The evening air was damp and raw as the wind blustered in from the sea. Even with the cover of the heavy cape, Callie shivered as she fumbled with the awkwardness of her skirts. She had dressed at Randall Hall and had no experience in the art of entering or exiting carriages with such a voluminous gown over multi layers of petticoats and side hoops. She was beginning to consider it a hopeless feat when Jonathan, short on patience, lifted her off her feet and stuffed her unceremoniously into the compartment.

She was still in the process of righting her skirts and finding her seat, when he jumped in beside her and signaled to the driver. Immediately, the carriage took off and Callie found herself sprawled across her husband.

"Madam, a lady usually finds the ride more tolerable in a seat," he remarked in a clipped tone. His manner was patronizing as he righted her and set her firmly beside him like a father with a wayward child.

"Sir, a gentleman usually waits until a lady sets her seat before instructing the vehicle to motion," Callie replied tartly.

Jonathan glared at her.

The hour-long trip passed slowly and awkwardly. Callie couldn't fathom Jonathan's mood, and Jonathan couldn't grasp this latest adjustment in his life. He was a man who liked predictability in his world, though he took pride in being unpredictable himself. And he found himself continually at war of late with the many unexpected changes that were being thrust upon him, changes that were beyond his control.

He stole a look at Callie now and again trying to recall the rapscallion she had been. The wit and the spirit were the same, but everything else about her was different—her manner, her appearance, her voice, even her figure. While he delighted in the transformation, he also found it daunting. With Callie the child, he had always known where he stood; with Callie the woman, he wasn't sure about anything.

Jonathan folded his arms across his chest, his manner aloof. He felt like a callow schoolboy with his first girl instead of a man well practiced, and the feeling did not sit well with him at all. Good Lord, he had handled the likes of Lady Westmont, but Callie…Callie was different. Theirs was supposed to be a relationship of checks and balances. The rules had been clear, the lines well drawn. Now, thanks to Mrs. Whithers' lessons and a twenty-minute ceremony, this was no longer the case.

"I suppose that I should thank you," said Callie, breaking the heavy silence.

"For what?"

"For helping me to secure my land and my release from my stepfather's guardianship."

Jonathan shifted in his seat, feeling a stab of conscience. He couldn't tell her that, caught in a weak moment, he had agreed to marry her only to save face.

"Surely, Lord Randall explained that, if I hadn't married, my stepfather would have been able to sell the farm," Callie continued when Jonathan didn't answer. "He was also about to petition my return to his authority under his roof in any case."

"Yes, yes, I can understand your problem," he responded curtly. "But why did you have to name me as the only man you would wed, when there are plenty of other young men better suited to your needs?"

"Were I interested in having a husband, I dare say that would be true," replied Callie.

Jonathan looked at her as astonished as he was bewildered. *If she were interested in having a husband...what the deuce did she think he was!*

"Under the circumstances, only you would do," Callie went on, unaware of Jonathan's confusion. "But you know that."

"No, I do not know that. Suppose you enlighten me."

Callie glanced at Jonathan wondering at his play of ignorance in the matter. "Well, 'tis certain that you have no more use for a wife than I for a husband," she said, a little less sure of herself.

"Go on."

"When I reach my majority, I need no longer fear my stepfather's authority, and I shall have my land. As I will have no more need of marriage then, I can file for an annulment," she explained matter-of-factly. "Even though we will be living apart when you leave for England soon, we shall be free legally as well to enjoy separate lives."

Jonathan was stunned by the cool calculation of her plan and rather miffed that her reasons for choosing him weren't a little more flattering. "And what is my reward to be for participating in your scheme?" he asked tightly.

Callie regarded Jonathan with surprise. "Lord Randall said, that after conferring with you, you were pleased to do me the favor—given all the trouble you have caused me."

Jonathan bristled at the familiar refrain but let it pass. "Indeed, Lord Randall seems to have said a lot of things," he said, seeing the truth of the matter.

They both had been cleverly duped into this marriage, but he didn't perceive Callie as being quite the victim that he was. She merely got tripped up in her own intrigue, for she had covered all the angles but two. He wouldn't be leaving for England any time soon, and this marriage was not going to be annulled. Apart from that, he was taking control now, and he vowed that Callie would not be let off the hook so easily. She had taken a husband; she would pay the price of a wife.

As the carriage bounced across the ruts in the road, Callie fought to keep her seat. But with part of her skirts caught beneath Jonathan's leg, it proved to be a difficult task. His manner was so withdrawn that she had no desire to intrude upon his mood a second time.

Once again, she wondered what ailed him. After Lord Randall had conveyed to her that Jonathan had agreed to the marriage, she had expected to see him before the wedding to clarify the agreement once more. But when he had made no attempt to see her, she saw no reason to question anything. Now, looking at his brooding features, she was beginning to wonder if that had been a mistake. Clearly, something was amiss.

When the carriage finally pulled up in front of the three-story brick house where Jonathan was residing, it was with great relief that both viewed the end of the journey from Randall Hall.

Jonathan jumped out of the conveyance and extended a hand to Callie. But, again, the wide hoops and extra petticoats proved to be an obstruction, blocking her exit just as they had impeded her entrance.

Muttering an oath beneath his breath, Jonathan slid his hand down one side of her gown to flatten the hoop and skirts underneath, then turned her and pulled her out against him. It rather reminded her of a cork being popped from a bottle, and unable to help herself, Callie burst out laughing. It seemed to relieve the tension between them as Jonathan, likewise, found himself amused by the absurdity of the situation.

"Consider yourself fortunate, madam, for I know of one woman who was forced to leave much of her gown behind in order to vacate her carriage."

For the time being, Callie was content to remain in Jonathan's arms as they shared a rare moment of humor and warmth in an otherwise tumultuous day. But all too soon, the spell was broken as the housekeeper, the cook, and Jonathan's valet appeared at the front door to welcome the new couple. Jonathan brusquely acknowledged the staff's greetings and escorted Callie into the house.

"Mrs. Bendel, please see my wife to her chambers and assist her accordingly," he said, handing their cloaks to the valet.

"Yes, sir," replied Mrs. Bendel with a bob and a curtsy. She looked at Callie strangely for a moment. The young woman seemed familiar to her, but the housekeeper couldn't for the life of her recall why. "This way, yer Ladyship," she said, leading Callie to the stairs. "Yer trunks just arrived from Widow Whithers and was sent to yer chamber."

Jenkins, for his part, was so taken with Callie that he stared after her with undisguised admiration, unaware of anything out of the ordinary about the new mistress.

Jonathan snorted. At another time, he might have found it amusing. Not now. "Jenkins, are you going to stand here all night acting the coat stand!" he barked.

Jenkins jumped and looked down at the cloaks in his arms as though noticing them for the first time. "N-no, sir," he stammered and quickly went about his business.

In ill humor again, Jonathan entered the drawing room to brace himself with a drink for the task that yet lay ahead.

CHAPTER TWENTY-THREE

Payment Due

The housekeeper stopped before a door at the top of the stairs. "I hope ye find the room to yer likin', Lady Trenholme," she said, a note of pride in her voice. "I shall show ye in and then fetch some water for ye."

Lady Trenholme. It was the first time that anyone had called her that. The full realization that she was a Lady and a Trenholme hit Callie with a jolt. The new identity sounded so strange to her ear and even more foreign on her tongue, and she was suddenly struck by the irony of it all. Disdainful of privilege and position unearned, she was now the beneficiary of both. For the second time, she found herself questioning the wisdom of her actions.

"Be there something amiss, yer Ladyship?" asked the housekeeper worriedly.

"Oh, no, Mrs. Bendel," said Callie. "I fear events of the day have taken more of a toll than I realized."

Mrs. Bendel nodded, satisfied that the young lady's distraction stemmed from fatigue than from disappointment with her new residence, and she proudly threw open the door to the bedchamber. Expecting an unemotional accolade in true British tradition, the housekeeper was, instead, treated to a shriek of joy as Callie spied the large, round figure standing by the bed.

"Lucie!" Callie ran and threw herself into the woman's arms with rare abandon. "Oh, how I have missed you and Old Joe," she cried.

As an equally emotional Lucie hugged Callie close to her bosom, the surprised housekeeper shook her head and went about her errand. She would never understand the relationship these colonists had with their slaves. They either treated them with total disregard or embraced them as family. And showing such affection for a servant most certainly wasn't practiced by the gentry class.

Callie stepped out of Lucie's embrace and stared in wonder at the Negress. "Lucie, how come ye to be here?"

"Lord Randall, bless his soul, thought as how ye'd have need of me. My, my, ye be as pretty as da dew at dawn with all the trimmin's of a lady," said Lucie, somewhat in awe of the accomplishment. "And married, too. I wouldna believed it iffen I didna see it with my own eyes. I peeked into the parlor when dat Sanders witch weren't a lookin'. Dat man of yers be a handsome buck," she said with a sly wink. "Didna I tells ye—"

"Lucie, hush! 'Tis a matter of business between us and nothing more. Marrying Trenholme was the only way I could keep Cane from selling my land and bringing me under his roof. As soon as I can get that scoundrel off my property and some huts built, you, Old Joe, and me are going back. 'Twill be just in time to plant the tobacco seedlings."

Lucie chuckled deeply. "I 'spect your man'll have somethin' to say 'bout dat."

"Trenholme will be returning to England soon, and I shall be free to do as I please."

The expression on the old Negress' face was one of skepticism, and she shook her head at her mistress' naïveté. "I see'd how he was a lookin' at ye when ye walked into dat room. And da way he kissed ye...honey, dat boy is all man, an' iffen ye thinks he jest gonna walk away from ye, ye best think again."

Heat that had nothing to do with the blazing fire in the fireplace fanned Callie's cheeks at the thought of Jonathan's kiss. The intimate caress during the ceremony had been nothing like the dispassionate kiss of the night of the ball, and she felt a ripple of something—she wasn't quite sure of what—but it aroused interest. A frown settled over her features as she, again, wondered if she had misjudged a few things about the man who was now her husband. In any case, she would have to keep a comfortable distance between them until he left for England, she decided.

"Yes suh, dat is one man dat ain't gonna walk away," said Lucie knowingly.

"Never mind," snapped Callie, refusing to discuss the matter. She would have better luck convincing the wall than Lucie once the woman got something into her mind.

She turned to survey the room. The bedchamber was very pleasant. A print of primroses covered the walls, and a thick carpet and damask rose-colored curtains replaced the rushes and lace material of summer. A four-poster bed with heavy bed hangings in shades of green and gold was centered in the room in front of the fireplace. Matching high-backed wing chairs flanked the hearth.

Too long, Callie had led the Spartan's life, and while her room at Mrs. Whithers had been far nicer than what she had been accustomed to, it was rather stark by comparison to this richly appointed chamber.

"Oh, the room 'tis lovely indeed," said Callie, testing the thick feather mattress with her hand.

She hadn't realized how weary she was until now and was looking forward to crawling beneath the down comforter. How easy it would be to become accustomed to such comfort, she thought with a sigh.

Mrs. Bendel bustled into the room carrying a large pitcher of water. "Yer pardon for takin' so long, yer Ladyship, but the water seemed not of a mind to boil." She set the pitcher on the washstand and dropped a knitted cozy over it to hold the heat until Callie was ready to use the water. "I fear the weddin' caught us unawares, or we would be more prepared for ye," said the housekeeper apologetically. "His Lordship told us of it only two days ago. Humph, I dare say 'tis time for the man to be settled," she declared as she busied herself with turning down the bed and plumping the pillows.

"Is that so," said Callie, amused by the housekeeper's bluntness.

"Yes, ma'am. Ye wouldna believed the shenanigans what went on here aforehand. Why an uncouth woman broke in upon his Lordship one day at a most untoward time to say that he—" Mrs. Bendel clapped a hand across her mouth. "B-Beggin' yer pardon, yer Ladyship," she stammered red-faced. "I didna mean to run on so."

Callie fought back a giggle, knowing full well the incident to which the woman was referring. "'Tis all right, Mrs. Bendel. No harm done." She wondered what the housekeeper would say if she knew that Callie was the uncouth girl who had so scandalously broken in upon Lord Trenholme's bath that day.

"If it pleases yer Ladyship, I shall see to the unpackin' of yer trunks now," said the housekeeper, eager to atone for her blunder.

Callie nodded as she pulled the pins from her hair and shook the heavy tresses loose. Her scalp felt like a pincushion and she gently massaged it before combing through the curls with her fingers.

"Lucie, would you please help me out of this gown?" she asked. "I am very weary."

In a short while, Lucie had Callie released from the gown, petticoats, and pannier hoops. Still clad in her chemise and stays, Callie moved nearer to the warming fire to remove her shoes and stockings.

"Here ye be, yer Ladyship," said the housekeeper.

Callie turned to find that the woman held up a voluminous white shift made of linen so fine and sheer that she could see the candle through it. Delicate lace trimmed the scooped neckline and long sleeves. It was unlike anything she had ever seen before.

"What is this?" she asked.

"Why 'tis for yer weddin' night," replied Mrs. Bendel somewhat nonplussed. "Jane said as how Miz Whithers had it specially stitched for ye to wear this night."

Callie fingered the thin, smooth material. "'Tis lovely indeed. I must remember to thank Mrs. Whithers for her kindness, but whatever was she thinking? A body might as well wear nothing at all, as well it warms one." She picked up a shawl and wrapped it around her shoulders. "Lucie, please find me my old shift."

"Beggin' yer pardon, ma'am, but I believe ye to be missin' the point."

"I do not care what the point is, Mrs. Bendel. I am not wearing that," said Callie politely but firmly. "Why, I could catch my death of cold in it."

"But, yer Ladyship—"

"Please do not call me that."

"Very well. Lady Trenholme—"

"And do not call me that either."

Mrs. Bendel looked at Callie, obviously flustered. "What would ye have me call ye, then?"

Callie waved her hand in a gesture of impatience. "Oh, I don't care. Just not that. I have no use for titles."

Mrs. Bendel was hard pressed to disguise her shock at the young woman's insistence upon dispensing with the very foundation of English society. Many a woman finagled for the honor of possessing a title. While one part of her admired Callie's lack of pretense, another had to wonder at the mental stability of the young woman.

Conscious of the passing time, Mrs. Bendel redirected Callie's attention to the exquisite bed shift and pleaded with her. "Mistress, we must make haste. Lord Trenholme will be coming upstairs soon, and whatever will he think?"

Callie yawned. "What does it matter what he thinks?"

This time the housekeeper didn't even try to hide her astonishment. The young woman really was an innocent. "Lady Tren—Madam—

this be your weddin' night," she said more candidly. "Ye should be lyin' abed in proper retirement as befittin' the occasion."

"Missy Callie, Miz Bendel be right," interceded Lucie to the gratitude of the housekeeper. "Ye be a married lady now, and Mister Justice will expect—"

"Oh, not you, too, Lucie!" exclaimed Callie in exasperation. "Find my shift and leave me to my peace. I am weary and have a great desire to test that mattress."

"But-but, madam," sputtered the housekeeper helplessly.

"I shall handle this, Mrs. Bendel," said Jonathan, strolling into the room. "You and Lucie may take your leave now."

He carried a decanter of wine in one hand and a goblet in the other and projected a more casual air. His hair hung loose, the cravat and waistcoat had been discarded, and his white linen shirt was open at the neck.

"What are you doing here?" Callie asked, pulling the shawl tighter around her.

Mrs. Bendel's jaw dropped, her stupefaction complete, as she stared uncertainly from Callie to Jonathan. A wife challenging her husband's right to be in her bedchamber and on their wedding night— it simply wasn't to be believed!

The housekeeper and Lucie stood rooted to the spot, wondering what the rest of the hours would bring, until Jonathan set the decanter and wine glass on a table and firmly ejected them from the room.

The night was turning bitterly cold. The wind rattled the glass panes in the window and howled eerily in the chimney. Callie moved closer to the small, open hearth.

Jonathan filled the goblet and brought it to her. "Drink this," he said.

"What is it?" she asked irritably.

"Claret. 'Twill ease the chill and relax you."

"'Tis a suitable shift and that comforter of which I have more need," remarked Callie testily, taking the drink from him.

She took a small sip of the red wine and tested it on her tongue. She liked the taste of it, but more than that she reveled in the warmth it was sending through her chilled body. And her next sips were not quite so small.

The shawl had slipped unnoticed from her shoulders and hung loosely off one arm as she became more relaxed. One long curl hung over her shoulder, beckoning Jonathan's eye to the cleavage that swelled above the ruffle of her chemise. Though she was not what some might term voluptuous, Jonathan found her measurement nicely proportioned to her petite frame, and his gaze lingered for a long moment before slowly sliding down to the curve of her hips.

The light from the fire illuminated shapely thighs and legs beneath her calf-length garment. And he was moved to marvel, once again, how a little nurturing could yield such amazing results. He was still having difficulty consolidating the image of the Callie of his earlier acquaintance with the one that presently stood before him, but he began to consider that he might enjoy getting to know Callie the woman after all.

"You have changed a good deal," he said, his voice husky.

Callie was oblivious to Jonathan's perusal, her interest taken up solely with the liquid in her glass. She felt as though she were floating on air. Jonathan's voice seemed to come from a long way off, and she blinked in surprise when she looked up to find him standing so close to her.

"What did you say?" she asked, suddenly aware that he had spoken. Her words were slightly slurred, her cheeks flushed, and she had an engaging lopsided grin on her face as she extended her glass for a refill.

Jonathan's mouth curved up in amusement. "Easy, Callie. The wine can be pretty heady for one unused to drink."

He reached out a hand to steady her as she swayed slightly off balance. The touch of his fingers on her bare arm sent shock waves through her that had an immediate sobering effect, and she closed her eyes for a moment to get a grip on her hazy sensibilities.

"Trenholme, what…what be ye…what be ye doing here?" she asked between hiccups. "I shouldn't want the servants to talk."

Jonathan nearly laughed aloud at this. She hadn't worried about the servants' reactions when she burst into his bath that day. "You seem to forget that you are my wife now, Callie, and this our wedding night," he said. "The servants would most assuredly talk were I not here."

Callie looked up at him in confusion. Her eyes suddenly widened and her cheeks turned a bright pink when she comprehended his meaning. In her mind, the marriage was a business pact, pure and simple, and it never occurred to her that anyone would consider it otherwise.

She gave a little giggle. "Oh dear, no wonder Mrs. Bendel was in such a tizzy over that silly shift. I thought everyone understood that—well, never mind. I shall set the matter straight in the morn that our marriage is but a temporary arrangement."

"You might want to reconsider doing that," suggested Jonathan. "A union requires consummation or there is no union. Should your stepfather suspect a ruse, he could contest the marriage or perhaps bring a charge of conspiracy against you to defraud him of his rights."

Callie thought for a moment. "Yes, I see. We shall have to be most careful in our actions so as not to arouse suspicion."

Jonathan took the goblet from her and set it aside. "No, Callie, you don't see."

His voice was low and held a seductive note that she had never heard before, and there was a look in his eye that, inexperienced as she was, she could easily read.

She stiffened and quickly backed further away from him, drawing the shawl tighter around her. "Surely, you are not suggesting that— now see here, Trenholme, the situation does not give you liberty to—"

"On the contrary, madam, that gold band on your finger and the documents you signed entitle me to all the liberties that I wish to take with you."

"But we struck a deal," she protested.

"You struck a deal with Lord Randall," Jonathan reminded her. "I was no party to it."

Callie moved away from him, massaging her forehead. She needed to think more clearly. "But when Lord Randall said that you had agreed to the terms, I thought you had accepted that this marriage was to be in name only."

"Let that be a lesson to you, Callie. Always negotiate directly with the principal. I do not know what terms you thought you had, but his Lordship put none of that nature to me."

"You mean to say that Lord Randall lied to me?"

"Let us say that he forgot to mention a few things."

"Well, it still does not give you the right to—"

"It gives me every right, madam, morally and legally. You know the law," said Jonathan smugly. *"THE LAWES RESOLUTIONS OF WOMENS RIGHTS* states: 'Just as when a small brooke is incorporated into the Thames, it loses its name, it beareth no sway, and it possesseth nothing; similarly, it is that as soon as a woman is married, her new self is her superior, her husband her master.' If I must have a wife, Callie, I intend to exercise *every* right that is mine as a husband."

Callie knew that she fought him more effectively with her wit than with her anger, but he had just exceeded the bounds of her restraint. "I do care not what Lord Randall did or did not tell you. I will have no master, and I will not submit to any man's rule—not now, not ever!" She pulled off the ring and slammed it on the table as though the action absolved her of any responsibilities.

"I am afraid it is not that easy," said Jonathan.

He seemed amused. The knowing half smile on his lips enraged her all the more, and she grabbed the goblet from the table and threw it at him. It narrowly missed his head and shattered against the wall. The startled look on his face instantly turned thunderous, and the steely glare would have been warning enough for a more prudent person. But Callie's temper was such that, once ignited, there was little room for temperance or fear, and he watched in further amazement as she cast around for yet something else to throw.

When she reached for the pomade jar, Jonathan swiftly closed on her and wrenched the jar from her fingers. Callie's response was just as immediate; he had to move quickly to stay her hand before she struck his face. Before she could make another move, he lifted her off her feet and both went tumbling across the bed. She thrashed beneath his weight, beating her fists against his chest in an effort to throw him off. He was surprised by her strength, and it was a few minutes before Jonathan could imprison her arms and position his leg across hers to subdue her.

"I told you before, Callie, you cannot begin an action and expect to walk away from the consequences," he said.

He wasn't sure what to do with her at this point; he would much rather take a switch to her. As he looked down into defiant blue eyes, the moment was decided. His mouth closed on hers in a kiss designed to establish his authority. After a few moments, she went still and her soft lips parted, seeming to invite more intimacy.

Drawing upon his experience and powers of seduction, he broke the kiss to move his lips along the column of her neck as he slipped a hand beneath her chemise to caress the soft flesh of her thigh. His hand moved higher, and his fingers played lightly across her sensitive skin before dipping down between her legs. There was a sharp intake of her breath, and he could feel her body quiver. In the next moment, Jonathan was shocked to see tears rolling down her cheeks, and it stopped him in his tracks. He had expected her to be resistant, but he thought he could bridge that gulf. Clearly, it was too soon for her to make the leap. Truth to tell, he wasn't sure that he was ready to make it either.

He moved off the bed, his mood heavy. "The initiative shall be yours, madam, the General Assembly be damned," he said.

Jonathan walked to the door. When he pulled it open, Lucie and Mrs. Bendel nearly fell at his feet.

"Yer pardon, yer Lordship," stammered Mrs. Bendel. "W-we was waitin' to see if there was anythin' more ye or her Ladyship might be needin'."

A wide-eyed Lucie nodded vigorously.

As Jonathan continued to glare at them, the women tripped over each other in their haste to reach the stairs.

CHAPTER TWENTY-FOUR

A Matter of Resolve

Callie stared moodily out the window, barely cognizant of nature's spectacular show, as dawn cloaked the night in the pinkish glow of a new day. She shivered beneath the warmth of the heavy shawl but was unmindful of the cold draft that seeped through the casement. She had passed a long, tedious night marked by confusion and uncertainties that had denied her sleep.

Jonathan's revelation that her bargain was not as she believed it to be gave her to know that she had not quite the command that she thought. His demand for his marital rights had made that clear. Callie blushed to think of it—the way he had touched her, where he had touched her, the sensations he had aroused before he stopped.

His actions had shocked and overwhelmed her. She hadn't been mentally prepared for any intimacy, most certainly not of that nature. Indeed, after Mr. Plinn's frenzied advances, she was repelled by the very thought of it. Callie knit her brows in bewilderment. But Jonathan hadn't repulsed her. She did not find his touch offensive, and she had no desire to thump him on the head with a book as was the fate of Mr. Plinn. At the very least, he had stirred curiosity and that did not bode well for her resolve.

He hadn't followed through with the consummation, and he had promised her the initiative from hereon, but it was her observation that men were not the most trustworthy when the mood was upon them. And it didn't seem to take much to trigger it. Lord Randall said Jonathan would be returning to England in five or six months. That was too long, she decided. She couldn't allow him to jeopardize her plan.

She moved decisively across the room and into the empty hallway. She didn't know which room was his but took a chance that it was the one closest to hers. Taking a deep breath, she rapped smartly on the door.

"Come in, Jenkins!" commanded Trenholme.

Even from behind the door, Callie could hear the contention in his tone. His mood was almost certain to be quarrelsome. She put her hand on the knob and was taking a moment to collect herself, when Jonathan flung open the door, and she was catapulted into the room. Had he not reached out to grab her arm, she would have landed in a very undignified heap.

Callie quickly disengaged herself from his grasp and modestly rearranged her shift.

"I-I am not Jenkins," she stammered, struggling to recover her composure.

Jonathan kicked the door closed and gave a sardonic snort. "I can see that. I trust that you passed a night equal to my own?"

"Yes, very much so," said Callie, taking his inquiry at face value, until a quick glance around the room revealed that neither had he passed the night in blissful slumber. The bed had not been slept in and an empty brandy decanter set alongside the wing chair that had been drawn up to the hearth. "I mean no, I slept quite nicely, thank you," she quickly amended. She didn't know what his source of torment was, but he couldn't know that he had been the cause of hers.

Jonathan had to smile in spite of his dark mood as Callie continued to avert her eyes from him. Lying was so alien to her nature that he had yet to know her to be able to look him in the eye with an untruth—notwithstanding the case of Mae Bailey, which hadn't been a lie by her definition but a fib for a noble cause.

When she finally met his gaze, Callie was annoyed to find Jonathan regarding her with a smile complacent and amused as though he was privy to some secret about her. "God's teeth, Trenholme! Must you look like the cat that ate the canary? How can I expect to have an intelligent discourse with you?"

"It depends. What intelligent discourse do you wish to have?" questioned Jonathan. "Do tell, madam, to what I owe the honor of your presence in my bedchamber before it gives me pause for reflection." He gave a meaningful glance toward the bed. "You may not find the conclusion that I draw at all to your liking."

Callie blushed at the inference and bit back a retort. To lose her temper now would accomplish nothing, she decided.

"I have not all day, woman," growled Jonathan, his patience running short. "Name your purpose. Knowing you, there is certain to be one."

Callie nervously bit her lip as she cast about for the right words. "Trenholme, I—"

"Madam, given the change in our circumstances, I suggest you call me Jonathan."

Callie took a deep breath and started again. "Jonathan, I think that both our interests would be better served were you to leave for England sooner than planned. I am sure that, with Lord Randall's assistance, the governor can be persuaded to grant you an earlier release."

Jonathan's silence and the now inscrutable expression on his face as he continued to regard her increased her level of discomfort and uncertainty.

"Well, how say you?" she asked brusquely.

"Perhaps you should think again," he said.

"Why?"

"When I set sail for England, 'twill be with *all* my possessions, Callie. Do you understand me?"

Callie understood him perfectly. She visibly bristled and her eyes flashed. "I am not one of your possessions."

"The law says that you are."

The smugness in his tone was positively galling to her. What was worse, he was right. "But my place is here and yours is in England. I assumed that you understood that," she argued with some desperation.

Jonathan folded his arms across his chest, his manner uncompromising. "That was your second mistake, Callie. You should never assume anything."

Callie drew herself up, her manner equally uncompromising. "I am not going to England," she declared resolutely. "I have a farm to rebuild."

"Then we shall consider the subject closed—for the present. Now, my dear, unless you wish to be a part of this morning's regimen," said Jonathan, again glancing at the bed, "I suggest that you seek your own quarters, for the day may not find me so generous as the night."

Callie wanted to slap his arrogant face. But the look in his eyes as he read her mind warned her against it, and it was with considerable effort that she curbed the impulse. "I should have known better than to try to reason with you," she said with an indignant huff.

As she flounced to the door, Jonathan called out to her. "Callie, proceed as you wish with the rebuilding of your farm, but you are forbidden to set foot on that land until my return. There has been the report of more attacks on that road."

Callie whirled about. "You are going somewhere? When?"

"This morning. I am being sent to a county court in the north for a month."

"A month! But 'tis time to plant the tobacco seeds now."

"Old Joe can see to the cold boxes."

"But—"

"'Tis not open to debate, Callie. I am warning you. Do not cross me on this."

"Or you shall do what?" she challenged defiantly.

"I shall forbid any further work on the farm, and we will set sail for England at first opportunity."

With a cry of exasperation, Callie stormed out of the room.

Her rage was all encompassing as she flew into her chamber. The man wasn't to be figured! Ever since his arrival in the colonies, he had been obsessed with returning to England and had continually cursed the day that their paths had crossed. And now he was showing little inclination to quit Virginia any time soon and was refusing to leave without her.

"That man is impossible!" exclaimed Callie, with a healthy slam of the door.

Lucie looked up startled. "What man?"

"Trenholme! Who else? He forbids me to go near my own land until he returns from some county court."

"He right, missy. Dat road ain't safe no more for a lady. Asides, Cane ain't gonna leave dat farm as pretty as ye please on yer say so. And ye ain't got yer papa's gun to speak for ye."

In the uproar of the past months, Callie had forgotten about that. Her father's hunting fowler had gone missing the day that Cane had viciously assaulted her, and she figured it to be in his possession.

"Just the same, Lucie, I will not be treated like a child," declared Callie peevishly.

"Then ye best start actin' like a woman," returned Lucie.

Callie glared at the old Negress. Her attention was drawn then to a disturbance outside, and she went to look out the window. Jonathan was preparing to leave on his trip. He threw his great coat about his shoulders and lithely swung himself atop the magnificent stallion. Sensing the audience of another, he looked up to see her watching. To any casual observer, he appeared to be a gentleman tipping his hat in farewell to his lady. But to Callie, the slow easy gesture of his hand, the half smile on his lips, and his unwavering gaze conveyed a much more significant message.

She looked down at her hand. The wedding ring was more than just a pretty band around her finger. Jonathan had made it quite clear that it was a band of ownership. She took off the ring again and placed it in a trinket box. She knew it didn't matter whether she wore it or not. She was still legally bound to him. But the gesture mattered to her.

CHAPTER TWENTY-FIVE

The Web Unravels

Abel Cane stumbled blindly about the crude hut collecting the last drops of liquor from the bottles that littered the dirt floor. With the loss of his guardianship over Callie and his right to sell her land, there came an immediate withdrawal of credit and no more prospects of funds.

"The bitch!" he snarled drunkenly. "The connivin' li'l bitch! I'll make her pay dear for this I will."

He stopped when he remembered something that his old drinking buddy Jack Bailey had once told him, and his puffy eyes took on a bright glow. Suddenly, his future no longer seemed so dim. Cane laughed and, with an unsteady hand, tipped the bottle to his lips to dribble the last dregs of rum into his mouth.

He dropped onto the wooden bench and fell into a heavy sleep. He had no idea how long he was passed out before a persistent pounding at the door penetrated his foggy senses.

"Who goes there?" he asked in a slurred voice, rubbing his bleary eyes.

The door slowly creaked open, and the silhouette of a man appeared in the entrance. "I was told this be the Hastings farm," said the man, holding his nose against the foul odor of the unkempt hut.

"So what if it is?" responded Cane belligerently.

"I got a letter for Callie Hastings. I was visitin' in Carolina and was asked to bring it to her on me return."

"Well, she ain't here. Now leave me be."

The man was torn. The young lady had instructed him to deliver the missive directly into Miss Hastings' hands, but he had already gone several miles out of his way and was most anxious not to delay his homecoming any longer.

"If I leave the letter on the table, will ye see to it that it finds its way to Miss Hastings?" he asked hopefully.

All Cane could manage before lapsing once again into a drunken stupor was an impatient wave of his arm.

A few hours later, the afternoon sun shining through the cracks of the shutter finally stirred Cane to consciousness, and he shook his shaggy mane in an attempt to clear the haze from his mind. As he became more lucid, he vaguely recalled that a man had been in his hut, and he scratched his head in confusion. He had nearly succeeded in convincing himself that he had dreamed the encounter, when his eye fell upon the travel-worn letter at the end of table. He had never learned to read passably, and he wracked his brain trying to remember what the messenger had said.

A letter from Carolina, the man had told him…a letter for Callie, he suddenly recalled. Now what would Callie be about to receive a letter from there or from anywhere? he wondered curiously. Cane ran a dirty hand across the weeklong stubble on his face as a nasty smile spread across his bloated features. Perhaps it contained something of value that he could use against her. He picked up the missive and studied it for a long moment. Surely, someone at the tavern in town could decipher this scribble.

Jonathan rode wearily into Williamsburg. It was late afternoon, and the air felt damper than usual. He had been away for five long, arduous weeks. Images of Callie had bedeviled him continuously, and in his less rigid moments, he would have sworn that they had even dared to taunt him. Now that he was home, he knew he had to deal with the problem, or he would know no peace.

Unquestionably, he was taken with her stunning transformation. Callie the child had exasperated him; Callie the woman intrigued him. The image of her on their wedding night clothed only in her chemise and stays, the firelight behind her exposing every curve of her figure to his eye, had burned itself into his memory. But he was still having difficulty transitioning his role. He felt like a guardian whose charge had grown up too quickly for him to grasp the reality. And he had realized at that moment on their wedding night that Callie needed time to grow into her new role as well—mistaken though she was about the nature of their union. He pulled up at Wetherburn's Tavern to regroup before facing her. He wondered in what frame of mind he would find her. With Callie, he never knew.

Trenholme made his way across the noisy, smoke-filled taproom, picking up a tankard of ale along the way. He had just settled himself in a chair by the fireplace when Lord Randall sat down across from him.

"You waste little time," said Jonathan.

"There is little time to waste," responded Lord Randall soberly. "I posted a boy to watch for your return and have spent the last four days in town. You are a week late."

"Spring snows made the journey difficult at times, and one can ill-afford to be casual these days about Indians."

"Just so. What news have you?" asked the earl. "Were you able to make contact with the scouts?"

"Aye, with one—Billingham. Halbertson drowned early on in a ford crossing, and Talbot was killed in an Indian raid on their camp. Billingham escaped and found refuge with the Mingos. He married one of their women and now resides with the tribe, which affords him great sight of French movements. He reports that a substantial military contingency is in place and that the fort in the Ohio Valley at the fork of the Allegheny and Monongahela Rivers has fallen to the French. They are erecting their own fort—Fort Duquesne—on the site."

Lord Randall sighed heavily. "Then it is as we feared. What about the Indians?"

"The French have been drawing them to their side with considerable success," replied Jonathan. "Billingham fears the Hurons and Tuscaroras are faltering."

"God's blood, if they side with the French, there could be uprisings on the border that may well spread throughout the colony," worried the earl. "How can this be? England has always commanded the allegiance of the Iroquois nation and at a rather handsome price, I might add. What do the French offer to persuade Iroquois tribes to ally themselves with the Algonquins? They have been great enemies for years."

"Land," said Jonathan. "According to Billingham, the French's primary interest in the territory is fur trading. They have no need or interest in moving Indians off these lands for settlement. I understand that the Tuscaroras were displaced from Virginia and Carolina by the English, and the Hurons fear the same fate."

Lord Randall nodded, his brow creased with concern. "Yes, I can see how that might work to the advantage of the French. They always were a good deal more tolerant of the savages."

"It also helps that an Englishman aids in their recruitment," interjected Jonathan.

"An Englishman aiding the French...the devil you say!" exclaimed the earl. "I would have thought it of a Scotsman or an Irishman but never an Englishman. Is he the same man who passes along our secrets?"

"'Tis not known."

"Have you a name?"

Jonathan shook his head. "He is quite clever.

"You have done well, sir. My apologies for taking you away from your bride so soon, but I think you can appreciate the urgency of the matter."

Trenholme toyed with his tankard. "Have you seen Callie?" he asked. "How has she fared these past weeks?"

Lord Randall sighed resignedly. "Callie is Callie. She still believes that you were sent to a county court and is most eager for your return."

Jonathan snorted and took a swig of his ale. "No doubt she looks to my return to begin work on her farm."

"Well, I did recently assist her in the hire of three field laborers and with the purchase of some supplies and materials," said Lord Randall.

Jonathan looked at him in surprise. "I had not thought her profits to be so generous from this year's tobacco crop."

"They weren't. She established credit in your name," replied the earl with a chuckle.

"What say you?"

"It seems that you had given her a note of consent."

"I did no such thing," retorted Jonathan.

"Well, whatever she presented, the merchants were only too happy to accept. Not to worry, sir," the earl humorously assured him. "She fully intends to repay you with next year's crop." He stood up to leave. "Now I must make haste to take your report to the governor. It is most concerning. By the bye, perhaps you should make inquiry into Callie's tea parties," he said in a parting comment.

As the earl left the tavern, Jonathan sat wondering what the devil had been going on in his absence.

"Ah, Lord Trenholme, just two and a half fortnights wed and already back with the men, ay. Well, can't say as I blame you, what with a house full of gossipy women every week."

Jonathan swung his attention to the gentleman planter. "I beg your pardon, sir?"

"'Tis of Lady Trenholme's tea parties that I speak—every week on this day. My wife is in attendance now."

"Mine as well," said another prominent gentleman, joining the conversation. "I know not what Lady Trenholme is serving up, but, from what I hear, the ladies are fighting to get on her list."

Jonathan's eyes narrowed. He had a pretty good idea what Callie was serving up. When the two men moved on, he quaffed his ale in a hurry to leave.

Abel Cane staggered into the tavern then.

"I got me this here letter what needs be 'ciphered," he announced loudly.

"Who'd be writin' the likes of ye, lessen it be the devil hisself?" joked one of the patrons.

"'Tis a letter fer me stepdaughter—from Carolina," said Cane, goaded into giving out more information than he had intended.

"Then, why not ye let the lass read the letter for herself?" challenged another patron.

"I jest wants to be certain there ain't nothin' she needs be spared is all. Her don't take kindly to bad news."

"Ah, go on with ye," guffawed another man. "From what I heard, ye be the bad news she don't take kindly to."

"Here now, perhaps I can be of some help," offered a well-dressed gentleman.

"And who might ye be?" demanded Cane warily.

The man's lips curled up in disgust. "Someone who needs no introduction to the likes of you, but I shall humor you just the same. I am Justice Smythe."

Cane scrutinized the man, undaunted by his air of superiority. There was something about the judge that he didn't like. Maybe it was his condescending manner, or maybe it was the intense interest that burned in his eyes as he looked at the letter. After a moment's consideration, Cane shrugged. If the man could read, what did it matter? He handed over the letter, his greed overcoming his distrust.

Smythe avidly scanned the parchment. The writing was crude, and he had great difficulty deciphering the misspelled words.

"Well, how's it read?" demanded Cane impatiently.

"I believe that is for my wife to say," declared Jonathan, holding out his hand for the missive. "I shall see that she receives it this time."

Neither man had noticed Jonathan's presence in the busy tavern, and they started at his sudden appearance.

Smythe stiffly handed over the letter. "Lord Trenholme, had I known of your attendance, I should have tendered it to you immediately."

"Yes, I am sure of it," replied Jonathan, his tone dubious.

When he swung a cold eye on Callie's stepfather, Cane drew back cowardly. Standing up to this Smythe was one thing, but Lord Trenholme was an entirely different matter. "I-I didna mean no harm," he stammered. "Jest lookin' to spare Callie an ill is all."

"Then spare her the ill of your presence on her land. After today, you shall not step foot on that farm again." Cane started to protest, but Jonathan crushed the man's brief moment of courage with one look. "If you do not heed my warning," Trenholme continued, enunciating every word as though he were addressing a simpleton, "I shall have you shot for a trespasser. Do you understand me?"

Cane's mouth dropped open, and his head bobbed up and down.

"Good. Then I bid you both a good day, gentlemen."

Smythe seethed with rage as he watched Jonathan leave the tavern. He had read enough of the letter to suspect that one old problem yet remained. If Lord Trenholme were involved, it would not be so easily remedied.

CHAPTER TWENTY-SIX

Nuanced

Callie had just seen the last of her guests to the door, when the housekeeper urgently approached her.

"Madam, the cook just returned from the market. She says Lord Trenholme was seen ridin' into town an hour ago."

Callie looked at Mrs. Bendel in surprise. "Be ye certain?"

"Quite," responded the housekeeper.

A smile tipped the corners of Callie's mouth before she quickly assumed an air of indifference. "Well, 'tis fair time, I dare say."

Mrs. Bendel followed her into the parlor. "Madam, we must make haste to set the room to rights before his Lordship arrives here."

"Miz Bendel be right, missy," said Lucie, hurrying into the room. "The justice ain't gonna be partial to yer gatherin's. As it is, I fear he'll learn of 'em soon enough."

"Nonsense," scoffed Callie. "He will not hear of them from the ladies, and we have won Jenkins to our cause."

"'Tis only because the poor boob is so besotted with ye that he keeps a closed mouth. But Lord Trenholme..." Mrs. Bendel shook her head. "He just seems to sense things. You would do better to—" The housekeeper stopped midsentence as a wide-eyed Lucie tugged at her arm and she looked over to find Jonathan standing in the doorway with the darkest look she had ever seen. She sucked in her breath sharply. "Uh, madam," she squeaked out.

With her back to the entrance as she moved a chair into place, Callie was oblivious to the housekeeper's strangled warning. "No need to worry about Lord Trenholme," she continued on blindly. "All he will hear is that I am having tea parties. Men never see what is beneath their noses unless 'tis pointed out to them. In any event, he can be handled. Now help me with this table."

Mrs. Bendel and Lucie thought Jonathan was going to explode at Callie's confident assurance that she could handle her husband. When he silently dismissed them, the housekeeper and Lucie scurried away, happy to leave Callie to her task.

"Mrs. Bendel…Lucie," called Callie impatiently. She turned to see what was keeping the women and nearly swallowed her tongue at the sight of Jonathan. "How—how long have you been there?" she asked haltingly, trying to recall what he might have overheard.

"Long enough," replied Jonathan tightly. "What have you been up to, Callie?"

She gave him a look of wide-eyed innocence. "Just a few tea parties," she replied.

"Tea parties that happen to include some instruction on the law?" When she didn't answer, he thundered: "Just what do you think you are about preaching law to these women?"

Callie drew herself up to stand her ground. "What I am about is informing women who wish to know of their legal rights…rights their menfolk have conveniently forgotten to mention that they have."

"Maybe so, but 'tis not your place to instruct them. 'Tis the duty of their fathers, guardians, and husbands to protect their interests."

"And what if through ignorance or greed or by design they fail to do so?" she challenged. "What man advised Lydia Stanhope to declare herself sole trader in order to save her business from her husband's weakness for gambling? And what man told Hannah Black of her right to claim benefit of clergy to save herself from—"

"Benefit of clergy—where did you learn of that?" demanded Jonathan.

"Mr. Plinn once told me that parliamentary statutes grant any Christian convicted of a felony for the first time the right to plead his clergy and escape punishment."

"Did Mr. Plinn also explain to you that the statutes make no mention of the condition applying to the colonies or to women?"

"It makes no difference," retorted Callie. "According to Lord Randall, the General Assembly passed a law of its own some twenty years ago allowing it and extending the benefit to women, blacks, mulattoes, and Indians."

Jonathan struggled to control his temper. "Hear me well, Callie, contrary to what you colonists would like to believe, only Parliament has the right to pass laws."

"And I told you before, sir, this is not England."

"Tread lightly," he warned sternly. "'Tis treason you speak."

Callie knew she had overstepped and paused to collect herself. "Trenholme, if women waited for their men to protect them—the same men who regard them as nothing more than possessions and servants to be bartered and view marriage as a means to an end—"

"Is this not the way you wish to view your marriage?" interjected Jonathan. "I dare say men alone are not to blame for the ill-use of marriage this day."

Callie's cheeks reddened, and she was momentarily thrown off balance. "Well, most women never have a say," she said, regaining her stride. "They go from being under their fathers' thumbs to being under the authority of their husbands. They cannot set the terms of the marriage as I have."

Jonathan nearly choked on the bold assumption of her last statement. Did she actually think that she commanded him?

"The truth of the matter—" Callie continued.

"The truth of the matter," Jonathan cut in curtly, "is that the menfolk of these ladies will not stand for this interference. I forbid you to hold any more of these 'tea parties.'"

Callie's eyes sparked with anger. "You forbid me! We shall see about that."

As she swept past him, Jonathan caught her arm. "I mean what I say, Callie. No more meetings."

"Or what?" she challenged brashly, pulling her arm free from his grasp.

Jonathan refused to take up the gauntlet. He was tired and hungry after his long journey and in no mood to continue this argument. Instead, he answered: "Now is a poor time to bring attention to yourself."

His tone was low and measured, his manner so serious that she knew this was no idle warning. A chill ran down her spine. "What do you mean?" she asked. "Is something amiss?"

Jonathan took the worn, folded parchment from his pocket. "This letter came for you. 'Tis from Mae Bailey."

Callie looked at him with a mixture of surprise and suspicion as she took the missive from him. "How did you come by it?"

"It was delivered to the farm, and Cane brought it to the tavern hoping to find someone who could read it to him. Justice Smythe was there and was happy to oblige. Luckily, I had stopped by the tavern for refreshment on my way here and laid claim to the letter. I am not sure how much of it Smythe had time to read, but this letter is enough to indict you and Whithers should he get his hands on it again. I would suggest that you read it and burn it immediately."

Callie felt the blood drain from her face. She nodded and hurried off to her bedchamber.

Jonathan lost no time gathering together the household staff to sternly inform them that if there were any more social gatherings without his prior approval, they could expect very unpleasant consequences. The servants sheepishly exchanged glances of the guilty during Jonathan's lecture, and, by the time he had dismissed them, he was certain of having put the fear of God into them.

At supper, he was greeted by Callie's empty chair, which faintly amused him; the lock struck on her bedroom door decidedly did not.

The next morning, when Jonathan encountered Callie's empty chair at breakfast, he beckoned the housekeeper. "Mrs. Bendel, please tell my wife that her presence is required at the table *now*," he commanded in no uncertain terms.

The housekeeper looked at him in surprise. "Lady Trenholme is not here, sir. She has gone off to see to her farm."

Jonathan was in a temper when he, once again, called the servants together. After the dressing down he had given them the previous day, they were treading lightly around him and were dismayed to find themselves in the middle of yet another dispute between Lord and Lady Trenholme. They withered beneath his glare as he fired questions at them. When did Lady Trenholme leave? Did she travel alone? When was she returning? Why was he not informed that she had disobeyed his orders?

"Beggin' yer pardon, sir," spoke up Mrs. Bendel timidly. "Lady Trenholme said yer instructions were that she was free to leave upon yer return."

Lucie nodded. "I tol' her ye wouldna like her goin' off without ye, Mister Justice, but ye knows how Missy Callie twists words to gets her way."

Jonathan continued to fix the nervous group with a stern eye, but he had to allow that Lucie was right. Callie had an uncanny ability to turn words to her advantage when it suited her needs. It had taken him months to catch on to her tricks. A staff of short acquaintance was certainly no match for her.

"Jenkins, see to my horse," he ordered.

A half hour later, Jonathan was galloping along the Yorktown road. His anger flared anew. By defying his orders, not only had Callie made it appear to the servants that he was not in control of his own wife, but she had also put herself at risk by traveling to her farm without his protection. In the time he had spent away from her, he had forgotten how exasperating she could be.

CHAPTER TWENTY-SEVEN

The Plan

Callie shielded her eyes with her hand against the morning sun. Memories—good, bad, and indifferent—washed over her, as she surveyed the dismal, blackened landscape of what had once been her farm. Only the tobacco barn stood as a poignant reminder. There was so much to be done in so short a time she hardly knew where to start.

"Where are the cold boxes?" she asked Old Joe.

"Yonder where da wind can't whip 'em. Don't ye worry none. The tobaccy seedlin's is safe."

"How long do we have?"

"'Til after da second full moon, I expect."

By Callie's calculations that meant she had six, maybe seven weeks to build suitable living quarters and cultivate the fields. It was a tall order but one she was determined to fill whatever the cost.

"Since we will require only two for now, we shall start with the cabins today," she said. "Tell the workers to unload the supplies and timber that we brought from the mill. Then tear down Cane's shack. I will not house even a field hand there. If the chimneys from the old structures are sound, make use of them and build the cabins around them. That should save time."

"Yes, missy." Old Joe grinned as she continued to bark out orders. At first, he had feared that her new life might have spoiled her instincts and spunk, but his Missy Callie was back again.

Within a few hours, one of the cabins was half finished. Callie busied herself with restoring the cornfield. Above the din of hammers and saws, Old Joe could be heard humming a spiritual and before long, the workers had joined in.

Callie closed her eyes and leaned on the hoe, giving herself up to the rhythm of the music. It was the first real peace she had known for a very long time. This was where her place was, she decided, lifting her face to the warmth of the March sun. She didn't belong in town and most certainly not in England. She belonged to the earth—this earth—where she answered to no one save God and nature.

Callie's sense of contentment faded as an image of Jonathan suddenly floated before her mind's eye. The frequency and ease with which the man trespassed upon her consciousness was disconcerting to her. Over the course of his long absence, she had actually missed him for reasons that went beyond her farm. "Why can he not return to England and leave me to my own," she muttered aloud to herself.

With a sigh, Callie opened her eyes to find the very subject of her thoughts glowering down at her in person. She started in surprise, reality and fantasy at odds for a few moments. But the dark emotion on Jonathan's face was real enough.

"What be ye doing here?" she asked in astonishment.

"I might inquire the same of you," he replied tightly.

Callie evaded his hard gaze and returned to her hoeing. "I know not your meaning."

Jonathan was in no mood to be trifled with, and he snatched the hoe from her hands and pitched it beyond her reach. "I warned you not to come here without me."

"You warned me to wait until your return, not your escort," she responded coolly.

"God's blood, woman, you knew full well my intent."

"Did I? Perhaps you should have been clearer."

"I had assumed—"

"That was your mistake, sir. One should not assume," said Callie, promptly throwing his words back in his face. She felt a measure of satisfaction when she saw him bristle. "Besides, Cane is gone and no longer a threat."

Jonathan didn't know if he was angrier because she had defied him or because she was so casual about her safety, and he struggled with an intense desire to shake some sense into her.

"You little fool, who knows who or what roams these desolate woods? What is so bloody important about this farm to take such a risk?"

Callie gazed at the landscape around her. "It is where I belong," she replied soberly. "This is where my family is buried. It is my past and my future and it needs be my present." She looked up at him with eyes free of guile or mischief. "This land is who I am, Trenholme— dust to dust like the Good Book says."

Jonathan was struck by her quiet reverence and by the conviction and eloquence of her words. He had a feeling that he had just gotten a glimpse into her soul, and, for the first time, he understood her.

"It does not change the fact that it is too dangerous for you to be here alone, Callie."

"I am not alone. Old Joe and the workers be with me."

"One old man and a couple of field workers armed with the tools of their trade are little defense."

"I can take care of myself," Callie responded stubbornly. "I might remind you, sir, that I was doing quite well before I made your acquaintance."

"Luck was with you then. Now there is more danger about."

"What danger?"

Jonathan hesitated for a moment. To explain what he knew about the situation with the French and Indians might invite questions into his actual whereabouts for the past month and jeopardize his mission.

"Do not past attacks in the area spell danger enough?" he asked. "That aside, you should not be here alone with a handful of workers anyway."

"Why not?"

"Because you are a—"

"A child?" threw out Callie angrily.

"No, because you are a woman, dammit, and a very desirable one at that."

Dressed in plain blue linsey-woolsey, an apron tied around her waist, her hair bound in a cap, and dirt streaked across her cheek, she had more the appearance of a field hand than a lady. But there was an earthy sensuality about her that fired the blood in his veins. He pulled Callie into his arms, and his mouth sought hers with the urgency of a man too long denied. Feeling her beginning to panic, Jonathan forced himself to a slower pace. His kiss became less demanding, instead coaxing and caressing with a care given to the arousal of his partner.

Callie soon felt carried away on a wave of oblivion, her careful control ebbing. They might as well have been the only living creatures present, for neither was cognizant of any other existence. There was no sense of time. His lips against her mouth, her ear, her throat pummeled her defenses with absolute accuracy. She leaned into him, and Jonathan eased her toward a tree out of view of the others. As he hastened to lift her skirt and shift, Callie suddenly stiffened and pushed him away.

"No, stop. We cannot do this," she gasped.

Her response to his actions had been hesitant at first, but Jonathan knew he hadn't mistaken desire on her part. "Why not?" he asked in bewilderment.

"It isn't part of the plan," said Callie.

"Then make it part of the bloody plan," he responded impatiently.

When he sought to embrace her again, she sidestepped him. "'Tis not possible. It would only complicate the situation."

"What situation? Look, Callie, whatever the problem, we'll deal with it later." He reached out to draw her back to him, but she turned and ran off across the field leaving Jonathan to stare after her in astonishment. "What plan?" he yelled out as she disappeared from sight.

Old Joe frowned in consternation as Callie rushed in from the field, her face flushed. His features cleared instantly when Jonathan strode into view, and he grinned knowingly.

"'Tis glad we is to see ye, sir," he greeted when Jonathan walked up. "Ye jest set yerself down on dat log whilst Miss Callie dish ye up some of dat rabbit stew."

Callie glared at Old Joe as Jonathan sat down, showing no inclination to leave. When both men looked expectantly at her, Callie let out a huff of annoyance and reluctantly scooped some stew on a plate. She affected a cool disposition as she handed it to him, but Jonathan knew better when she refused to meet his eyes. If he had learned anything about her, it was that she was not very good at masking her emotions.

When Jonathan had finished eating and got to his feet, Callie eyed him guardedly. Would he insist upon her going back to town with him? No matter what he said or did, she had already decided that she would stand her ground on this.

As he approached her, she dug in her heels. Instead of engaging her, he wordlessly walked past her to Old Joe. Surprised and apprehensive, Callie watched the two men talk for a few minutes. When Old Joe signaled for the laborers to stop work, her chest heaved with anger and she clenched her fists. No one was going to interfere with her reconstruction—not even her husband!

She stomped over to tell Jonathan just that when, to her astonishment, he took off his coat and waistcoat and ordered two of the workers to begin construction on a second dwelling. Callie was dumbfounded. The man simply wasn't to be figured.

An hour before twilight, the thatch roof was added to two small clapboard huts. They were crude, but they would provide shelter.

"'Tis too dangerous to travel these roads after dark. We shall all stay the night here," said Jonathan, unknowingly echoing Callie's intentions. "Old Joe, you and the field hands take one hut; Callie and I shall take the other."

At this, Callie's head shot up, and she quit her task. In her planning, Jonathan had not been included. Once he had arrived, she had given no thought to it, never considering that he would stay the day to work.

"The night promises to be cold, so have a care to light a fire," he continued. "Luckily, the chimneys are in good working order."

He gave the field workers instructions to finish unloading the wagon, then he and Old Joe went to see to the horses.

As Jonathan had predicted, with the setting of the sun, the air quickly turned cold, and Callie shivered as she jabbed at the sparks on the hearth in a vain attempt to force them into a respectable fire.

When Trenholme entered the hut, he frowned as he took in the nature of the supplies that the workers had transferred from the wagon. It suddenly dawned on him that staying the night had been Callie's plan all along. Weary to the bone and not trusting his temper, he said nothing. Tomorrow would be soon enough to tell her that she was not going to be residing on the premises, he decided.

Callie turned and caught the scowl on his face. Mistaking the nature of his disapproval, she quickly explained: "I took the liberty of charging the supplies to your account."

Jonathan walked over to the hearth and stooped down to raise a fire of greater warmth. "So I heard," he remarked humorlessly.

"I intend to see you fully recompensed when the tobacco is next harvested."

Jonathan didn't respond. As he continued to work the fire, a silence stretched between them. It wasn't like him to say nothing, thought Callie nervously. This new, silent anger was more unnerving to her than his outbursts of temper. Words she could parry, thoughts she couldn't.

"I am within my rights. I am your wife after all," she continued.

Flames leaped to life, and Jonathan stood up to face her. "'Tis a fact you seem wont to remember only when it serves your purpose," he observed critically.

"Regardless of the circumstances of our marriage, I am entitled to some considerations and amenities."

"You are entitled to my name, my bed, and whatever else I choose to give you," he reminded her coolly. "I trust you know the penalty for forgery, madam."

Callie's brow furrowed in bewilderment. "How mean you?"

"It is of the note you presented to the merchants that I speak."

"Oh. Well, you were gone for such a long time, and I needed to start—"

"You presented a false note of credit."

"No, I made the request in my own hand and affixed the seal from your ring—"

"You used my signet ring?"

"Yes."

"You went into my desk drawers?"

"Yes—no—I mean I was looking for note paper."

Jonathan struggled to hold on to his temper. He had left behind the ring to protect his disguise as a French trader while on his mission, never imagining that Callie would find it and be so bold to use it. He should have known better.

"So you see I forged no signature," Callie was saying, proud of her cleverness. "I cannot be held responsible if the merchants made assumptions upon sight of your seal."

Once again, Jonathan was amazed by her calculating manner. "Madam, I suggest you consult your law book more closely."

"Why?"

"You would find that the seal from my signet ring is considered a signature," he informed her crisply. "Your use of it counts as forgery. Were I a lesser husband I would beat you within an inch of your life for theft. The court is not so lenient. It would see you confined to a day of shame in the pillory and an 'F' or a 'T' branded upon your forehead."

Callie looked at him, searching his features for any sign of guile. Finding none, the smug expression faded from her face. "Surely, you would not report your wife…would you?"

"I am a justice of the court, madam. I cannot have my wife running amuck ignoring the very laws that I must enforce against all other people," he lectured sternly. "You cannot shade the law when it does not suit your purpose, Callie. If you continue on this course, I will not be able to shield you, and Justice Smythe is biding his time waiting for that moment. With that note from Mrs. Bailey, it may be at hand."

Sobered by the gravity of his tone and demeanor, Callie nodded visibly apprehensive.

Satisfied that he had put the fear of God in her, Jonathan made a bed for them before the fire. She picked up a blanket to retire to the far corner of the room, but at the no-nonsense look he gave her, she thought better of it. She couldn't afford to antagonize him any further and lay down on the pallet, putting as much space between them as she could.

The wind picked up and whistled through the chinks in the walls. The day had been unseasonably warm, and in her haste to be on her way that morning, Callie hadn't thought to pack a cloak and shivered beneath her blanket.

Jonathan pulled her closer to him. "Be still, Callie, I seek only to warm you," he said when she put up a struggle.

He rearranged the blankets around them for more insulation. When he lay back down on his side and rested his arm across her, she held her back stiffly to him. As the heat from his body began to warm her, she snuggled closer before giving into the drug of sleep. Jonathan smiled and tightened his arm around her.

The next morning, Callie stretched languidly beneath the covers, loath to come fully awake. She felt warm and peaceful. Suddenly remembering the circumstances, she quickly roused to find that Jonathan had left the cabin. Wondering what he was up to, she jumped up from the pallet, tidied her appearance, and hurried outside. She was much surprised to find him in earnest conversation with Lord Randall.

The earl broke into a smile when he saw her. "Callie, my dear, how well you look. The state of marriage appears to be agreeing with you," he said with a chuckle.

Callie blushed. "Lord Randall, how come you to be here?" she asked.

"Lord Randall has brought the loan of three of his field hands and an overseer," interjected Jonathan.

Callie looked off in the distance to see four more men working the fields. "My thanks for your kindness, sir. I shall try not to require their services for too long." She looked at Jonathan. "We shall have to construct another hut."

"How so?" asked Lord Randall. "I should think these two to suffice very well for the workers that you have."

"I think you misunderstand, sir. I intend to—"

"He understands quite well," cut in Jonathan before Lord Randall could tip his hand. He hustled the surprised earl to his carriage. "I shall see you on the morrow, sir."

"Oh, yes, quite," mumbled Lord Randall, climbing into the conveyance.

As the carriage took off, Callie eyed Jonathan suspiciously. "Why did you chase away Lord Randall? What was he about to say that you didn't want me to hear?"

Jonathan hesitated. "That you will not be staying here this night or any other night," he said, bracing himself for the storm. "The farm is in capable hands now. The overseer shall see to the cultivation of the fields, and Old Joe will tend the tobacco seedlings."

Her hands on her hips, her blue eyes blazing, Callie declared resolutely: "I am not leaving."

Jonathan returned her gaze unflinchingly. "I am bound that you are. I will not have my wife at risk, nor shall she make her lodgings in a hut. Now, you can either make a dignified departure, madam, or I shall pick you up and throw you into the wagon. Which shall it be?"

Callie's determination waned in the face of his ultimatum. As he advanced toward her, she scrambled to take her seat on top of the wagon.

CHAPTER TWENTY-EIGHT

Necessity Makes Not the Best Bargain

Tension hung heavy in the house, and the staff, including Lucie, walked softly.

The divide between Callie and Jonathan seemed to be growing wider. Meals were largely eaten in silence, and he noticed that she wasn't wearing her wedding band. The gesture was not lost on him. He had expected Callie to be angry when he refused to allow her to remain at the farm, but he hadn't thought that she would carry it on this long. But, then, it wasn't the first time he had underestimated her stubbornness.

Sitting across from her at supper this night, she looked especially fetching to him. The light from the candles and the fire in the fireplace reflected the highlights in her hair and made her eyes sparkle like sapphires, and the emerald-green gown brought out the sensual earth tones of her coloring. Neither did he miss the effect of the laced stays as her breasts swelled provocatively above the bodice. It was a twisting torment to his sensibilities each time she leaned forward.

With other women of his acquaintance, the taunting show was a deliberate part of the game, calculated to titillate and end in a mutually agreed upon dalliance. With Callie, he knew the effect to be unconscious, an uncomfortable nod to fashion, and he struggled to make his interest less apparent. If he weren't careful, he would send her running back to her buckskins, he thought wryly.

Jonathan furrowed his brow in perplexity. The few times she had let her guard down he knew there to be a spark of desire, but as soon as he moved to ignite it, she retreated. If he had been concerned about keeping her at arm's length to protect the secrecy of his activities, he needn't have worried. Callie maintained a distance between them these days quite well. Her inexperience and distrust of men might be a consideration, but her mention the other day of some plan gave him to wonder what else was at work.

Fighting her own battles, Callie toyed with her food eating little. While she was still angry with Jonathan for taking her away from her farm, more troubling to her were the thoughts of that day and night they had spent there, for they refused to be banished. She could still feel the press of his kiss upon her lips and the warmth and safety of his arms around her. With each touch, he was changing the dynamics of their relationship, and every minute she remained under his roof was a danger to her goal.

Callie finally gave up the pretense of eating. She excused herself and hastily left the dining room. As Jonathan watched her leave, he wondered how to break through that wall.

A storm blew up later in the night, which only added to Jonathan's restless mood. He unconsciously swirled the amber liquid in the brandy glass as he sullenly stared out the drawing room window. The servants had all retired; the house was deathly still. He swallowed the brandy in a single gulp and set the glass aside, then purposefully strode into the foyer to the foot of the stairs. With his hand on the banister and one foot on the step, he stared up the staircase. He was the master; Callie was his wife. Yet, here he stood waiting to be beckoned!

He turned away in frustration. His pledge to let her take the initiative hung over him like a curse. Judging from her mood at supper and the bolt on her door, there was as much chance of her inviting him into her bed as snowballs in hell. A furious clap of thunder shook the windows, stirring Jonathan's already heightened emotions. God's blood! If he waited for Callie to make the first move, he would be an old man. He turned on his heel and bounded up the stairs.

Slumped in a wing chair, tapping her fingers on the arms of the chair, Callie was faring no better in harnessing her emotions. Sleep had been impossible, and she no longer tried.

There came the trying of the door knob and she tensed.

"Callie, unlock the door," ordered Jonathan. "We have a need to talk."

"I am abed. Go away," she called back.

A splintering of wood suddenly shattered the silence as Jonathan kicked open the door. Callie jumped up from her chair incredulous. Was he mad, drunk, or both? she wondered in wide-eyed alarm. But the firm set of his mouth, unwavering gaze, and resolute manner bespoke more a man of purpose than of madness as he crossed the room to her. His handsome features held no anger or censure, just a calm assurance of one having come to an irrevocable decision.

She gasped when he wordlessly scooped her up in his arms. "What are you doing? Put me down!" she yelled.

The commotion brought Jenkins, Lucie, the cook, and Mrs. Bendel on the run from their quarters on the third floor, and all gaped in astonishment as Jonathan carried a loudly protesting Callie to his chamber. To the disappointment of the staff, he kicked the door shut on them, forcing them to rely on whatever they could divine through the walls.

When Jonathan set Callie on her feet again, she quickly moved away from him.

"Are you mad!" she cried. "What the deuce ails ye? What must the servants think of such a display to say nothing of the owner upon the report of his damaged property?" She unleashed days of pent-up frustration that actually had little to do with his actions of the moment.

Jonathan said nothing as he waited for her to finish her tirade as a father might ride out a child's tantrum. Finally drained of all protest, Callie moved to the door. When she pulled it open, he reached above her to slam it shut.

She whirled about, furious. "I cannot fathom you, sir. What is the meaning of this?"

"Some things need to be settled between us, Callie, and I mean to see them settled tonight," he stated unequivocally.

As she looked up into strong, angular features and gold-flecked brown eyes, the air seemed to go out of her and she swallowed hard. "What things?"

Jonathan took her firmly by the shoulders. "I think you know."

Before she could react, he lowered his head and swiftly took command with a kiss that was intimate and sensual. She put up no resistance, but when he moved a hand to further engage her, Callie broke away from him.

Jonathan let out a deep sigh of frustration. "Callie, look at me. Can you honestly deny that have no desire to lie with me?"

Callie slowly lifted her eyes to him, clearly conflicted. "No," she said in a quiet tone.

"Yet, you thwart my every attempt. Why? If you are afraid—"

"It is not that."

"Then, pray tell, what is it?"

"It is not part of the plan."

"That again. What plan?" he asked impatiently.

"You know of it. You are to go back to England and I to my farm," said Callie.

Jonathan looked at her in disbelief. "This is why you hold yourself distant from me, testing my days and nights? Madam, I fail to find the problem."

"Surely you see that, under the circumstances, nothing must occur between us."

"No, madam, I do not." He pulled her back into his arms and caressed her neck with feathery kisses.

"Jonathan, stop. I cannot think," pleaded Callie, her senses swirling "Did ye not hear what I said?"

"Aye, ye have a plan. But I have learned that life doesn't always go according to plan," he murmured huskily against her ear. "And something very much is going to occur between us this night."

He ran his hands over her body, feeling the curves through the fabric of her shift, and it was with some difficulty that she disengaged herself from him again.

"Callie, what is the problem?" demanded Jonathan.

"If we engage in this act, I will not be able to file for an annulment."

"What does it matter now?"

"You know the law. A single woman has more rights. When you leave—"

"God's teeth! If that is all that keeps you from my bed, woman, I will grant you whatever rights you wish. You will have no need of an annulment." He tried to move her to the bed, but she continued to balk. "What is it now?"

"After the misunderstanding of the terms of the marriage, perhaps we should put this in writing," said Callie.

Jonathan regarded her with exasperation. "Must everything be a negotiation with you?"

"It was you who said to always bargain with the principal and to never assume—"

The rest of her words were lost when he captured her lips again in a kiss that ended all debate. He was done with argument. The electrical energy of the storm that raged without sparked the heightened tension within, igniting the smoldering passion that hung between them. And Callie finally gave into it. Her arms went around him, and she ardently returned his caress. As her body melted into his,

Jonathan quickly steered her onto the bed before she could raise any new points for discussion.

She felt a moment of uncertainty when he shed his clothes and lay down beside her. Sensing her withdrawal, he brought her into the circle of his arms and resumed his well-honed practice of seduction and arousal.

She stiffened again when he started to remove her shift. "Mrs. Whithers said a lady of good moral standing does not remove articles of clothing during such times," she said, primly lowering the garment to below her thighs.

Jonathan looked at her in surprise. Since when was Callie Hastings concerned about anyone's opinion of her moral standing? But he could see that she was nervous and conceded the point without comment, however much it would hinder him.

When he slipped his hand underneath the garment to explore her body, she started but didn't object. She sucked in her breath as he lightly caressed, fondled, and massaged points that shocked and excited and sent impulses through her body she didn't know existed. Overwhelmed by the intensity of the sensations that washed over her, she started to pull back.

"Surely, this must be wicked," she gasped.

Jonathan assured her that it wasn't, strategically plying her with kisses and further stimulating erogenous areas until she didn't care if it was wicked or not.

He directed her hand to him, showing her how to stroke him. At the reaction of his member, she jerked her hand away. He coaxed it back. It would seem that Whithers had omitted the finer points of this instruction as well, thought Jonathan wryly. In truth, she hadn't, but as it was another one of those lessons Callie didn't see as pertaining to her goal, she hadn't thought the need to listen to it, this being a temporary marriage of convenience.

Shyly, she followed Jonathan's instruction until he could no longer hold back. Making certain that she was ready as well, he quickly positioned her beneath him. As he entered her, Callie tensed and uttered a cry at the discomfort, and the web of arousal that he had so carefully woven around her threatened to dissolve with her distress.

He quickly slowed his movement, soothing and encouraging her with words of assurance and distracting her with caresses until she began to move with him. The discomfort eased, and Callie soon matched Jonathan's movements as wave after wave of pleasure intensified with each thrust before reaching a climatic tension that begged for release. When it finally came, Callie felt it from head to toe, the raw force of it leaving her shaken. Jonathan's release came minutes later, and any image that might have lingered of Callie the child was banished from his mind forever.

Neither spoke, as they lay side-by-side catching their breath in the aftermath, allowing the moment to settle around them.

"I am going to go to hell," declared Callie solemnly.

Jonathan looked over at her. "How so, madam?"

"The Reverend said that to enjoy the pleasures of the flesh is to follow the path to hell. Surely, I am damned."

Jonathan laughed. "Were that the case, my dear, you would know plenty of company. And you might be surprised to see who precedes you on that path."

"Mrs. Whithers said that only a lady of low morals experiences any satisfaction in—in what we just did." Callie didn't remember much of the old matron's instructions about the marriage bed, but she remembered that. She turned her head to Jonathan. "Trenholme, do you think me a lady of low morals?" she asked him worriedly.

"Whithers seems to have said a lot of things," replied Jonathan with a touch of annoyance. "To allay your concerns, my dear, you are just as I desire you to be in such matters. In this, Whithers is wrong. And so also is the Reverend. A body would not be capable of such feelings if it were not meant to be."

"But he says it is the devil's temptation testing the weak and tricking the stalwart."

Jonathan snorted. "The Reverend is trying to keep unmarried lasses in line and married women from straying from husbands who do not meet the challenge."

Callie fell silent for a minute as she considered all of this. "In that case, sir, you will not find me wanting to stray," she said in all seriousness.

Jonathan was hard pressed to suppress a chuckle. "Indeed, madam, I shall endeavor to make certain you never feel the need."

She was lying nestled contentedly against him in the circle of his arms, when another recollection and a new concern suddenly assailed her. She bolted upright and bounded out of bed.

"Callie, what are you doing?" asked Jonathan in surprise. "What is amiss?"

"It has just come to me that Mrs. Whithers said the purpose of the marriage bed is for procreation."

"Well, I wouldn't say that it was for that purpose alone," he replied, amused. "Now, come back to bed."

"Jonathan, we cannot come together again."

Jonathan looked heavenward for patience. "Callie, I thought we had settled the matter of an annulment. If you wish, I will pen a bill of rights."

"It is not that."

"What then?"

"I cannot get with child."

"'Twould be hardly a scandal. 'Tis a natural condition that usually follows marriage," he quipped.

"I have a farm to see to, and you are returning to England. A child is not part of the plan and would only complicate matters."

Jonathan groaned. The plan again. "Callie, hold on—"

But Callie wasn't listening and ran out of the room.

He blinked in astonishment and jumped out of bed to rush after her. "Callie...Callie, come back here!"

He was about to run into the hall, when he encountered a wide-eyed Jenkins taking in the whole curious scene.

"'Tis just dawn, Milord, but do ye wish me to help ye to dress for the day?" asked the dumbfounded valet.

Realizing that he had no clothes on, Jonathan glared at the man and slammed the door on him.

As Jenkins scampered off to report this latest development to the staff, Jonathan was busy trying to figure out how the bloody hell he was going to fix this latest dilemma. Abstinence was out of the question now.

Over the next several days, Jonathan called up every trick to woo and seduce Callie, stealing opportunities to kiss her and touch her, putting his hands intimately on her waist to help her into or out of a carriage, tucking her arm in his when they walked, or putting an arm around her in a casual embrace. Callie was not immune to his efforts but stopped just short of his ultimate goal.

It was not an easy task. His slightest touch called forth the memory of the sensations of their night of intimacy, and she was beginning to wish she had not partaken of the fruit at all; it was too hard not to want more, particularly with him being so much in her presence. As the tension built, the household staff found themselves treading softly once again.

It was an intolerable situation, and Callie did the only thing she could think of. She went to see Mrs. Whithers for advice.

Mrs. Whithers blushed and blinked in astonishment as Callie quite frankly put forth her problem and informed the older lady that, by the way, she—Mrs. Whithers—had had a few facts wrong about the marriage bed.

"So unless you have a solution, Madam, Trenholme and I shall just have to continue to withhold ourselves from each other," Callie ended pragmatically. She sighed with a measure of desperation. "I pray that his return to England is soon."

Mrs. Whithers was shocked on so many levels she didn't know what to say. After all this time, she still hadn't gotten used to Callie's candor. As Callie looked at her expectantly, she cast about for a way to address the delicate matter.

"Well," she began haltingly, "an engagement of this nature does not always result in such a condition. There is always the possibility that one party may not be able to contribute in such a manner as needed to create progeny." It wasn't the best advice, but it was all the poor woman could think of at the moment to keep peace in the marriage.

After some thought however, Callie found the information most helpful. She returned to the house and walked into Jonathan's bedchamber, surprising him.

He smiled. "Madam, to what do I owe this visit?" he asked hopefully.

"You have known women before in the biblical sense, have you not?" she asked.

"Yes," he replied tentatively, wondering where this was leading.

"How many?"

"Enough," he responded shortly. He had no wish to discuss his other affairs with anyone, least of all with his wife.

"Have you any issue?" Callie continued to question him.

"If you mean children, no."

"Good. Then I can share your bed."

Jonathan's brow furrowed in confusion as he tried to follow her logic. "Madam, while I welcome your change of heart, you shall have to explain it."

"'Tis plain enough," she responded matter-of-factly. "Mrs. Whithers said that some parties are not up to the task of creation. As you have been with women before and have not produced any issue, 'tis safe to assume that you are unable to do so, and I need not worry to share your bed."

Jonathan stared at her dumbfounded. He didn't know if he was more shocked by her lopsided logic, annoyed that she had discussed their private affairs with his old governess, or angry that she had called into question his virility. But when Callie smiled up at him with open invitation and took his hand to lead him to the bed, he forgot his annoyance and wounded pride quickly enough. He still had to settle the matter of England with her, but that could wait, he decided.

CHAPTER TWENTY-NINE

Trust vs. Trust

The governor was giving a dinner ball in honor of Major Washington before the young man departed with a colonial army to confront the French in the Ohio Valley, and carriages lined the circular drive in front of the Governor's Palace to drop guests at the gate entrance.

Callie and Jonathan's carriage drew up and the footman opened the door. When Jonathan stepped out of the carriage and reached out a hand to her, Callie knew her first real misgivings. She had never thought to be an invited guest here, and the distance that she had traveled from her world to this was suddenly overwhelming to her.

Seeing her uncertainty, Jonathan moved to reassure her. "You will find no one here this night to rival you, my dear. Major Washington shall have cause to regret your presence for the attention you are sure to command away from him."

Callie gave a nervous laugh. "I fear, sir, you are biased."

Jonathan helped her from the carriage, his gaze roaming lazily over her. "Washington will not be alone in regretting the attention you will attract," he said, his voice husky.

He lowered his head and was about to kiss her, when the footman loudly cleared his throat.

Callie giggled. "I believe we are delaying other guests."

"The man has no humor," quipped Jonathan as they walked through the royal gates.

"Indeed, it seems to be an affliction of Englanders," she replied, giving him a sidelong glance.

Jonathan raised a brow. "As stubbornness is an affliction of colonists," he shot back.

Another footman stood at the palace doors and directed them into the entrance hall. Callie stared in awe at the arsenal of pistols, muskets, and swords. Arranged on the walls and the ceiling in grand display, they, nevertheless, stood in readiness to protect the king's authority from uprisings against the colony or foreign invasion.

From here, Callie and Jonathan followed other guests through an arched doorway and up the grand staircase to the audience room where the governor greeted his guests.

"Lady Trenholme, how pleased I am to see you in attendance this night," said the governor when it came her turn. "If I may say, you look quite lovely."

Callie lowered her eyes, feeling self conscious. "You are too kind, sir," she replied.

The governor shifted his attention to Jonathan, catching the young man's admiring eye on his wife. "It would seem that your marriage has benefitted us *all*, Lord Trenholme," he remarked pointedly.

Jonathan stiffened, still annoyed by the interference of the governor and the General Assembly in the matter. "Indeed," he responded in a stilted tone.

Callie found the exchange and Jonathan's reaction odd and tried to ask him about it, but he brushed it off and quickly escorted her back down the stairs to the ballroom. Upon entering the room with its high arched ceiling and elaborate moldings, Callie forgot all else in the grandeur of her surroundings. The candles in the crystal chandelier bathed the bright blue room in a soft glow, musicians played, and couples danced to a minuet. She had thought the holiday ball at Raleigh Tavern special, but this was magical.

A tall, strapping young man with reddish brown hair and penetrating blue-gray eyes approached to greet them. An inch or two taller than Jonathan and some years younger, he was attractive and carried himself with an air of confidence.

"Major Washington, I should like you to make the acquaintance of my wife," said Jonathan.

George Washington bowed gracefully for a man of his size and took Callie's hand in a courtly manner. "Lady Trenholme, permit me to say that were all the eligible young ladies as lovely as you, I might not be so quick to extricate myself from their presence."

His smile was warm, his manner sincere, and Callie felt the familiar heat rush to her face at the compliment. "You are too gracious, sir," she responded, "though I fear 'tis not the young ladies you seek to avoid but rather their mothers' intentions."

Washington's wide set eyes twinkled with humor. "I dare say there is more than an ounce of truth in your observation, Milady. And now, Lady Trenholme, if I may intrude upon your good nature, might I have a word with your husband in confidence?"

"But of course, Major Washington," replied Callie.

"I pledge it to be a short time. A lady of your charms should not be left too long to her own devices, else Lord Trenholme may have to fight his way through the throng of admirers."

"Most assuredly so, sir, were my wife to make use of her fan," quipped Jonathan.

Callie knew that he was thinking of the holiday ball when three young men had misinterpreted her desire for solitude for a summons, and, again, she felt the damnable flush stain her features.

As Jonathan and Washington moved off, she could hear Washington's hearty laughter, and she gave Jonathan a mental kick as she rightly guessed that he was explaining the miscue to the major.

"Might I assume a lady in distress before me, madam?" inquired a voice lightly behind her.

Callie turned to see Charles Smythe and smiled, relieved to encounter someone he knew. "I must confess to being a bit overwhelmed," she replied. "The palace is so grand and this room so beautiful."

He looked about him. "I suppose. This must be your first time here."

She nodded. "Is it so obvious?"

He smiled. "It is refreshing to find one who still appreciates the splendor. I fear the rest of us have become rather blind to it. 'Tis an unfortunate symptom of entitlement." Smythe paused. "But where is Lord Trenholme? Surely, he is not so foolish as to leave your side."

"Major Washington requested a private audience. He should not be long. And how does this evening find you, Mr. Smythe?"

"Alas, much better. I had thought to pass a tedious evening until I saw you." His gaze slowly moved over her. "Permit me to say that you look stunning tonight, Milady."

"You are most gracious, sir," she replied, still feeling uneasy with such compliments. "Will you be dining this evening?"

"No, I fear I must take my leave soon. Business beckons me elsewhere. I came only to pay my respects to Major Washington. May we meet again, Lady Trenholme, when time is less pressing."

Nearby, Jonathan was hard pressed to keep his mind on the matters at hand as his eye found Callie in conversation with a young man. It was the man he had seen talking with her at the Christmas services. She was smiling, and Jonathan felt a stab of irritation for it seemed to him that she was a little too familiar with the fellow.

Washington soon became aware that he no longer held Jonathan's attention and was amused. "I think, sir, that were the lady my wife, I would lay claim to her before she is overwhelmed by admirers. We can talk of this matter on the morrow."

Jonathan gave the major a grin that was at once grateful and sheepish, and he immediately started off. Jealousy was an emotion that he was unaccustomed to experiencing. That he should be that settled was one of several revelations he had encountered since his marriage.

He hadn't gotten very far across the room when Lilibeth intercepted him. "Lord Trenholme, how wonderful to see you again." She spoke in a breathy whisper, coyly batting her eyelashes and waving her fan.

Jonathan looked down at her, barely registering the low-cut neckline. "Miss Sanders," he acknowledged.

When his gaze immediately returned to Callie, Lilibeth's rouged lips turned down in a pout. She made another attempt to engage him, but his attention remained fixed.

"Who is that with my wife?" he asked, as the man took Callie's hand and lingeringly pressed his lips to it.

Lilibeth huffed and nearly stamped her foot in vexation. "'Tis Justice Smythe's son Charles," she replied peevishly. "He divides his time between a plantation up north in the colony and here. I hear tell that—" Lilibeth stopped in midsentence as a thought cunning and malicious came to her. "I hear tell that Callie was seen with him on several occasions while you were away," she said with sly innocence.

Jonathan's features darkened, and he immediately set off at a determined pace. Lilibeth smiled. She had overheard her uncle comment on the couple's clash of tempers, and her mother had learned the actual circumstances of the marriage from the wife of a burgess. She should have no problem ending this union. If a divorce simply wasn't to be had, she would accept being Jonathan's mistress, she decided. Mistresses of the nobility lived quite well.

Jonathan was only a few yards from Callie in the crowded room, but it seemed to him that she took no notice of anyone else but her admirer. Charles Smythe was the son of a man who would yet hang her and Mae Bailey if given the chance. Was Callie out of her mind? What secrets had she divulged to him? he wondered, suddenly angered by her carelessness.

"Lord Trenholme," hailed Lord Randall, "the governor wishes a word with you and Major Washington."

Jonathan groaned. God's teeth! Was he destined never to reach Callie's side this night? But Callie didn't lack for company. As Charles departed, another admirer stepped in to take his place. To Jonathan's mind, she appeared not to mind her husband's absence one whit. Throwing a last glance at her over his shoulder, he reluctantly followed Lord Randall from the ballroom.

While it was true that Callie begged for no one's attention, she possessed little knowledge of this world and felt increasingly ill at ease in these surroundings. She scanned the crowd for Jonathan, but he seemed not to be anywhere in the room. After an hour, she went in search of her husband, much provoked that he should leave her alone for so long. As she stepped outside the ballroom, she heard masculine voices coming from the top of the grand staircase.

"The traitor must be found," the governor was saying.

"Indeed. The success of our campaign depends upon it," replied another man, whose voice Callie recognized as being that of Major Washington. "The French are expecting a military response. They must not know our approach or the number of our company," he said. "The loss of surprise could be deleterious to the cause."

The governor sighed heavily. "The French must be expelled at all costs. If those devils win the Indians to their side, I fear the massacres we shall see in the colony."

"Neither can we forget that if there is an uprising of the Indians against the colony, so might follow the slaves," interjected Lord Randall.

Callie had heard rumblings of problems with the French on the colony's far western frontier, but she had no idea that matters had progressed to this point. As the men descended the stairs, she quickly ducked back into the ballroom. She had the feeling that they wouldn't welcome her discovery.

When Governor Dinwiddie, Lord Randall, and Major Washington entered the room, a servant announced that supper would be served. Callie again searched for Jonathan, but saw no sign of him.

As people began moving into the next room, Lilibeth came alongside of her. "Good evening, Callie."

Callie eyed the young woman with suspicion. "What do you want, Lilibeth?"

"There is no need to be unpleasant," Lilibeth replied sweetly. "I have accepted the fact that you have won, even though Lord Trenholme was forced to marry you."

"It is no secret that ours began as a marriage of convenience, but no one forces my husband to do anything if he is not so inclined."

Lilibeth put a hand to her mouth in a gesture of surprise. "Oh, dear, then you don't know. Everyone else does. I just imagined that you did as well."

"Know what!" snapped Callie impatiently.

"That the governor and the General Assembly refused to release Lord Trenholme from his obligations here, unless he married you and stopped your meddling in the affairs of the court."

Callie felt the blood drain from her face, and she fought to keep a mask of indifference in place. "Should that have been the case," she said, forcing a complacent smile, "my husband is not regretting the bargain I can assure you—and neither am I—if you understand my meaning. Please excuse me now. I must find my place at the table."

Callie moved on, and Lilibeth's mouth dropped open. This wasn't the response she had expected.

As a footman showed Callie to her seat, it took every ounce of fortitude that she had to maintain her composure. Fool that she was, she thought that she had engineered the marriage and that Jonathan had agreed to it as a favor to her when, in fact, it had been a clever trap laid by the General Assembly. Lord Randall cleverly overturning her objections to marriage by offering her land as a dowry and allowing her to keep ownership; Jonathan's surliness throughout the wedding and his odd exchange with the governor this evening—it all made sense to her now. If she hadn't been so desperate to save her land and escape her stepfather's authority, she might have seen through the ruse.

Mrs. Whithers had tried to warn her that the town fathers would not sit idly by while she dispensed legal advice to their women and pressed their cases in court. Now, too late, she realized the consequences. But not before she had opened her heart again. She looked up then to see Jonathan slip in through the garden door as though trying to avoid notice. She might have found his actions curious, but her emotions were in too much turmoil at the moment to consider anything other than Lilibeth's revelation.

As Jonathan took his seat across the table from Callie, he observed that she was looking strained. He gave her a wink and a smile, but she didn't respond.

The dinner was twelve courses long. As one dish was taken up and another brought in its place, Callie thought it would never end. She barely tasted anything and had difficulty following conversation.

Jonathan tried to catch Callie's eye, but she patently ignored him. Something was wrong. Mayhap she was upset that he had left her too long alone. He had been reluctant to leave her side when they arrived, but he had had no choice, and she seemed to be handling herself well enough. He would make it up to her this night, he thought with a smile at the prospect.

Finally, dinner ended and guests were invited to return to the ballroom to dance. Callie saw Jonathan making his way to her, but Lilibeth diverted him long enough for her to slip away. As she ran out into the night, she gave in to tears. She hadn't even stopped to collect her cloak. How could she have been so foolish to trust him?

As though the night were made for casting doubts, she suddenly recalled the long absences when Jonathan claimed to be advising county courts and the strange meetings over the past month when he was supposedly seeing about supplies for the farm. Yet, each time they visited, she saw little change.

And what of the odd little man dressed in buckskins with whom she had seen Jonathan conversing recently outside a tavern? When she had asked Jonathan about the incident, he shrugged it off and said that she must have mistaken someone else for him. Since they were just coming to terms with their relationship, she had let the matter drop.

Given these questionable events, what she now knew about the truth of the marriage, and the conversation she had overheard between the governor, Lord Randall, and Major Washington, her heart sank. Was Jonathan helping the French to avenge himself on the governor and the General Assembly for forcing him into this union with her?

Once again, she was struck by how little she really knew about her husband. She never did learn the fate of the couple in London who had dared to cross him, but it must have been serious enough for the king to exile a member of nobility. Try as she might, she couldn't consolidate the image of a man of such dastardly deeds with the man who had made love to her with such care and passion. Whatever he was or wasn't capable of, she decided that she was taking no more chances.

The footman at the gate glanced curiously at her. "Be ye well, madam?"

Callie nodded. "I require a carriage," she said.

He signaled a carriage for her and helped her in. By the time the driver pulled up in front of the house, Callie had firmly closed the door on her heart and sensibilities.

When she walked through the door of the residence, Lucie suffered an inward chill at the sight of her mistress's tear-stained face and the implacable set of her features. The fact that she was alone was more cause for alarm. The look that Callie leveled on her warned her not to question, and the old Negress quietly followed her mistress upstairs to help her undress. Lucie sent up a silent prayer as she left Callie staring into the fire.

Callie didn't know how much time had passed before she heard Jonathan burst through the front door and race up the stairs, nor did she care. The frame on her door had been fixed, and she would have bolted the lock now if she thought it would have done any good. When he entered her room, she didn't move.

"Callie, what has happened? You hardly spoke throughout dinner, and Mrs. Carter said you left the reception without a word—without even your cloak. And Lucie is downstairs moaning some nonsense about evil spirits. What's amiss?" he asked anxiously.

When she remained unresponsive, he pulled her to her feet and shook her. "Answer me! What is wrong?"

Callie's eyes slowly focused on him, and she drew herself up and slammed her hand against the side of his face with a resounding crack.

Jonathan stared at her, stunned for a moment. When he spoke, his voice was low and controlled; his temper simmered just below the surface. "I will never strike a woman, Callie, but if you ever try that again, you will not enjoy the consequences. Now, what the deuce is wrong with you? I thought that we had come to terms."

"Nay, it was you, the governor, and the General Assembly who had come to terms," she shot back. "Oh, how very clever you all were. The only way the General Assembly could think to silence me was to see me married because a married woman cannot petition the court." She gave a short, bitter laugh. "I had thought to be worth more than just your release to England. Why didn't you tell me that the General Assembly had forced you into this marriage?"

"What does it matter the circumstances?" questioned Jonathan. "I am free to return to England. You have recovered your land and escaped your stepfather's custody. And yes, the General Assembly has stopped your interference. We have all used each other, and we have all gotten what we wanted into the bargain."

She couldn't deny the truth of his words, but the brutal honesty of them stung. She didn't know if she was more upset that she had been duped by the General Assembly or that Jonathan, as unwilling a partner as he may have been, had been a party to the trap.

"'Twas still trickery by whatever means you measure it," she charged. "You should have warned me."

"To what avail? We were both forced into a position where marriage was the only choice."

"Yet, you allowed that you were doing it as a favor to me."

"I never allowed any such thing," Jonathan corrected her firmly. "If you remember, that part of the bargain was struck between you and Lord Randall. I was not consulted."

That was a point that Callie found herself regretting more and more. "The General Assembly will not find their victory so handily won," she warned. "This marriage will not stand."

"On what charge, madam? You know that a consummated marriage cannot be annulled. On that point, I need not refresh your memory."

Callie suddenly understood his strange reference to the General Assembly the night of their wedding. "Was that part of the plan, too?"

"That may have been their instruction," admitted Jonathan, "but what has passed between us is not of their making. As I have no grounds for a divorce yet—"

"What is that to mean?"

"Stay away from Justice Smythe's son, or at least do me the honor of being discreet."

Callie blinked in surprise. "Charles? You think that we are—why, I scarcely know the man."

"For a casual acquaintance, you certainly appeared comfortable in his company tonight."

Callie was stunned and hurt that he could think her capable of such deceit, especially after the intimacy they had shared.

Jonathan faltered for a moment at the look on her face. "God's blood, Callie! His father would put the noose around the necks of you and Mae Bailey if given half a chance. How do you know that Smythe did not send him to gather information from you?"

"Charles has never questioned me about Mae. Besides, he holds no affection for his father, and I see no reason to judge him by the yardstick of Justice Smythe," retorted Callie.

Jonathan looked at her in disbelief. Where was the Callie who had found his every move suspect when she had much less to lose than her life? He caught Callie roughly by the arm. "Are you having a liaison with young Smythe as Lilibeth Sanders hinted?"

"Lilibeth!" A shadow of pain crossed Callie's features that he would trust the word of the spiteful young woman on such a matter, but, in tune only to his own anger, Jonathan took no notice of it.

As they faced off against each other, eyes blazing, tempers clashing, Jonathan didn't know what he was going to do if she gave him an admission of guilt. When her answer finally came, it gave him little relief.

"'Tis truth Charles holds my attention," she responded with cool deliberation, "as much as Lilibeth Sanders holds yours."

What the bloody hell did that mean? Was she telling him that Charles meant as little to her as Lilibeth did to him, or did she possibly imagine that he was carrying on an affair with the young Sanders woman?

Jonathan visibly struggled to bring his temper under control. "I must leave on the morrow for several days. We will talk of this further when I return," he said.

Abruptly, he turned on his heel to escape the room before he strangled her.

From the bottom of the stairs, Mrs. Bendel, Lucie, and Jenkins stared up at him expectantly, making him feel all the more powerless.

"Jenkins, bring a decanter of brandy and be quick about it!" he bellowed. Uttering an oath, he stomped into his bedchamber and slammed the door so hard that the servants feared it no longer remained on its hinges.

As Jenkins tore up the stairs with the brandy, the housekeeper and Lucie exchanged nervous glances, wondering what had passed to shatter this new, much welcome peace in the house.

CHAPTER THIRTY

Treachery

Jonathan followed the Fall Line Road from Richmond to the Carolina border. After three and a half days of hard riding, he was five miles from his destination.

A deep frown furrowed his brow as he struggled to keep his thoughts on the task at hand. Instead, they seemed bent upon Callie as they had for the most part of the journey. In the past, had a woman proved to be troublesome, he merely bid her farewell. But he didn't want to leave Callie. The uncomfortable truth was that he loved her.

He had stopped to see his old governess before leaving town ostensibly to learn of Mae Bailey's whereabouts and ended by venting his frustrations with Callie. Just as Whithers had predicted, now that a cooler head prevailed, Jonathan dismissed the likelihood of Callie having an affair with Charles Smythe. Lilibeth was hardly an impartial witness, and it was not in Callie's character to be so deceitful. She was exasperating and clever and frequently bent words to her purpose, but she was not dishonest in her deeds. It was as Whithers had said—pride was the culprit here.

Jonathan suddenly reined in his horse, his senses on hair trigger alert. He went still, his eyes slowly scanning the woods. There was only the sound of small creatures scurrying about, but he knew that he had heard something else—a distinctive clicking sound. He was about to dismount to seek cover, when an explosion scattered the birds. Jonathan felt something hit his side, and he looked down in surprise to see blood oozing through his coat. He fought to remain conscious but blackness soon enveloped him, and he slumped forward on his horse before falling to the ground.

* * * * *

"Callie, do sit down before you set the room on end," grumbled Mrs. Whithers. "Neither do I wish to have a path worn in my carpet. What troubles you so?"

The old matron grimaced as Callie dropped into a chair in a most unladylike fashion.

"Oh, Madam, the marriage is a mistake," she blurted out. "Would that Jonathan's and my paths had never crossed. The man is impossible."

"If memory serves, you were most insistent upon marrying Lord Jon, were you not?" questioned Mrs. Whithers.

"Yes, yes. But that was when it was put to me that marriage was my only option and Jonathan seemed the best choice. As it turns out, the marriage was all a clever ruse by the General Assembly to prevent me from petitioning the court on behalf of women, and Jonathan was a party to it."

"I see. Well, you did safeguard your land and escape your stepfather's authority, and Lord Jon will soon be off to England. Was that not your intention?"

"Yes, but—"

"Well then, you have gotten everything you wanted," said the old matron.

"Yes—no—oh, Madam, matters have become complicated," groaned Callie.

Mrs. Whithers smiled to herself. She had had an earlier similar conversation with an equally agitated Lord Trenholme. She had had her doubts from the start about this union. But now, like Lord Randall, she was finding the match very much to her liking.

Whether the young couple realized it or not, each had already had a marked positive influence on the other. Callie had flowered into a beautiful, young woman from a lonely, embittered child, and there had been a glow about her these past few weeks that Mrs. Whithers was quite certain Jonathan had had a hand in. As to her previous charge, Jonathan was much less the self-indulgent, arrogant, and insensitive product of his narrow society. It tickled her to no end that it had taken an uneducated slip of a girl to effectively shake his cool self-possession and open his cynical heart.

"Well, Callie, your paths did cross," said Mrs. Whithers, matter-of-factly. "And regardless of the circumstances, you and Lord Jon are married. Sometimes a man and a woman need time to know each other."

"Jonathan and I shall never know each other," responded Callie brusquely. "He actually accused me of having a liaison with Charles Smythe—on Lilibeth's say so."

"Too often pride looks only to emotions and refuses to acknowledge reason, my dear. I will warrant Lord Jon already sees the error of his thinking and will tell you so upon his return," Mrs. Whithers assured her.

Callie looked at her mentor skeptically. "Even should that be the case, he is a man of too many moods."

Mrs. Whithers raised a brow. "Yes, I am quite familiar with the type."

"And he has secrets," Callie continued.

"Secrets? Lord Jon?"

Callie nodded. "Aye, I dare say that you do not know him as well you think, Madam. He goes away to county courts of late—or so he says."

"What makes you think that he goes not to county courts?" Mrs. Whithers asked guardedly.

"He has taken to wearing buckskins sometimes and has more the appearance of a hunter than of a traveling justice. For another, it comes to me that county courts do not sit when the General Court is in session, so he cannot be going to county court now. And that is not all."

"Dear me," mumbled Mrs. Whithers, alarmed.

"There are meetings in which he claims to be attending to matters of the farm, yet each time we visit, there is little changed," continued Callie. "Then, I chanced to see him meeting with this little man. At the governor's dinner, I overheard Lord Randall, the governor, and Major Washington say that there is a traitor in their midst supplying the French with information. There can be only one conclusion, Madam. Trenholme is a spy for the French."

Mrs. Whithers nearly fainted, and she set her fan in furious motion in an effort to compose herself. "Callie, you must pay no heed to your suspicions, for they are groundless. But, if raised, they shall spell certain danger for Lord Jon."

Callie glanced up sharply at the anxiety in her mentor's voice and drew herself up to perch on the edge of the chair. "What goes on, Madam? You may as well tell me everything, for I shall not leave until you do."

If Jonathan Trenholme had difficulty controlling the indomitable Callie in the face of her determination, an old woman was certainly no match at all, decided Mrs. Whithers. Reluctantly, she explained Jonathan's mission for the governor, as he had been forced to explain it to her before she would tell him the whereabouts of Mae. Mrs. Whithers stopped short of telling Callie that Trenholme had gone to Carolina to talk to Mae regarding information that had arisen about her husband Jack Bailey.

Callie left Mrs. Whithers and walked home in a daze, stung by the fact that her husband apparently felt more comfortable confiding in his old governess than in his own wife. She had been ready to believe him a traitor, just as he had been ready to believe her an adulterer. What was wrong with them that they were so quick to think the worst of each other?

"Be ye Lady Trenholme, ma'am?"

Callie roused from her thoughts and looked down at the ragtag little boy with the thatch of red hair and a yard of freckles.

"Aye, I be Lady Trenholme."

"A man give me this here note for ye," said the boy.

He shoved a slip of paper into her hand and dashed off before Callie could question him. Glancing around, she had the eerie feeling that someone was watching her, and she hurried the remaining distance to the house. Once inside, she examined the stained, rumpled note. It filled her with curiosity as she unfolded the parchment; fear seized her when she read it.

I know about Mae Bailey. If ye wants my silence, come to the room at the back of the stables after dark. Tell no one and come alone.

It was signed Abel Cane.

* * * * *

Callie quickly drew on her blue linsey-woolsey skirt over top her shift and pulled the drawstring tight around her waist.

"Ye ain't goin'," declared Lucie flatly, her hands on her hips, as Callie slipped on a dark blue bodice and laced it up the front. "Dat Abel Cane be up to no good, and with Mister Justice gone away, 'tis too dangerous. Da note can't be from him anyways. Dat man don' take pen to paper no better'n me."

Callie threw a cloak around her shoulders. "He must have had someone write the note for him. Now hush, Lucie. I cannot think clearly with you jabbering like a magpie."

"Humph, iffen ye goes there in da dark, ye ain't thinkin' at all. Dis be Publik Time, missy. All manner of men be roamin' the streets full of drink an' mischief."

"I have to know what he is up to." If Cane knew anything, how much did Justice Smythe now know? wondered Callie worriedly.

Lucie shook her head in disapproval, her eyes full of concern as Callie pulled the hood over her head. "Ye be careful, missy. And take dis witch's bag with ye."

Callie wrinkled her nose at the odor of the sachet of weeds and herbs and firmly pushed the good luck charm aside. "I will be fine, Lucie. Tell Mrs. Bendel that I have retired for the evening and do not wish to be disturbed for any reason."

With Lucie anxiously looking on, Callie slipped out of the house unnoticed.

The evening was cool. Wispy clouds obscured much of the full moon as she cautiously made her way to the edge of town, skirting revelers who spilled from the taverns.

When she arrived at the stables, she found that a lantern was lit. Horses snorted and whinnied as she passed through to the room in the rear. Her legs shook and her heart thudded when she knocked on the wood-plank door. No one answered. She knocked several more times. When there was still no response, Callie lifted the leather strap latch and peered cautiously into the gloomy darkness. The small room was empty, and she hesitantly stepped inside to await Cane's return.

The stale, sour odor of mold, decaying refuse, and an unemptied slop jar assaulted her senses, and she nearly retched in disgust. The low fire provided a dim light in the darkness. In the center, stood a rough table littered and stained from food and drink; in the corner near the hearth was a pallet.

Callie jumped when the door suddenly opened and Cane staggered in on unsteady feet.

He came to a sudden halt at the sight of an intruder. "'Ere now, what be ye doin' in me room?" he growled.

When Callie shoved the hood back from her face, his scowl turned into a sly smile.

"Well, if it ain't me girl comin' to see her stepdaddy," he said, moving closer to her.

Fear swept through Callie, and she immediately knew that she had made a mistake in coming. "I am here because of your note," she said, striving to keep her voice steady. "Tell me how much you want for your silence, and I'll be on my way?"

Cane looked at her blankly for a moment, but as his besotted mind was capable of registering only one thought at a time, his eye returned to her person. He yanked the cloak from her shoulders and grabbed her by the arms to pull her to his chest.

"What's the matter. That gentry buck ain't man enough for ye, ay." He snickered and his mouth sought hers.

Nauseated by the smell of his sour breath, Callie turned her face away. As she struggled to break free, he shifted an arm around her waist to bring her tighter against him. With the other hand, he impatiently unlaced her bodice and groped at her breasts.

Marshalling her strength, she pushed him away in disgust. "Get away from me, you animal!" she spat, wiping her mouth with the back of her hand. "You aren't fit to wallow in pig slop."

Cane's eyes narrowed menacingly. "Always the bitch, ay, Callie. Well, 'tis time ye was taught some manners."

He blocked her departure and fell upon her, bending her backwards over the table and pinning her beneath him. Callie gasped. His weight on top of her crushed the air from her lungs. Cane yanked up her skirt and shift and forced her legs apart. As he fumbled with the front of his breeches, Callie desperately groped for anything to thwart the attack. Her fingers finally made contact with a long, slender object. When it cut into her hand, she realized that it was a knife.

Her energy nearly spent, she grabbed the handle of the knife and blindly struck at him. As the blade sliced deep into the flesh of his shoulder, Cane let out an enraged bellow and jumped back from her.

Shouting a string of oaths, he swatted the knife aside and viciously backhanded Callie twice across the face. He moved to strike her again, when there came a deafening blast. His eyes bulged in astonishment, and his body slumped lifelessly over top of her. Blood spread across his shirt from the knife wound she had inflicted and from where gunshot had entered his back.

Dazed from the blows her stepfather had dealt her, Callie was cognizant only of the fact that there had been an explosion and that the assault had stopped. It took a minute for her to comprehend that her stepfather had been shot and lay unconscious or dead on top of her. Whimpering hysterically, she shoved Cane off of her and struggled to her feet.

CHAPTER THIRTY-ONE

The Confrontation

Jonathan awoke with a start to find himself in a bed with a huge man standing guard over him. He winced as he struggled to lift himself up on one arm. When the cover fell away to reveal a bandage around his chest, his face reflected confusion.

"Have a care, mind ye," said the man gruffly. "Ye lost a bit of blood."

Jonathan shook his head to clear his mind. "Where am I?" he asked hoarsely, falling back against the pillows.

"Right where ye was headin', Lord Trenholme," said an elderly woman entering the room.

Jonathan blinked and stared at the woman in disbelief. For a moment, he thought he was hallucinating. She was rougher around the edges and a good deal less fashionable, but she was the image of her sister.

He smiled weakly. "Whithers failed to mention you are twins."

The woman laughed heartily. "Well, Martha ain't left much unsaid 'bout you, sir. She said ye was a handsome buck but tough, smart, and trustworthy. She weren't lyin' 'bout the first two, and I shall take her word for the rest else ye wouldn't be lyin' here so comfy. My name be Priscilla Bates. The big man over there is Jake Tyler my overseer."

"How do you know who I am?" asked Jonathan.

"Jake went through your belongings when he come upon ye and found Martha's letter to me. 'Twas lucky for ye that he was out huntin' and heard the gunshot, or might be no one would have found ye for days, mayhap weeks. The ball lodged in yer side, but we managed to get it out without doin' more damage." She walked over to Jonathan and pulled back the linen bandage. "The wound looks clean now. Yer fever broke. Ye should mend quick enough. Jake didna see who done it. Most likely a poacher."

"What day is it?"

"Ye been here nigh on four days. What brings ye?" asked Priscilla guardedly.

Jonathan studied the woman for a long moment. She was a shrewd old bird just like her sister. She was going to make him show his hand first. He realized that if he was going to get past her, nothing less than the truth would do.

"I trust Whithers wrote you that I have come to see Mrs. Bailey," he said.

Priscilla Bates didn't bat an eye. "There ain't no one here by that name."

"Whithers told me differently."

At this, Priscilla and Jake exchanged guarded glances. The gesture was subtle, but Jonathan caught it.

"Miz Bates be tellin' ye right," said Jake at length. "Ain't no more Mrs. Bailey. She be Mae Tyler, my wife. She has a child and a new life now."

"I am not here to return your wife for punishment," Jonathan quickly assured the large, burly man. "I seek information about her first husband."

"What about him?" demanded Tyler sharply.

"There is evidence to suggest that Jack Bailey was helping to recruit Indians of British alliance to the French cause on the western frontier. There be also the suspicion that he relayed sensitive information from a spy in the colony to the French Command," explained Jonathan. "I do not suspect your wife of any involvement, but she may unknowingly have information that would yield the identity of the spy."

"'Tis Virginia business. Ain't got nothin' to do with us," said Tyler.

"There is the danger that uprisings may spread to other colonies if the Indians switch alliances."

"Why would tribes allied with England side with the French?" asked Mrs. Bates.

"King George wants colonization, and his troops have forced tribes off their ancestral lands in Carolina and Georgia. The French are interested in fur trading, not land acquisition for settlement," said Jonathan. "Who would you side with?"

Mrs. Bates looked at her overseer. "Ye best fetch Mae."

Jake hesitated for a moment. He regarded Jonathan closely, taking careful measure of his character. With a grunt of grudging acceptance, Tyler left the room.

Several minutes later, the huge man returned with a shy young woman carrying a smiling pink-cheeked baby four months short of a year. The affection in his eyes, as he placed a reassuring hand on the woman's shoulder and lifted the playful child from her arms, made Jonathan yearn all the more for the intimacy that had been lost between Callie and himself.

"Justice Trenholme," said Mae softly, "Mrs. Whithers has written me of yer part in my escape and of yer marriage to Callie. If Callie had trust enough in ye to marry ye, I owe it to her to trust ye as well. How might I be of help?"

Jonathan squirmed uncomfortably at such blind faith. As Whithers had obviously seen fit to omit the finer details of Callie and his union, he also declined to mention the true circumstances of the marriage and that Callie didn't trust him any more than Jake probably did. And he was conscious of an immeasurable loss that he was determined to recover.

As Mae honestly and forthrightly answered Jonathan's questions, even he hadn't been prepared for the scope of her confidence. When put together with what he had suspected and the facts that he knew, it revealed a picture that would, at last, lay this nasty business to rest.

"I fear, Mrs. Tyler, that information of this nature shall require your presence before the governor," said Jonathan, bracing himself for protests.

Priscilla Bates said nothing; the worried frown on her weathered features spoke for her.

Jake's response was a flat out "no," immediate and final. He passed the child to Mrs. Bates and moved to stand protectively beside his wife. "God's teeth, man! This Justice Smythe would have a rope around her neck as soon as she stepped one foot into town."

"I will protect your wife well. Under the circumstances, I am certain of obtaining a pardon for her," said Jonathan. "I must warn you, Mr. Tyler, I suspect that the traitor now knows of your wife's existence and general whereabouts. The attack on me was more than the work of a poacher. Someone followed me here. I fear that Mrs. Tyler will be in danger wherever she is until this person is apprehended with the help of her testimony."

"I can take care of Mae. You will have to find another way."

"No, Jake, he is right," said Mae. "I must go back. If what Justice Trenholme suspects is true, you are all in danger here until this man is caught. I will not have people I care about at risk on my account." Mae placed her hand on her husband's arm and looked up at him, beseeching him to understand.

Finally, Jake nodded. "If ye are so determined to do this, then I'll be goin', too," he said with firm resolve.

"Miss Priscilla needs ye here, Jake. Justice Trenholme will see me safe."

"Stuff 'n nonsense," interceded Mrs. Bates. "Virgil can take over for Jake while he is gone. The boy has been hankerin' to prove his worth anyways."

Mae threw the woman a grateful smile and turned to Jonathan. "We shall leave when you are well enough to travel, sir."

Jonathan could hear the strain in her voice and see the fear in her eyes, but she didn't waver in her decision. He respected her courage and could now understand why Callie and Whithers had risked so much to help her.

By the week's end, Jonathan decided that he was strong enough to travel. As he watched Mae tearfully give her baby over to Priscilla Bates' care and the emotional farewells of the two women, it struck a chord with him. And he pledged to himself that he would keep this lady safe at all costs. He fervently hoped that he would be able to expose the traitor in their midst without having to betray the secret that Mae had confided to him. It was as Callie had said, the woman had suffered enough.

With pistols drawn, Jonathan and Tyler carefully guarded Mae as they made their way along the isolated trail to the Fall Line Road. When they crossed into Virginia, their senses were especially alert to any unnatural sounds or untoward movements. Jonathan's pace was slower this time around. Four days later, the little band arrived on the outskirts of Williamsburg without incident and went their separate ways as prearranged.

Jonathan's thoughts immediately turned to Callie. Whithers had told him that when he was able to admit one truth, he would be able to see the others. The sage old governess had been right. He was seeing things very clearly now and was anxious to get home to Callie to set things right between them.

It was late afternoon by the time he had stabled his horse. The stableman was unusually solicitous toward him this day, and the people Jonathan encountered as he walked to the house greeted him with uncertain solemnity as one might greet a friend who had just had a death in the family. Indeed, he perceived an air of expectancy over the town, but of what? Everything was too quiet. A feeling of uneasiness raised the hair on the back of his neck, and he picked up his step. Every beat of foreboding seemed to spell out *Callie*. His second indication that Callie was in trouble was when a weeping Mrs. Bendel, a hysterical Lucie, and a downcast Jenkins met him at the door.

"I tol' her to take da witch's bag with her," wailed the Negress. "But she don' never listen to ol' Lucie."

Jonathan ushered them all inside the house, frantic to make some sense of their incoherent jabbering as each endeavored to give him a different piece of the story at the same time. His alarm increased all the more when he was finally able to make out that Callie was not in the house. He thanked Providence when Lord Randall suddenly arrived. Perhaps now he could get to the truth of the matter, though he took little comfort in the fact that the earl was pale and drawn and greatly distressed.

Jonathan quickly took the older man into the privacy of the drawing room. "What has happened?" he asked anxiously, pouring the shaken earl a bracing glass of brandy. "Where is Callie? Has she been hurt?"

Lord Randall took a gulp of his drink. "Worse than that, my boy, worse than that. Callie is being held for murder in the gaol."

Jonathan felt as though the air had been sucked out of him. "Murder! Whose?"

"Abel Cane…a week after you left town. And, Jonathan, there is strong evidence against her."

Jonathan stared at the earl in disbelief. Callie a murderer—it was too ridiculous to consider even if the victim was Abel Cane. "What evidence is there?" he demanded to know.

"The man was shot in the back with Callie's hunting fowler."

"I thought she lost the rifle months ago."

"Whatever the case, it was found on the floor near the body along with Callie's cloak," replied Lord Randall.

"Where?"

"In the room at the back of the public stables."

"The public stables—what the bloody hell was Callie doing there alone and at night?"

The earl took a crumpled piece of parchment from his pocket and handed it to Jonathan. "Lucie says a street urchin passed this note to Callie. She thought Cane was after blackmail and went to confront him."

Jonathan quickly read the note. The knot of apprehension in his stomach tightened as he clearly saw the case from a prosecutor's point of view. "I shall have to argue that the rifle and cloak were placed there to incriminate Callie," he said, mentally preparing her defense. "Did anyone see her there?"

Lord Randall nodded. "A passerby saw her running out of the stables."

"What does Callie say?"

"Nothing. She refuses to talk about what happened that night, but Mrs. Bendel and Lucie said she arrived home in a state of shock. She had blood on her clothes and a gash across her palm, most likely from a knife. As it happens, Cane was also knifed in the shoulder. Until the sheriff arrested Callie the next morning, none of us had guessed the scope of the incident."

Jonathan was incredulous. "Callie has been in the gaol all this time?"

"I tried to have her released," said Lord Randall. "But Smythe wouldn't hear of it. He said he could not allow special favors."

"What of the governor or a quorum of justices?"

"Dinwiddie has been in Alexandria, and the justices refused to act in your absence. I fear that Smythe means to see the job done this time, Jonathan. He will not allow Callie any visitors. The Widow Whithers and I both have tried. The widow is very upset. I was with her when that woman arrived with her husband from Carolina. Jonathan, I know not the whole of the story yet, but you must be mad to have brought that woman back here. Justice Smythe has enough against Callie now without adding—"

Jonathan signaled to Lord Randall to be silent. "Suffice it to know, 'twas necessary," he said in a lowered tone. "But there must be no discussion of the matter or mention of Mrs. Tyler's presence here until I allow it." At the earl's nod, Jonathan moved on. "Now, what of the trial? The spring session of the General Court is over. Smythe cannot mean to keep Callie in the gaol until the court sits again in October."

"'Tis exactly what he intended," the earl replied angrily. "But, in this, the other justices intervened out of deference to you and have extended the session. Even so, they have bowed to Smythe's insistence that Callie's trial be set for the morrow. I believe it is Smythe's hope that you would not return in time." Lord Randall shifted uneasily as he considered how to break this next bit of news. "Jonathan, there is something else you should know."

Jonathan looked at Lord Randall in dismay. "There is more?"

"Sadly so. Lucie and Mrs. Bendel suspect that Callie was attacked by Cane. In addition to the wound on her hand, she has bruises on her face and other areas of her body. And—" Lord Randall stopped and took a deep breath. "Information has come to me that Cane was found with his britches undone."

Jonathan had heard enough. He turned on his heel and was across the room in three quick strides. When he pulled open the door, he was brought up short as the entire staff nearly fell at his feet.

"Have ye nothing better to do than to listen at doors!" he thundered.

"B-Beggin' yer pardon, sir," stammered a white-faced Mrs. Bendel. "We wasn't listenin' fer gossip, sir. We be worried about the mistress."

As the others bobbed their heads in unison, Jonathan was struck by the effect that Callie seemed to have on the lives of people around her, however brief the acquaintance. She had certainly placed her mark upon his. And he nodded, acknowledging the staff's concern.

"Jenkins, help Mrs. Bendel and Lucie prepare a bath for Lady Trenholme in her chamber," said Jonathan. He turned to the cook.

"Mrs. Forsythe, make ready a meal. I shall return with her Ladyship within the hour. Lord Randall, see if you can get a quorum now for a statement of custody and meet me at the gaol with a closed carriage." Jonathan had barely finished issuing orders before everyone scattered, relieved to have something to do to help.

It was four blocks across the commons to the gaol. As he stormed out of the house, Jonathan was alternately filled with rage that Callie had been hurt, guilt that he had not been here to protect her, and fear that the Callie he had come to know and love might have become lost to the violence she had experienced.

The temperature was pleasantly warm and the breeze gentle, a day made to lighten the mood of troubled spirits. But Jonathan's features were set in a grim line, his manner determined as he walked swiftly down the street. Since the news of the murder and Callie's arrest, the whole town had been awaiting his arrival to see what he would do. When he strode past onlookers, they jabbed at each other and a small group began to follow him, soon growing to twice the size as others fell in along the way. But Jonathan took no notice. His mind was bent on one thought.

All held their breath as Lord Trenholme walked up to the gaol and banged on the door. "Tom Wilson, be ye here? Step forth!" he commanded.

Hesitantly, the door creaked open and the gaoler looked out, surprised to see Jonathan and dismayed to see the crowd that had collected behind him. He had known that sooner or later he would have to contend with the husband of his notable prisoner, but that it would be in plain view of the town was something he hadn't counted on.

"Justice Trenholme, I—uh—that is—Justice Smythe has refused your wife visitors," he stammered out nervously. The look on Jonathan's face caused him to quickly reconsider the matter. With a deep gulp, he opened the door wider to allow Jonathan to enter.

Inside, a brood of children, including the gangly Willie, stared open-mouthed at the tall, imperious stranger.

"This way, Justice Trenholme," said Mrs. Wilson, taking control of the situation.

"Now, Mrs. Wilson, ye know what Justice Smythe said," her husband warned her.

"The devil take Justice Smythe!" she exclaimed to her family's astonishment. "'Tis his mean spirit what keeps Lady Trenholme here. That young woman ain't no more'n able to kill a body, however much the blatherskite was deservin' of it, than I am." Mrs. Wilson looked at Jonathan worriedly. "She be needin' ye, sir. Lady Trenholme ain't been right these past days. She don't eat much or talk. She just stands there starin' out the window."

"Mother, I have my position to consider," the gaoler anxiously reminded her.

"'Tain't worth the life of an innocent woman. And me pride demands more than threats from a lizard," she declared stoutly.

The gaoler looked fearfully over his shoulder. "Mrs. Wilson, mind yerself."

Time was wasting, and Jonathan held up his hand to stem any further argument. "I am not without influence of my own. I shall see to it that you suffer no penalty for my actions. Now, sir, I would have the key."

Hesitantly, the gaoler relinquished his key to Callie's cell.

Inside her prison, Callie stared dismally out the window. Ironically, it was just over a year ago that she had shared these same four walls with Mae and the irreverent Sally. Maybe she had been too young or naive then—no, she had been too angry that long ago day— to feel the helplessness she felt now.

She could abide feeling hopeless, for her indomitable spirit usually refused to allow her to accept it for long. But to be powerless—that was something altogether different; it meant a total loss of control.

She had honed her instincts to recognize and sidestep questionable circumstances that might lead to it. Why hadn't she foreseen this one?

Callie wasted no sympathy on Cane. She felt only revulsion. She could still feel his hands pawing at her, painfully squeezing her breasts, groping under her shift. And she wrapped her arms around herself to block out the memory. She winced as a salty tear trailed down her cheek to sting the cut on her lip. For the first time, she could fully understand Mae's state of mind when first they had met. Powerlessness was like an illness that reached out to grip the mind and paralyze the senses. It caused one to give up.

Callie leaned her head against the damp wall. She wondered what Jonathan's reaction would be when he returned to find her jailed for murder. Would he renounce her to protect his family name? They had parted on such angry terms that, in retrospect, she couldn't blame him if he did wash his hands of her.

It was true that she had drawn him into the marriage for her own purposes, and if, in the process, she had been tricked by the General Assembly, she couldn't fault Jonathan. Even if he had told her the truth of the matter, it was as he had said. Marriage still would have been her only alternative. As for his hurtful accusation that she was having an affair with Charles Smythe, how could she expect him to trust her when she didn't fully trust him? If only they had it to do over again.

The key clanged in the lock, but Callie's spirit was so low that she paid it no attention. It was a common daily disturbance as the keeper brought meals and fetched prisoners for an hour of airing in the yard.

"Callie," a deep voice called softly.

For a moment, Callie thought she was dreaming, and she slowly turned. When she saw Jonathan standing there, a strangled cry escaped her. She desperately wanted to run to him, but she wavered. How would he receive her? When he moved toward her and held out a hand to her, Callie ran to him. She didn't question what she might be compromising. Her pride no longer cared that he might reject or pity her. She only knew that she had to feel his arms around her to erase the memory of Cane's assault if only for a moment. As he gently enfolded her in his embrace, sobs shook her body and tears rolled unchecked down her cheeks.

"I did not kill him, Jonathan. I did not kill my stepfather," she cried. "And Charles—"

"Hush," said Jonathan. "We can talk of this later. I'm taking you away from here."

Jonathan was so shaken and enraged at the sight of the ugly bruises on her cheek and forearms and the nasty cut on her lip that if Cane weren't already dead, he would have killed the man himself. He lifted her up in his arms and carried her out of the gaol into the fresh air.

Murmurs erupted when the couple appeared, and the group pressed closer for a better view.

"Over here," shouted Lord Randall, pulling up in a closed carriage.

The crowd respectfully cleared a path for them.

Jonathan had just handed Callie into the conveyance when Justice Smythe rode up with the sheriff in tow, nearly trampling anyone in his way.

"I heard you had returned to town. I thought you might try something like this, Trenholme. Your wife is a murderer and her place is in the gaol until her fate can be determined by the court."

"'Twould seem, sir, that you have already determined her fate," responded Jonathan, a hard edge to his tone.

"No more than you have proclaimed her innocence with a preponderance of evidence against her," returned Smythe.

"Perhaps we both should step down from this case, as our minds seem to be set. There is a quorum without us, Smythe."

Smythe clearly heard the challenge in Jonathan's voice, and he bristled at the inference that his verdict might be less than impartial. "I am led by the evidence, sir, not by emotion."

"Make certain that is the case," warned Jonathan. "Until her fate is determined by the court, Lady Trenholme shall remain in my custody."

"Prisoners in your custody tend to disappear," Smythe remarked snidely.

Jonathan didn't flinch. "I recall only two previous incidences of custody, sir. In one, the defendant reappeared as scheduled; in the other, the woman died in childbirth."

He had taken a calculated risk confronting Smythe in this manner, but he was gambling on the chance that the man wasn't ready to tip his hand yet. Judging by the furious glare that Smythe threw him, Jonathan knew he had gauged right.

"Justice or not, you have no authority to release this woman," said Smythe, taking a different tact. "Sheriff, tell him!"

The sheriff shifted uneasily in his saddle, not wanting to get caught in the middle between these two powerful men. "My apologies, Lord Trenholme, but it appears that Justice Smythe is correct. I regret that your wife shall have to return to the gaol."

"I beg to differ," spoke up Lord Randall from the carriage. He held out a sheet of parchment. "This will set the matter straight."

"What is it, sir?" asked the sheriff.

"'Tis a statement of custodial release for Lady Trenholme signed by the required number of justices."

Smythe's lower lip quivered with rage. "Enjoy your moment of victory now, Trenholme, for 'tis the last you shall know when all is made known." With that, he sharply wheeled his horse around and galloped off.

Jonathan climbed into the carriage and drew a trembling Callie back into his arms. With the confrontation over, the group of townspeople dispersed. No one had been disappointed. The clash between the two justices was all that it had promised to be, and everyone eagerly looked forward to what would come next.

CHAPTER THIRTY-TWO

Unburied Secrets

Callie leaned back against the tub and closed her eyes, allowing the hot water to do its magic. She didn't want to think beyond the moment. And she almost sighed with contentment as the soothing warmth bathed away the dirt and eased the pain of the past days of horror. Her hair had been freshly washed, and Lucie sang to her softly as the old Negress brushed out the long, burnished tresses to dry by the heat of the fire. Fortified by the soup, cakes, and tea that Mrs. Bendel had practically force-fed her, Callie began to feel the fog lift from her mind.

She didn't want to spoil the serenity of the moment by inquiring after Jonathan's whereabouts or his manner of mood. He hadn't spoken a word on the carriage ride home, and the fact that he had handed her over to Lucie and Mrs. Bendel the minute they had stepped through the door was answer enough that he had washed his hands of her. And Callie resigned herself to the probability that she was no longer going to be a part of his life.

As to her present predicament, she could plead benefit of clergy. It would be tantamount to an admission of guilt, and she would be branded on the hand to prevent her from pleading it a second time, but she had no way to prove her innocence and could, at least, escape the rope.

In the corner of the room, Lucie and Mrs. Bendel quietly conversed. They had noticed the subtle changes in Callie's body, her listlessness, and her aversion to food and odors. But both agreed that now was not the time to raise this point of discussion with her.

Downstairs, Jonathan restlessly shoved away the plate of quail set before him. His thoughts were centered on what was happening upstairs. Was Callie on the road to becoming her old self, or was she retreating to a place inside of herself where he would never be able to reach her again? He had seen it happen before with female victims of assault.

He didn't yet know Callie's emotional state, but he had found that in such matters women preferred the company of other women until the shock wore off. It had been with great difficulty that he had surrendered her into the care of Mrs. Bendel and Lucie in hopes of mitigating the damage already done. Now, as he watched the housekeeper bustle up and down the stairs without sparing him a glance, her features set in a grim line, his heart sank as he feared the worst. It was all he could do to quell the impulse to bolt up the stairs to Callie's room and see to her himself.

"Callie will be fine," said Lord Randall. "She has always been a strong lass."

"Everyone has a limit—even Callie," replied Jonathan. "If you remember, 'tis the meek who shall inherit the earth. They accept and endure, while the stalwarts are weakened and felled by their battles."

"I think you will find that Callie will survive. If you have done with your meal, let us retire to the drawing room. We have much to discuss before the trial."

Jonathan nodded. He stood and led the way into the small paneled room. There, he poured two glasses of brandy, passed one to Lord Randall, and motioned him to a comfortable chair by the fire.

"I was waylaid on my journey to Carolina," said Jonathan, seating himself across from the earl.

Lord Randall looked at him in surprise. "To what end?"

"Someone put a shot in my side."

"Dear God!"

"I am fine," Jonathan assured him. "I was well tended."

"Why would anyone do such a thing? Do you think it an accident or perhaps a hunter whose shot went astray?"

"No. I believe it was an attempt to keep me from learning the identity of the spy. I suspect it was he who ambushed me."

Lord Randall sat forward in his chair. "The devil you say. Have you a name? I must make haste to tell the governor. He has requested that the king send over troops from England. 'Twill be some weeks until we have word of the particulars, and I'll warrant the scoundrel would love to carry that information to the French."

"Hold fast, sir. The culprit will be made known in court."

"At Callie's trial? But what has one matter to do with the other?"

"I cannot say just yet, for I have not the proof I seek. Suffice it to know that if we are to absolve Callie of any guilt, the matter must be left to me."

Lord Randall settled back into the chair. "I bow to your judgment, sir. I know of no one more capable to whom I would entrust Callie's life."

Jonathan eyed the earl speculatively. "If that be the case, sir, will you tell me now, or must I wait to hear it from another quarter?"

Lord Randall looked at Jonathan nonplussed. "I beg your pardon."

"I have sensed that there is something you have been trying to tell me for some time. Judging from Smythe's parting threat today and your reaction to it, I would guess that he knows of it, too, and intends to use it against Callie."

The old earl sighed. "You are right. There is something. But 'tis not only Callie that Smythe intends to hurt by this but me as well. It would seem that I have opposed him on too many issues. I believe that he hopes to compromise my influence with the governor and minimize my power by forcing my resignation from the Council."

"You are one of the few men the governor trusts. What information could be so damaging to you and Callie?"

Lord Randall paused and took a sip of brandy to marshal his courage. Finally looking Jonathan in the eye, he said: "Callie is my daughter."

Jonathan was stunned. He had been prepared for almost anything but this, and he was silent as he worked to absorb this latest development and the impact it might have. "Perhaps you had better start at the beginning," he said at length.

The earl nodded. "Mine was an arranged marriage you understand."

"Yes, I am well acquainted with the condition," Jonathan remarked dryly.

Lord Randall gave a slight smile and continued. "Mary was a good woman, but we were ill suited to the match. I was heavily indebted to those merchant leeches in London and decided to immigrate to the colonies to better my fortune. Mary refused to accompany me. Callie's mother was a young colonist hired out by her father to be a member of my domestic staff." The earl smiled wistfully. "I will never forget the first time I saw Anne. She was a beautiful creature with titian hair and smiling blue eyes…so bright and such a wit. Callie is very much like her. Suffice it to say, Anne and I came to love each other. I would have married her—"

"But you had a wife in England," interjected Jonathan.

"Yes. Then I received word that Mary had died in a carriage accident, and I travelled back to England to settle her affairs," went on Lord Randall. "It was my intention to ask Anne to marry me upon my return, but when I arrived back in Williamsburg, I found that she had married John Hastings, an indentured carpenter and joiner I had brought from England, and there was an infant. Callie was a few months old then."

"Indentured servants are not permitted to marry without approval of their masters," pointed out Jonathan. "How is it possible that John was able to wed Anne without your knowledge?"

"Hastings had finished his indenture before I left for England," replied the earl. "Needless to say I was devastated. When I was finally able to confront Anne, she said that a marriage between us could never be possible because of our class difference. I had always suspected there was something else, but I didn't discover the truth until much later."

He paused to take another sip of his drink and collect himself. "For Anne's sake, I awarded John the land for a tobacco farm and continued to hire him for work at Randall Hall," he continued. "Callie often accompanied him on his trips to the plantation. A lovelier child I had never seen. From the first, she claimed a place in my heart. But Anne was always careful to keep a distance." Lord Randall shook his head. "It would appear that the Fates were aligned against us, for it was my great misfortune to be in England when John died, and Anne married Abel Cane. I did what I could to ease her lot, but she was a proud woman."

"You never suspected about Callie?" asked Jonathan.

"I did ask Anne about it once," said the earl. "She denied it. Even so, I always wondered."

"How did you learn the truth?"

"Anne summoned me to her deathbed and told me. She asked that I look after Callie, but she made me promise to never force the child into my world."

"Then she didn't forbid you to tell Callie of her parentage?"

"No. But Callie knew one man as her father. I had no wish for her to go through the pain, confusion, and humiliation of having to know another. And I suppose there was a fear of rejection. I already enjoyed a relationship with Callie based upon mutual respect and trust, and I did not want to risk losing that."

Jonathan nodded. He could understand that. Now all the earl's machinations to keep Callie on her land and to see her well married began to make sense. If he wasn't permitted to bring her into his world, he would leave it to Jonathan to do so. All along, he had been seeing to his child's welfare as best he could without betraying Anne's wishes.

"How did Smythe come by this information?" asked Jonathan.

Lord Randall's features tightened with anger. "Olivia, I suspect. I had changed my will to acknowledge Callie as my daughter and legal heir and had foolishly left the document on my desk one day when the overseer called me out."

"And Olivia saw it?"

"Yes. We had quite an argument over it. She denies it, but I am certain that she has been conspiring against Callie ever since to secure the inheritance for herself and Lilibeth. No doubt, she enlightened Smythe in hopes of strengthening the case against Callie." The earl ran a hand across his face with mounting anxiety. "Jonathan, I fear Smythe is going to argue the case that Callie killed her stepfather to keep him from exposing her parentage or her part in the Mae Bailey business rather than submit to blackmail."

Jonathan stared into the fire. All the pieces refused to fit so neatly together. For one thing, how did Cane know that Mae was still alive? He hadn't been able to read any of the letter Mae had sent to Callie, and, even if he had later learned of some of the contents from Smythe, he had been in Alexandria at the time of Mae's trial. It was highly unlikely that he could have pieced together the details himself of the Bailey case and of Callie's part in secreting Mae away from Williamsburg. The man wasn't that bright, and certainly Smythe wouldn't have shared his trump card.

"I dare say that Cane did not send that note to Callie," said Trenholme. "Someone else lured her there."

The earl looked at Jonathan in surprise. "Who and to what purpose?"

"I'll know that when I find out who wrote it."

"But how? There is so little time. What can I do to help?" asked Lord Randall.

"Find the boy who passed Callie the note, and arrange an audience for me with the governor in the morning before the court sits."

Lord Randall nodded. "What about the use of Callie's parentage as a motive?"

"Is it possible that Anne Hastings had confided her secret to Cane after marrying him?" questioned Jonathan.

Lord Randall shook his head. "She swore to me that I was the only one she had told."

"'Tis unlikely that Olivia would have given that information to Cane. It was more to her interest to keep it a secret from him. As there is no reference to it in the note, I think I can discredit it as a motive for blackmail, unless there is evidence to the contrary."

Lord Randall's brow was furrowed with a new worry. "Jonathan, given Cane's state of undress when found, Smythe may also try to use rape as a motive. You know how harshly the justice system deals with a woman who even accuses a white man of rape. Good God, imagine the penalty for a woman who is convicted of killing a man for it."

Jonathan hadn't thought about that. It was a far more damaging and dangerous charge, and, where Callie was concerned, he knew Smythe would leave no stone unturned to convict her.

"It is the more difficult charge to discount," he admitted. "I shall have to make certain the issue is not raised." Jonathan looked at Lord Randall. "I suspect there are two forces at work here. One has nothing to do with the other, but both stand to benefit at Callie's expense. The key is the lad who passed her the note. He must be found." Trenholme paused. "For now, there is the task of telling Callie that you are her natural father. She must be prepared for the possibility that it will come out in court."

The earl sighed heavily. "Would that I could spare her this last burden. She has known too many already."

"And it would seem that I am yet to know another," said Callie.

Jonathan and Lord Randall had been so deep in conversation that neither had noticed her standing at the door. Her eyes were huge and luminous in chalk-white features, and she bit her lip to keep it from quivering. Both men could only stare at her; neither knew what to say.

Callie turned and fled up the stairs. When she burst into her bedchamber with a look of anguish on her face, Lucie anxiously fingered the amulet around her neck and mumbled one of her many incantations.

"What now, missy, what now?" she cried fretfully.

Callie rounded on Lucie. "Did you know? Did you know that Lord Randall was my true father?" When the old Negress evaded her gaze, Callie felt the energy ebb from her body, and she grabbed hold of the bedpost for support. "So 'tis true, then," she whispered raggedly.

Lucie slowly nodded, grateful to be relieved of the burden she had been carrying for so long. "While yer mama lay dyin', she took on at times 'bout havin' to tell Lord Randall that he was yer papa. I thought 'twas the fever. When she recovered enough, she sent Ol' Joe to fetch him. The man come away from her bedside in such a state I know'd it must be so."

Callie recalled that day. It was true. Lord Randall had emerged sorrowful and shaken from Lucie's cabin where her mother lay near death. When he saw Callie, he stopped and gave her a considering look and a sad little smile, then climbed into his carriage and left. Callie had thought at the time how odd it was that the earl should be so affected by her mother's condition, but she had been too busy trying to dispel her brother's anxieties, as well as her own, to give it any further thought.

"Does Old Joe know?" she asked.

Lucie nodded. "Said as how he always know'd. In his cups one night, Mister John told him he suspected as much afore he married yer mama, but he had always loved her and couldna bear to see her suffer the punishment of deliverin' a bastard. He said it made no matter to him, but he ne'er told her he know'd."

Nothing Callie had endured these past several months—being hauled before the court on a false charge of infanticide, nearly losing her land to her stepfather, or being tricked into marriage by the General Assembly—had been as staggering to her as was this web of deceit.

Though her other problems had seemed insurmountable at the time, she had always managed to rise to the challenge and go on, just as she would meet this latest challenge of being falsely accused of murdering her stepfather. But this lie about her parentage threatened to undo her. It didn't demand a solution. It was just there—the ugly truth that she was a nobleman's bastard—to be acknowledged or ignored but unable to be denied. She didn't know with whom she was the more angered—Lord Randall for his dalliance with a woman he was not in a position to marry; her mother for accepting the favors of such a man and keeping her daughter's lineage a secret; or the man Callie had believed to be her father for quietly abetting the lie.

Suddenly, all her emotions bubbled together and boiled over. In a fit of helpless rage, she snatched up the jar of pomade and threw it against the wall. She watched it shatter and with it her sense of self. Sinking to the floor, she gave into wracking sobs. Only Lucie heard the knock on the door. When she opened it to Jonathan, relief flooded her round features. He motioned for her to leave, and she scurried out the door.

Jonathan stood silent for a moment, trying to decide how best to handle the situation. He cursed fate that this disclosure should come so closely on the heels of her other misfortunes. She was so vulnerable now. He decided to appeal to her temper, for he had long ago realized that therein lay the core of her strength for rallying her spirit.

"The Callie I knew never had time for self pity," he commented.

"'Twould seem, then, that you have as little knowledge of that person as I do," she responded bitterly, choking back sobs.

"This doesn't change who you are, Callie. It matters not."

She jumped to her feet, wiping away tears. "It changes everything—everything that I thought I knew about myself," she retorted. "What of you? How long have you really known that Lord Randall is my father? Mayhap you agreed to the marriage thinking that there was more to be gained from it."

"If you remember, my dear, I signed away all rights to your dowry and future inheritances. If that is not proof enough, you shall have to take me at my word that I knew nothing of your parentage until tonight."

Callie gave a cynical laugh. "I have been betrayed by the best."

"You have not been betrayed," said Jonathan, taking a firmer stance. "You were being protected by honorable people who loved you."

"If Lord Randall was so honorable, why did he bed a servant girl he could not marry?" she challenged. "Why was my mother not honorable enough to refuse him?"

"Unfortunately, we cannot always dictate with whom we fall in love, and life is not simple or fair. You know that. To that end, your mother made decisions that she thought best for all of you. And Lord Randall and John Hastings, for reasons of their own, allowed them to stand."

"Did she ever love John Hastings, or was he merely a convenient solution to a problem?"

"Perhaps you can best answer that question. Is it possible for a marriage of convenience to become one of love?" Jonathan asked her.

Callie looked at him, startled for a moment; she grasped the point he was making. How could she question her mother's honesty when she, too, was guilty of using marriage as a means to an end? And Callie understood the question he was asking her. She closed her eyes to focus her thoughts. She felt so confused, and she still felt betrayed and uncertain. She wasn't ready to trust again or to let go of her anger.

"The intimacy that passed between us was true, Callie. I have not played you false, and I never will," said Jonathan, slowly closing the distance between them.

The cadence of his voice was hypnotic, enfolding her like a warm cloak. His large hand cupped her face, and he bent his head to lightly press his lips against hers. If he couldn't surmount her wall of anger and suspicion, Jonathan sought to circumvent it on a level where he knew her defenses to be weak. Given Cane's attack upon her, he didn't know if she would reject him, but he decided to take the gamble. As Callie was so determined to spar with his every word, it seemed the best way he knew to get through to her. She didn't protest his action, and he felt encouraged. His kiss became more passionate, but when he moved to untie her robe, Callie stayed his hands and broke away from him.

"I heard what Lord Randall said about Cane's state of undress," she said.

"It matters not, Callie."

"It does matter. It matters to me that you know the truth." She looked at him, her eyes unwavering. "He did not rape me, Jonathan. It was his intent, but he was shot before he was able to. Whoever killed him, though he has held me to the deed, did me a great favor."

Jonathan felt an inward sigh of relief that she had not been violated, not owing to his sensibilities but because it gave him hope that her emotional healing would be easier and quicker.

"If Smythe makes this charge of rape, shall I have to prove my innocence in this as well to a jury of matrons?" Callie asked with heavy sarcasm.

Jonathan smiled. "I doubt it will come to that. We both know the matrons will not find what they are looking for this time around."

A blush-stained Callie's cheeks, and she averted her eyes for a moment. "If I am convicted of the murder, I shall have to plead benefit of clergy," she said.

"Trust me, Callie. I will defend you well. You shall not be convicted." Jonathan reached out a hand to lightly stroke her cheek. "Let us have this night together to put our differences behind us," he said, his tone and manner becoming seductive.

He slipped off her robe in a slow, fluid movement and lowered his head to lightly trail kisses from her neck to her shoulders, ultimately reclaiming her lips in a gentle caress. He could feel her responding. But as he deepened the kiss and started to lift her bed shift, she again turned away from him.

Jonathan frowned. He thought he had broken through her wall of defense. "Callie, what is wrong?"

"I—I know that you are planning to return to England," she said, reluctant to say it aloud. "Regardless of what happens tomorrow, I will not fault you if you petition for a divorce as well. I'll warrant that your father will not be happy to hear of this new scandal."

"Let us take one matter at a time," responded Jonathan. "This night is for healing. After the trial, we will talk of other things."

To Callie, it was an admission that he was, indeed, planning to leave.

She appeared to be trying to make up her mind to something, and Jonathan waited for her to make the next move. When she turned back to him, it was with a more settled air of one having come to a decision.

"You asked me a question," she said, gazing into his eyes. "My answer is 'yes.' I have it on good authority that a marriage of convenience can become a marriage of love."

He smiled as she reached up to remove his neck cloth. "Madam, might I assume that you are seducing me?"

"I believe it was you who taught me that one should not assume, sir."

"I also warned you that actions have consequences—most especially ones of this nature."

Jonathan took her in his arms and kissed her, the light caress becoming more urgent when Callie readily responded. As she began to take more of the initiative, he followed her lead, until, with a low moan, he broke away and pulled off his shirt.

Callie gasped at the fresh scar on his side. "You have been hurt! Jonathan, what has happened?" she cried, her blue eyes wide with alarm.

Anxious to preserve the fragile moment, Jonathan brushed aside her concern. "'Tis nothing. I shall explain later."

"But Jonathan—"

"Not now, Callie. This time is for us."

He quickly removed her shift and the rest of his clothes and pressed her onto the bed. His lips marked a sensual path from her neck to her shoulder and down to her breasts, while his hand slowly traced the curve of her waist and thigh before moving lower to play teasingly between her legs. When he heard the sharp intake of her breath, his moves became more deliberate. His touch was gentle and unhurried, considerate of her emotional scars and physical bruises, but yet so finely tuned to her needs.

Callie met him halfway and moved her hands unabashedly across his toned body. She faltered when she came to his wound, but he urged her on, and she resumed her exploration with a touch that was bold and sure. Jonathan's kisses and caresses became more demanding, intensifying her desire until her body begged for more. Finally, he pulled her beneath him. Even in his own urgency, he moved slowly to penetrate that most intimate and guarded part of her, carefully positioning her for optimum pleasure.

Her times with Jonathan had always been comfortable and pleasurable, but deep in her subconscious had remained a fear of loss or betrayal if she shared too much of herself. Tonight, however, come what may, she felt compelled to answer him with an abandonment that was with her total being.

At the culmination of an explosive union, neither wanted to surrender the moment. When Jonathan reluctantly parted from her, Callie turned away and tearfully buried her head in her pillow. How could even a small part of her bear to lose him now? Laying her emotion to her latest ordeals, Jonathan reached out for her and gathered her close to him. Emotionally drained, she cuddled against his chest and soon fell asleep.

Looking down at her, he had the feeling that she had been entrusted to him by something greater than fate, and he tightened his arm protectively around her. Abel Cane's murder was a complication he hadn't counted on. Contrary to his earlier assurance, he had to acknowledge that the situation didn't look good for Callie. But now that she was his again, he would be damned if he was going to lose her. He would have to revise his strategy. Jonathan gently eased her aside and rose from the bed. There was much to do this night.

The next morning, Callie awoke in dismay to find Jonathan gone. She jumped out of bed, threw on her robe, and hurried to his room but found it empty. She was about to start down the stairs, when she heard him talking with Lord Randall in the foyer and stopped. She wasn't ready to face the earl so soon after his disclosure that he was her father. As she turned to retrace her steps to her room, part of their conversation caught her ear.

"The *Homeward Bound* is in port from Charleston to pick up wares and orders for goods from the merchants," the earl was saying. "The ship is bound for England. You shall have to come to a decision. I've received a missive from your father. He wishes you home. I fear that much has reached his ears."

"When does the ship sail?" asked Jonathan.

"The captain is hoping to sail on the morrow with the tide. His wife is with him. I think she would make an admirable companion for Callie on the journey. You know, Jonathan, it strikes me that you and Callie would have much in common with the Deverauxs. They have quite a story to tell themselves.

"Indeed. I shall more closely consider the matter. For now, there is the concern of Callie's trial," Jonathan reminded him. "The outcome is not yet determined."

CHAPTER THIRTY-THREE

Paying the Piper

Callie was conscious of time repeating itself as she stood, once again, before the General Court in a room filled to overflowing with curious onlookers. The only difference of note this time was that one of the justices was missing from the jurists' box; Jonathan now sat in the bar with the accused as Callie's representative.

Looking about the courtroom, Callie was surprised to see that she had many supporters here—friends she had once thought never to need. Mrs. Whithers, Jane, Lydia Stanhope, Mrs. Bendel, Jenkins, ladies to whom she had given legal advice over the months were all present sending her signs of encouragement. Charles Smythe, too, smiled reassuringly as he took a seat up front near the railing. Callie squared her shoulders feeling stronger.

All talking ceased as the secretary announced in a loud, toneless voice: "Callie Hastings also known as Lady Trenholme, present yourself to the court."

Callie and Jonathan stood and approached the railing in front of the secretary.

"You stand charged with the murder of your stepfather Abel Cane. How does the accused plead?"

When Callie started to speak, Jonathan put a hand on her arm to stay her and spoke in her stead. "Lady Trenholme pleads not guilty."

"Mr. Procter, present your case," said the secretary.

The attorney general rose. "Your Honor and justices of the court, Lady Trenholme's relationship with her stepfather—"

Smythe impatiently cut him off. "Lord Trenholme, the accused was seen by a responsible witness to be running from the stables shortly after a shot was heard—the shot that killed Abel Cane. Must you waste the court's time by entering a plea of innocence?"

"Did anyone witness the accused firing the shot?" asked Jonathan.

"Lord Trenholme has a point," interjected a second justice.

"I remind you both that Lady Trenholme's cloak and rifle were found beside the body," replied Smythe brusquely.

"I am not contending that the defendant was absent at the time of the murder, merely that she had no hand in it," said Jonathan.

"And I suppose the boy with blueberry stains on his mouth isn't the culprit who snitched the pie from the sill."

Jonathan smiled smugly. "My point exactly. Even Justice Smythe is willing to concede that the boy had innocently eaten the berries off a bush and was unjustly accused."

Smythe's fleshy face turned red. "I concede no such thing!" he shouted furiously. "Mr. Procter, are you going to prosecute this case or not?"

"I am trying to, sir," replied the attorney general with a tinge of annoyance. "As I was saying, the relationship between Lady Trenholme and her stepfather was known to be contentious and on the evening of—"

"Fellow justices," broke in Smythe again, "Lord Trenholme would seek to twist words and waste our time with stories to cloud the fact and confuse the issue that his own wife committed murder rather than submit to blackmail. Blackmail, gentlemen, by a man who knew her to have duped the court by aiding the escape of a fellow prisoner—one Mae Bailey, also convicted of murder," declared Smythe, raising his voice to be heard above the loud murmurs of the crowd. "Blackmail by a man who knew her to be the daughter of someone—"

Callie closed her eyes against tears of humiliation as she saw her mother's memory about to be maligned before the whole town."

"Justice Smythe!" intervened Jonathan sharply. "I suggest you refrain from speaking before you taint the case, or I shall be forced to petition the governor to dismiss it."

Smythe's face turned purple as Jonathan once again backed him into a corner. "I think Lord Trenholme forgets just who is on trial here!" he exploded.

"On the contrary, 'twould seem that Justice Smythe is intent upon trying truth with suppositions instead of facts," countered Jonathan.

"Mr. Procter, what are the facts?" inquired another judge impatiently.

The prosecutor looked helplessly from Smythe to Jonathan and shrugged. "I am not sure," he said. "I appear to be lacking a few."

The judge looked at Jonathan. "Perhaps, I should be addressing myself to you, sir. What are the facts, Lord Trenholme?"

"For one, the accused was lured by this note to where her stepfather made his lodgings," stated Jonathan. He held up the parchment to view and handed it to the secretary.

The secretary read it aloud. "I know about Mae Bailey. If ye want me silence, come to the room at the back of the stables after dark. Signed Abel Cane."

"Lord Trenholme, the note does suggest that Abel Cane possessed some knowledge with which he was intending to blackmail the defendant. I fail to see how this helps Lady Trenholme's case," said the judge to Smythe's immense satisfaction.

"Milord Justice, Abel Cane did not know how to read or write. I contend that another party made it appear that the note had come from the deceased in order to lure the defendant to Cane's room and frame her for a murder that he, himself, intended to commit."

"Cane could just as easily have had someone write it for him," pointed out the justice. "The fact is that Lady Trenholme did respond to the note, lending credence to Justice Symthe's argument."

"What is this reference to Mae Bailey?" asked another judge gravely. "By my recollection this woman died in childbirth before her sentence could be carried out."

"I shall get to that, Justice Wrenner," said Jonathan.

Smythe smiled, confident that he now had Jonathan where he wanted him. "Yes, pray tell that you do."

"Lord Trenholme, what evidence have you to offer that Cane is not the author of this note?" Justice Wrenner continued to question.

Jonathan signaled to the bailiff. A freckle-faced urchin appeared and was sent forth, clearly apprehensive about the summons.

"Is he the lad who approached you?" Jonathan asked Callie in a whispered tone.

Callie nodded. "How did you find him?"

"Lord Randall and Jenkins were out at dawn working to turn up the boy." Jonathan readdressed the court. "Milord Justices, this is Finch, the lad who delivered the note to Lady Trenholme. But you did not receive the note from Abel Cane, did you, Finch?"

The boy slowly shook his head.

"Who gave it to him, then?" asked the justices in unison.

"A man who sought to rid himself of Cane and found a most convenient way to divert suspicion by framing a person with a more obvious motive—Lady Trenholme," said Jonathan. "As Mr. Procter pointed out, the rancorous relationship between the accused and her stepfather was common knowledge. The real killer knew that, if he could lure Lady Trenholme to Cane's room, suspicion would naturally fall on her."

"But what reason did this person have to kill Abel Cane?" asked another judge, confused.

"Abel Cane's intention was to blackmail someone, but it was not Lady Trenholme," said Jonathan. "He was intending to blackmail a man whom he knew to be selling information to the French concerning British movements in the Ohio Valley."

As murmurs and gasps erupted once more around the room, Smythe rapped the gavel sharply to restore order. "Bah! Lord Trenholme seeks to turn attention once more from the charge at hand to stories that confuse the issue."

"How did this Abel Cane come by such knowledge?" inquired one of the other justices, ignoring Smythe's protest.

"Cane and Jack Bailey frequented taverns together," replied Jonathan.

"What has that to do with anything?"

"A trader saw Jack Bailey in a tavern one night. He overheard Bailey arguing with a man over the pay he was receiving for the risk he was taking. In light of information that has come to me, I submit that Bailey carried information from the traitor to the French. Becoming increasingly disgruntled with the arrangement, he confided his activities to Cane. He either disclosed the name of the traitor to Cane or Cane guessed it and decided to use the information to his advantage."

"I hear no facts, just suppositions," remarked Smythe snidely. "How come you to know any of this? Cane and Bailey are both dead and cannot bear witness to the fact."

"The traitor and Cane were known to be frequent visitors to the Bailey farm," said Jonathan.

"By whom? Is not Mae Bailey also dead?" asked Smythe slyly.

"Your facts do strain credulity, Lord Trenholme, when all who could bring testimony are deceased," remarked Justice Wrenner.

Undismayed, Jonathan again signaled to the bailiff. A hush fell over the crowd followed by murmurs of disbelief as the bailiff brought in a young woman and walked her to the front of the room to stand beside Finch.

Callie gripped Jonathan's arm. "How could you!" she whispered angrily. "How could you bring Mae here?"

"Step back, Callie. You will have to trust me," he said firmly.

Smythe nearly climbed atop his chair in his frenzy to make himself heard. "Guards, arrest that woman! Arrest her, I say! 'Tis Mae Bailey. She is alive, just as I have always suspected. And you have Lady Trenholme to thank for it. I submit, my fellow justices, that if you cannot bring yourselves to condemn this woman for the murder of her stepfather, you must condemn her for her part in a travesty against the Crown."

"Nay, Milord Justices, Lady Trenholme was part of a well-worked plan to secret Mrs. Bailey away under the guise of death for her own protection, until enough evidence could be collected against the traitor."

"'Twas by a miscarriage of justice!" shouted an outraged Smythe.

"'Twas by order of the governor," countered Jonathan smoothly. He didn't think it necessary to mention that the secreting of Mae had occurred before the fact, and that it was only after being told the truth of the matter that the governor was persuaded to lend his authority to the story.

"You are lying," charged Smythe.

"Lord Trenholme speaks the truth," said Governor Dinwiddie.

"Lord Trenholme, if you please, name the spy," demanded Justice Wrenner impatiently.

"That is not necessary."

Gasps filled the room as all eyes turned to see that Charles Smythe had hopped the railing into the bar and held Callie at gunpoint.

"Easy, Trenholme," he warned, training the pistol on Callie's head as Jonathan started toward him. "Now, unless you wish to see your wife dead, too, I suggest you give us safe passage." There was no hint of the dandy about Charles now. He was a cold blooded killer capable of any act.

Callie's eyes were wide with shock as Charles wrapped his other arm around her waist and pulled her backwards with him through the opening in the railing into the gallery. Every muscle in Jonathan's body tensed, and he readied to spring with the first opportunity, but none presented itself.

The governor jumped up from his chair. "Young man, I demand that you unhand Lady Trenholme and relinquish your pistol," he ordered. "Bailiff, take this man into custody."

"Your pardon, Governor, but I take my orders from the French now," said young Smythe. He looked at the approaching bailiff. "Stand down," he warned. "You may be able to overtake me, but not before I put a bullet in the lady's brain."

Jonathan quickly waved the bailiff back.

The other jurists looked on in shocked silence.

Justice Smythe's eyes bulged as he rose from his chair, incredulous. "Charles, for the love of God have you lost your mind?"

Charles laughed with bitter humor. "You never did give me much credit for anything, did you, Father? How does it feel to know that you have been the dupe all this time, unknowingly supplying me with all the plans that the General Assembly voted—the plans that the French needed to know to strengthen their hold on the colony's frontier? Yes, that is right, Father. Who would have ever suspected the son of a most righteous judge of the General Court and a member of the General Assembly? Justice Smythe feared and disliked by all, hated most by his own son."

Charles turned his attention to Jonathan. "Father told me that the governor suspected a spy somewhere and had petitioned the king for an emissary. It took me awhile to realize that the emissary was you, Trenholme. You were quite clever."

Jonathan struggled to maintain a cool disposition. "Might I assume that it was you who ambushed me?"

"Yes, that was unfortunate. Father told me of the letter from Carolina and that he suspected Mae Bailey was alive and living there. I dismissed his silly notion until I spotted you heading down the Fall Line Road from Richmond. I happened to be in the city then and followed after you to see where you were going. Mae never knew what Jack and I were up to, but I couldn't take the chance that you might get enough information from her to put things together if you were, in fact, going to see her. I really didn't want to have to shoot you, Trenholme. I rather like you. But when you crossed into Carolina, you left me no choice. It's about survival you understand. My first mistake was in not making certain that you were dead."

"What about Cane?" pressed Trenholme. The longer he kept Charles talking, the greater the chance Smythe might let his guard down. "He guessed you were the traitor and was trying to blackmail you, wasn't he?"

Charles gave a snort of disgust. "I had just returned to Williamsburg, when the drunken fool approached me in the tavern. I thought I had tied up all the loose ends, but it appeared that one yet remained. Bailey couldn't keep his mouth shut."

"Why did you have to involve my wife?"

"She had the most obvious motive," replied Smythe matter-of-factly. "I needed more time to find out when and how many soldiers were due to arrive from England before leaving. I did not know that Cane had stolen the rifle from Callie. That was a stroke of luck." He paused. "You know, Trenholme, it occurs to me that you owe me a debt. I had intended to put a knife to Cane when your wife left the stable, but, when he started to attack her, I spotted the rifle and shot him before he could—"

"And what of Jack Bailey's death?" broke in Jonathan, moving to forestall any mention of the attempted rape.

Charles smiled with a measure of appreciation. "Figured that one, too, ay."

"Mae said you had been at the farm earlier that day and had quarreled with Bailey," said Jonathan. "You never left, did you? You hid in the barn waiting for the right moment."

"Jack threatened to expose me. What a pity we are adversaries, Trenholme. Together we might have controlled the frontier ourselves. We seem to think along the same lines."

"I do not betray my countrymen and leave innocent women to hang for my crimes, Smythe."

"The latter was regrettable," admitted Charles. "Jack was drunk and meting out one of his usual beatings to Mae, when he lost his footing and fell on the pitchfork that she had picked up to defend herself. When she ran for help, I saw my chance and finished the job for her. Jack never did right by her anyway. Mae was better off without him."

He shifted his attention to the shocked woman. "Apologies, Mae. I always had a great fondness for you. Under the circumstances, I never expected that you would be convicted or that Father would hand you the rope. There was nothing I could do, then, without tipping my hand," he said, regarding her with as much contrition as one of small conscience was capable of feeling.

Tightening his hold on Callie, Charles turned back to Jonathan. "When I was far enough away in French territory, I planned to send a letter of confession to the governor absolving your wife and Mae of any crimes. Where would be the fun if Father didn't know how clever his son had been?" he asked with a laugh.

Jonathan slowly moved closer. "Your father must have told you that I had returned to town. You knew that your attempt to kill me had failed. Why did you risk coming here today?"

"I had to know how much you had pieced together…how much you could prove…how long I had to collect information before I had to leave. And I suppose 'tis the danger that excites. A man like you would understand that, Trenholme. Truth to tell, I never figured you to turn up Finch though. When a man's wife is on trial for murder, he tends to be more emotional than pragmatic. I underestimated you. That was my second mistake. Enough talk now. Clear us a path and be quick about it. Careful, Trenholme, stay your distance." For emphasis, he cocked the flintlock to half position, resting the barrel against Callie's temple.

"Charles!" shouted Justice Smythe. "You have ceased to be my son."

"Your son!" Charles laughed harshly. "I was never your son. I was someone you kept near to remind you of how my mother had shamed you…a whipping boy on whom you vented and fueled your hatred of a woman who had dared to defy you." A look of pain and confusion came over his face. "I never understood why she didn't take me with her."

He shook off the bitter memory and dragged Callie from the courtroom through the door. The spectators followed after them. Lord Randall and Mrs. Whithers were ashen-faced, and each seemed to be supporting the other, while Mae tried to console them however she could.

Jonathan motioned Jake Tyler to him. "You are a fair shot?"

"I am. What would you have me do?"

Jonathan took out the pistol he had hidden under his coat in expectation of a showdown with Charles and handed it to Jake. "Take this. Go out the back and work your way around. I will go out the front and try to distract Smythe long enough for you to get a clean shot at him. The crowd should cover your movements. Now that he thinks himself to hold all the cards, he is bound to let his guard down if only for a moment."

"A moment is all I need," Tyler assured him.

Quickly, Jonathan shoved his way to the front of the crowd as Smythe edged his way down the steps outside to a nearby horse, using Callie as his shield. If this nightmare was to end, something had to be done now. Careful not to give himself away, Jonathan searched for Jake's position. He sighted the large man behind a tree at Charles' back, his arm raised in readiness to shoot. Jonathan knew it was up to him now to create the opportunity.

"Charles," he called out in a clear, level voice, "I assume that you intend to join the French at Fort Duquesne. 'Tis a long journey from here. A woman will slow you down, and surely you must know that a band will follow after you. Why not trade Callie for one of us men?"

"Yes, Charles, take me in her stead," pleaded Lord Randall, pushing his way to the front.

Charles laughed. "An old man for a comely young woman—what kind of a fool do you take me for, Trenholme? The French will pay handsomely for her. They don't see many white women."

Callie was terrified, and she fought to keep her wits about her. Charles' arm across her chest, as he continued to drag her backwards, was so tight she could scarcely breathe. Her eyes locked pleadingly on Jonathan's.

It was the moment he had been waiting for. He gave her a slight nod and steadily held her gaze.

"Look at her, Smythe. She is near to *collapse now*," said Jonathan with emphasis on the last words.

Callie understood the message and immediately went limp.

The sudden, unexpected dead weight on his arm threw Charles off balance, causing him to loosen his hold on her and to discharge the pistol into the ground. As he struggled to regain his footing, Jonathan moved quickly to pull Callie from his grasp.

Suddenly, the sound of another gunshot split the air, and Charles staggered and fell to his knees. Young Smythe stared in wonder at the blood spreading across the front of his waistcoat, then looked up at his father who stood in front of him with a smoking pistol in his hand.

A hush descended over the people as Justice Smythe put a single word to his dying son. "Why?"

Charles smiled and his laugh came out in a gurgling sound as blood spurted from his mouth. "'Twas my greatest revenge," he rasped out before keeling over at his father's feet.

Justice Smythe seemed to age before their eyes, and the crowd gasped as he suddenly grabbed his chest and collapsed beside his son. No one had to check for signs of life. Providence was balancing the scales. In the distance, Callie heard the unmistakable song of the whippoorwill.

CHAPTER THIRTY-FOUR

Reclamation

Horrified by the events of the day, Lucie and Mrs. Bendel had decided that this was one trauma too many. When Callie, Jonathan, and Lord Randall arrived home weary and drained, the women firmly took charge of Callie. They practically tore her from Jonathan's arms, unequivocally stating that she needed rest and nourishment.

"I believe that I can adequately attend to my wife's needs," he responded in annoyance.

"Beggin' yer pardon, sir, but Lady Trenholme needs *rest*," said Mrs. Bendel, giving him a pointed look.

Jonathan's jaw dropped at the bold inference, and he gave her an icy glare. "Mrs. Bendel, may I remind you that I am the master of this house, and I shall decide—" He broke off in disbelief as Lucie and Mrs. Bendel ignored him and whisked Callie up the stairs. When the bloody hell had he lost control of his household?

Lord Randall chuckled and handed Jonathan a drink. "Let the women to their fussing. Sometimes they know best. And Callie has been through a great ordeal."

Jonathan snorted, greatly perturbed, and downed the drink in a single gulp.

Upstairs, Lucie and Mrs. Bendel saw to what they decided were Callie's needs. When she balked at the food set before her, Lucie and Mrs. Bendel exchanged knowing glances and nodded in agreement. Now was the time to confide their suspicions to her.

Given all the turbulence of the past weeks as well as certain assurances that she had assumed, it had not crossed Callie's mind that she could be with child. And she met the news with great shock, disbelief, and denial. It wasn't supposed to be possible. It wasn't until Mrs. Bendel put a few questions to her that Callie was forced to accept the obvious—Mrs. Whithers had been wrong again in her information.

Throughout the day, Lucy and the housekeeper diligently guarded their mistress' privacy. Mae and her husband stopped by on their return to Carolina, and the girls had a tearful reunion. They talked for a long while, but Callie didn't divulge her secret. She was still trying to come to grips with it herself.

Evening had fallen before Lucie and Mrs. Bendel bowed to Jonathan's insistence that he be given entrance to his wife. Callie's needs were primary to them. Lord Trenholme's needs decidedly were not. As the women reluctantly withdrew, Jonathan was further shocked when Mrs. Bendel admonished him not to press his wife too sorely, again reminding him that she was more in need of the rest. As Lucie nodded her head in full agreement, Jonathan met their advice with a frosty glare and firmly shut the door on them.

Callie was staring out the window at the moonlit night, her manner pensive, as she tried to sort out her emotions. She was still stunned by the news of her condition. And Lord Randall's selfless act in offering himself as a hostage in her place had touched her heart. She knew that, in time, she would be able to make her peace with him. But what of Jonathan and her?

"What troubles you so?" asked Jonathan, coming to stand behind her. His hands caressed her shoulders, then slid down her arms to encircle her waist and draw her back against him. "Is it that Charles Smythe is the father of Mae's child?"

"Partly," said Callie. "She told you, too?"

"Aye, when I went to see her in Carolina. She had already told Jake before their marriage, and she thought that you had a right to know as well. That was what Smythe and Bailey had argued about that day at the Bailey farm. When Mae could no longer hide the fact that she was with child, Bailey knew the child was not his. The man was not able, shall we say, to rise to the occasion. Bailey may have been a drunk, but he wasn't a fool. He beat it out of Mae that Smythe was the father and threatened to expose him as a spy."

"But to deceive her husband with Charles—that is not Mae's character," said Callie.

"'Tis not a question of character or deceit," said Jonathan. "Charles gave her affection and kindness when she most needed it. Indeed, they were both, no doubt, in need of it. Coming from similar backgrounds of abuse, they were probably able to lend each other the solace that no one else could. I suspect that, in his own twisted way, Charles did love her as much as he was capable of loving anyone. He did tell his father that the child was his, hoping to get Mae's sentence set aside. But given his obsession for punishing women and fearing that such a scandal would threaten his position, Justice Smythe became that much more determined to see her hanged for her crime. In the meantime, he bought her silence about Charles' paternity in exchange for the welfare of her child."

"Mae once said that she had bargained with the devil," recalled Callie, "but I had never guessed such a truth. 'Tis luck that the knowledge never came out in court. Now Mae can truly embrace her new life. But Charles…who would have ever suspected him of being a spy when he was never known to put a question to anyone?"

"A man as clever as Charles Smythe knows how to elicit information without seeming to make inquiry."

Callie shook her head. "'Tis all too incredible to believe."

"So long as human nature is what it is, there can be no givens," said Jonathan. "Callie, is there something else that troubles you?" he asked, when she fell silent again.

Callie took a deep breath, the moment upon her. "I overheard your conversation with Lord Randall this morning. Jonathan, I cannot go with you to England. My home is here."

Jonathan sighed. "I know." He moved her hair aside and brushed his lips lightly across the nape of her neck. "Come to bed," he murmured against her ear. "We have taken care of the business of others. 'Tis time now to tend to ours while we can—assuming that it meets with the approval of Mrs. Bendel and Lucie," he added with a measure of annoyance. "They have become quite the mother hens. I am going to have to reassert my authority with those two."

Callie gave a light laugh. "You would do better to talk to the wall I fear. It appears that they have a mission."

Jonathan turned her in his arms. "So, madam, have I."

He captured her mouth, his lips caressing hers until they parted to invite a more passionate and intimate embrace. As he gently coaxed her to the next level, she totally gave herself up to him, returning his advances with an ardor that surprised him given her harrowing day, and further putting to rest his fears that the physical and emotional trauma she had suffered might have lasting effects. Without delay, he lifted her up in his arms and carried her to the bed. Again, she held nothing back. She touched Jonathan with a comfortable familiarity that needed no prompting and allowed herself to love and be loved without reservation as she sought to block from her mind all thought and concept of time.

As they later lay in each other's arms, Jonathan made the announcement she had been dreading. "I shan't be here in the morning when you awake, Callie. I have to make contact with the ship in Yorktown. I think it a good time for you to visit your farm tomorrow, and I have made arrangements for Lord Randall to escort you."

Callie went still. It cut across everything she was to beg, and she loved him too much to make him stay against his will. She had thought about changing her mind and going with him, but the sad simple fact of the matter was that she belonged on her farm in Virginia, and he belonged in his castle in England. The baby would remain her secret. She ran a hand protectively over her stomach. History seemed to be repeating itself all over again, she thought, as it came to her how closely she followed in her mother's footsteps. Both loved a man they couldn't have.

Callie's sleep was fitful at best. She awoke several times throughout the night to make certain that Jonathan still lay beside her. Perhaps she had dreamed that he was leaving her—just one more of a long line of nightmares of late. But the reality was there to greet her in the morning when her hand found only empty space this time. At least with the child, she would always have a part of him with her.

A somber mood settled over Callie. Her body felt heavy, her mind dull and listless. She would have stayed abed the entire day had not Lord Randall arrived to take her to her farm. Not even the prospect of seeing her land again or the beauty and warmth of the spring day could lift her spirits.

As the carriage bounced along the road, Lord Randall became increasingly alarmed by Callie's desolation. Her eyes held a distant look of such sadness, and she was totally devoid of spirit. Mistaking the nature of her mood and the source of her distress, Lord Randall desperately searched for a way to bridge a new understanding between them.

"Callie, about your mother and me," he began awkwardly.

"I understand," said Callie, continuing to stare vacantly ahead. "At first, I blamed both of you for the decisions you made, but I have come to see that one who judges the actions of others may someday be faced with the same choices."

The earl's hopes were raised that all was not lost between them. "Then you have forgiven your mother and me?"

Callie nodded. "I have."

Lord Randall looked at her, perplexed by her emotional state. "If that is the case, what is distressing you so?"

"Jonathan left this morning," she said quietly.

"Yes, I know," replied Lord Randall, still mystified. "That is why he asked me to bring you to the farm."

"I was too late. When I awoke, the ship had already sailed for England. He did not even say goodbye." Her words tumbled out and tears spilled down her cheeks.

"Oh, I see," said the earl, suddenly comprehending the situation. He handed her a handkerchief. "Well, I shouldn't worry, my dear, for I have it on good authority that you shall see him again. Obadiah, turn here," he instructed his servant.

"Where are we going?" she asked, blotting her eyes. "Why do we follow this trail?"

Lord Randall smiled. "I thought perhaps we might explore the boundaries of your land along the way. Now that you have more help, you might think about increasing the acreage you have in cultivation."

"'Tis the parcel I had sought to sell," said Callie, looking around her. "I had once dreamed of building a fine house on the other side of the hill overlooking the river."

As the carriage rounded the hill, Callie stared in disbelief at the sudden materialization of a two-story brick house in the Georgian tradition. It was still under construction; there was scaffolding about. Workers were applying pine shingles to the hip roof and inserting windows in the dormers, but the exterior of the grand home looked to be nearing completion.

Boundary lines were sometimes vague and often in dispute, but this was the last straw for Callie. "Am I destined to always fight for my rights? What man takes my property now!" she exclaimed, forgetting her despair for the moment.

"Perhaps we should go and see," said Lord Randall. "Obadiah, make haste to that house."

When they drove up to the entry, Callie sprang from the carriage. She ran up the steps and pounded on the door. "Open up!" she shouted. "I would know who seeks to steal my land."

When the door opened, Callie's jaw dropped. "Lucie! What are you doing here?"

Lucie beamed. "I is openin' the door for the mistress of this fancy new home," she explained self-importantly.

"You have left me to serve another mistress?" asked Callie.

"Ain't done no such thing, missy. Mister Justice is buildin' this place for ye as a surprise."

Callie looked at the woman thunderstruck. Lord Randall came up behind her, and she turned to him for confirmation.

The old earl smiled. "'Tis true. Jonathan had the devil's own time of it keeping the secret from you. 'Tis why he could not let you stay at the farm."

"And all the supplies that he said he was ordering for the farm—"

"Were for this house."

Tears glistened in Callie's eyes. Jonathan had said goodbye after all. As Lord Randall escorted her into the house, she stared in awe. Work was just beginning on the interior, but she could clearly see the vision. She felt as though she had stepped into a dream, and she was glad when the workers, Lord Randall, and Lucie absented themselves to allow her time to herself to adjust to it all.

"I'll warrant this will be the handsomest dwelling in Virginia when all is done," said a familiar deep voice.

Callie felt her heart skip a beat, and she whirled about to see Jonathan. A myriad of emotions registered on her delicate features before she let out a cry and ran into his arms.

"I thought you had sailed this morning for England," she said, choking back a sob.

"Where did you get that idea?" asked Jonathan in surprise.

"Your conversation with Lord Randall…and when you said that you had to meet a ship this morning, I assumed—"

"That I was departing?" When she nodded, Jonathan chuckled. "Perhaps we need to learn to state our intentions more clearly, as we seem so prone to false assumptions. To set your mind at ease, I was seeing to the delivery of a letter to my father to inform him that I will not be returning to England, except perhaps to visit."

Callie looked up at him, her blue eyes wide and luminous. "You are staying?"

"Unless you wish to accompany me to England, my dear, this shall be our home. Any land that can breed character such as yours bears closer scrutiny," said Jonathan. "By the bye, Olivia and Lilibeth Sanders sailed on that ship, so you won't be bothered by them anymore." His manner took on a more serious air, and he placed a hand beneath her chin to be certain of her full attention. "Know this and know it well, Callie. I love you. I have no intentions of ever leaving you."

She didn't have to say anything. Her face radiated happiness. For the first time in a very long while, she could believe again.

Jonathan lifted her left hand. "I see that you have found your wedding band, madam."

"I have, sir, and I hope not to lose it again," she said with a twinkle in her eye. "But, Jonathan, you must understand that it encircles my heart, not my being."

He regarded her for a long moment. "I would have it no other way," he replied solemnly.

There was something different about her, he thought, studying her closer. She had a glow about her. He couldn't put his finger on it, but he found the effect most appealing.

"Were there a bed here, madam, I would seek to test its mattress with you," he said, a telltale gleam in his eye.

"I fear, sir, that we have tested one bed too many," responded Callie. "As it stands, you have seven months to advance this house to a livable state, else our child shall be birthed in a cabin for it will be born on this land."

Jonathan looked at her, the momentary shock on his face replaced by a pleased smile. "Are you certain of it?"

"'Tis what Mrs. Bendel and Lucie tell me."

Jonathan laughed. "No wonder they have been circling you like mother hens. It would appear that Whithers' premise did not hold," he remarked smugly, the question of his virility now put to rest.

Callie's brow was knit in perplexity. "Yes, I shall have to inform her that her advice was wrong on this matter as well. Madam seems to be wrong on many things of this nature."

Jonathan chuckled. "I think we shall be seeking our own counsel from hereon. With a child and a farm to keep you busy, I trust that now you will leave the practice of law to me. I have decided to step down from the court and stand for the defendant—you will not have a hand in it," he quickly added when he saw her eyes light up and imagined her mind churning with the possibilities.

"But I can help you," she protested. "I may not be able to petition the court anymore, but I know how to argue the law."

"And it has gotten you into much trouble," he pointed out.

"Smythe is no longer a concern."

"Madam, I forbid—" Jonathan stopped himself. He had learned he could not use that word with her. It usually generated the opposite result. "Callie, as your husband," he said, rewording his resolve, "I do not give you leave to—"

"I remember a time when my husband promised me all the leave that I wanted," she cut in pertly.

Jonathan groaned to himself as he recalled the brash promise made in a moment of desperation. "At the time, you required the persuasion of certain assurances," he said.

"Are you saying that you employed a lie to bring me into your bed?"

"No. I would call it a fib," he replied.

"A fib can be used only in the furtherance of a just or noble cause," she pointed out.

"Exactly, madam. That was just the way I saw it."

Callie bristled with indignation. "I would hardly call satisfying your needs a noble cause, sir."

"That is a matter of perception, my dear."

"Trenholme, you cannot take such liberties with my words," she sputtered. "You cannot twist them to suit your purpose."

Jonathan cocked a brow. "It appears to me that this is a case of the pot calling the kettle black."

Callie pursed her lips and glared at him. "It still does not give you the right to—"

"What the devil is that?" demanded Jonathan, cutting short her protest as a sharp malodor filled the area.

When investigation revealed Lucie industriously hanging malodorous witches' bags about the house, Callie and Jonathan forgot their argument and burst into laughter.

"With ye both bein' as prideful and tempered as ye is, I ain't takin' no more chances. Dis gonna be a peaceable house," Lucie roundly informed them. "Now what is we gonna call dis here place anyway? 'Tis bad luck not to give it a proper name."

"If this house possesses half the strength of its mistress," remarked Jonathan dryly, "'twill long endure. And as neither will know the authority of another, it shall be called *Callie's Way*," he declared.

As Jonathan drew Callie back into his arms, both considered how much they had to teach the other about life.

About the Author

Kathy Keller is the author of eight books that include historical fiction, historical romance, and time travel. She graduated from the American University, Washington, D.C. with a BA in journalism. A native of north central Pennsylvania, she is a long-time resident of Florida and currently resides in Ponte Vedra with her husband.

Books by Kathy Keller

The Homeward Heart
A Love too Proud
Destiny's Shadow
Millionaires' Row (co-author with A. J. Billman)
Millionaires' Row: The Legacy (co-author with A. J. Billman)
The Paradox
A Little Gentle Persuasion
Lady of the Sea

www.KathyKeller.com